Fool—he is a fool.

Rain dribbles down out of a dark sky as Night heads down the walk to the Lincoln where his partner waits. He has absolutely no idea what he will say. None. Derek will want answers, and he has none for him.

What he does have is two rooms in a house with a dealer and a check that will bounce if he doesn't get to the credit union after work.

What has he done? That he should have been so out of control scares him, thrills him, too. He can't say why, but he feels more alive than he has in a long time. Like a man coming up from deep water for a gulp of air. But it's insane to think he can move in with a dealer under investigation and hope to get away with it.

It's stupid.

It's dangerous.

It could cost him his job.

Then why is he smiling?

Also by D.W.St.John

FICTION

A Terrible Beauty
Sisters of Glass

NONFICTION

The Nasty Little Writing Book
(with Madelyne Simone Rovenhauer)

See Night Run

A Controband Novel

D.W.St.John

Poison Vine Books

Distributed to the trade by **Poison Vine Books** an imprint of

Elderberry Press
1393 Old Homestead Drive, Second Floor
Oakland, Oregon 97462-9506

Publisher's Catalog-in-Publication Data
See Night Run / D.W.St.John.
ISBN: 1-930859-17-1
1. Police——Fiction.
2. Crime——Fiction.
3. Romance——Fiction.
4. Marijuana Laws——Fiction.
5. Drug War——Fiction.
I. Title

COVER PHOTOGRAPH © WONDERFILE/DIGITAL VISION

This book was written, printed, and bound in the United States of America

To Libertarians
for having the courage
to speak the truth—
even when no one is listening.

With thanks to
Officer Layne Frambe of the Springfield Police Department
for sharing an insider's view of law enforcement,
Dr. Bailey for generosity describing the effects of,
and treatments for neuroblastoma,
Pam Wilds for uncompromising line editing,
Warren Cooley for perceptive editorial assistance and advice.

Quis custodiet custodes?
(Who watches the watcher?)

Juvenal [1st-2nd century, A.D.]

The ruler sees what he chooses.
The citizen what he is allowed.
The outcast what is.

Pé Ku Vang [1968-]

ONE

From across the street Night Hume watches the woman through a rain-spotted windshield.

It's her.

Miserable, he wrings rain from a sopping ponytail.

In the back seat Derek yelps. "Hey, watch it, man, you're dripping."

Resenting the rain, Night ignores him, cracks the window, peers out. June in Oregon. Can't turn on the wipers without attracting attention he doesn't want. It's her all right. It's the one they are here for. But something is wrong.

From Derek a sigh. "What's she doing now?"

Night cranes his neck to look at his partner, smiles at what he sees. Five-eight in his boots, hundred-fifty pounds, half white, half black, calls himself a zebra. Derek—the only guy he can stand to share a car with all night, seven nights running and not get to hate the sight of, the stink of.

Night watches his target unload groceries from the Volvo, jeans clinging to long legs as she strides up stairs and inside. He frowns, fingers an ear stud. Can't be right.

Unconsciously Night reaches to the neck of his sweatshirt to tug down a vest that isn't there. Fingers finding nothing, he sighs. The Kevlar may be in the trunk, but the habit he carries like a scar, like the mange. Useless gesture. Dead give away if anybody knew what they were looking at. They don't.

He watches her move as she returns for another load. "Have any professors look like her when you went to college?"

Derek reads the paper in the back seat, feet up, toothpick filling the gap in his front teeth. Earphones dangle from his ears. "Never one looked like that. Never dealt either." He turns the page without a glance up, wrinkles a wide black nose, "Your car smells like something died. What you been doing, moonlighting for the coroner?"

Night scans the street—she's still inside. "Mouse chewed up my lunch, found the napkin all torn up in little bits on the seat. Making a nest."

Derek grimaces, "What you do, shoot him?"

Night keeps his eye on the Volvo, hatchback still yawning. Still inside. "Of course I didn't shoot him. Poisoned him."

Derek looks up. "Poisoned him? What's the matter with you? You don't poison mice in a car. You trap them. Where the hell you raised, boy?"

Night wishes she would hurry up. "Where we didn't have mice in the car."

Derek's paper rattles. "Say what? That sounds like a racial slur to me."

Still no action at the house. Doors still wide on the boxy Volvo 980. Professor's car. Classy, yet staid—the slacks and silk blouse of station wagons. The thought of this woman driving it lends it an aura of sex.

"Any more of that I be axing IAD to do something about certain racists in this here po-lice department. That's what I be doing."

Something about the way she moves. What is it? He's seen it before somewhere. "Get my name right this time."

"How's I supposed to do that, youse all looks alike to me." Derek tosses the paper away, lays a hand on the back of the seat palm up. "Sports."

Night watches as she strides out the front door, down the steps to the car. "Ducks took the play-offs sixteen fourteen."

Brown fingers wag. "Pass that sucker back." Night does, and Derek takes a look out the window, sighs again. "What you waiting for? Get your ass over there and save U of O's sex-puppies from the evil professor peddling them green dope."

Not willing to be hurried, Night finds him in the mirror. "Read your paper and let me do my job, huh?"

Derek blows air, goes back to his reading.

Behind her the house stands, a domestic fortress. Eyebrow dormers frown down at him from above a wraparound porch as he plots its downfall. Across the slope of a park-like front lawn oaks stoop, branches pendulous. Castle in the sky. Domestic charmer. Close to U of O. Steps from public transportation and shopping. The kind of house that doubles in price every five years in the hot Eugene market. Too much to lose selling a few finger bags. And to your students—how stupid can anybody be?

Derek taps the paper with a nail, "Look here, says they did a poll and sixty-eight percent of voters in Oregon favor initiative 82. Can you believe that?"

Night watches her take in another load, body moving like a dancer. In control. Never off balance or overextended. Night frowns, thinking. "That the one about logging?"

"Nonono." He glances up, appalled. "You sure is one ignorant ass white boy, ain't you? It's the one legalizing pot. Don't you read the paper?"

He doesn't. Doesn't want to know what they call news, what they call cops in what they call news. "Not lately."

"Oh, yeah, you been elbow deep in gypsum dust, haven't you? Well, I tell you what, partner, that one passes, we be working a garbage truck."

Night releases his seat belt and it whines as it slips away. "No, no, you'll be working the garbage truck. I'll be warning hot little coed's not to drive their Beemers too fast on their way to class."

Derek sneers and the paper crackles. "One lousy year of seniority. Where are quotas when you need them?" Again he glances out. "Nice neighborhood, anyway. This where you picked up that fixer, isn't it?"

Night nods, attention across the street. "One block down." The neighborhood is wrong. Again Night checks his pad. On it he finds the address given him by the informant he'd met at IHOP that morning. Usually reliable, Linda had seemed clean and lucid. He'd checked her eyes, her scarred hands, the veins between her fingers and had found nothing. If he's wrong, he'll find out soon enough.

"I'll have to come check it out."

Night isn't listening. "Sure."

"Tell me again how you can afford something over here?"

Night watches the professor lean over to retrieve a bag. Three years with Interagency Narcotics Enforcement Team and he's seen thousands of white dope freaks. He knows the walk, the talk, the type—she isn't it. Everything about her screams education, class, restraint. None of the twitchiness of the tweaker, nothing slatternly. He finds Derek in the mirror. "What did you say?"

"How'd you get it?"

"Probate sale, heirs wanted out. Ray turned me on to it."

With this load the Volvo is nearly cleaned out. Night flexes his right elbow, working feeling into buzzing fingers. Nights are the worst. Cold curls his fingers into claws without the strength to grasp his Glock. Three surgeries later it's no better. At forty, the scars, the aches are piling up.

"Your ex's husband, Ray? Why would he do that?"

"He's a nice guy, that's why." He wishes he weren't. Might make him easier to hate. Night reaches into his jacket for the compact .40, drops out a magazine the size of half a Snickers, taps it against the steering wheel to seat the cartridges—more super-stition than necessity. He slips it in, cracks the slide to spy the nickel glint of casing, hides it away, opens the door. "I'm gone."

From behind his paper Derek grunts. "Watch yourself, man, she looks dangerous. One slip, she be messing you up."

Night laughs, hoists himself out of the sedan, knees stiff from a vault over six-foot chain link the week before. He glances down the street. Nice neighborhood. Noth-ing like the trailer park he goes home to every night. Halfway across a rain-slickened street, kinks almost worked out of his knees, he thinks of Jade, and piranhas of guilt swarm in his gut.

Thirteen. So smart she scares him. What kind of home can he offer? In a trailer the size of a shower stall? Working the hours he does? His daughter sleeps in another man's house, Ray's house. A man who makes ten times what he does. A man who keeps his hair short and clean, who wears suits to work, who doesn't carry, who doesn't ever think about where he sits in a restaurant. A man who plays golf.

Night makes the sidewalk as the professor breezes out. Screen slamming behind her, she spots him and does what most women do—looks away, goes on with busi-ness. Big mistake. The sixties' gift to the predator—a never-ending offering of vic-tims. How many women die, how many suffer because they've been trained it's wrong to judge by looks? Smart is what it is, the secret to long life and good health.

He cuts across lawn to reach her and she glances up at him. That's right, it's you I'm after. At least she has that much on the ball. So why is he nervous? Small buy. In and out. Just enough to justify the warrant. All he needs to do is get the message to his gut.

With a glance over her shoulder, she heads inside, arms loaded. Mistake number two. A maggot would be right in after her, door slammed behind him, knife at her throat before she could drop the bag.

On the porch, boards enameled gray squeak under his sneakers. He raises a fist to rap and out she bangs, nearly bowling him over. She brushes past, screen door ping-ing behind her.

Taller than she looked from across the street. Five-ten anyway. Lithe, trim—not wasted like the meth-addicted tweakers he lives and breathes. Nice head of hair, even wet. Early thirties is his guess. Very early.

"Hello," she says, smiling wide.

Okay, nobody's perfect, thirty-five. Lipstick, yes, and freckles. Hair the color of hand-rubbed butternut to her shoulders. No perm, no bleach, no makeup. Clothes nothing to write home about—jeans and pullover—but worn well. Searching her eyes for signs of fear, he finds none. "Hi."

"Here to have a look?"

That he is. What he's seen so far he likes. Still, it's an odd remark. Dope is dope. What's to look? It's good or it's stems. "Actually, I was—"

"Just be a sec." A watermelon heavy as a toddler she drops into his arms. "If you wouldn't mind getting that, I can get the rest in one trip, then I won't have to come back." Python eyes wrap him up. And squeeze.

"I don't mind."

She hesitates just long enough to make him wonder how much she sees. Then the smile widens. "Come on in. Can't stand buying fruit from Chile, all the spray they use. We outlaw them here, then sell them over the border and buy the fruit they raise with it—insane. So when I saw this was raised in Hermiston, I had to get one for Alex."

Husband likes fruit. Night files it away under Useless Information as he follows into the kitchen. She puts groceries away as if it were the most natural thing in the world for a maggot to be standing in her kitchen cradling a watermelon.

"Do you know what I paid for that stupid melon? You probably know better than to buy the first ones of the season, right? You look it anyway. Seven bucks. Seven dollars, can you even imagine?"

In a world where people pay $20 for a sack of shriveled bud he can. Ordinarily, he would have spoken up, said what it was he wanted, but here he stands, marveling at his own inaction, watching her move.

She laughs, winces, pressing fingertips to her temple. "I know it's dumb for me to be telling you, but I just couldn't believe it. But then it's true of everything, isn't it? I mean what isn't high, right?"

Your students are, anyway. It's time to drop some names. Whether she'll go for it or not is something else again. "I hear from Andy and Clarise that you—"

"You know Andy?" She lets out a deep breath, seeming relieved. "Andy, good student, pre-med, smart, hoho, very smart, and Clarise, well...struggling through Bio right now, but she'll make it, I think. You know them, that's great. Just a sec while I get the milk put away and I'll show you the room. My God, hasn't the weather been rotten? I wish to God we'd get some sun. I mean it is summer, even in the Willamette Valley."

What is it about her that keeps him here like a fly in amber? It's as if he hears a familiar strain of music through a wall. She affects him that way, as if there's something he should recognize about her, something he should know. It's funny. He never has a problem taking charge of a conversation, guiding it where he wants it to go. Why now?

"Did you know use of a heated pool is included in the rent? And kitchen and living room privileges." She slams palm to forehead, "Damn! I forgot to put that in the ad. I did, didn't I? I forgot."

Rent? "Actually, I was—"

Her hands fly to rest on slender hips. "Oh, I know, so many places in Eugene are for rent you can't see for the forest of signs. I don't blame you for looking around. I know I would. Oh, God, I'm sorry." She snatches the melon from his arms. "Thanks, but for the price, this place is great. I think you'll like it, I really do." She rushes off, waving him after, "Come on, I'll show you."

He follows, watching hips move under her jeans as she leads him through a living room and up wide stairs. Why should a nice looking woman's hips be so damned good to look at, anyway? He has no intention of taking the room. Good business to play along. Time spent now will soften her up for the pitch, bring her one step closer to losing her house—maybe her freedom. What harm can it do? Eventually he'll get what he wants.

She leads the way into a bedroom, draws curtains wide. The walls are papered with a trellis of rose and twining ivy. "I love this paper, don't you?"

Wallpaper he dislikes. This he hates. "Nice."

"Not a man's style, I know. Anyway, a space in the garage is yours." She opens a door. "Your own bathroom with shower, and I mentioned the pool, didn't I?"

He nods. Something about this woman makes him want to smile. Not as in funny. As in comfortable. It's obvious how bad she wants to rent the place. Why? With a job like hers? With a house like this? Dealing, too? It makes no sense. She can't need the money. Why, then? "You know, you shouldn't be doing this."

She looks up, eyes frank. "What?"

"Showing a place by yourself to anyone that wanders in. It's dangerous. Woman alone. Man she doesn't know. Things happen."

She turns to him, unaffected, open, a little worried maybe. Again her hand goes to her head. She sighs. "Oh, you're right, you're right. I'm new at this. I should have someone here." She heads for the door. He moves out of her way, feels the heat of her as she passes. She doesn't stop until they are back in the kitchen. "That's pretty much it." She opens the fridge. "This shelf is…would be…yours." She smiles, looks away. "Once the melon's gone anyway." Hands on hips, she sighs, mouth widening into a worn smile. A smile that says she's tired of waiting for life to surprise her pleasantly. A thought he's had often himself in the three years since his divorce. Since Jade was ten. Three years of her childhood lost.

Arms braced on the counter, her shoulders sag. "I'm not very good at this, am I?" Another sigh as she palms her brow, blowing air. "Well, I'll get better. You're the first, and I've got two rooms to show. Practice makes perfect. That's what they say, anyway."

He finds himself smiling. If she sells dope the way she rents out rooms, she'd better keep her day job. "What about the neighborhood? Is it quiet?" Why is he asking this? He knows damned well it's quiet. He's patrolled it.

"Couldn't be quieter."

Except for kids running in and out buying dope, she means. He has to remember he's talking to a player. Might make it easier if she looked the part.

"Lot of traffic?" He's getting his voice back anyway.

"Where in this city isn't there? People walk a lot in the evening here. It's nice." She leads him to the door. "Well," she says, voice disappointed, "I just put the ad in, so I'll be showing it all week. If you don't see anything better…." She shrugs, lets her shoulders drop like an eight-year-old. "Stop on by and take another look."

Anything better… He's got nothing better. What he has is a job to do. It's time to make his play. No way she'll shy now. The buy is as good as his. One hour and he'll have the affidavit written. Three and they'll have their warrant. She's already penciled in for tomorrow at six. Knock-knock.

I was wondering if I could pick up some bud while I'm here —that's the line. He thinks it, but his mouth is cemented shut. What the hell is he doing? "I was wondering…"

She stops, head up, receptive. "What?"

Right now is when he does it. Hand warm on the twenty in his pocket, the dope is his, all he has to do is ask. Something he's done a thousand times. Say the words. Say it and it's over. Say the words.

Why doesn't he? He needs that bag in his hand when he goes out the door or he needs a good reason why he doesn't have it. So far he has neither.

He tries again, and it's as if he's forgotten the language. Do carpenters forget to swing a hammer? Do whores forget the pitch? He's got to think. Why can't he think?

"I was wondering…"

Hint of a smile on her face. "What? What were you wondering?"

Comes a tingling up the nape of his neck to the crown of his head and he knows. He doesn't want what he came for. He wants something else. "Can I see the room again, both rooms?"

Her eyes widen.

"I want…." What? What does he want? "I want to check something."

Puzzled, she shrugs, "Sure."

Mounting the stairs, he trembles, a familiar burning kindling in his gut. The feeling he has when he's too far out a limb. In the room, feeling foolish, he presses the mattress as she watches from the door.

"The bed in the other room was my son's. It's a lot better. Want to try it?"

The second bed is softer, the wallpaper footballs and helmets. Voice screaming in the back of his head, he has to move fast. Before reality, before sanity presses too close. He rises, faces her. "How much?"

Unsure, she laughs. "You're kidding."

"I'm not kidding."

"There is just you?" she says.

Lost again. "Just me?"

"You live alone?"

What does he say now? "I…" Night, the banter king. Never at a loss for words. Never short a line. Where's your line, now? Nothing occurs but the truth. "I have a daughter."

Lines form on her brow. "And will she be living with you?"

Used to be Jade would plead with him every time he took her out for the day. No more. Learning what a flake Dad is. "She might."

She looks disappointed. "I advertised for one person. They're small rooms."

He sees where she is going with this. "We wouldn't be sharing."

"Oh, I see." Shock flares in her eyes. "You mean both rooms. How old is she?"

"Thirteen." He finds himself wanting to make a good impression, to be found acceptable. Why? "She lives with her mother now." Why is he telling her this? He doesn't talk about Jade with dealers.

She considers. "I'll bet she and Alex will get along fine."

Now that's weird. "Your husband?"

She laughs. "My daughter, Alexis. She's eight."

In his belly a spark glows, ignites. It has to be now, right now. He has to move fast. "How much for both?"

She sees he is serious and her smile fades. "You're not kidding are you." Her hand goes to her throat. "Well… I put each one in for five hundred, room and board. I suppose I could let you and your daughter have them for… nine, I guess? Utilities, trash, water, cleaning—all included."

He can't believe what he hears. The tin can he lives in now costs him six. Breathless with fear. Afraid of himself, of what he'll do next, he feels the weight of an avalanche press him hard, numbingly cold.

He can not do this.

He will not do this.

He will buy his finger bag and he will get his ass out the door. His eye strays to her bare left hand.

This is nuts.

He knows this is nuts.

Herrera finds out he'll have his guts for a necktie. He takes a deep breath. Too far out on sagging ice to make it back, he presses on before his nerve fails. "How much to hold them?"

She speaks as one dazed. "First month would be fine."

He thinks. Or tries to. How can he think with a brain encased in ice? What is there to think about, anyway? He is jeopardizing an investigation, risking his job. And for what? For what Derek would say is a chance at a piece of tail? But is it? He doesn't think that's it.

"I could hold it for less."

"Nine hundred?" He says the words, listening for sense and hearing gibberish. She nods, confused.

Mouth dry, he talks, not believing what he hears. "Okay... yeah, okay."

Her jaw drops. "You mean..."

He nods. "We'll take it...them...both of them...one for me...one for Jade."

Her mouth widens into an incredulous smile as she loses her breath in a rush, "Oh...that's great!" She laughs. "I'm...that's just fine! Come down, I'll brew us some tea. I can't believe it! The first person I've shown and you take both rooms, I just can't... Oh." In the kitchen she turns, offers a hand. "I'm Ceridwen Lawrence."

Her grip is dry, firm. "I'm Night, Night Hume. Take my check? It's local."

She waves a hand as she fills the teakettle. "I trust you."

He pauses, pen in air. Still numb from what he's done, he appraises the woman before him. This is a dealer talking? Nothing about her fits. Nothing. He's used to finding out what he wants to know without asking. Her he can't read. "I make it out to..."

"Me, please." Quick smile, gone just as quick. "It's just me and Alex. And you?"

He thinks of Derek waiting in the car for him to make a quick buy, and, mouth dry, scribbles out the check. He folds it back along the perforation, smooths it with a finger, rips it out before he has a chance to think. "Just us two. Sign of the times. I'll get you a copy of my credit report."

She turns, hand on hip, considering. "Don't bother."

He wants to laugh. "You serious?" The dope dealer conducts business.

That shrug again. "Sure."

"Ever been a landlord?"

"No, why?"

Babe in the woods. "I have." He stands. "Always look at a report. Save yourself a lot of heartache. I'll drop a copy off tomorrow." He hands her the check. "Interesting name, Ceridwen."

She shrugs. "Welsh. My father was from Aberystwyth, little town northwest of Cardiff."

"What's it mean?"

"Well..." She raises her eyes, "Cerdd means poetry, gwyn, blessed." She pulls down two large glasses for tea, avoiding his eye. "So, blessed poetry, I guess." She laughs, saying it as if it were all a silly mistake.

He watches her as she puts away dishes from the washer. No mistake. "Speak much?"

"Welsh? Me? No no. Three words only—*pronounda, osgwelghunda, and juju.*"

He's sure if he wanted he could get her to go for a sale, now. Too late. She has his check. That he could never explain to Herrera. How does he explain it to himself?

"What do they mean?"

She smiles, ticking them off on her fingers. "Please, thank you, and oh my goodness!"

He laughs. "Probably get along pretty well with those."

She turns to look at him over her shoulder as she sets dishes up on a cabinet shelf. "What about Night? Hardly something you hear every day."

"About that you'd have to ask my father, and I'm afraid you're about five years too late."

To his relief she doesn't say she's sorry. His check she holds out to admire in both hands. "I can't believe you took it, I just can't. I was counting on showing it a hundred times. And you've got a girl too." She props the check in the window, goes back to her dishes. "Beginner's luck, I guess, huh? Oh, damn!" she says, peering into the dishwasher, exasperated. "I hate this thing! I can never get it to drain." Leaning inside, she bails with a measuring cup.

Unable to resist, Night rises. "Mind if I look?"

"It's the disposer. It hasn't worked in a long time."

He flips the switch. Nothing happens. He should go. The longer he stays, the harder it'll be to explain coming away with no dope. He should have left fifteen minutes ago. One look at midnight blue eyes and he gives up. "Got a mop?"

"A mop?"

"A mop, doesn't matter what kind."

She frowns, fetches it. "Are we going to make a mess?"

Night turns the mop upside down and hands it to her. He has already made one. Up close she smells of soap, of perfume subtle as buddleia. Her hands are cool, dry. Being near her is like the long second before an entry. That loaded with potential, that frightening. "I hope not. Move it around counter clockwise." He watches her pry.

"Like this?"

"That's right. Feel anything?"

Just then something gives and she laughs.

"Reach down, see what you find."

She looks worried. "Should I do that?"

He pulls the cord from its socket, shows her. "Go ahead."

She comes up with a piece of chewed gold. "My God, it's my wedding ring! I lost it two years ago. Will it work now?"

He plugs it in. "Try it."

It whirs. "I can't believe it! It's been broken forever. You did it."

He watches the way the small gold chain she wears around her neck lies over a freckled collar bone. He thinks of where he is and an itch starts in the pit of his stomach. He dries his hands. "No, you did."

Slowly, a smile grows at the corners of Ceridwen's mouth. "I did, didn't I?"

The front door slams and Night jumps, right hand moving to his jacket pocket. A small girl with large eyes blows into the kitchen, heads for the fridge. Coke in her hand, Alex drags to the table, drops her backpack. Night she watches with ancient eyes, eyes that miss nothing. "Did what?"

"Fixed the disposer." Ceridwen reaches over, turns the switch on and off, dusts her hands. "See that?" She displays the mangled ring. "Guess what I found down there, Babe? My ring."

Alexis falls into a chair, eyes drooping with ennui. "Whoopee. It's not like you need it." Cynical eyes pivot to Night. "Who the hell is he?"

"Alexis…" Ceridwen reprimands her with a stern look. "This is Night. He's going to be living here. He has daughter just a little older than you."

Interest flickers in Alex's eyes and is gone. She swigs from the two liter, huge in her small hands, heavy-lidded eyes on him. "Knight, like in dragons?"

Like as in he's got to get the hell out of here, and soon. He edges to the door. "Like in dark."

She thinks this over, looks away. "Nicetameecha, Night."

"What is it you do?"

He's used to lying about what he does. It doesn't usually bother him. It does this time. "Lane County Sanitation."

This throws her. He's not surprised. "Sanitation." She says it as if she's trying not to sound disapproving.

"I'm a garbage man." Not so far from the truth. What does he do but take garbage off the streets? Dope and the people that sell it. The lie he's used to. What surprises him is the regret he feels telling it. "Pay's fair, work's steady. No danger of us running out. What about you?" He knows what she does—she deals.

She hands him his tea. "I'm sorry, is that sweet enough for you? I have lemon, if you like."

"It's fine." He won't be staying long enough to drink it.

"I teach at U of O."

"Oh? What you teach?" He would guess English, drama, dance maybe.

"Biology."

"Biology?" A day for surprises.

"Yup." She says it like a kid.

"Like it?"

She keeps her eyes on her glass. The hand goes to her head as if she doesn't realize she's doing it. A habit. Meaning what? Migraines, he guesses. "I do. And do you have only the one daughter?"

"Just the one. You?"

"I've got Alex, and a son in college, Grant. He's a sophomore, now."

"Junior," Alex says without looking up.

"She's right. You'll meet him. he'll be home in a few days. He spends part of the summer with me, and part with his dad." Her smile falters. "What about your daughter?"

"With her mother." Night imitates her, pressing his temples between thumb and fingers. "What's this about?"

She frowns, puzzled. "What?"

Alexis doesn't bother to look up. "She always does that."

"Oh, this?" She does it. "Just some allergy thing. Got some pills for it, but they don't do anything but put me to sleep." She laughs, wincing. "Here it comes again."

He backs down the hall. "I should go."

"You haven't finished your tea." She shuts her eyes. "Damn this headache."

"Mom!" Alexis fixes her with jaded eyes, "Don't say, damn!"

"I'm sorry, Baby."

Outside, he lets the screen shut behind him, turns, "Thanks for the tea, Professor Lawrence."

From inside the screen she watches him. "It's Ceridwen. I think I will lie down for a while. I'm sorry," she laughs. "You were here ten minutes, and you fixed half my kitchen."

Feeling Derek's eyes on him, he backs to the stairs, raises a hand.

Suddenly she is serious. "Night, my washer leaks. There's a shower that won't drain, and a whole room where the lights won't come on. The whole house is falling apart. My boyfriend says he'll fix it, but he won't. He's too busy. He isn't any good at it anyway." She looks embarrassed. "I never realized how much everything costs. Keeping this place up is like maintaining the Hult Center. They want sixty dollars just to come look at the washer. Look, I know you haven't even moved in yet, but could I pay you to check it over sometime?"

"Sure." Fool. He is a fool. "I'll be by tomorrow to move my stuff in. I... could look at it then."

"That would be great, see you tomorrow, then."

Rain dribbles down out of a dark sky as Night heads down the walk to the Lincoln where his partner waits. He has absolutely no idea what he will say. None. Derek will want answers, and he has none for him. What he does have is two rooms in a house with a dealer and a check that will bounce if he doesn't get to the credit union after work.

What has he done? That he should have been so out of control scares him, thrills him, too. He can't say why, but he feels more alive than he has in a long time. Like a man coming up from deep water for a gulp of air. But it's insane to think he can move in with a dealer under investigation and hope to get away with it.

It's stupid.

It's dangerous.

It could cost him his job.

Then why the hell is he smiling?

• • •

Ceridwen watches Night walk down the drive. "Hear that, Alex? He's going to look at the washer."

"That's what Len said, too."

Guilt hits her a blow as she shuts the door. "I know." Back in the kitchen, she dumps his untouched glass of tea. "God, I can't believe it. We might not have to spend Sunday at the laundromat."

Alexis leans on a hand, pressing her face out of shape. "If he's not a flake."

Ceridwen frowns. "Why do you say that? You just met him." Suddenly worried, she presses a hand to Alex's forehead, feeling for the heat, infection, relapse. Feeling none, her heart drops back to its place under her breastbone and she draws Alex to her.

Alex pulls away. "Will you stop it? I'm fine."

Used to the rebuff, Ceridwen smiles, "Try to be a little more positive, huh?"

Alex shrugs. "Yeah, sure, the world's a swell place."

Cer opens her mouth to respond, thinks better of it. "Staying in?"

Alex sags. "Uh, huh. Mr. Hix gave us three pages of addition. It's so stupid!" She slams down her pencil. "Three pages!"

An ice pick of pain drives through her temple. No way she is getting into that with her today. "Can you get your dinner, babe? My head's driving me nuts."

"Yeah, sure." Alexis looks up, concern on her face. "You want anything? I could mike some soup or something."

Staggered, Ceridwen feels her way to her room. "No, honey, all I want is for this headache to go away." She kicks out of shoes, squirms out of jeans, stepping on them to yank her legs free one at a time, leaving them where they fall. She calls behind her down the hall, sound of her own voice unbearably loud. "Kiss me good night later?"

"Uh, huh."

Crawling between cool sheets, she brings up a knee, presses pillow to cheek and, almost at once the pain lessens. Eyes closed, she rubs her foot up and down over cotton percale, soothing herself. Her mind turns to the day everything changed, the day she became a single woman. She had just taken a deep dish lasagna out of the oven after a day battling the pasta machine over egg noodles when Jeff had felt the urge to spill his guts.

He is in love with one of his graduate students.

Stunned, she turns, hot Pyrex in her hands. There he sits at the counter cradling Scotch and water in two hands. Suddenly everything makes sense to her. All the pieces that hadn't fit fall into place now. Humiliation warming her face, she sees it- —all she has done her best to ignore. Is she really so shocked?

"Did you hear me?" he asks, voice low, face concerned, the sensitive professor even now.

"How long?" She says it calmly, dish still in her hands, heat burning her through oven mitts.

"Almost two years," he says. He is glad she takes it so calmly. He goes on, eyes on his glass of Scotch, dunking ice with a finger as she stands numbly, hands burning. He'll be moving out. He would like a divorce. They will be getting married as Lisa is pregnant. "Put that down," he says. "It's hot."

Pregnant. Bubbling lasagna in her hands, smell of melted cheese turning her stomach, she staggers, nearly folds, catches herself. He will be starting another family. Moving on after eighteen years, trading up.

"Cer, put it down, we need to talk."

Lisa—what name could be more perfect? Twenty three, but very mature—he says that. She fights the urge to laugh. Of course maturity is what he craves.

"Will you come and sit down?"

The lasagna she hurls against the wall. For one timeless second it stays, then slides to the floor, leaving a bloody smear of sauce. He spills his drink, watches her warily in stunned silence.

In no hurry, she pours herself a glass of iced tea, takes a chair at the table across the kitchen. There sits her husband, forty-year-old full professor, head of foreign languages, looking as if he's not quite sure whether to run or stand his ground. No mystery what attracted Lisa. A good looking man. She sips her tea, finds it needs sugar, adds a spoonful, stirring. The sugar swirls but does not dissolve. Too cold. So, this is the mid-life thing.

"I had hoped we could work this out calmly," he says, much less confident, now.

She notices perspiration beading his upper lip. "I'm calm," she says contemplating her reflection in the mirror behind him. Thirty-eight. Hair still all right, but the face, the eyes… She smiles at the woman in the glass. Never will she be mistaken for twenty-three again. Thirty-eight does not compete with twenty three.

All so predictable, so banal, so drearily commonplace. She watches him pour more Scotch. He wants her to ask, needs her to. About them. How they had met, how guilty he feels, what it was like to lie for all those months, their plans, how they make love. Oh, yes. He wants to share his conquest. The son of a bitch wants to share.

Her palms itch to bounce something off his skull. How like him. He would relish this high drama. He is prepared to take the high road—to be the calm one, the superior one. She's seen him play the part so many times in committee and he is so very good at it. He wants to see the fear worm its way though her bowels. He wants her to beg, scream, cry. In the mirror behind him she meets her own eyes, feeling herself turn hard and cold.

Like hell she will.

Voice low, she speaks, eyes on the man across the room who was once her husband. Mind void, words come of their own. "I want you out of my house. Now. Tonight. Today's Thursday. You have tomorrow to get what you want. My furniture stays. Saturday I have the locks changed. Whatever you leave goes to Salvation Army."

He reaches across the counter, "Now, Cer—"

She slams both palms down on the clear glass table top and he jumps, says no more. She takes a deep breath, calming herself. "I want the house and I want Alex. Other than that I don't care. Have Ron draw it up. I'll sign it."

He opens his mouth and she stops him with a raised hand. "It's that or we go to war." She snatches up her coat on the way out. "I'm going for a walk. Be gone when I get back."

That quick one life was over and another began. Now here she is. She smiles into her pillow. Rooms rented. Disposer working.

Only reasonable anyone who could fix a disposer could fix a washer.

Maybe her luck isn't so bad after all.

Pain in her head a dull throb, Ceridwen gropes her way toward sleep.

• • •

Crossing the street Night weighs his options.

He can get out from under this one. He can. All he has to do is make the buy before the check hits the stratosphere. He takes the cold door handle in his hand and he knows he won't do it.

He slides behind the wheel, rain trickling down his neck. What he will do is lie. And why not? A lie is a lie. Lie to dealers. Lie to dopers, tweakers, lie to women—anything to get what you want—which is usually not what they want. So this time he lies to his partner.

Derek looks up, sighs. "What she do, grow some for you?"

"Talker."

"How'd it go?"

It went great. That's how it went. He blew a thousand bucks and a career all in twenty minutes. All for a woman he knows nothing about. No, that's not true. He knows she has a boyfriend and a daughter and he knows she deals. Derek moves to the front seat and Night pulls them out and away from the house. Now all he's got to do is kid the kidder. Lie—to Derek. "No problems."

"You ought to try this, man." Mouth full, Derek offers a gooey dark slab, "Tofu carob brownie."

Night cringes, swallows. "I won't tell you what that looks like."

"You're missing out. Sure you don't want some?"

"I'll try to resist."

"So…" Derek sucks brownie off his thumb, works his way down his fingers, "Let's see it."

Night turns left, taking them downtown. "Didn't get it."

Derek cocks his head, jerks earphones off by the cord. "Say, what?"

"I said…" Night looks right at him, "I didn't get it."

"That's what I thought you said. Why not?"

Because he didn't ask. Because he's never seen a woman that could smile like that. Who knows why? Night knows the body language of liars. He knows how they avert their eyes. That he can beat. It's that cop's sixth sense he worries about. He looks Derek straight in the eye. "Out until next week."

"It took you an hour to find that out?"

Night glances as his watch. He had been in her house twenty-seven minutes. "So I stayed a half-hour. What was I supposed to do, ask for it through the screen door?"

"That would work."

"Well I don't, not that way. I was building up rapport."

Understanding crosses Derek's face as Night catches the last scrap of yellow, taking them through the intersection of Fifth and Willamette. "Ah, so, she looks good up close, too, huh? I get it now."

Derek's ribbing has never bothered him before. "We talked. She made tea. Her kid came in."

Derek sips from his can of Diet Coke, brown pinkie extended, "Oh, tea, jolly good show. So you're old chums, now, what? No doubt the purchase shall come off smashingly next week eh, old bean?"

Downtown Night parks behind the hidden INET office, noses the Lincoln in toward a brick wall recently sandblasted back to red clay. He takes the key, looks over at Derek in the quiet car. "Yeah. Right."

They head in. The scent of baking bagels lies heavy on the air from the bakery down Willamette. Inside, Night heads for the toilet. Alone in the room, he faces the mirror, standing still as a hare in the glare of headlights.

First lie to his partner.

They say the first is hardest.

It wasn't.

It was easy.

Too easy.

• • •

Nine o'clock that evening, Night spots a unit on a stop across the street from a crank house and pulls over.

Two dealers from California. Late twenties, cruising in a lowered Caprice with a local girl, cute thing, fourteen. One dealer produces no ID, gives a bogus name. If he'd only known it, he could have walked away and they would have had to watch him. They have nothing. But he doesn't know. No rocket scientists, maggots.

Under a tangerine streetlight the dealer stands, rips his shirt off over his head to show he's clean. Rain sparks orange as it falls past the streetlight to bead and run on the dealer's dark skin. It beads, too, on Night's jacket as he uses his quiet voice, one man to another. Up close and confidential. Reasoning. Cajoling. The con game. The waiting game. A contest of wills. Night perches on the hood of the car, spins the line he's famous for. If it takes all night he'll find out who this guy is.

When he has what he wants, Night slides off the hood and, hair dripping rain, calls one of the uniforms over out of the light. They run them both, come up with warrants. As the cops cuff and belt them in the back seat of the cruiser, Night keeps an eye on the girl.

Skinny thing, hair same color as Jade's. On the front seat he finds her balled up pantyhose, scales, bags. Everything but the coke she's hidden. End of story.

Woman across the street—a crank dealer Night knows from his time on the street—comes out on her porch to watch the excitement. Turns out she knows the kid. She assures Night she'll call her parents and get her home. Not liking it, but with no reason to hold her, Night leaves her there. All one big happy family, Eugene. It takes a village. It sure does.

Back in the car, they drive, Night's head churning. Same age as his daughter. Dealers twice her age. Thousand dollars of white dope up her skirt. Tomorrow—if the baggie doesn't break and OD her—she'll be nodding off in school. Ask her to concentrate on long division after her big night out? Sure thing. If this world makes any sense he sure as hell doesn't know what it is.

Derek suggests Chinese, and though he's no longer hungry, he takes them there. A smiling man smaller than Jade takes their order.

"Why so quiet?" Derek says, pouring them tea.

Night nudges the bowl of tea around with an index finger on the slick table top. "Awful young."

"Same age as Jade." Derek's dark eyes read him. "That's it, isn't it?"

Night says nothing. Friends since grade school, they read each other like ticker tapes. Food comes, steam rising off a mound of bean sprouts. Derek digs in, eying him, curious. "You going to eat?"

Night grunts.

"Call her."

Again, he has read his thoughts. Night sighs, blade of guilt working its way between his ribs.

"Go on." Derek motions, mouth full. "I'll watch your food."

Night slides out. "That's what worries me."

The booth is dark, light burnt out. Night presses the numbers by feel.

"Hello?"

He's disappointed to hear Rita's voice. "Can I talk to her?"

Rita's trademark—as Kleenex owns tissues, Rita owns that sigh. "It's ten o'clock."

"I know… I know what time it is, Rita. Can I talk to her?"

"She's in bed. She has school tomorrow."

He shuts his eyes, breathes out, breathes in, forcing himself calm. He raises his voice, she'll hang up. He wants to talk to his daughter he'll have to play. That's the way it is. Baksheesh—the toll on the bridge. He thought he'd given up resenting it years ago. He hasn't. "I know it's late, Rita. Just for a minute."

"Did something happen?" The old concern in her voice sounds tinny, out of place. "Never mind, I don't want to know." Another big sigh, "Just a minute."

"Rita."

She comes back, "What?"

"Thanks for being a good mother, Rita. You were always that, always a good mother."

"Yeah." Her voice is edgy. "We've all got our good points. Hang on. And Night, take care of yourself, will you?"

The phone bangs down. Rita saying this to him… Been an odd day all around.

"Daddy?" It's Jade—sleepy, surprised, worried—the one voice in the world that turns him to grape jelly. Before today it was. He tries to answer but his voice refuses to cooperate. The jelly cop. The thin purple line. What a flop his life is. What a complete write off.

"Daddy, you there?"

"I'm here."

"Something happen? You okay?"

"I'm fine, Booboo," he lies. "Nothing happened. Just wanted to hear your voice. You can go back to sleep now."

"Oh, Daddy." She laughs, still half asleep.

Face hot, scalp tingling, he's grateful for the dark. "You snug?" he begins the ritual.

"As a bug."

"Homework done?"

"Yup."

"That kid, what's his name, the one who pushed you off the bench last week?"

"Sonny?"

"He bother you any more? He does, I'll come down there and have a talk with him."

"Dad, he's not bothering me."

"He pushed you, didn't he?"

"That's because he likes me."

"Likes you? What's the matter with him? How old is he, eighteen?"

"Seventeen."

"Well, you just tell him your dad's a cop, okay? You tell him he better not even look at you. Do that for me, okay? If he ever touches you again—"

"Daddy, he won't bother me again."

He frowns into the dark. "Yeah, why not?"

"I told him I didn't want him to touch me."

He thinks that over. "You said that?"

"Sure."

"That's…" His nose reacts as if he snorted horseradish. He pinches the bridge between his fingers hard, phone cradled at his neck. Head against cold steel of the booth, eyes shut. Teeth he clenches hard enough to make his jaw ache. The air of the booth is stale and smells of the butts ground out on the floor. "That's my Booboo."

"It's late, where are you?"

"Spring Garden with Derek catching some dinner."

"You're okay, though, you sure?"

Now he is. "I'm okay."

"Then I better go. Spanish quiz tomorrow."

"Another one?"

"She gives us one every Monday. She's tough."

"She is, huh? You want I should maybe break her kneecap?"

"Daddy, she's sixty years old!"

"What, you don't think I can handle her?"

"Oh, Dad."

He loves hearing her laugh. He's missed that laugh more than anything else the last three years. "Listen, baby, I…" He wants to say this right. "How would you feel about spending the weekend with me?"

Silence. He shuts his eyes, kicking himself for asking. He's such a goddam kid.

Why can't he learn to wait?

"The whole weekend? In the tin can?"

He smiles at their code for the travel trailer he lives in. "Not in the tin can."

"Where, then?"

"You'll see."

"Dad, tell me."

He has her attention. "Oop, being paged, got to run."

"Dad, stop goofing around. What do I bring?"

"A swimsuit would be a good idea."

"A swimsuit?" Her voice is electric. "We're going to swim? In the rain?"

"Afraid to get wet?"

"What time?"

"I'll pick you up at school, wait for me."

"You sure?" He hears the old hesitance in her voice and despises himself for it. Too many disappointments. All the times he's promised to meet her and not shown. So what if it was work. As if that made it okay. It won't happen this time. Not this time. "Promise."

"I'll be waiting."

"Sleep tight."

"Don't let the bedbugs bite."

He hangs up, sits in the dark.

Night Hume plays daddy from across town in a phone booth in the back of a Chinese restaurant at ten at night. He pushes his way out of the booth and heads back to his cold chow yuk.

Some dad.

• • •

Next morning Ceridwen's head throbs.

As she bends over to slip on her shoes, the top of her head feels as if it may come off. She's heard people describe the feeling, but has never felt it. Breakfast is aspirin gulped with orange juice. With relief she hurries Alex out to ride her bike to school with a friend, grabs her bag and hurries out the door.

She can make it through today. She has to. Today is lab day. She doesn't trust a grad assistant to set up the culture media the way she likes it. In spite of the throbbing behind her eyes she will get through the day. And then she will come home. And then she will die.

The drive to the college she survives, one hand holding her head together. At lights, eyes closed, she pants, working hard to convince herself she can ignore the pain. Several times she loses track of time. A horn behind reminds her where she is and, concentrating on the license plate of the car in front of her, she forces herself to drive.

Will power and black coffee get her through morning labs. In the department office, she runs into Dr. Pickering, head of Life Sciences. A bird-like woman of middle age, with the carriage of an Oxford don, she perks up as soon as she claps eyes on her. "Good God, you look like the plague. Allergies again?"

Ceridwen collapses in a chair, winces from the shock of sitting, head a bruised muskmelon. "My head feels like it's going to go off like a bomb."

Concern plain on her face, Pickering lays a hand on her shoulder. "Well, you just get on home, then. Jo and I'll take care of your afternoon classes."

Jo, department secretary, a tall woman with close-cropped blond hair, grabs a phone. "I'll get a G.A. to cover for you, and you should see someone about that headache. How long have you had it?"

Ceridwen makes the effort to speak. "Ever since that cold a couple weeks ago."

"Sinus." Jo wags a finger. "I tell you it's sinus."

"You mean to tell me you haven't been in yet?" Pickering says, Bristol accent out of hiding. "Why ever not?"

Ceridwen groans wearily, annoyed with herself. "I don't know, haven't had time. I spend half my life at the laundromat."

Pickering props a hand on one round hip. "And why haven't you seen to the washer, then?"

"Money, why else?" She sighs, head pressed in the vise of her hands. "I've had to let two bedrooms."

Jo lets the phone sag at her ear, "Running a boarding house, now?"

Pickering casts Jo a frown, "Well, it doesn't cost a penny to go to the health center, and that's precisely where you're going."

"I hate missing labs. We're wrapping up cloning callus cells in media and I—"

Pickering snorts through a pug nose. "Oh, bosh! You're not as indispensable as all that, your G.A. can muddle through. Some antibiotics and a warm bed are what you want."

Jo drops the phone into its cradle. "Got her in for one o'clock, so she needs to get right over. Oh, and Joan's taking your afternoon labs."

Through a fog of pain, Cer levers herself upright. Joan was good. It would be all right. "Okay, okay, you win, I'm going."

At the health center, she sees an intern only a few years older than her son. Nice kid, he's very serious as he offers her a thick penlight. "Close your lips around this."

Smiling at the vaguely sexual suggestion, she complies.

He darkens the room. "Something funny?"

"Uh, uh, no," she says around the tube, face burning.

"There it is."

"Ere hut ih?"

Incredibly, he understands her. "A dark spot in your left sinus—infection." He presses it gently with a finger, making her wince. "We'll knock it out." He hits the lights, writes a prescription for ampicillin.

"What about the pain?"

Still writing, he digs in his coat pocket, drops a couple sample packets of ibuprofen in her lap. She sees what he gave her, groans under her breath, disappointed. With the size of the ache in her head, these would be like using a BB gun against King Kong. "Thanks."

The prescription he waves in the air between them, "Take this seriously. It doesn't clear up you may need surgery."

At home, she takes the pills, crawls into bed, trying to sleep. No use. All she can think of is them going in up her nose with something long and sharp and cold. Right now she would lie at the feet of a road worker, let him drill into the front of her head with a jackhammer if it would stop the throbbing. At least no checks will bounce this month. Night took care of that. Doubt washes over her, dark and smothering.

Did she do the right thing renting to him? When she'd first seen him out on the street her impulse had been to run. But his eyes made her forget the hair, the jacket, the unshaven face. His voice, too, reassured her. Somehow she was sure he was a man she could trust.

She thinks of the work he does and cringes, then again with guilt for the revulsion she feels. She sighs, sinking deeper into her pillow, pain at ebb. So he hauls garbage. It's honest work. Decent work. Someone has to do it. She wishes it helped. It doesn't.

Then there is the daughter. She should have had Alex meet her. A teenager. She pictures tattoos, tongue stud, spiked hair, leather. She should have met her before she rented to them.

Too worn by the ache in her head to resist sleep, she sinks deeper.

Dear God, let the girls get along.

• • •

Feet up on the old couch in the second floor INET briefing room, Derek reads the paper as Night drags in.

"About time."

"Overslept." It was a lie. The night he had spent in a cold sweat.

"The sleep of the just." Derek rises, tosses the paper aside, strikes a heroic pose. "Well you might tremble, evildoers, for we is on our way."

Derek leads down a hallway heavy with the smell of leather and polish and through a workshop where a woman labors over an inverted boot. They emerge into bright overcast through a door marked Sole Survivor Shoe Repair. Night takes them out onto Willamette, homing on their first drive through of the day like frog to water. He knows exactly what he will do. He will fill Derek in on his plan to rent the rooms in order to soften her up. Sure, makes sense. She was suspicious. He was losing the sale. He needed a way to loosen her up. Unconventional, maybe. Derek will want to know why he didn't tell him. But he is sure he can make it fly. Tonight a quick trip over to let her down, to say he found another place, and he'll be out from under. It will work. After all night going round and round with it, It's the only way out he can think of.

Night drives them to Taco Charlie's, orders coffee. "Want anything?"

"Don't drink it any more."

This is news. "No coffee, now, huh?"

"That's right." Derek smiles a superior smile. "Julie read it causes colon cancer." He makes a Richard Pryor grimace. "And who needs that, right?"

Doing his best to look serious, Night nods admiringly. "I think that's great. She's going to have you living forever. It'll seem that way, anyway."

"Come on, come on, we got work to do."

"What work is that?"

"Meeting Linda. I want to ask why she didn't tell us about the professor being out of product."

Night's palms go cold, tightening on the wheel. Not good. He has to be the one to change the story, not Linda. Night takes the car up to the pick up window. "What's the rush? Next week's only three days away."

Derek glances inside the window where a girl pours Night's coffee. "Don't like leaving things hanging, that's all."

Is that all? Night gets his coffee, peels off the lid, makes a show of inhaling the aroma, eyes closed. "Mmm… Is there anything like the smell of fresh-brewed coffee?" He remembers and is at once sympathetic. "Oh, sorry man, I forgot." He smiles, simulates ecstasy, "Oh, man." He looks up to see Derek watching. "It's not that good. Really. When we meeting her?"

Derek scowls. "Ten."

"Ten? You know she's never up before noon." Usually true. In Night's experience, strippers are neither healthy, nor wealthy, nor wise. "You wake her up, she won't be able to remember who she is until she's had her coffee and whites, you know that."

Night slips it in drive and Derek slams it back in park, leans over to Night's window, calls to the girl at the register, "Can you do that again?"

She's confused. "I forget one?"

He hands her a bill. "I told him two but he's…" He taps his temple, "You know, thanks."

Night puts on a puzzled face. "But I thought—"

"You're right," Derek takes his cup. "Let's give her a couple hours."

So he has two hours. Night takes them out onto Seventh. It's not much, but it's enough.

"When you showing me that fixer?"

At the light Night thinks it over, decides it may give him the opening he needs. "How about now?" Night pulls out onto Fifth and east toward U of O. "Sure you want to see it? It's a hell of a mess."

Derek squints at him over his coffee, "You growing dope in the basement? Yeah, I want to see it."

He takes them up from Fifth, turns on Fairmount, sweeps up and around the hill past the house where he will sleep tonight. From the corner of his eye he sees Derek watch it as they pass.

"Two cars out front. There she is talking to a kid on the porch." He cranes his neck as Night cruises by. "She gave him something, you see that? She passed him something. Didn't you say she was out?"

He shrugs, keeping his eyes on the street. "That's what she said."

Derek watches him. "She suspect you?"

Of course she didn't suspect him. He gave her no reason to. Night shrugs, feels the long cold fingers of the lie feel their way through his guts. This is the moment. This is the cue for him to tell the truth, to clear away the lie, to make it good. It has to be now. Right now, or he is lying again with silence. "Don't think so."

Derek broods as they head up the street.

That quick the chance is gone. "Maybe it wasn't what it looked like."

Derek gapes. "That a joke? I know what a goddam buy looks like, so do you. Tell me that wasn't a buy. Go on, tell me."

He can't.

"I don't know what happened yesterday, how she resisted your charm, but that was a goddam sale and you know it. I'll see what Linda has to say."

Lead in his belly, Night pulls to the curb in front of his house.

Derek stretches his back, looks it over. "This is yours?"

"It's mine."

"You one of them crooked cops I read about?"

Night sees he's kidding, breathes, the fist clenched around his heart opens. Not until yesterday he wasn't. Inside, the stench of mildew and ammonia hits them.

"What's that, cats?"

Night slides open a glass door for air. "Husband had Alzheimer's. Twenty years they let the place go."

Derek tries a light switch. "No power, either?"

"They'll be out Monday."

Night leads a quick tour. It's a mess but it's his mess. And it won't be a mess forever.

In the kitchen, Derek opens the oven, pulls a dried mouse out by the tail. "He done."

Night laughs, the lie for the moment forgotten and follows Derek out.

"You won't have to worry about filling your idle hours for a while, anyway."

Night locks up behind them. "That I won't."

"When you be moving in?"

"Couple months if things go right."

Derek takes a last look from the street. "The American dream." He claps Night on the shoulder. "You made it, man."

The rest of the morning they search power company computer records for a house out at felony flats for anomalies in power consumption. Big drop means a harvest. Surge means wide band greenhouse lights back in use for another cycle. Boring work, made bearable only when one of the attractive single computer data entry operators is assigned to help them. Today Night draws the one Derek calls The Hag—and not for her looks.

It's a long afternoon. Neither finds probable cause for a search. At noon they wait for Linda at their usual meet by an ugly red metal sculpture off Seventh near the Beltline on-ramp. Derek sits as Night paces the block, praying she won't show. He's on his tenth lap when Derek pulls up in the Lincoln. "It's one. She was going to show she would have by now. If you're done with your aerobics, let's go."

Relieved, Night is curious to see they are headed downtown. "Where to?"

"Her apartment. I'll roust her out of bed if I have to."

Night waits in the car as Derek tromps up to the door. If Linda's home it will all be over in just a few seconds. When on the third ring there is no answer, he slumps in his seat, takes a deep breath, eyes shut.

Derek slams his door, "Off on a binge somewhere."

Night promises himself to slip her a twenty next time he sees her. "It happens."

Disgusted, hissing under his breath, Derek pulls out, grinding gravel, "Tweakers."

• • •

After work, Night drops by a copy of his credit report and Ceridwen offers him the key. He tells her he'll be moving in Friday night and that he'll look at the washer then. That night he boxes up what little he has and falls asleep mouthing the dialogue along with *The Maltese Falcon* on the tube.

The phone brings Night out of deep sleep.

Through gaps in aluminum foil lining the windows of the travel trailer he sees light and groans. He feels for the phone on the floor, finds a shoe, a box of crackers, an open jar of peanut butter.

Insistently the phone trills.

He finds it, snatches it up, "Night."

"Get dressed, I'm on my way."

Only Derek. "What you talking about?" Night lifts his wrist, focuses sandy eyes on his watch, "Yesterday was my Friday. I'm picking Jade up after school."

He can hear Derek chew—something disgustingly healthy he guesses. "No problem, you still can, it's only, what, ten thirty? We'll serve the warrant on Childs and you can be home by two easy."

Night sighs, passes the receiver to his left hand, licks peanut butter off his fingers. This is not happening. He can't let it. He goes and he knows what will happen. He knows. "Derek…"

"Hey, buddy, I'm asking a favor here, Hutto's out with the flu. I need you on this one."

"I promised, man, I promised. I won't disappoint her this time."

"Cross my heart we'll have you out by one, one thirty at the latest. What do you say?"

Night presses the heel of a hand to his forehead hard enough to make veins on his forearm stand out. "You know it never works that way. I'll miss her again."

"Cross my heart, man. We'll get you to the school on time if we got to use a strobe and siren to do it, you've got my word on that."

Night groans and it turns into a yawning stretch.

"Good, now get dressed. We've got bad guys to catch."

Disgusted with himself for letting himself be conned, Night chokes down dry cereal, then loads the last of the boxes into his trunk. Derek is there by eleven. They pick up the informant, a tall, skinny half-Indian, and Derek takes into traffic.

"Staying clean, Ricky?" Derek asks.

Rick removes his fedora, sets it on the seat. "Yeah, man, I'm clean, I'm clean." He strips his shirt over his head, shows tattooed arms, emaciated stomach, scarred back.

Night looks him over, hands back a twenty for the buy.

Rick stares in slack-jawed confusion. "Where's mine?"

Night shakes his head and sighs. Some winners he deals with. This guy is sad. "When we get the balloon, Rick, that's when."

He huddles in the back seat of the Lincoln, trembling as Night watches. This guy should be a poster boy for the drug war. Put him on every toilet stall. Weak souls like him dope chews up and spits out.

"When you eat last, man?"

"Don't remember, day before yesterday, maybe."

"What you have?"

Rick stares out at the street, eyes dead water. "Bologna sandwich, at the mission."

Night looks at Derek, sees what he feels reflected there. What was a little more time? "Want something?"

Rick turns, eyes seeming to focus through the back of the front seat and about ten yards past. His brow creases in thought. He decides. "Yeah, I could eat."

Derek swerves into the drive through, where a fat Mexican on a tiny burro asks him for his order in the voice of a nineteen year old girl. Derek orders Night his regular taco burger. He turns to Ricky, "What you having?"

Back to the door, arm on the seat back, Night watches him. Wherever he is, is a long way from here.

"Big Mac."

"Wrong," Night says. "How about a taco burger? they're pretty good."

"No, man, give me a cheeseburger." He slurs his words like a man asleep. "With everything, extra catsup and mustard."

Night watches his eyes light with an idea.

"And pickle."

"And pickle," Derek repeats.

"You're not eating?" Night asks him.

"You kidding? That stuff's poison." Derek pats his brown bag on the seat beside him. "Tofu pudding for me."

"Poison?" Ricky says, red eyes lit with suspicion, "What you mean, poison?"

"Don't worry, man, figure of speech." Night calms him, gives Derek an unhappy look. "It's good, you'll like it."

They collect their order, park around the corner off the drag under a catalpa tree to eat. Night pictures Jade standing on the street waiting for him. He looks at the time—noon. He watches Rick unwrap his burger, set it in the waxed paper in his lap, spreading the wrapper out smooth with filthy hands. Then he rips open one of the ten catsups, pinching it between dog-yellow teeth. As if he's performing brain surgery, he squirts it over the open face of the patty in a geometric pattern. Night watches him do this six times. Night stuffs what's left of his taco burger in his mouth, wads the wrapper.

Night checks the time. He's already pissed ten minutes away. This keeps up it'll be one o'clock before he'll be ready to start eating. Night pictures Jade out waiting in front of her school, kids, cars thinning out. It's happened before. More than once. It won't this time.

Halfway through the pile of mustard packets, burger looking like something by Dali, Night reaches back, folds it up, tosses it out the window. "Let's go."

Derek pulls away and Rick looks up at him from under a drooping fedora, mouth open, face puzzled. "What'd you do, man?"

"I threw out your masterpiece is what I did, Gauguin. Here." Night tosses a twenty in his lap, "We get done, you can get yourself another one and a forty ouncer, my treat. Right now we're in a hurry."

Around the corner, they park, send Ricky on his errand.

When he's gone, Derek sighs. "What's eating you? That was the first thing he's had to eat in two days."

Inside Night boils. He catches another glance at his watch. "I gave him a twenty, he'll be all right."

Derek's not satisfied, "That's not like you, Man."

"Look…" Night's had all he can take. "I need an aura reader, I'll call one. You see what he was doing? Did you? He was playing with his food. We'd still be there. I don't have time for that crap. This is my day off. I got to be somewhere."

Derek won't let it go. "We've known each other a long time. You've never been a horse's ass."

At this point Night wants one thing—to be on his way to Jade. Behind it all is the lie—prodding, eating. He looks out the window, "Maybe I was and you didn't notice."

"Maybe you're right."

Rick comes back around the corner, tosses the balloon of crank in through the window, grabs his twenty and keeps walking.

Derek drops by the office, prints out a warrant and they run it by the judge's office for a signature. A call to the team and they meet down the block, pile into the van. They ram the door at one thirty. Night is third one in, like always. Third because he's the only one with no wife to worry about. Third because when things go to shit that's the guy gets whacked. First guy goes in, the suspect's watching the tube.

Second guy goes in, he reaches for his piece. Just about the time the third comes by he gets his gun up, and bang—no more number three. Night likes the slot, counts on his luck and his speed to bring him through. So far it has.

This time nothing hits the fan but air. Ten seconds of bedlam and everybody's down, everybody's calm. When they're cuffed, Night takes the man of the house back into a bedroom to pitch him. Nothing overt, nothing anything like coercion, just the bit about them forfeiting their home, about the possibility of doing time, about them losing their kids to Services to Children and Families.

"You screwed up bad, you know that. SCF will be out. You got anything to say you think will make it better you've got five seconds to say it." All the time Night's hoping he won't turn anybody, praying he'll just keep his mouth shut. He rolls, he'll never meet Jade by three. Never.

So far so good. All he gets is the blank stare. Treading eggs, Night heads for the door.

"Okay, man, I'll give up my supplier. He ripped me anyways. He's at the Blue Moon, he—"

Night raises a hand to stop him. "Wait a minute," Night says, waving him quiet, backing away, "just wait." Outside he slams a hand against the wall, sending a picture crashing to the floor. "Dammit!"

"Derek comes running. "What, man, what?"

"The SOB gave him up."

Derek laughs, "Just a minute, let me look that up in my little book. Yup, uh huh, says right here that's supposed to be good."

"Yeah, great."

"Oh," Derek turns serious, "I forgot about Jade, sorry, man."

"Thanks." Right then Night hates him. "Me, too."

"What you going to do?"

Night sighs, "Call Rita—again."

The second warrant leads to a third. Third to a fourth. It's nine when patrol units transport the last of the suspects to jail. Derek drops him at the trailer and cursing himself, the job, and whatever else is handy, Night loads the last of his stuff into the trunk. Ignoring the drunken yelling match in the trailer next door, he slams the door to the tin can for the last time.

The drive over he whips himself bloody. He's a lousy father, a lousy husband. The one thing he's good at is being a maggot. As a maggot he's a natural. Why fight it, that's what he is. Maggot with a shield, but still a maggot. The worst part of it is that he's let Jade down. Jade—the one thing in his life that's good. He grew up without a dad and now she is. Because he's a flake. Because he can't keep his promises. This stuff just doesn't end. It keeps on going right down the line.

He whips the Lincoln into Rita's driveway, slams it into park. Dreading the scene coming, knees stiff, elbow sending numbing jolts up his arm, Night drags himself up the circle drive. Spotlight-illuminated walls rise two stories above him at the crest of a knoll, reminding him of the castle at Disneyland. On his way up he laughs, shakes his head. The Magic Kingdom. Who would want to live in a stucco castle? Rita, that's who.

Conscious of his hair, jeans, leather jacket, aware that with his puffy face, withthe extra twenty pounds he's put on to look the part of a junkie he looks like the scum Ray must think he is, he presses the buzzer.

Rita answers, scowl darkening her face. "It's eleven o'clock."

He leans against the jam. "My watch works. She ready?"

"She's been ready for eight hours."

He's been on the receiving end of that voice plenty. "I was held up, okay, you know what that means. Like you were held up at the office when you were a legal secretary. You remember that, don't you?"

"Let's not get nasty." She gives him one of her best looks. The threat's there— the door opened, can close as easily.

He drops his head, takes a breath, runs fingers through snarled hair. He hates it when she's right. "Okay, I'll start over. I'm here to pick up my daughter that the court said I had a right to visit every weekend I wasn't working. This weekend I'm not working. I would appreciate it if you let me take her. Please."

Rita ratchets the hate down a notch, sighs. "She's getting her things, now. She fell asleep." She looks closely at him, "Have I ever made seeing her hard for you?"

He hangs his head. He prefers Rita angry to Rita offended.

"Have I ever kept you from her? Have I?"

In her voice he hears what may be the germ of hurt. And hurt he doesn't want to deal with. He is done dealing with hurt from Rita. He throws in the towel. "No, Rita, you haven't, you never have. I'm just tired, that's all."

Her voice changes. So do her eyes. Around them is the old worry. "You okay?"

Rita wants to know if he's okay. The overfed shyster's wife in her million dollar mansion on the hill wants to know if the maggot slime X on her porch is okay. "I'm fine." It's not like the old days. He can't stay angry with Rita now. He's not sure why. Maybe because she's so forgiving. Charity of victor to vanquished. "I'm just tired. I just want to get Jade and go, that's all."

Now the great doctor of jurisprudence, the great defender of downtrodden co-caine dealers and green dope smugglers, comes to the door, slips an arm around Rita's ample waist. "Hey, Night, how's business? Come on in. I'm just watching a replay of the Atlanta game. Got a cold one for you in the fridge."

Why does he have to be so goddam nice? "Thanks, Ray, but I'm beat. I just want to get home. Rain check on that beer, huh?"

"Sure, how's the house going? Got that sheet rock torn out yet?"

A prod to remind him of a favor or genuine interest? Night can't tell which. "Not yet." He peeks around the door. Still no Jade. Damn.

Ray pulls at his bottle of beer. "You look like a train wreck, you know that? Ought to try sleeping once in a while."

Night smiles despite himself, leans back against sandpaper stucco, crosses his arms. "Thanks for the advice, Ray, I'll try it."

"Hey, no problem," he says, heading back to the TV.

Jade comes to the door, Rita kisses her, and they head down the hill to the Lincoln. It's started to drizzle. Perfect.

He tosses her bag in back, and they go.

• • •

The air in the car is frigid.

And not from the open window at his elbow.

He tests the waters. "Sorry I'm late, Babe. Got tied up."

She watches the wipers work.

"Babe, I'm sorry."

"You said that."

The words go in a needle stiletto. What's he supposed to say to that? He waits at a light, rain an idiot percussionist working the roof of the car with spastic fingers. "As a dad I make a pretty good dope dealer, I know that. You'd be better off with Ray." The light changes and he takes it out on the Lincoln.

"No, I wouldn't."

"Sure you would. He's a great guy."

"He's horrible."

"Horrible? We talking about the same Ray?"

"He's…bossy, he thinks he can tell me what to do."

"He can tell you what to do. You live in his house."

"I hate him."

He looks at her. "That's malarkey. You hate him, come on, you're talking trash, now."

"All right, maybe I don't hate him, but I have a father."

He pulls on Beltline, the V-8 purring, taking them up the ramp at 70. "I don't know what it is about fathers. My dad was no good at it. I think I scared him."

Flashing blue and red comes close in the rear view. Night hisses under his breath, heads for the shoulder.

For the first time tonight she looks at him. "You were going too fast, huh?"

Resigned, he sits back, ID ready. "Yeah."

There's no guarantee the cop will know him. He rolls down his window, switches on the dome light, holds his ID out in the glare of the headlights. The cop edges up, staying behind the door, takes his ID.

"Night, that you in there?" He shines his light in his eyes, then over at Jade. "You look like shit."

It's Phil. Hotshot. Night's never much liked him. Too mouthy, too much of a player. "Thanks, would you get that out of my face?"

"Sure, who's the babe?"

He grabs back the offered ID. "She's my daughter, Phil."

"Oops," he says under his breath, and leans down to see into the window, "Well, hello there. So you're Jade. Last time I saw you you were—"

"Yeah, Phil, she grew. Be seeing you, huh?"

"Sure, but let me give you a little advice, huh?"

Night keeps his teeth clamped so hard they groan.

"The way you look, in that car, I'd watch how I drive, you know?"

"I will, thanks," he says, and pulls away, leaving him by the berm.

"You know him?"

"I know him."

"Don't like him very much, huh?"

"Not much." He squints at her through the dim, "You could tell?"

She gives him a tired guffaw, "You don't hide it very well."

For a block she's quiet, but he can tell she's got more to say. "Your dad was scared of you?"

He thinks he knows what's coming next. "He never said it, but I think he must have been."

"And are you scared of me?"

The 64 thousand dollar question. He drives, taking his time, not wanting to screw this up. Since he wised up a year after the split he has lived his life for her. His eyes he keeps on the road. "Maybe."

He can feel her eyes on his face in the dark. "Of what?"

What good is a voice if it fails at all the wrong times?

She reaches for his hand on the gear shift, squeezes, "You're a good dad. If I could live with you, I would."

He whips them down the ramp onto seventh. Heart stopped, he watches her in the near dark, "You would? Even after everything?"

"You know I would. Next week's my birthday. I'll be thirteen. I can come live with you, if I want, can't I? They let twelve-year-olds decide for themselves. That's what you said."

Not trusting himself to open his mouth, he takes them up Seventh past motel no vacancy signs.

"Where are we going?"

"You're sure about that? You're sure you would?"

"You should know. I don't bring it up because I know you don't have room. But, Dad, when? You've talked about this for so long. When will we have a place?"

He squeezes her hand on the seat. This is going to be good. This is going to be so damned good. "We've been over this and over this, haven't we?" He works at keeping his voice stern.

"I know…" She nods, eyes on the floor, voice a bored sing song. "You're working on the house and when it's ready we'll move in, but a cop doesn't make what a shyster does so I've got to be patient."

"That's right. That's exactly right." He can't help smiling. "You know you do that very well."

She stares ahead. "Thanks."

"Well, you'll never guess what happened yesterday."

She looks up suspiciously, not daring to hope. "What?"

He pulls up the slope to the driveway and into the carport.

"Where are we?"

He kills the engine, turns to her in the silent car. "Home. I got a place."

"You did? " Her mouth falls slack. "You got a place?"

"I got a place."

"I don't believe it." From the wariness in her voice he can tell she doesn't.

"I don't either, but I did. Want to see where you're going to sleep?"

Excitement vibrates through her like current as he opens the trunk. Her eyes take every inch of it in. "Oh, Daddy, here? It's so big!"

"Don't expect too much. It's just an old house and we're sharing it. We've each got our own room."

"I don't care. Is it nice?"

"It's okay." Wanting her to like it as much as he does he leads her along the path to the back and through the gate into the yard.

She stops dead with an intake of breath. "It's got a pool." She runs, stoops to dip her hand. "And it's warm." She rises, crushes him in her arms, "I want to stay. Can we?"

He holds up the key. "I'm paid up. Open the door while I get the blankets."

Through a dark house he leads her. Upstairs in the glare of the overhead light her room looks spartan. He desperately wants her to like it, though it can't compare to her room in the castle. "It's not much, I know."

She drops her bag to explore. "Oh, I like it. I've never had wallpaper. It's nice."

He makes her bed while she changes in the bathroom down the hall. Shaking out the sheets he revels in the smell of laundered linen. In spite of everything. In spite of all the lies he had to tell to get them here, it has been worth it. He tucks the sheets tight, shakes out a thick wool blanket. Pillow pinched under his chin he shakes it into a case, tosses it on and looks over the bed he has made. For Jade. Something he should have been doing for the last three years.

Jade returns in sweats, digs Puppy out of her duffel and and jumps in bed. Night tucks her in, kicks off his shoes, unclips the Glock in its holster from the inside of his jeans and lays it on the bedspread, curls up next to her. He reaches to tweak Puppy's nose and she slaps his hand away. "Don't hurt Puppy."

The game they have played since she was four. It never changes. "I was just playing with him, is all."

She clutches him tighter. "He doesn't want to play with you."

"Why not?"

"Cause you're mean, that's why."

"What do you want him for? He's old and he's ragged and he's dirty and he's—"

"He's Puppy and I love him."

"I know, but I think now that you're growing up we should throw him away, don't you?"

"No."

"He'd be easy to get rid of, Puppy would."

"No, he wouldn't."

"Sure he would. We could put him down the garbage disposer."

"No."

"We could bury him under a rosebush like that vicar did with cats."

"I said no."

"We could drag him behind the car until he's just a little ball of dirty stuffing."

"He stays right here."

He sighs, beaten. "He does?"

"Yes, he does."

"If you say so."

"I say so. "

Puppy under one hand, her other wrapped up in his, she talks. About school and girlfriends and things only women care about—all the she-said-this-but-really-meant-that stuff. He basks in her voice and pretends to listen. It doesn't take long for her to run down. Soon she fights to keep her eyes open—and loses.

He watches her, this incredible person right here in front of him and he keeps on looking as if he could soak her up through his eyes. All Ray has to offer, everything his income can buy, and she wants him. She wants a room in somebody else's house and her maggot father. Awed, he watches her breath slow.

He reaches out to touch a single finger to her brow—incredible.

Failed marriage. Failed husband. Failed cop. But Jade is his daughter.

No way he deserves her.

No way he ever could.

• • •

Ceridwen awakens to a clanging from down the hall.

Head throbbing, she puts her feet to the floor, shuffles downstairs, steadying herself as she goes. At the end of the hall she finds Night with his head in the washing machine. "What time is it?"

His head comes out. "Morning."

She winces, raises a hand to hold off the sound. "Not so loud."

He looks up at her, appraising, concerned. "Sick?"

"Fighting a sinus thing."

He nods, smiles. "Sorry about the noise, had to do a little persuading with one of these hose clamps. Rusty as hell. You'd think they'd pop for stainless but I guess they saved a couple cents."

"Whatever you need, I'll pay you back." Reaching out, she steadies herself against the wall holding her head together over her eyes with a hand.

"Head feel like it might explode?"

She nods carefully, amused. Why shouldn't he know about sinus headaches? It seems everyone does but she.

"Thought it might. Been to the doc?"

"Went today. He's got me on antibiotics. Says if it doesn't clear up he may have to send me to a surgeon."

He nods as if he has heard this before. "I know that tune. What about the pain?"

She winces. "Worse. I'm just going to stay in bed."

He seems to consider. "Doctor young?"

She frowns, "Why?"

"They love the pills and the knives, the young ones. Let one of them dice up my arm. Wish I hadn't, now. They've got their Mercedes payments to make, bless their little avaricious hearts."

"All moved in?"

He levers himself to his feet, calls to Jade. Ceridwen winces at the sound of his voice. Must he yell?

"Sorry."

In she comes, Alexis at her heels. "What, Dad?"

Ceridwen forces herself to open her eyes to look, and sees that her fears were needless. She only wishes she looked less a hag. "You're Jade."

"Yeah, hi."

"Hi." Ceridwen tries to smile, but can only grimace.

To Jade he says, "Grab me a couple clean towels down the hall, will you?"

She goes as Ceridwen watches him through squinting eyes. To her, he looks nauseatingly vital. "Why towels? Is it leaking?"

"Look, I know you probably just want to get back in bed…"

He is right about that.

"… and we'll be going out in just a couple minutes and let you sleep, but if you like, I could show you something that'll help."

Inside she cringes. She doesn't want to be rude, but some weird home remedy she doesn't need. Without the slightest hope that what he says is true, or the slightest interest in hearing it, she tries her best to smile, hoping her dread doesn't show. "What's that?"

"You need to lie down. "

She forces herself to peer through the fog of pain to see if he's kidding. He's not. "Lie down?"

"The couch will work fine."

She doesn't have any idea what he's talking about. Nevertheless, she allows him to lead her to the living room. "I think I'll just go to bed."

"It'll help. I promise."

She's curious and a bit wary. She doesn't want him popping her neck or anything even vaguely painful. She doesn't want anything but her bed. "What are we talking about here?"

Jade comes with his towels.

"A home remedy that works." He opens his hands with a self-deprecating sort of non-laugh. "Look, I don't want to be a pest. I know you don't know me at all."

Right again. Carefully, so as not to allow the top of her head to fall off, she lies back, thinks it over. Their daughters are here. She trusts him not to do anything stupid.

Another twinge hits her. It's as if a giant's boot heel grinds her eye socket. "Why not?"

"I'll just be a minute."

Another throbbing pain washes over her. She doesn't want it whatever it is, but she isn't worried. She'd known when she saw him on the porch the first time that he was nobody to worry about. A little rough looking, maybe, but she trusts him. After seeing Jade she trusts him more. Maybe she's being stupid, but she does.

In the kitchen she hears water run, then the microwave drone. It beeps and in he comes with a steaming towel.

She holds him off, squinting into morning light flooding in at the window. "That's it? A hot towel?"

He nods. "You need hot and cold compresses. Now if I just tell you that, and we leave, you won't do it. I know you won't. I wouldn't."

"I can't argue with that."

"I've had this, I know how it feels."

Try as she may she can think of no reason why not. She gives up, leans back, "Okay."

"Here, careful, it's hot. Put it on as hot as you can stand it. Press it right where it hurts." He lays it on her face. "How's it feel?"

Hot. Very hot. Good, too. "Get a bigger towel." She moans as the heat works its way into the great ball of pain that is her head. Yes. She doesn't know how she knows it, but she does—this is the right thing to do. She can't see him, but his voice she trusts. It's a voice that, like the scalding towel, may be good for her. An odd thought. She pushes it away. "This is Heaven."

"Thought it might be. I'm going to crawl back under the washer and make sure what parts we need. Just…stay there."

If she could laugh without dislodging the top of her skull she would. "I'm not planning on running away." She lets the moist heat relax her. It seems he fixes more than washers. She smiles into the towel. Stupid, she knows. Home remedies are fine, but how can a hot towel cure what only antibiotics can? Okay, so she humors him a little. What can it hurt? She has to admit, it feels good.

"Mom?"

It's Alex. Ceridwen gropes, finds her hand, draws her close. "Yeah, Baby?"

"What are you doing?"

"It's something Night is doing for me to help my head."

"A wet towel? How's that going to help?"

"I don't know, but it feels good."

"I met Jade."

"Oh, and how are you getting along?"

"Okay." She pulls away. "Be back in a minute. I'm showing her my room."

She revels in the heat, thoughts drifting. At least the girls are getting along—so far. She feels his tread on the carpet beside her and wonders how long it's been. Gently he lifts the towel, replaces it with one shockingly cold, and every muscle in her body contracts. "Get that thing off me, it's too cold!" She pushes it away, squinting painfully up at him. "Give me another hot one."

"It's got to be ice. Sorry."

She'd trusted him and now this. It's nightmarish. She's helpless and she doesn't like the feeling. "Why? It's sadistic!"

He smiles down at her . "Because it does. Just for a minute. Come on." He presses it to her face gently. "Just put up with it for a minute while I get the hot one ready."

"Well, hurry up, will you?"

He catches her holding the icy towel off her face and gently presses it down, "No cheating, hold it on."

She grits her teeth, regretting ever going along. The cold burns where heat soothed. Having it on her is misery. Then the ice is gone and the heat is back. She melts and runs down between the cushions, soaking into the couch like hot wax. "Oh, that's so much better." Comforting—the heat and his voice both. Alex is there to hold her hand and for the first time in a week the pain is bearable. Now why would that be?

"Here comes the cold one."

She wants to cry. "Already? I don't want it."

"I know you don't want it. You need it."

She holds it off, but he presses it gently on her and she lets it come. It lights her head with cold fire. "I hate this!"

"I know, but you can take it, just for a minute."

From under the corner of the rag she sees Jade standing by to rush the warm towel to the microwave. Hot, cold, hot, cold. It goes on for what seems an hour. It's just after Jade lays a fresh hot towel on her face that her head turns inside out as a tsunami of liquid under pressure sweeps through her sinus, agony and ecstasy mated. She moans, reaching to feel for a head she's not sure is still there. "Jesus, oh, Jesus!"

"What is it, Mom?"

He's there smiling down at her. "Worked, didn't it?"

She squints up at him, not believing the pain is gone. "It did it! It broke! I felt it go down behind my palate! Just like that the pressure was gone! Oh, my God, it feels so much better I can't tell you." Wanting to cry with relief, she sits up, hugging Alex to her, head a deflated balloon.

He hands her a box from his shirt pocket. "Here's some spray decongestant I picked up. Use it. It's open, now. Keep it that way."

Her heart sinks. "You don't mean it'll close up?"

"It can. As long as you can breathe through your nose you should be okay. Jade and I are going to get more of her stuff. I found the trouble with the washer. It's the pump. I'll pick up a new one on the way back if they're open Saturdays."

She looks at him through new eyes. The absence of pain changes her, changes everything. It's as if a vice has been unclamped from around her skull. "I'll give you a check."

He follows Jade to the door, "You can square with me later. See you tonight."

She rises, follows Alex to the window, head not pounding for the first time in a week. Alex is uncharacteristically quiet. "You like her?"

Alex nods.

"She seems nice, huh?." Ceridwen watches them back down the drive in his old Lincoln.

As she watches she wonders.

Is there anything he can't fix?

• • •

On the way to Rita's, Night wrestles with asking Jade to lie.

He doesn't want to, doesn't want to have to explain why. He doesn't want to ask her, but the thought that she might have told Alexis he was a cop chills him. He's got to say something, and it's got to be soon.

Rita meets them at the door, looking puzzled and none too pleased. "I thought she was staying the weekend."

Night hedges. "We came to pick up some things."

Jade heads upstairs and Rita corners him in the kitchen. "So, what's this all about?"

He dreads what is coming, doesn't see any way round it. "She wants to live with me, Rita, has for a long time, you know that."

"I've seen where you live. You adding on a bedroom?"

He won't let her do it to him, not this time, won't let her sucker him in. He sheds his leather jacket, hot in her house. Rita and he fought the thermostat war for five years. He lost. Whatever cost the most money, that's how she had to have it.

Night looks at her, really seeing her for the first time in the three years since she left. What he sees does nothing to him at all. She's become a woman he wouldn't glance twice at. Hips spread to fill the leather seats of her Mercedes, designer jeans in size 14. Even the long sweaters she wears can't hide the ravages of comfort and affluence. "I found a place."

"You did? Where?"

"Up the hill from U of O on Fairmount, near the fixer."

She frowns, puzzled. "You can't afford that, and anyway, she's still eleven. Ray wants her here. He loves her."

"So do I, Rita."

She sighs, "I know you do. But sometimes, Night, love just isn't enough."

She isn't just talking about Jade, now. "It is with us."

Jade pads silently downstairs to hesitate in the doorway. Night sees her, Rita does not.

"Ray will stop you. You can't fight him, you know that."

"You're wrong, Rita." He hopes she's wrong. "Ray wants her to be happy, and she'll be happy with me."

In her face he sees the gloves coming off. "Oh, and what about all the nights she gets to spend alone? What about all the mornings she gets up to an empty house because you're still out somewhere, maybe dead? What about school? What about gymnastics? Have you thought about any of that? Have you?"

"I'll be okay. Dad can drive me to gymnastics, can't you, Dad?"

Rita turns, surprised, "How long have you been there, young lady?"

She looks down, "Not long."

"Go on out, Baby," Night says. "I'll be out in a sec."

Jade gone, Rita springs to the attack. "You're driving her in that Lincoln? Does this sound like a better idea to you than it does to me? Maybe some doper you bust will take a shot at you, huh? That'd be nice."

He backs away and she comes close enough to whisper. "You sure you want to do this? Are you really sure you're ready? You know, kids aren't something you do until you get tired of them. They're there every day, whether you feel like it or not. Don't disappoint her again, Night, don't. Don't do it."

Guilt rises, a dark tide inside him. He deserves this. And more. "Look, Rita, I know I'm not the best dad in the world, but can we just give it a try, just give it a couple weeks? I can't work it out, I'll bring her back."

"You will?"

He stops, takes a breath. "This has never been about fighting over her for us. We've never let you and me get in the way of what's best for her. I won't start now. Just let me try it. Ray could tie me up in court in a New York minute, I know that. Talk to him for me. Get him to give me one shot. Just one. I've got a good place in a good neighborhood. Not too far. She can come over any time she wants. Any time you want. You can come over and check on her. Here, I'll give you the address." He uncaps a marker, scrawls it on the message board on the front of the fridge. "There, you've got my cellular number. Come on, what do you say? Couple weeks, that's all I ask."

She's not happy, but he can tell he's got it. "I want her home in a couple days to talk it over with her. When do you go back to work?"

"Monday."

"I want to see her Monday."

"I'll drop her before I go to work, around five."

Rita crosses fleshy arms. "I don't like what I hear, she stays."

Knowing better than to try for the last word, he heads out.

They are as far as 30th Street before Jade speaks. "She doesn't want me to go, does she?"

"She loves you, you know that."

"I know, but I've lived with them for three years. In a week I'll be twelve. I'm not going back. I don't have to, do I?"

He looks at her, clamps a hand on her neck, "Not if you don't want to." He has no idea where the money will come from to hire a lawyer to fight Ray if it comes to that. All he knows is that short of sending him to jail, they won't be able to make him send her back. "Not if I can help it."

She looks thoughtful. "So tell me about her."

"Tell you about who?"

"Alex's mom, she's divorced too, isn't she?"

He watches her, speculating. "How do you figure out all this stuff so fast?"

She shrugs, a woman thing.   "How long has she been divorced?"

"Couple years, I guess."

"Think she'll get married again?"

"How would I know? Maybe. She says she has a boyfriend."

She looks up at him, blue eyes searching, thinking… What? He can't tell. Her mind is working, though, he can see that. "Mama got married right away, huh? After…"

She'd been eight years old. Too young to know the details. He sees no reason to drop them on her now. So what if Rita ran out on him with her boss? Rita's no angel, but she loves her daughter, is good to her. He would never sour that. "Within a few months, I think."

"What about you?"

"What about me?"

She rolls eyes turned dark. "You know—will you ever get married again?"

In the five years since his divorce he's dated several women, none of whom he could picture living with for the rest of his life. Then there was Sam. If everybody has a weakness, Sam is his. "How should I know, baby?"

He takes them by the parts store, then to the fixer where he plans on explaining to her about the necessity for the lie. She helps him fill a dumpster with carpet they rip up in pieces. Two hours later they're filthy and he still hasn't brought it up.

She passes with a roll held at arms length. "This stinks like ammonia."

"Cats." He follows her out with a load and knows it has to be now. "Can I ask you a flavor?"

She passes on her way back in for another load. "Shoot."

Inside, they each wrestle up another armful. "You remember what you used to tell people I did for a living?"

"Sure, why?"

"Well…" He's going to have to say this just right. She's very sharp and he doesn't want her guessing. "Some people are a little bit nervous around cops, you know that…so I just thought…"

She stops, rests her load against the wall, frowns. "You don't want me to tell them."

"You think you could do that for me?"

Her mind is working again. "You don't trust her?"

Now what? She should be the detective, not him. "I trust her just fine…" Liar. "…but I still don't want her or anybody to know I"m undercover."

In Jade's eyes, suspicion. "Dad…"

"What?"

"This feels funny. I mean you rent from her, she seems nice, and I mean, look at her house, you really think you have to worry?"

"I'm a worry wart, you know that, just—"

She raises a hand, "I know, I know, just do you a favor. Okay, okay, you're a trash man."

Conscious of having dodged a bullet, he follows her to the dumpster with another stinking armful of carpet, jute backing sanding the skin off his arms.

He got away with it this time.

How long until she puts it together?

• • •

Ceridwen is on hands and knees weeding in a flower bed when they drive up.

Close by, Alex sits cross-legged, hand on chin, looking bored. When she catches sight of them, she jumps up.

"Oh, Dad," Jade says, "I like it here. It's even better in daylight." Jade squeezes his scrambled arm, bounding out the instant he stops. She and Alex run to the house. Massaging his elbow, he watches Ceridwen work. What would it be like to come home to a woman like this one? Best looking dope dealer he knows. What is he doing bringing Jade into this? What is he doing here himself? How can a professor who peddles to her students—okay, to her adult students—look as decent as she does? For the hundredth time he wonders why she does it.

He props the door wide with his foot, sighs. Okay, so he's done something very stupid. It's just until he gets the house done. Couple months max. He can get through it. The important thing now is that he just keep his distance. He does that, he'll be fine. Derek's another problem, but he'll work it out.

Ceridwen sits back, wipes her brow with the back of a gloved hand, "Guess they've broken the ice."

"No fur flying yet." Going to her, he holds up a plastic bag. "Got the organ right here, I'd better get to the patient."

She leads the way to the washer, "I can't wait, got laundry piled to the ceiling."

Back against the wall, he can feel her eyes on him as she watches him work. "I asked the guy what was likely to need replacing and he sold me a filter and a couple hoses, too."

She shakes the bag. "How much was all this stuff?"

He strains to free a hose clamp with a nut driver. "Don't confuse me. Not too bright, only think about one thing at a time." The hose comes away in his hand. "That puppy was a leak waiting to happen. I guess the old guy wasn't kidding." He points to his tool chest. "Hand me a pair of pliers?"

She does. "How does a sanitation worker know how to do all this?"

Sanitation worker. That's always killed him. "Don't be polite. I know what I am, I'm a garbage man. It's not glamorous, but somebody has to do it.

She raises her hands in surrender. "Okay, how does a garbage man know appliance repair?"

"My mom taught me."

"Your mother?"

He enjoys the surprise on her face. "She raised me. We ran a little hardware store out in Coburg. Sundays we'd fix stuff around the house. There was a lot to fix, the house was old even then." He hands her the old pump and she gives him the new one. "See, she had the idea that if she cussed and listened to the Dodgers games on the radio and taught me to fix things, use tools, stuff like that, then I wouldn't grow up queer. She was scared to death of that." He sees her reaction and laughs, raises a hand to stave it off. "I know, I know, it was the fifties. Cut her some slack."

He rips open the bag, sets it in place. "What do you know, it fits. Accidents happen."

"How'd she do?"

He laughs again. "Not too bad other than I can't stand baseball." He watches her face with amusement. "To her way of thinking, she failed." He reaches out, keeping the part in place with the other. "Got that Phillips?"

She lays it on his palm. "Failed how?"

He seats six screws as hard as they'll go. "She wanted me to take over the hardware store. I wanted to be a cop. I used to work there as a kid, stocking and working the counter. I learned a lot doing that. I was only eight or so when I started."

He digs a hose out of the bag and works it over a barbed fitting. "Dad worked the catalogs. He had the counter covered with fifty books in a rack. The days before computers, right? Mom ran the office—billing, the books, the cash, all that, but he was the man. He was the one loggers came to when they needed something—case-hardened national coarse one-by-twelve bolt and hex nuts, say, or bronze ring-shanks, all the weird stuff you could ever think of. He could find any of it in those books of his. Dad could tell you if it was made, how much it cost, and how long it would take to get it. He had most of it out back in the warehouse anyway. Now you call some-where and if the system's down nobody can tell you anything. There's nobody who knows." He shrugs, "Progress. Dad—he knew."

Going to his toolbox, he puts together a ratchet and socket extension and begins tightening hex heads on hose clamps. "I'll always see him like that—rail thin at his counter, phone cradled at his neck, cigarette hanging out of his mouth, flipping through his catalogs. I'd get some guy asking for something I didn't know and I'd wait and, here he was busy, always busy. He'd bend down and ask me what I needed. And, I don't care what it was. He knew. He'd tell me, and I got to tell the guy."

Night works the new filter gently into its tube. "These guys knew him, they knew what was going on. These are guys with work to get done. They played along. That was something for a ten-year-old, I can tell you. But the thing was, he always knew the answer. "

He lowers the front of the washer, sets the screws at the bottom, tosses the screwdriver into his chest. "He died of a heart attack one night working late. They said he was dead before he hit the cement." He gathers old parts into the bag. "I just wish I had his trick for knowing."

Her eyes go wide. "You mean it's fixed…right now…like that?"

"Like that." He sets it back against the wall, turns on supply valves, plugs it in. "Try it."

She turns the dial, pulls it out. It begins to fill. "I can't believe it, after six months…. Can I do a load?"

"We can keep an eye on it to make sure, but it should be fine. What else needs work?"

She opens her mouth to answer and the doorbell rings. She leans to glance out the window, then back at him, eyes bright with what may be panic. "Just a minute. One of my students…." She hurries down the hall.

He's been expecting this. Funny her reaction. Bad liar. As if he could live here and not know. Can the dealer be ashamed of dealing? That would be a new one. Keeping well back, he watches out the window, sees the book he hands her with a twenty as bookmark. Nice touch, the book. Another book she hands back, crack in the pages where the finger bag of bud keeps it open. What could be any more normal than a professor giving one of her students a book? To the untrained eye no money changed hands. Slick.

He hears the door shut. What a jerk he is. What an absolute idiot. Here he is pouring out his soul to a dope dealer after he promised himself he would keep his distance. What is wrong with him?

She finds him waiting perched on his tool chest.

Without understanding why, she feels obligated to offer an excuse. "Forgot his book."

He nods. "Forgetful, kids."

She searches his eyes, is unable to read his thoughts. "They can be."

"What else?"

She fills the washer, adds detergent, lowers the lid on the most wonderful sound in the world. "You don't have to do anything else. This is more than enough."

The girls scream down the hall in their suits on their way out and Alexis freezes, open-mouthed at the miracle. "It works?"

"Don't worry," Jade says as she passes. "If Dad says it's fixed, it's fixed."

Over her shoulder, Alexis says, "Mom, have him fix the lights in Grant's room."

Night picks up his tools. "Where's the box?"

"You don't have to—"

"Lead on."

She gives up, leads him to the back porch and he opens the breaker box as she watches. "I know what you're thinking..."

He looks as if he doubts it.

"No, I do. What a dumb woman. She doesn't even know how to reset a circuit breaker, but I do. It won't go back on. I've tried it a hundred times."

He switches off the main breaker. "That wasn't what I was thinking."

She watches as he pries the circuit breaker out of place. "You didn't even try it."

"Why should I? I believe you. We'll assume it's the breaker." Crooking a finger, he raises it to the light. "See that?"

She moves close, notices his hands. Hands like her father's—hands that can do anything. She forces her eyes to the black box he holds. "What? That black screw? It looks burnt."

He tosses it into the trash. "They burn out like everything else."

"So I'm not dumb after all, am I?"

Eyes smiling, he squats, rummages in his chest. Matter of opinion. "No, you're not."

She examines exposed wires in the dismantled panel. "Now if I'd just turned this big one off up here..." She reaches inside to trace the cable with a finger. "...then I..."

He grabs her so fast it hurts, jerking her back hard against his chest. It knocks the air out of her, makes her heart race with fright and indignation. Her hands push against arms irresistible. "What? What is it?"

He releases her. "I'm sorry, I looked up and saw you reaching. I didn't know if you knew it could kill you. I'm sorry I grabbed you."

A finger of ice traces her heart. "It could kill me?"

"You knew that."

She doesn't follow. "You turned it off. I saw you."

"Yeah, but see," he points to big cables at the top, "those cables are right off the pole. They're still hot."

"Even with the main breaker off?"

"Even."

Shame rises, heating her face.

He shakes a new breaker out of its box, connects wires, sets the cover. "So now you know. Don't worry about it."

She slides down, suddenly weak, to sit, back against the wall. Don't worry about it. If he were Len, she would be hearing a lecture now.

Watching him, she thinks of something. "How on earth did you happen to have one of those in your little box?"

He fits it into place, replaces the cover. "You said you had lights that didn't work, so I came prepared. Turn it on. And keep your fingers crossed."

She reaches out, hesitates, looks back at him.

"It's safe, now."

She switches it on, and when she sees lights come on down the hall, feels sudden wealth. She laughs. "It works." She watches him, running her tongue along the inside of a molar the way she does when she thinks hard about something. "You knew it would."

He shrugs, snaps his box shut, "You said you had a shower didn't work."

"You'd better be keeping track of all this stuff, so I can pay you back. You are, aren't you?"

"Have no fear." He nods seriously. "I keep track of everything."

Now what does he mean by that? "You do, huh?"

"Sure. Lead the way."

She freezes, remembering, slaps her forehead, "I forgot, it'll have to be another time, I've got to go out tonight." She doesn't like the way that sounds. Much too close to the way she feels. She glances at the time, sees she's late, backs away, feeling rude. "I've got to get ready. A sitter's coming in so it won't be any trouble for you. There's dinner in the fridge and if there's any problem Heather knows where to get me."

Feeling his eyes on her back, she rushes to shower.

• • •

On the way out to the car Ceridwen pummels herself with guilt.

Disappointment—that's what she felt the moment she realized it was Saturday. She can't get over it—disappointment. Well, she will prove herself wrong. Tonight she and Len will have a good time.

Len takes her to the Pasta Factory—again. Tonight he's excited about his latest physics demonstration, and goes into great detail describing it. Something to do with velocity increasing as an object falls. She follows him that far, but loses him when he trots out the formulas. Round about the time he takes out the mechanical pencil she tunes him out.

Making all the right noises and facial expressions, she lets her mind wander. Fascinating how much people enjoy talking about themselves. What's amazing is that it doesn't seem to matter to most of them whether anyone listens. Chin in one hand, glass of chianti in the other, she contemplates the man across the table.

Len Goldbloom—six-two, fit, forty-eight, not bad looking, just the thing for her. Of course he wears glasses, and although she knows it is shallow of her, she wishes he didn't. He wears his usual black slacks, white oxford with wingtips. Winter, spring, summer, fall, the outfit never changes. If anyone had ever told her she would be sleeping with a man who wore wingtips she would have laughed out loud.

He makes a point about something and she nods, smiles as if she understands, and he forges on. How can you not notice that you are boring someone to tears?

They met at a faculty Christmas party soon after her divorce was final. He took her home and, at the curb, did not press her for a kiss. That impressed her. When he stopped by the department the next day to ask her out, she said yes. That was nine months ago. They have gone out every Saturday since.

Although she doesn't anticipate their evenings together, neither does she dread them. As pedestrian as they are, they at least take her out. She doesn't much care for spaghetti, but then he doesn't know that. He has never asked. She smiles at Len as she hears her mother's voice urging her to speak up for herself. But it's easier just to go along. They are only noodles, after all. Bland. Flavorless. But better than nothing. Like her Saturdays.

She drains her glass, refills it. Why should she expect more? So what if Len bores her? When she was twenty, she would have been disgusted by anyone who played life so safe. But she isn't twenty. The lines framing her eyes no cream can take away, and in spite of her swimming, bras are no longer optional. Since her divorce she has spent time alone, but has never liked it. Not evenings alone, not the silent house, not the time to herself. At twenty, being alone was exciting. Now it is just being alone. She wonders if that makes her shallow or, God forbid, dependent. Must wanting to share your life with someone be a character defect?

Len passes over a pad filled with clever-looking, but to her, meaningless diagrams and formulae, and she nods, smiling appreciatively. Satisfied, he carries on. Full professor with twenty years in, seventy-five a year. There, sitting across two plates of soggy pasta are the treatments that will cure Alex. She hates thinking this way, but if there's another way out she'll be damned if she knows what it is.

No more zip bags filled with curled bud. No more knocks on the door. No more forgotten books. The sooner she can stop dealing the better. Though she takes no chances, still she worries. Still, she feels guilt. Why guilt when she knows she hurts no one? For some reason today, selling in front of Night was the worst.

She catches herself anticipating tomorrow, and guilt slaps her. Len had asked about her headache first thing. True, he hadn't let her tell him much before launching into his monologue, but he'd asked. What does she know about Night, anyway? Divorced, with a teenage daughter. A garbage collector with a tool box. A joke, that's what it is—asinine. She should never have rented to him.

Len had offered to look at the washer when it first stopped working. Feeling the traitor, she pictures his fumbling. Unable even to open it, he had given up. What difference does it make? So he isn't the handiest guy around. He isn't some clunk making ten bucks an hour humping garbage cans. Len is a physicist. Why does a physicist need to know how to fix a washing machine? Len would buy a new washer without batting an eye. Probably use his American Express card. Then why does her mind keep slipping back the greased slope to tomorrow?

Guilt gnawing, she interrupts. "I think it's wonderful that you do such exciting things in your classes, Len. I do."

He reaches to squeeze her hand. "Listen, Cer, I'll stop boring you with this. I want to know how you got rid of your headache."

Surprised, she leans forward, eager. "You do?"

"I mean you had it for weeks."

"Well, it was the hot and cold towels that did it. They really worked. I couldn't believe it."

"Hot and cold towels? Like for a sprained ankle?"

She poured herself another glass of wine. "Yeah, compresses. They really work."

"And who did all this for you, the doctor at the health center? It doesn't sound like them. Usually they write a prescription and bolt for the door."

"No, no, it was my boarder."

"Your boarder?"

From the tone in his voice she can tell she may have made a mistake telling him. She nods.

"So you decided to go ahead and let the rooms? You didn't tell me."

When had she the chance? "Must have slipped my mind."

Utilizing fork as spindle, spoon as bearing, Dr. Goldbloom winds spaghetti noodles for his next bite. Ceridwen marvels at his talent, reminded of the way he makes love. Jeff had always just stuffed noodles into his mouth, slurping in any trailers, but Len is in another class altogether. He's tried to show her how, but to no use. A man that can eat spaghetti like that can find a way to pay a half-million dollar medical bill for experimental therapy. Slipping past her best defenses, a question worms its way into her mind. How would Night eat spaghetti? Would his way of managing noodles reveal something about him? Has she happened upon a heretofore untapped psychological mother lode? Man and noodle—key to the psyche.

"Is that smart?" Len asks.

She has to scrabble to find her way back to their conversation. "Oh, no, Night's okay, really. His daughter's living there, too. It's okay." She thinks of something. "I reviewed his credit report."

He looks unconvinced. "And he gave you this home remedy?"

"He and his daughter."

"Well, it was a nice thing to do, all right. I'll have to thank him when I see him. I just wonder if you should be getting that friendly with a boarder, that's all. I mean what do you really know about this guy?"

She knows he's a garbage collector that drives an old boat of a Lincoln, can fix anything from an infected sinus to a washing machine, and that he has the broadest back and sexiest hair on a man she's seen in a very long time. "Not much." She drains the bottle into her glass. He's hardly touched his. She will drink it for him when hers is gone. He won't mind. "His credit history is unblemished."

He flashes her a condescending look, wipes up the last of his sauce with a piece of garlic bread. "I mean, Cer, he could be anything."

She smiles reassuringly as she squirms in her seat. For a reason she can't name she doesn't want Len talking about him. "He's okay, Len. Don't worry about it."

He returns to his diatribe. She returns to her wine.

An hour later they are at his apartment. Ceridwen undresses, lays her clothes over the back of a chair. In the bathroom Len's electric toothbrush whines. She slips between cold sheets and waits for him as he gargles. Each time it's the same. She doesn't mind really, not as long as she's had her wine. It takes hardly any time at all. All very businesslike, very quiet, very mechanical. Neither speaks. What's to say?

When he's finished she lies watching the clock until she's sure he sleeps. At ten, she dresses, lets herself out. She wants only a shower and her bed. On the drive home she gropes for a feeling, any feeling, finds none. It isn't so much that she's hollow as she's stuffed with bubble wrap. Stuffed tight with it where her heart and lungs and insides used to be. The bubble wrap woman drives home after her night out.

She pays the sitter, sends her home, checks on Alexis as she passes. Finding Alex asleep with Mr. Frog crushed in a headlock, Ceridwen kneels to stroke her hair, and sadness wells up to choke her. Eyes brimming, she sags against the mattress, smothering her gasping breath in Alex's pillow.

Her life is a trailer park after a tornado. She hates what she is, what she does. If it weren't for Alex she would have nothing. And unless she is very very smart, she may lose her.

She's seen rats in a double bind, shocked either way they move, seen them driven insane by it.

Eyes unseeing, she smooths Alex's hair as she sleeps.

God oh God oh God…

What is she going to do?

• • •

When the sitter shows, Night leaves Alex and Jade in the pool.

At the fixer, under the glare of work lights, he rips out wallboard. What a jerk he is. To risk his job for a dope dealer. To bring Jade into a house where dope is sold off the front stoop.

She is with her boyfriend right now. And here he is.

A nail catches him on the knuckle, raking a gash, and he hurls his hammer across the room where it embeds itself halfway up the handle in the wall. Swell. Another hole to patch.

Tugging at a stubborn sheet he thinks of Sam and at once the room grows stifling. Sam... What a mess. Wanting one woman. Needing another. Trying too late to be the father he should have been from the start. Risking everything on a woman he doesn't know.

Prying the hammer from the sheetrock, he glances at his watch. Sam's on tonight. He can catch her between shows. They can talk. He can see how she's doing at school. He stands, stretching a kink from his back, looking down at the hammer in his hand. And afterward—what? Gently, he sets it on the counter. His hand he flexes to bring back feeling. Afterward nothing.

He walks the block back to the house, showers, and an hour later walks into the Squire. He finds an empty table far from the door, where he sits back to the wall. A dancer struts and thrusts her way across the runway. He waits it out, watching the men around him. Men who have paid to watch from the dark. Sad. Yet here he sits among them. The music changes and he looks up to see Sam.

Willowy with white Irish skin and ash blond hair, Sam is 100 percent real. Graceful as water, she moves in short skirt and vest, legs flashing white above black thigh high stockings. Looking a fast fifteen, among dancers she's day to their night. None of the braggadocio that leaves him cold. None of the gross sexuality, the sneering come on. Sam is innocence. Sam is vulnerability. Sam is who tugs at his sternum.

To the waitress he passes a note. When she takes it away he goes out to wait in the car. He doesn't like watching her up there, doesn't like the way it makes him feel. He's never liked it. Not when they were close. Not now. Too much like picking at a scab.

He hasn't been in the car long when he sees her come out wearing a long coat over her costume. He flashes the lights and she crosses the lot to the far end where he waits.

She slides in, drops her purse, sheds her coat and, without hesitation, straddles him. She tastes of cherry, smells of smoke. Long lean Irish legs bare above her stockings glow in the dim.

He holds her face in his hands. "Sam, I came to talk."

She laughs, voice hoarse. "Isn't that what we're doing?" She goes to work on him and he has to pin her hands.

"Be a good girl."

Her mouth jumps his, "I am."

He reaches for her hips to lift her off and his hands slide under the hem of her skirt and against the cool flesh of her flanks and that quick he loses the determination he came with. Sam is his drug, his addiction. Around her he is a junkie. The feel of her skin under his hands cocaina pura, the whiteness of her splayed legs the prick inside his elbow.

"Oh, you're bad," she says in a way that makes him feel he's the one pursuing. Makes him feel it's him forcing her astride him. His hands find her and she squeals into his hair. No thinking now. He needs her, is frantic for her. And by her frenzy he can tell she needs him.

When she sags against him, he pins her arms just above the elbows and with a fury born of loneliness, of want, of emptiness, of hopelessness, struggles to join her to him. At last he clamps her to him for the last time as he loses his soul through the base of his spine. Dazed with self-loathing, he lets his head loll back on the seat.

She straightens her blouse, slides off. From the box tissues on the dash she takes two, wipes herself. Pressing close she laughs. "Wow. You needed it bad."

Guilt, a filthy wave, washes over him.. "Why do you let me do that?"

"Let you? I didn't let you do anything. We…we did it."

Through a throat constricted he swallows. "I came to talk, just to talk."

"Looking in the rearview she combs her hair with long nails, turns to look at him. "I didn't."

He's got nothing to say to those honest eyes.

"I'm a big girl. I decide what I want and if this is what I want then that's the way it is, know what I mean?"

He looks at her and wishes again he could love her. Wishes he felt something more than fondness and an irresistible electric potential of need. He doesn't. "I can drive you home."

"I've got three more sets. She glances at her watch. "I'm on in ten, got to go." She struggles into her coat. "You want you can come home with me at one and we can get to all that talking you came to do."

He's tried it before. The problem is not lack of opportunity. The problem is they have nothing to talk about. He reaches out to run his fingertips down the curve of her face. Lovely empty-headed child. "Can't. Jade's waiting."

Does he see hurt in her eyes?

She slips on her heels. "No problem."

"How's school?"

She shrugs, grunts.

Sensing something, he watches her closely. "You keeping up?"

"Got to go." She pecks his cheek, slides out, evading his grasp.

He rolls down the window, calls after her. "Are you keeping up?"

She flashes a crooked smile, "Yeah, okay? I'm keeping up. See you."

He watches her go, shame mingled with rekindling desire. It ends up like this every time. She is impossible. A female body like hers is impossible. As impossible as her willingness to tend to his need.

Why does it have to be so damned hard? Why always so far between where he is and where he wants to be? Sam needs a friend. Why can't he be it?

Next time he will.

Next time.

He scents her on his fingers and his eyes shut.

It won't happen that way and he knows it.

He starts the car and heads home.

• • •

Late Sunday morning Ceridwen mashes a clove of garlic under the flat of a knife. Alex bolts for the door. "They're here!"

Ceridwen hears the front door open, close. The girls tear through, headed for the pool. She looks up to find Night watching her from the doorway. "Spaghetti will be ready in fifteen minutes. You and Jade are eating with us, aren't you?"

"As good as that smells? You're kidding, right? What can I do?"

"You don't have to do anything. Meals are included, remember?"

"I'd rather do something."

She has to smile. "Okay, I won't argue, wash your hands."

Feeling clever, she takes down a pack of spaghetti from the pantry, leaves it on the counter by the stove where a pot boils. This will be a test, of what she isn't sure, but how he eats spaghetti will reveal something important about him. Whatever it is, she hopes it will make it worth eating spaghetti again. "Mind tossing in the noodles? Then you can help me with the salad."

"Sounds like a job I can handle."

Behind her she hears him open the package and then the sound of breaking noodles. She turns to see him snap them between his hands into finger length pieces and drop them into the water.

Stunned by the collapse of her plans, she stutters. "What are you doing?"

He freezes, noodles poised over a steaming pot. "Putting noodles in to boil. Isn't that what you wanted?"

Knife in one hand, cucumber in the other she motions. "But… you're breaking them. You're breaking them all up into little pieces."

He stops, confused, "You prefer them long? I can take these out."

So much for clever subterfuge. "No." She laughs, feeling silly. "They're okay. I've just never seen anyone do them that way is all."

"I have ever since Jade was born. It was easier for her to eat them that way, and you know, they're a lot easier for me, too. I've got to warn you, me eating long noodles is not a pretty sight. So, am I putting them down the sink, or what?"

All at once she realizes her plan was not a failure at all. "Go ahead, dump them in."

He hesitates. "You're sure?"

She is not sure. Not about noodles. Not about anything. "I'm sure."

They crack under his hands and the water swallows them. "What now?"

"Why don't you sit down and let me fix you a drink?"

"Tea is fine. How about if I help with the salad?"

This is a battle she has never had to fight. "You can grate carrot, if you want." She hands him grater and carrots, and watches him as she works. His movements are sure, his hands steady. She likes watching him, likes being with him. It's easy. She wants to reach out to tuck the hair out of his face as he works.

He looks up to catch her watching him. "I doing this right?"

She jumps as if she's been caught doing something she oughtn't. He doesn't seem to notice. "Yeah, yeah, you are."

"So, tell me about your work."

Unsure she heard aright, "My work?" There he goes again, smiling—not with his mouth, with his eyes.

"Being a prof, what's it like?"

She sighs, tosses in a handful of cut cucumber. Where to start? What can she say that won't embarrass them both by outdistancing his understanding? "I…teach classes, run labs, supervise doctoral candidates, serve on doctoral committees…"

If he's uneasy, he hides it. "What do you like best?"

She thinks. It has been so long since anyone asked. Len never does. Well, nearly never. When he does she knows he has no interest in her answer. He can't wait for her to finish. With Night it's different. She studies his face to be sure, finds him awaiting her answer. She hesitates, blade of the chef's knife resting on the board. "You want to know. You're not just making conversation?"

He seems surprised she asks. "I want to know…" He shrugs. "…if you want to tell me."

She does. It's odd, but she does. Though it's a little like trying a new dance step—talking about herself. She's had little practice. Especially in the last two years. "I like teaching." She hesitates, voice quiet, eyes on the cucumber under her hands. "The students I enjoy." She looks up, and under his frank gaze she drops her eyes, laughs. "Cliche, isn't it?"

"So what if it is?"

She searches his face for a sign of impatience, finds none. "Everything's so new to them, so full of promise and possibility. I get to teach them about life, about everything living. That's what I love. Everything else is just a job."

His eyes smile, but not at her. There is nothing mean about those eyes. She can't picture them ever laughing at her.

"I thought you might say something like that. I'll bet you're good at it."

She thinks as she works. "I try."

"Your students are lucky to have you. Not every professor would take a forgotten book home with her."

Pleasure gone, she turns to see him busy over his grater. What does he know? What does he mean? Face burning with guilt, she fetches onions and celery from the fridge.

"I've been wondering, though, why did he give you a book?"

Passing by him she scours him with her eyes, wary now. He misses nothing. She will have to be very careful. "He took the wrong one."

"I see."

What does he see that he stares at her so? The bell buzzes and she starts, but stays where she is.

He watches her. "Someone at the door."

Why now? Why would it have to be now? It rings again and she gives up, drying her hand on a towel. "I'll get it." Passing him is like passing something statically charged. It is a young man she has seen but does not know. She hurries through the transaction, face scalding. Why this bothers her she can't say. She knows that when a person blushes it is the body's way of denying appearances. But what is there to deny? She does sell dope out of her house and, until now, it has never bothered her.

Done, she slips the book onto the top shelf of the closet, the twenty into her pocket and returns to her cutting block.

"Another book?"

She can read nothing in his face. Can she really expect him not to know? "That's right."

Night nods as if he accepts her explanation and comes to rinse celery at the sink beside her. They watch the girls in the pool. Usually Ceridwen dreads Sundays. Today doesn't feel like that. Today it feels like she has a friend over for lunch, something she hasn't done in a very long time. "Jade's good with her."

"They seem to be doing fine."

In spite of his questions, she can relax with him. It is as if he were Jo, or Pickering, or George—a friend, someone to talk to, someone who isn't always watching, always judging. The girls circle each other like sparring cats, absorbed in a water fight. "Alexis acts jaded. She's not. The divorce was hard on her. It's tough for a six-year-old when Daddy moves away. He hasn't spent but a couple of Saturdays with her in the last two years. He's got a new little girl, now."

"My parents divorced when I was six."

She frowns, puzzled. "But you said they worked together."

"They did. They weren't about to ruin a good thing. She still had my old man over once in a while for dinner, too. I think they still loved each other."

"Then why?"

"They could fight over what day of the week it was. He'd come over on a Saturday night, bring some porterhouses to barbecue in the backyard. First thing she starts in on him about the steaks being lousy. And she hammers, and she hammers. Finally he says fine, they're no good? He puts them down the disposer. She's yelling and cussing and pounding on his back, he's a big guy, you know, and he's stuffing the meat down the sink. And me, I'm the peacemaker. Six years old, I'm pushing my way in between them and asking them, "Can't we just love each other?" He smiles out the window. "Funny the things stick in your mind."

She can see it, see him as a kid. "That must have been hard."

He shakes his head. "Kids don't think like that. They accept whatever happens. They don't know any better. As far as I knew, my mom, my dad, they knew all the secrets, they knew everything. I would never have guessed that they were really as scared, as confused as I was. Never in a million years."

His musing is infectious. "Now here we are."

He looks at her, smiles, turns back to the window. "Here we are. I remember once, after the divorce, my mom was seeing this guy and I went out with them for some reason. I don't remember why, maybe they picked me up from the sitter, I don't know. We ended up at a bar and grill on Willamette, gone now. Front of the place was all glass. We had a table by the windows. I was in heaven—burger, fries, shake. What else does a kid want, right? Well, Dad drives by and sees my mom's Fairlane parked outside, and her with this guy through the window, and he flips out." He looks at her, shakes his head. "I shouldn't blab so much, I'm sorry."

She sets her knife on the block, grabs his arm above the elbow with a wet hand, shakes him. "No, don't stop. I want to hear it."

"I'm talking about myself too much. I don't usually do that. I don't want to bore you."

She blows air through compressed lips. "Bore me? Do you know what most men talk about? They talk about things—about jobs, cars, how great they are." She gives his big arm one last shove, taps on his chest with her fingers. "This comes from in here. Don't you dare stop."

Her assertiveness shocks her, but she means it. For a moment they watch the girls, now perched together on a boulder at the edge of the water. They turn, look over their shoulders at the house, return to their conversation.

"I wonder what they're cooking up?" she asks.

"Scary, isn't it?"

"You start boring me, I'll tell you. Deal?" She offers a wet hand.

The only sound is the plop-plopping of the sauce, the rumbling simmer of the noodles.

He takes her hand. "Deal."

Suddenly self-conscious, she returns to her slicing. As she works, a thought makes her smile. Here she is making a salad with this man, her boarder, and enjoying it. "Well, I'm waiting."

"You're shaking your head."

She smiles, onion in her hand. "I am?"

"Yes, you are."

Desperate, she points at the pot. "Pasta's ready."

"Where's the colander?"

"Under there, now go on."

He drains the noodles, steam rising to pillow against the ceiling. "Okay, but don't cut that onion yet."

She hesitates, knife poised. "Why not?"

"You have any matches? The wood kind?"

"In the pantry, why?"

He fetches one, sticks the wood end between her lips. "There, now your eyes won't burn."

She laughs, doubting. "You're sure about that?"

"That is wisdom passed down through many generations of Humes."

"Hmm…" She speaks around the match. "Does it work?"

"Not that I could ever tell. Doesn't hurt either. Not a highly educated bunch, my family. Fruit pickers, mostly, back in the depression. Itinerant farm workers is what they would call us now."

She slices. "Maybe it's supposed to distract you."

"Working?"

She glares through watering eyes. "Just get on with the story?"

"Oh, yeah, well, my dad flips out, and gets into my mom's car and opens the hood, and just rips all the wires out of the engine with his bare hands—plugs, coil, battery cables, everything. I'm maybe seven or eight at the time. That made him Superman in my book. My old man can rip a car engine out with his bare hands. Then he comes in and sits down at the table with us. His hands cut up, bleeding. I remember him sticking his cut finger into this poor guy's drink. I asked him why and he said it was to kill germs. Now I see it was to insult him. But I believed him. No big deal. Just another shouting match, this time in the middle of a restaurant. I remember her threatening to call the cops, and he finally left, promising to fix the car. I don't know if he ever did."

She works at catching up. "I thought you said they were divorced."

"Yeah, but I don't know how much it changed things for them, really. She always loved him, and I think he always loved her. They just couldn't live together." He rifles the refrigerator drawer. "Mushrooms?"

"Uh huh, why not?"

In the sink he washes them in his hands under spray. "You said the divorce was hard on Alexis, how about you?"

She shrugs. "Eh…"

"I shouldn't have asked."

She turns on him. "You get too personal, I'll tell you." She watches the girls in the pool, presses a wrist to teary eyes. "I don't know how you're supposed to feel when your husband dumps you for a twenty-three-year-old child. Maybe it's a tonic to some women's self-esteem. It hasn't been for mine. You see young kids flailing around looking for someone, and you feel smug, because you've got someone. And you thank God you don't have to go out looking today with all the disease and jerks out there. And then…you're single again. And suddenly all the lines and sags you didn't worry about because the man you've been with for twenty years loves you—they matter. Now it matters that you're not so slender or so supple or thin or, or, or. Who wants a divorced woman pushing forty when they can have someone with no black marks on her record? If a woman is dumped by her husband it means she's either frigid or a bitch, right? And who's out there looking, anyway? Everyone any good is taken. Am I wrong? "

He smiles down at his mushrooms.

"Am I?"

He laughs. "Thanks, I'm really encouraged. You've really got these pep talks down."

She laughs at the bleak picture she has described. "Well, it's true, isn't it?"

"We'll have to get you to talk to Parents Without Partners. Really give everybody a big lift."

Together they laugh. "Oh, just ignore me. Jo's always telling me I'm too negative. I just feel that way sometimes. Manic-depressive I guess."

"So neither one of us has a chance, then, huh?"

"Well, I've been lucky. I met Len." Even as she says them, the words taste tinny on her tongue.

Smile going rancid, he does his best at a sincere nod and a part of her wishes she hadn't said it. But why not? She is lucky to have him. She tosses salad with her hands. Sprouts cling to her fingers. "What about your divorce?"

Back to her, he dishes noodles. "You don't want to hear about it."

She does. "Come on, spill. All the gory details."

"There's not much to it. Rita went to work for Ron, they hit it off, and that was that. We wanted different things. I don't blame her."

"Awfully magnanimous of you."

"It worked out for the best."

"You really try to see the good side, don't you?"

"Why not? Whining doesn't change anything. So…" He watches her. "If you could have him back again right now, would you?"

She opens her mouth, shuts it, takes a deep breath. She sees no reason not to be honest. "A year ago I would have." She shakes her head. "Not now. Around the first of the month when all the bills come piling in, I wouldn't mind if he stopped by just long enough to write a few checks. Other than that, no. You?"

"We've been divorced for three years. She's part of my past, someone I talk to on the phone to arrange Jade's visits. We're not friends, but we get along okay, now. Probably better than our last year together." He scoops up a hand full of sliced mushrooms, dumps them in the salad bowl. "You know, to tell the truth, it doesn't seem like we ever could have been together."

She is curious. "Why not?"

"She's a shyster's wife, now. She lives the part. They live up on Spring Boulevard in a house that costs as much as a cruise missile, and their neighbor's bathroom window is close enough that if they run out of TP they can reach over and borrow a roll. She drives the Mercedes she's always wanted, and she's put on twenty pounds. She's changed a lot in three years. She's taken up golf, for crissake—golf."

"What's wrong with golf?"

"Nothing, nothing's wrong with it. What is it but bowling for the upper class? At least it's outside. It's just something I can't picture a woman of mine caring about.

Why, you play?"

"Not yet."

"Don't start. Anyway, looking back with 20/20 I guess things didn't turn out so bad."

Ceridwen calls the girls in and he sets as she serves. On her way to the table she works the cork from a long-necked bottle of cabernet, "Take a glass?"

He refuses and she pours herself one. When they are seated, Jade offers her hands. "Will you say it, Dad?"

He hesitates. "It's not my house."

She looks to Ceridwen. "We say grace when we eat together. Is it okay?"

Ceridwen is surprised. She hasn't eaten at a table where grace was given in twenty years. "Sure you can."

Jade's hand Night takes in his right, Ceridwen's in his left. "Lord, we thank you for this meal, these friends and these children. Amen."

Not sure what to expect, Ceridwen exhales, relieved.

"Mom, cut my noodles."

Night watches Alex push her plate to her mother.

Odd, an eight-year-old asking her mother to cut up spaghetti that doesn't need cutting. Fascinated, Night observes interaction between mother and daughter.

Ceridwen runs a knife through the tiny portion on her plate several times. "There, now."

Jade frowns, "But they're already broken up. My dad always does them that way."

"Oh," says Alexis, "I didn't know that."

Night watches as Alex spreads spaghetti sauce around her plate with her fork as if painting. If she eats any he misses it.

"So, Night," Ceridwen says, "tell me more about your work."

He knew this was coming. "What's to tell? People leave their cans by the curb, I hump them into the truck, we haul it down south and build ourselves a plastic covered Matterhorn by the freeway. If it were up to me I'd hose the whole mess down with gunite and throw up a roller coaster."

"A roller coaster?" Ceridwen frowns.

"Sure, like Disneyland."

"Mom."

"Couldn't look any worse, I guess," Ceridwen says.

"Who knows? Might make some money. Ride Garbage Mountain!"

"Mom."

"You don't mind the work?"

"Mom."

He shrugs, understanding her puzzlement, "Well, it's a dirty job, but somebody's got to do it. Even maggots have a purpose, right? I mean, all the lawyers could be wiped out in a night and who would miss them? But if something happened to the garbage men, well, we'd be in a world of hurt, wouldn't we? Like somebody said, "The poets have been mysteriously silent on the subject of cheese."

"Mom."

She laughs, "What's that mean?"

"It means that we're all watching the pretty stuff, the flourish of the magician's hand. Nobody's watching what's important."

She smiles at him, chin in her hand. "Like garbage."

"Like garbage." For him, garbage collection has always worked pretty well as an analogy for drug enforcement. "Okay, I get my hands dirty, but the job's important. I keep the world clean so poets can spend their time contemplating those rosy fingers of dawn they talk so much about."

"Mom."

"But you seem intelligent…"

He smiles and she stalls.

"Mom."

She really is doing her best to ignore the little darling. It's more than he can do. Her voice is a fingernail prodding a fresh wound. He takes his dish to the sink. "So if I'm not stupid I should be ashamed of what I do?"

"Mom."

With an exasperated sigh, she whips around, "What, Alex, what? What do you want?"

"I'm full, can I have some ice cream, now?"

"Eat your spaghetti, it's good," Ceridwen says, and to Night, "I didn't say that."

He shakes his head. "Somebody's got to do it."

"Mom."

He busies himself with the pot, suppresses the urge to scream, wonders how she can put up with this.

Ceridwen says, "You're misreading me. I didn't mean to suggest you should be ashamed."

It is entertaining watching her tap dance around the issue. "Ever read *Atlas Shrugged?*"

"Mom."

She nods, "In college, didn't everybody? 'Who is John Galt?'"

"Mom."

She drops her fork to clang on her plate, "What?"

"I don't like pisgetti." She whines in baby talk, "I want ice cream."

Defeated, she pinches the bridge of her nose. "Oh, all right."

To his amazement she dishes her a bowl. Jade gives him a look and he works at not smiling. At least somebody is firmly in control. What if it is eight-year-old who can't feed herself?

"Would you care for some, Jade?" Ceridwen asks.

Finishing the last of her dinner, she nods. The girls take their bowls out by the pool. When the door shuts, Night takes a deep breath, relieved.

Ceridwen grimaces with embarrassment as she clears the table, "Sorry about that." By his side at the sink she sighs, watching Alex and Jade out in the pool. Jade tows her around the shallow end. "You were telling me something."

Mind blank, he laughs, "Was I?"

"Atlas Shrugged."

"Oh, yeah."

She watches as he runs a sink of hot suds, drops in plates. Striking a dramatic pose, she clears her throat, "Oh please… don't do that. That sound sincere?"

He scrubs, enjoying the feel of hot water on his hands. "Needs work."

She leans on the counter. "That was the best I can do. I hate doing dishes. If I could afford it, we'd eat off paper."

"Anyway—Atlas Shrugged—you've read it, then you know that I'm really one of the geniuses running the world from the bottom up."

She peers at him over the top of her wine glass. Her smile he loves. "You are?"

"I mean, what better cover? The lowest of the low."

"Oh, so you're one of the world manipulators, huh?"

"Oh, yeah, to the uninitiated I may be just a crud slinger, but in actuality I'm orchestrating the next economic boom and bust cycle in my head at this very moment."

"Uh huh. And where will the smart money be next year?"

"Prisons."

"Prisons?"

"Yup, growth industry, prisons. Privatization should yield high dividends."

"Sounds like a fortune cookie."

He shrugs, "Who do you think writes those?" She smiles again, a smile he likes way too much. He sets a plate in the rack, "On my breaks."

"A man of vast talent." She takes the rag from his hand. "Come on, we're done."

"Shall we watch them swim?"

"Watch? What are you, an old man?"

He rubs his arm, "Feel like it, sometimes."

The doorbell rings and the smile wilts on her face. He can't help but find something funny in her discomfort.

Out she storms. "What now?"

From the kitchen he listens to his third deal in two days with a fire in his gut. This puts him in deep. Her lawyer would have fun with this. IAD would have fun with it. But for him, it would be no fun at all.

Troubled, she comes back to wipe down the table. Watching her, e's puzzled. If he didn't know better he would guess she was ashamed. Dealer ashamed of dealing? What next, blushing strippers? "Forgetful students, biologists," he says to see her reaction. "Hope they don't go pre-med. I'd hate to have one of them losing one of their books inside my gall bladder."

She wrings the dishrag, tries a smile, gives it up. "I…"

He has the feeling she wants to tell him something. "You what."

In her eyes he sees something fade and she tosses aside the towel with a tired sigh. "Let's go get wet."

"Appreciate the offer, but—"

"But what?"

"I haven't been swimming in…I forget how long."

"About time then."

He's not so sure. "I don't even own a pair of trunks."

She looks him up and down appraisingly. "What do you wear, a thirty-four?"

He laughs. "After spaghetti, thirty-six."

"Grant's are out, then. You mind wearing an old pair of Jeff's?"

"Not if he doesn't."

"I was going to tear them up to dust with anyway. Hang on, I'll get them."

TWO

At the side of the pool Night dangles his feet in the water.

Perfect. Just warm. Around him in the gathering twilight oaks stoop low to a sculptured lawn under a sky turned the color of lead. So restful this place. So hard to believe that barely a mile away U of O bustles. Another world from his trailer park with its screaming children, drunks and tweakers—so many people trapped together in the American version of a refugee camp.

Alexis turns on the pool light, and, seeing it come on, Night feels the same thrill he felt as a child. Their lives have changed in three days.

Jade swims over. "Isn't this great?"

He has to admit it is.

"I don't have to go to school the last week, do I?" She clings to his feet, pushing off from the side with her own.

"Yes."

"Oh, Daddy."

Alexis dog paddles over in a life vest and tags Jade. With a conspiratorial smile, Jade pushes off to follow. He looks up to find Ceridwen beside him in a black one-piece

"Well?"

He is careful to keep his eyes on hers. "Well, what?"

She spreads her hands wide. "What do you think?"

"I, uh…" He is unprepared for the question. "I think you look great."

His response seems to strike her as funny. "Thanks, but I was asking about the trunks."

"Oh…" He moans, presses his eyes. "Oh, boy."

"Well," she slaps him on a knee, "they fit or don't they?"

"They fit okay. And I love the design." He glances down at blue seahorses prancing amid a tumble of orange pineapples. "Sophisti
cated yet, primitive."

"They're fifteen years old at least. Not that that's any excuse."

"Has his taste improved?"

"In women, at least." She slides into the water, swims away.

"Coming in, Dad?"

He slips in and it is like stepping into a tepid bath. He comes abreast of Ceridwen. "What's it cost to heat a pool like this?"

"Too much, but Alex loves to swim and it's good for her."

Her suit clings, light shimmering on wet nylon. He pries his his eyes away. "You have a beautiful place here."

"A white elephant mortgaged to the flying rafters is what I have here."

The girls disappear inside. Water sloshes against tile, quieting. Crickets chirr, jasmine weights the air. Night looks up to see a clear sky. Warm June night in Eugene. Who says there's no such thing as miracles.

"I do twenty laps a night." She calls from the far end. "It gets old doing them alone. Swim with me?"

His arm bothers him tonight, but swimming might be good for him. "Why not?"

Silently, they swim, pace neither fast nor slow. He stays abreast of her, but it isn't easy, and before long he is conscious of his breathing. Ten laps into it his elbow complains. Unwilling to let her draw away, he keeps on. Fifteen laps and a stitch eats into his side. Grimly he plows on, cursing himself every stroke. Out of shape and towing around twenty pounds he doesn't need, what does he expect? Here he is dragging his sorry butt back and fourth in a pool so he won't look like he's as out of shape as he is in front of his sexy dope dealer landlady. Sad. Very sad.

He's lost count long ago. At last she stops and he drags himself to meet her through water turned viscous. Weak, dizzy, he clings to a stone big as a king size bed, sucking air as if he's been pearl diving. It isn't supposed to be like this. The good guys are the ones with the long wind and the svelte bodies, the dopers the ones ravaged. He thinks it over as he waits for his heartbeat to drop from Sing Sing to something recognizable as a heartbeat.

"I want to be clear with you."

He notices she looks worried, and very sincere. Always a sign bad news is on the way. "I'm in favor of clarity. Hard to argue with clarity."

"I'm seeing someone, you know that, a physics professor. Len's a nice guy, incredibly bright. I told him about you."

He fights the urge to smile. This is where she makes sure the dumb ass garbage collector gets the message. "Serious?"

"We're serious."

He nods, bracing himself on his elbows at the edge, breathing slowly coming back to normal. He feels as if his body has gone to sleep. The pins and needles haven't come yet, but they will. They always do when the blood comes back.

She watches him. "Well?"

"I heard you mention him. I'm happy for you."

She seems relieved by his response. "I didn't want you to get the wrong impression."

Again he fights the smile. Considerate. She may have a shot at the most sensitive dealer of the year. "That you were interested? In me? I didn't think that." He hoists himself to sit on the edge. Looking down at her he sees nothing in her face to dislike. "I do envy you, though. Finding someone who can make you lose track of time, lose yourself in the moment. Rita and I had it—once. It didn't last. I don't know what it is. I've known women, smart women, pretty women. In spite of all that was right, something just wasn't there." He lets his eyes lose focus amid the reflections dancing on the bottom of the pool. "And when it isn't there, you don't conjure it."

She nods. "I know."

"Then tell me, will you, what is it? What is it makes one plus one more than two?"

She keeps her eyes on the water as she slides her hand hydroplaning along the surface, "It's love, isn't it."

Of course she's right. "Love. Most misused word in the language. More definitions than round. Just think of the trouble, the heartache in the world that could be avoided if people could choose who to love." He levers himself to his feet. "But we can't. It's hit or miss. Chemicals, pheromones, you should know. Is that all it is?"

She shakes her head, eyes distant. "I'm the wrong one to ask."

"That makes two of us. Thanks for dinner."

Without waiting for a reply, he snatches up his towel and goes in.

In the pool she glides to the deep.

There she stands letting water tickle her upper lip. Cheeks burning, she watches the pool light shine on the underside of the trees overhead. She sees the light come on in his room. Who is this man living in her house? Who is Night Hume? In the back of her mind he nettles, uncategorizable. Though he has to know her story about forgotten books is a lie, he doesn't call her on it. She makes it plain she's not interested and, expecting resentment, she gets… what? Air. Nothing, certainly not hostility. It's as if having dropped a stone down a well, she hears nothing.

What kind of a man is that?

• • •

Night claims a desk in the circle at Monday morning briefing.

The dozen men making up INET sprawl about him. After an hour pushing weights he is pleasantly tired, radiating. "Jesus," he says to no one. "Didn't we just go home?"

It was two by the time they wound up the paperwork from last night's bust. Not unusual, but a pain the night before a briefing. Running on three hours sleep isn't as easy as it used to be. A wall of fatigue towers over him, held off by power of will. In the back of his mind crouches dark fear—is he too old for the job?

Herrera, the flyweight lieutenant in charge of INET, bustles in, banty rooster with hemorrhoids. "Okay, before we get started…" He passes around a stack of copies. "Initiative 82 made the ballot for November. I don't know how many of you have read this thing. It legalizes small scale growing, possession and sale of green dope to anyone over 18. This thing is a time bomb. It passes, you'll all be bumping somebody down at the jail for a spot handing out tampons and toothpaste. Do what you can to get the word out."

"So…" Herrera flips through the sheath of investigation status reports. "Night, Derek, what's coming down?"

Of all his grating traits, none bothers Night as much as Herrera's insistence on speaking in what he considers street vernacular. Night supports a head of tangled hair with both hands, hoping he looks as bored as he is.

Derek answers. "We're working Rick for a big shipment of coke. Don't know when or if it will come through, but he's convinced it will."

"We hope so," Herrera says, flipping to the next sheet. "What's the sit-rep on the professor? Why no affidavit?"

Night looks up. It's his turn. "Carla gave us some bad information. She was out of product when we went by. We'll try her again this week."

Another step. Another lie. This time to Herrera, a puke, but a superior officer puke. Night looks him in the eye, finds it easier than with Derek. Maybe because he doesn't respect him. Maybe he's just getting good at lying. He doesn't know.

Heading out to the Lincoln he wonders.

How is it he only counts these?

How are these lies different from the lies he tells every day, from the lie he lives? What is his life but lies?

• • •

Spotting her fondest hope, Ceridwen hurries through a crowd noisy and young to an empty table the size of a three dollar postage stamp as Jo and Pickering scurry in her wake. Catsup smeared, but within mere feet of the window—a find during normal session worthy of inclusion in the oral history of the Bio Department. "I can't believe it, I found a table."

"This burger belongs in a mausoleum somewhere."   Jo taps the open face of her burger patty with an emerald enameled talon. "What do they do, boil them?"

Ceridwen is tired of hearing Jo run down the food. "As a matter of fact they steam them in trays the size of the Titanic. If it's so bad why do we keep coming back?"

Pickering exhales, "Oh, stop. It's close, it's fast, it's easy. You want good too?"

Perched on her chair, Pickering wraps her burger neatly in a napkin before taking a bite. Ceridwen smiles at her optimism. As if this withered dead thing could possibly contain any juice to soil her immaculate suit. Hope does indeed spring eternal.

Jo slaps her bun down with a disgusted sigh, "I don't know why I just don't bring a sandwich."

"I don't either," says Pickering, and to Ceridwen, "What I want to know is what you're doing back so soon? I wasn't looking for you before Wednesday."

Jo arches a penciled eyebrow, leans conspiratorially close, voice high to be heard above the din, "What did that young intern do for you, anyway? Isn't he adorable, though?"

"It wasn't him, it was Night."

Pickering frowns, bag of catsup pinched between her teeth, "Night? What happened to Goldbloom?"

Ceridwen waves a hand as she chews, "This has nothing to do with Len. Night's my boarder."

Pickering leans forward in her chair. "Your what? Since when did you become a landlord?"

"Since I needed the money. I thought I told you. The empty bedrooms...I'm renting them out."

Jo's eyes light, eager for gossip, "Who is he? What did he do?"

"He fixed my disposer, then he fixed hot and cold compresses for my head, and it worked. I can breathe, see?" She demonstrates, plugging a nostril and inhaling. First one, then the other.

"Wow," Jo says, impressed.

Pickering wipes her hands, "What is he, a shaman?"

Squirming in the seat of her chair, she dreads telling. The words don't tell the story, don't begin to tell who he is, what he is. Truth it may be, but she's beginning to see that truth can lie. "He works for the county."

"The county?" Jo frowns in thought. "What is he, a sheriff?"

"No."

"Building inspector?"

Ceridwen sees no way out but to tell it. "Sanitation."

This stops them cold.

"You mean he's a garbage man." Pickering says.

"A garbage man?" Jo laughs, sputtering, mouth crammed full.

For some reason Jo's laugh offends her. "That's exactly what he is."

Jo is first to recover. "You're kidding, right?"

"No, Jo, I'm not kidding." Ceridwen stares her down, "He collects garbage, drives the truck, cleans up all our messes. It's honest work."

"Your prejudice is showing, dear," Pickering taunts Jo with an amused smile.

Jo backtracks. "So he's a garbage man. Somebody has to do it, right?"

"He gave me a check for nine hundred dollars. You know what that means?"

"We pay them too much?" Jo says.

"It means I might actually make it through the month. And he fixed my washer."

Jo flashes Pickering a cynical look. "A Mr. Fixit, huh?" Her eyes gleam, suspicious. "What's he look like?"

Ceridwen frowns as if to consider, wishing they didn't know her so well. "Don't pay much attention. About forty, tall, longish hair, moustache, brown eyes, average build, good size arms and chest, a little heavy maybe, nothing exercise and good food wouldn't cure."

Pickering hides a smile behind a paper napkin.

"Didn't pay much attention, huh?" Jo says, teasing. "The FBI doesn't pay that much attention."

Embarrassed, Ceridwen shrugs. "You asked."

Pickering chases a smear of catsup around her plate with a fry. "And how are things with your physicist? You saw him, Saturday, yes?"

"Mr. Excitement," Jo says to the air.

Annoyed, Ceridwen pushes her plate away. With Jo every man is Mr. something. "Everything went fine, why?"

Pickering's eyes widen. "Just making conversation."

Jo daubs on lipstick to match her nails using a mirror from her purse. "So why do you think this guy's being so nice, huh? can I ask you that?" She raises a hand in Ceridwen's direction, "I mean, really Cer, you're so naive. Divorcee, I'll bet with your house, he thinks you're rolling in it."

Ceridwen nearly aspirates her water, "He's after my money?"

Pickering is the first to get up. "Oh, piss off, Jo. He's probably just a nice guy. They exist. They must—somewhere."

Jo knocks back her chair, plasters her lips to the edge of a paper napkin, leaving the pink imprint face up on the table. She laughs with a hiss, "Yeah, right, just a nice guy, a nice garbage man. I want a sure thing, I'll stick with the lottery."

Their doubts resonating with her own, Ceridwen follows them up the stairs and out.

●   ●   ●

Monday afternoon Night swings by to pick up Jade at school.

"How'd it go?"

"Okay."

"What's that mean, okay?"

"It means okay."

"This is like pulling teeth. From a chicken."

She sighs. "Everybody wanted to know why I wasn't riding the bus and I told them I moved."

He watches her, can read nothing in her eyes. "And?"

"And nothing."

"Miss Jeannie, huh?"

She nods.

"You can see her whenever you want. I can take you over there anytime."

She looks down at her hands in her lap. "I know. That's not it."

"Then what is?"

"Nothing."

Night has been around enough women to know what that means. "Tell me."

"There's nothing to tell."

"You told them you moved…" He feels his way. "And they asked you where…"

She nods.

"And you said with your Dad…" He sees it now. "And they asked you what your dad does for a living, right?"

In her silence is her answer. No matter what he does, or how he does it he ends up hurting her. There is no way out of the loop. He thinks it over. "They didn't know, after three years?"

She looks out the window. "It never came up."

He smiles, understanding how she would make sure it didn't.

"And now they all know you are a garbage collector."

There is hurt in her voice, and shame. Neither is easy to take. He takes a deep breath and turns up the drive where he kills the engine, lays an aching arm along the back of the seat. Bad arm day. He rubs it with his left hand as he turns to face her. "You know, kiddo, everybody can't be a brain surgeon in this world. Somebody has to collect the garbage. If that makes you ashamed—"

"I'm not ashamed."

"Well, I want you to know I love you."

"I do."

"But whether you're ashamed or not, I do what I do. Sometimes it doesn't thrill me either, but that's my life. And I do it."

"It was hard," she says, mouth muffled in his jacket, "I didn't want to tell."

She presses her ear to his chest and he lays a hand on her hair. "I know."

Inside they find Ceridwen taking dinner out of the oven.

"Dinner's ready."

It smells good. He thinks of how long it's been since he has come home to a meal, any meal. "Didn't you teach today?"

She bustles by him, "Sure."

"Then, how—"

"Don't be too impressed. It's just enchiladas, homemade fast food. Jade, if you could get glasses maybe I could con your father into getting plates." From the doorway into the living room she calls out past Night. "Alex, dinner. Could you get out the milk?"

Night watches Alex where she lies in front of the TV as if she hasn't heard. Ceridwen passes, snatches up the remote, turns it off. "Alex, will you please get out the milk?"

She doesn't bother to turn. "I don't drink it, why should I get it?"

Sighing, Ceridwen gets it herself and they sit. Alex drags in, slumps in her chair, curls her lip at her plate. "Yuck."

Night and Jade link hands. Night offers a hand to Ceridwen, who takes Alex's.

Night says, "Thank you, Lord, for this food. Amen."

Alex smiles a drunken smile, "That's funny."

Ceridwen gives her a look. "There's nothing funny about saying grace, Alex."

"Yes there is, it's funny."

Rage claws at Night's insides as he forces himself to sit quietly. He has never in his life seen a better candidate for a good, hard swat on the behind. In embarrassed silence, they eat.

Alex takes up her fork, flattens her food. "Mommy."

Face hot, Night eats, chews, swallows, tasting nothing.

"What is it, Alex?"

"Cut up my food."

Night watches, amazed. This is an eight-year-old?

"Alex, it's enchiladas, it's soft, you can cut it with your fork."

"Cut my food, Mommy."

Ceridwen cuts it. "There you go."

More mud pie slapping with her fork. "I don't want any, it looks gross."

"Alex, you have to eat if you want to get well."

"But I don't like it."

With an effort Night keeps his eyes on his plate and his mouth clamped shut. He doesn't and he'll do something, say something he shouldn't.

Alex drops her plate into the sink, goes to the fridge, takes out a box of cookies and a 2-liter of cola, hauls them into the living room. The TV blares a commercial, shockingly loud.

Ceridwen sighs, looking embarrassed, "I don't know what to do with her. I…can't get her to eat anything but junk."

A glance at Jade tells him she knows what he wants to say. Jade's face also tells him she's hoping he won't. With an effort of will, Night keeps his mouth shut. Escaping the awkward silence, Jade buses dishes, heads for the living room. Night calls after her. "Homework first, right?"

"Okay."

When they're alone, Ceridwen pours herself wine. "There's something you need to know about Alex."

That he doubts. He already knows more than he wants to. No longer hungry, he takes his plate to the sink.

"I'm sorry about that, but she's a sick little girl and I have to be very careful she gets enough to eat."

That explains the remark about getting well. As if anybody could eat that way and not be ill. "Sick, from what?"

"Neuroblastoma."

An ugly word. She has his attention. "I'm not much with Latin. Sounds bad."

"Greek, and it is."

In spite of the disgust he feels for inept parenting, he understands. Hard to set limits when you are convinced a kid may starve herself to death. "What is it?"

"A tumor that starts in the liver."

Picturing Jade in the same world with it, his guts clench. "I had no idea."

That's why she's so pale."

He keeps rinsing dishes. "That's why she won't eat anything but sweets?"

Cer smiles a sad smile, "That's my fault, I'm afraid. I can't stand for her to go hungry. I know I shouldn't give in."

"Will she be okay? What do they say?"

She sighs, with a wary glance at the living room doorway, "They say there's hope. We didn't catch it until late—she was almost five. By then there's a high rate of regression, nobody knows why."

In his stomach Night feels a stone drop cold and heavy. Cancer…Jesus. It explains a lot. Maybe everything. "You mean she could die."

She seems to turn inward, "There's something, a new treatment. They inject the tumor cells into mice, then inject the antibodies from the mice back into Alex. It's long, it's difficult, and it's painful."

"But it works?"

"They say it does."

He wonders at the hopelessness in her voice.

"It also costs a million dollars."

"You have insurance, though, right? through the University?"

"It's got a two million dollar benefit cap. In the last two years we've gone through three quarters of it."

One point five million. In two years. "So what's that mean?"

"It means unless I can come up with five hundred thousand dollars she doesn't get the treatment. That's what it means."

He doesn't know what to say.

"I've accepted it. It's just the way things are. Right now, she's doing fine. I just wanted you to know, that's all." She goes upstairs, leaving him alone in the kitchen.

He finds Jade studying for a final and kisses her good night, then heads back to finish his shift.

• • •

The week drags on as they wait for Rick's truckload of white dope.

Jade he sees for a couple hours in the evening between shifts. Each time the same scene is repeated with Alex. The more he thinks about it the more he regrets having committed himself to a month here. Several times he comes close to saying something. Each time stops himself. It can only make things worse.

Wednesday night for some reason Alex doesn't come down. Without her, dinner is bearable, if strained. Ceridwen keeps watch on the doorway. Still Alex doesn't show.

After dinner Ceridwen disappears to her office. He and Jade settle in downstairs to read before he has to get back to work. It isn't long before Alexis clomps down to slump deep into an easy chair. Peering at them from under sagging lids, she frowns. "What are you doing?"

Annoyed, knowing what's coming and aware there is nothing he can do to stop it, Night looks up from his book, "Reading."

That blank, jaded look shedding ennui like dew. "Why?"

"Because we enjoy it."

She laughs through her nose, "You like to read?"

He doesn't trust himself to look up. "That's right."

She reaches for the remote and their quiet time is over. Seething, Night calmly sets a bookmark, lays aside his book, stands.

Alexis casts him a sly what-are-you-going-to-do-about-it glance.

Trumped by an eight-year-old, he kisses Jade and lets the screen bang behind him. Home sweet home.

• • •

Friday night finds Night in the back of the raid van.

He shrugs into a vest, cut down twelve gauge across his thighs. Warrant service on a green dope house downtown. He has taken to eating out again, and a taco burger weighs on his gut like a bundle of tire weights wrapped in baling wire.

Derek hunkers, elbows on knees, opposite him. The six men in the rear lurch, tilting dominoes, as the van halts for a light.

"Damn!" Derek hauls himself off Sid, calls to the driver. "Hey, Ace, it turns yellow before it turns red."

Night fights a rebellious stomach. "Anybody got some Rolaids?"

Three rolls emerge from three different vests and Night laughs, taking Derek's. Occupational hazard. The tablets lie chalky and insipid on his tongue. "Julie had a kid when you met her, didn't she?"

Derek nods. "What about it?"

Night slips into his jacket, pulls down the flap in front with POLICE in six-inch bright yellow lettering. He smells cheap cologne, recognizes it. "Dammit, Sid, I told you not to wear my jacket."

Leaning back at his elbow, Sid shrugs. "Your day off, mine was at the cleaners. Dog brains all over it from that pit bull we had to take out last week. What's the big deal?"

"The big deal is this effluent you call cologne."

"Why, want to borrow some?"

Night gives Sid the finger, leans forward, mouth close to Derek's ear. "I need some advice."

"Advice to the lovelorn, market timing tips, name it, I'm your man."

"Any problems working things out between you?"

"About the kid?" Derek laughs, "Problems? you bet your lily white ass there were."

"What kind?"

"What kind don't we have? If I told her to do anything it was 'you ain't my daddy.' Swatted her once for her smart mouth and it was World War III."

Night thinks. "But you worked it out?"

He shrugs, "It was rough sledding for a while, but yeah, we did. Why, you seeing a woman got kids?"

He'll have to choose carefully what to give up. "She's an acquaintance."

"But you'd like her to be more."

"Maybe."

"How many?"

"Kids? At home—one."

Derek blows air. "That's something, anyway." He elbows the man next to him. "Jenaro, how many kids Anita have when you met her?"

Jenaro doesn't bother to open his eyes. "Three."

Derek whistles. "Now that's an hombre got some cojones."

Torn between the need to tell and the need not to, Night succumbs. "Jenaro, what do you do when the mother's in the habit of letting the kid get away with murder?"

On Jenaro's wide face a smile spreads. "We're in counseling."

"Help?"

"Must have, I haven't run out on her."

Derek pulls on a hood. "So who is she? Why haven't you said anything?"

Conscious of Derek's eyes on him, he hesitates. "It's nothing serious." Like hell it isn't. If risking career and friendship isn't serious, what is? They joggle along, the need to talk smoldering in Night's gut. "What about the first time you met Julie?"

"What about it?"

Night lowers his voice as much as he can and still be heard. "Did you feel normal, act normal?"

"Hell, no." Derek smiles, remembering. "We were at The Granary Brew Pub, remember? You were there. Sid, Jenaro, too. Friday night, four of us having a beer."

"I don't remember."

"Yeah, I know," Derek says, warming to it. "You were watching the game. I was watching Julie. She was there with six or eight people from her office. Some guy was hitting on her pretty hard. I waited until he went to the head and I went over and sat down."

Night smiles at his nerve. "Just like that."

Derek nods. "You know me, you know I don't do that kind of thing. I was the only black at that table. Hell, I was the only black in the place. And there I was, everybody gawking at me like I was from Mars. They all shut up so they could listen, and I've got maybe a minute and a half to get to know her."

Night shakes his head, amazed. "What'd you say?"

"Hell, I don't know, anything I could think of. I had two minutes, I used them. Told her I was a cop, told her where I grew up. When I saw the guy heading back to the table I handed her a card, asked her if she knew any cops. She didn't. I told her she   did   now. Told her she had any problems she could call—about anything."

Night smiles, picturing the scene. "Come on."

"So help me."

"And did she?"

"Hell, no."

Night frowns, confused. "Then how…"

"Month later I saw her again. Same place. Same crowd, this time sans the guy."

Night points. "I remember that. You went over and sat with her again, didn't you?"

"She wasn't too happy to see me. Again everybody stops and stares. I ask her how she's been and hand her another card and tell her that if she ever needs a cop she can call me."

Night has to smile. "Gutsy."

"She looks at me and says, 'How do I know you're a cop?' So I show her my ID. Then she says, 'Anybody can have one of those printed, can't they?'" Derek smiles, teeth glowing in the dim van. "Smart, huh? I say, yes, but if you call that number you'll get Eugene Police and they can tell you whether or not I'm legit. I am. She says do I carry a gun? and I say yes I do, but that I don't flash it around. She thinks about that. Then she tells me about this neighbor in the apartment upstairs that wakes her up dancing at three every morning. She asks me if there's anything I can do. I say if she wants I can talk with him." Derek shrugs. "She wants."

"You never told me any of this. What then?"

Derek shrugs. "The guy turns out to be gay as the ace of spades."

"He was a spade?"

Derek shakes his head, "He was as much a cracker as you are. Nice guy, explains he's exercising to an aerobics tape. I explain the situation to him and he agrees to switch to another room where he'll be lunging over the laundry room instead of her bedroom. And that's it."

"No, it's not," Night says. "How can that be it? Something else must have happened. You're engaged."

Derek rocks a magazine into his MP-5, checks the flashlight in the hand guard, flashing it on at the ceiling, then off. "Week later there she is again at the Granary. You were there that time, too. She keeps looking over her shoulder at me. Almost as if she expects me to go over." Derek smiles, shakes his head. "I don't. Next thing I know, there she is on the stool by me. Says she wants to thank me. I tell her it was no big thing, part of the job."

Night laughs. "You didn't."

"I did. I expect her to get up and she almost does, but then she asks me why I gave her my card, do I do that often? I tell her no, I don't, that she was the only one before or since, which is true, too. She thinks about that, and then she goes to fetch her purse. We had a nice talk." The smile on Derek's face is one of pride, of contentment. "A week later she sits at my table. So, yeah, to answer your question, if she's the one, it can make you a little crazy." Derek's eyes narrow with curiosity. "Why? How was it when you met this one?"

Night hesitates. "I surprised myself."

"That can be good. If I hadn't, I would never have met Julie. So, things heating up? Come on, let's hear it."

The van pulls up at the curb and Night is relieved to have an out. The word comes to go and the doors open.

"Anything develops you'll be the first to know."

At least so much is true.

• • •

Day off, Night rolls out of bed at dawn, rouses Jade with a knuckle on her door.

They slip out for breakfast. Across the booth she moans, wiping bleary eyes. "You got me up so early."

The waitress sets coffee in front of him and he watches her go. "Good for you, getting up early."

Face bleak, she laughs, "Sure it is."

Coffee scalding his throat, he rubs his hands, "We've got to get the place ready for the sheet rockers. They're coming a week from Monday."

Her eyes brighten, "You mean they're going to put the walls back on?"

"That's right"

In front of each of them the waitress slides hotcakes.

Jade stares. "They're so big!"

Mouth already full, he grunts agreement.

She watches appalled. "Dad, why don't you ever put on syrup?"

"Don't need it."

"But you're supposed to eat pancakes with syrup."

"I like them plain."

"It's not normal."

So like Rita is Jade he has to smile. "I'm not. Ever noticed?"

Frustrated sigh. "What do we have to do?"

"Add some outlets, backing, tear out some appliances." He smiles. "And somebody needs to sweep out."

Her shoulders sag. "Bet I can guess who."

"I didn't raise any dummy, did I?"

In her face he sees clouds gather. "You don't like Alex, do you?"

He knows she enjoys being with her. He also knows he can't fool her if he tries. "I'm not in love with the way she acts."

"This whole week it's like I haven't seen you at all."

He opens his mouth to protest and sighs instead. It's true. She hasn't.

"I know you've driven me to school and picked me up, but other than that, most of the time you're at the fixer or working. I never see you."

The sandbag of guilt drops hard on his neck. "I…" He raises hands in surrender.

"You can't stand being around Alex. I know that's it."

"You're right."

"Then do something about it. Don't just disappear."

He takes a long breath, lets it out even more slowly. "She's not my daughter. I'm a boarder in her house, for crissake. Her house. Her mother doesn't want me disciplining her. I say one word she would turn on me like a mother lion. Anyway, it doesn't matter. We're out of there in three weeks."

The chagrin in her face takes him by surprise. "Dad, I like it there. Can't you talk to her about it?"

"Oh, sure. By the way, Cer, your kid's a spoiled brat and you are a washout as a mother. How? She's been sick. She thinks she has to baby her. I can't change that."

"I don't know, maybe you're right. But I like Alex. I don't think she wants to act like she does. It's almost like…" she struggles for words, "…she has to…because she can get away with it. You know what I mean?"

He can see the glee in Alex's eyes right now. No. Alex loves getting away with what she does. Alex loves being in control. "Let's just suppose for argument's sake that deep in her little rotten heart she bleeds to be an angel. How does that help us any if she acts like the brat from hell?"

She thinks this over. "I don't know. But I know you'll think of something."

• • •

Ceridwen watches, relieved, as Night comes up the drive with Jade.

Skin powdered white with gypsum dust, arms laden with groceries, they take the walk around to the kitchen. Ceridwen meets them at the door, looks them over. Until now the morning has been as blah as the overcast sky. "Somebody's been working." She peeks into their bags as they pass. "What's all this?"

He unloads, "Parmesan, spinach, Ricotta, fresh basil—"

"Opening an Italian deli?"

He lays out his spoils. "Ground sirloin, egg pasta."

Dread wells from the pit of her stomach, "You're cooking? Tonight?"

Filthy as he is, he makes a little bow at the waist and she has to laugh. "Mia lasagna especiale."

Inside, she squirms. Wrong night, wrong life, wrong everything. "Just my luck."

He takes down a skillet, "It's not that bad, really."

She has to laugh. "That's not what I meant." Why does it have to be Saturday? She doesn't want to tell this. "I mean I'm sorry to miss it."

On his face is confusion. "Miss it?"

When she answers, she has trouble getting her words to sound like anything other than a death sentence. "It's my night out."

She sees his face fall, sees him hide it. After this horrible week she had wanted to try again to get to know him. She sees now how hopeless it is. What chance do they have? What chance have they ever?

He avoids her eyes. "My fault. Forgot it was Saturday."

She moves opposite him at the island, "I wish—"

"No problem. It'll be good tomorrow. We'll save you some."

It's no use. He won't let her say it. As if she knows what it is she's trying to say, anyway. She thinks of something. "I thought maybe since Jade's so good with Alex, I might cancel the sitter. I could pay her."

Jade rushes up, "Could I?"

He dices onion on the block. "Up to you. I'll be here."

"You're sure it won't interfere with your plans."

His look tells her she already has. "I'm sure.

In the shower, Ceridwen clenches inside with pleasure as she thinks of him going to the trouble to make dinner for her, and of the disappointment in his face. Shampoo thick in her hair, she blushes hot under the spray. Can it be possible she would rather stay here and eat lasagna with this near stranger than go out with the head of the physics department? It is not. Fiercely she scrubs her scalp. Her life is on course, and it's going to stay that way.

She passes through the kitchen on her way out, and drawn by an aroma to die for, peeks in the oven. Cheese bubbles, golden, meat sauce over-dripping the dish to pool, sizzling on the floor of the oven. Seeing what she's missing, she finds herself scrambling for a plausible excuse for Len. Laughing at herself, she meets them by the pool. "Okay, now you're sure you and Jade don't mind."

He looks up from a book. "Ask her."

They're out in the deep end, Jade bearing Alex piggyback. "That's okay, I don't want to interrupt." For a moment she hesitates, marveling at what she is leaving behind to be with Len. She is so clever at getting what she wants. So clever.

"Don't worry," Night says, "I know the rules—no parties, no sneaking food out of the fridge, no boyfriends."

Even now he can make her laugh—it's disgusting. "How reassuring. Okay, I'm going." To Alex she raises her voice, "Now, baby, while I'm gone Night's in charge. Mind, okay?"

Purposely ignoring her, Alex keeps up her splashing, "Bye, Mom."

• • •

Round the table the tone is morbid.

No one speaks as Night dishes lasagna. Across from Jade, Alex slumps, head on chin. No mystery why. It's right there, a presence in the room. He feels it himself and doesn't like it—they miss her. They all do.

"Aquí es, bambini mio, Night's famous three-cheese lasagna. Prego…manga."

Alex cocks her head, "What's man-ja?"

Listlessly, Jade says, "It means eat."

Alexis snorts through her nose. "Whoopee."

"It's good," he says, "you'll like it."

Alex pushes away from the table, fetches a bowl. "I'm having ice cream."

Night snatches the dish from her hand, sets it back. "Uh, uh, you want anything else you'll have to eat this first."

She readies a tizzy, screwing up her face.

"No point putting on a show either. It doesn't impress me and Mom's not here. I've been promoted to baby sitter and I'm power mad. What I say goes. She said it. You heard her. Live with it."

She strikes him as desperate. "If you starve me she'll be mad."

Inside he smiles. So far he's a jump ahead of her. "Maybe. That doesn't help you now, does it?"

She stands her ground. "Then I won't eat at all."

He sits, shrugs. "Up to you, but I guarantee you, you don't eat my lasagna, you eat nothing else. And that means nothing. And no soda either. Water, that's all."

She looks up at him, small pointed teeth bared. "You can't starve me. It's cruel."

"I'm not starving you, there's food on your plate. Eat it."

She's scandalized. "I'm sick, you know, I've got cancer. You know what that is, huh? do you?"

Getting nastier. He was waiting for that. "Don't be so dramatic. Sick people need good food too. You starve yourself, it's your decision. You're not a baby. You're old enough to decide for yourself."

He reaches out to Jade and they link hands, wait for Alex. She doesn't budge from where she stands in the middle of the kitchen. "You don't say grace with us, you don't eat." He's way out on a limb here. The last thing he wants is for her to miss a meal.

She keeps those eyes on him. Jade sends him a silent plea. Under them both he breaks, "Okay, Alex, let's deal. Sit down, say grace with us, take a bite and just see what you think."

Hand on hip, she glares. Looking daggers is no empty phrase with this kid. Strippers he busted have looked at him that way. It's strange to see the look on the face of an eight-year-old. "One bite?"

"Come on, Alex," Jade says. "Try it."

She doesn't buy it, raises a finger. "One."

He has worked out plea bargains with less haggling. "One or two. You might like it, you know."

"Oh, I'm so sure." She smirks, cynical glare aimed at him. "I'm going to like lasagna."

Seeing her face, he would guess the odds somewhere between slim and none, "Stranger things have happened."

Hissing through her teeth, she reaches with small cold hands, "Right."

Relieved, Night takes Jade's hand in his right, Alex's cold small hand in his left. "Dear God—"

"Why do you pray? You a fanatic or something?"

"Not particularly."

"Then why?"

Night thinks, mind gone vacant. "It feels right."

"Oh." She keeps those eyes on him.

"Dear Lord, we thank you for this food—"

"Why do you say that?" Her lip curls. "Why thank Him for the food? You bought it, didn't you?"

Night is numb. "Yeah."

She shrugs, "Then what's He got to do with it?"

Night's no good at this. There are people could answer her right. He isn't one. "Food comes from God."

"Those are hydroponic tomatoes in that salad. I read the label. They came from Holland. God didn't grow them."

He's got no answers, and now she's making him mad. "I'll tell you what, you just keep quiet and listen, and then you see how it makes you feel to thank God for your food, okay? Think of it as a learning experience."

"I still don't get it."

Night understands how parents flip out and whack their kids. A kid like this could do it. "That's okay. Right now what you need to do," he says, voice low, "is keep quiet and listen. When it's said, we can talk about it for the rest of the night if you want."

She shrugs, "Sure, no problem, go ahead, say it."

A deep breath and he can go on. "Dear Lord, we thank you for this food and this day. And if you've got the time, please, God, protect the children. Amen."

She drops his hand and squints, "Protect the children? Why children?"

He can see in Jade's eyes she wants to tell why he says it. Wants to tell about his years on the fatal accident team, his time working sex crimes. Wants to badly. Instead she takes a bite. How he rates her he'll never know. "It's something I feel, that's all."

"And that amen stuff, what's that mean? Why is it ah men and not ah women? That's what I want to know."

Night looks at Jade and suddenly they're laughing.

Alex stares, offended, "What? What's so funny?"

"Nothing," he says.

"Come on, what are you laughing at?" She's laughing, now, too. "I want to know!"

"You're funny," Jade says.

"Why?"

"You keep asking these questions that nobody can answer," Jade says, "and it's almost like you don't really even want to know the answer. It's like you're asking just to ask."

"I do so want to know."

"Do you?" Night asks. "I'm not so sure. I think what you want is attention, and you've already got it. So relax, why don't you?"

Alex stares at her plate as they eat. Jade tries to entice her with a bite off her fork and she takes it.

In silence Night watches her chew. "Pretty god awful, huh?"

She picks up her fork, "No," she says, voice small, "it's not."

To his amazement she takes another bite.

It's as if a pressure relief valve has blown somewhere. They can breathe again. No one is any more relieved than he. Denying her dinner. That would have sounded great. He promises he won't put himself in that position again.

Alex drops her fork. "Why does Mom have to go out with that jerk?"

Night's not sure what to say. He can hardly say he feels the same way. "People go out to have a good time."

She looks at him, eyes narrow. "Then why aren't you out?"

She's leading him onto thin ice. Maybe hoping he'll fall through. "I'm having a good time right here."

Those eyes again. The kid has a stare. "Sure you are."

"So," Jade says, voice upbeat, "let's not forget gymnastics tomorrow, okay?"

Grateful to her for breaking up their duel, he takes a bite, "Yeah, sure, remind me."

Alex's eyes home on Jade. "Gymnaxtix..." she says, getting it wrong. "You take gymnaxtix? What's it like?" In her voice lurks high octane interest.

"It's fun. We tumble, learn to do flips and cartwheels, even get to work on the beam and bars. It makes you strong, too, here," she offers her arm, "Feel."

Alex's eyes widen as she squeezes. "I want to do that." She sags in her chair. "Mom will never let me."

Jade frowns, "Why not?"

She makes a face, mouthing the words through a mask, "Because I'm sick."

Night reads Jade's eyes, "We can ask, can't we?"

Alex looks up, eyes electric, "You will? You'll ask her?"

He shrugs, "You don't ask, you don't get."

"She might say yes if you asked. You fixed the washer. She might let me!"

It's the first time he's heard her excited about anything. He decides to take advantage. He points to her lasagna with his fork. "Gymnasts eat."

She regards him with ill-concealed disappointment and picks up her fork. She cuts off a big bite, raises it to her mouth. Another bite and another as Night watches in disbelief. Plate clean, she sets down her fork.

"And..." He may as well test the limits. "...they drink milk."

"For strong bones," Jade says. "Got to have strong bones to be a gymnast."

Alex sighs, "You too, now?"

"Well, you do."

She sighs, raising her glass, "So, I'm drinking already." She drains half of it, sets it down, "Talk my mom into letting me go, okay?"

Night smiles, an idea taking shape in the back of his mind. "I can live with that. And just what do you do?"

"What do you mean what do I do? You want me to polish your boots or something?"

"My boots are fine."

"Then what do you want?"

Night considers. "I'll tell you what I'll do. I'll not only talk your mother into letting you go, I'll drive you to the lessons."

"Yeah!"

"I'm not done yet."

"Sorry."

"And I'll pay for them."

Her eyes narrow under half-closed lids,"Why? Why would you do that? You must want something."

Night smiles. "Smart kid. Want to know what it is?"

"It won't be fun, will it."

He waits.

"Okay, okay." She sighs. "What?"

He rises, hauls plates to the sink, rinses them under a stream of hot water. He'll take a chance. "I want you to stop acting like a brat, that's what I want. I want you to start eating right. I want you to help your mother clean up without being asked. I want you to start getting yourself up in the morning."

Aghast, she laughs, "All that?"

"There's more. I want you to start acting your age and not like some eight-year-old infant. I want you to kick the idiot box habit and read with us at night. That's what I want. That's what it'll cost to take gymnastics."

He looks back to see her turned away. He stacks dishes, regretting the gambit. He went too far. When would he learn to keep his mouth shut? Jade comes to the sink with glasses and Night is surprised to see Alex at his elbow, reaching for the dishrag. She holds it under hot water, rings it dry. He watches as she wipes the table down, puts the milk back in the fridge. Can it be possible she'll bite? He won't risk asking.

Kitchen in order, he follows the girls into the living room. The TV squats, an omnipotent idol, huge and silent across the room, a fount from which noise and light has always flowed. Alex goes upstairs, returns with a quilt, drapes it over the TV, sits forlorn. She sighs long and hard.

Night smiles at her hopeless expression. "You think it'll be easier if you can't see it?"

She nods. "What now?"

Night sets down his book. "Is it raining?"

Jade goes to the window, looks out, "Not right now."

"Good." He rises, "Let's walk."

Alex gawks. "You crazy?"

"Come on, I'll show you something."

From under drooping lids, she peers up. "What?" She says it almost suspiciously. "What are you going to show me?"

"Should we, Jade?"

She catches on. "You mean that? We're going to show her that?"

"If you think we should."

"What?" Alex looks from one to the other. "What?"

Jade pretends to consider. "I don't know. It depends on whether or not she can keep a secret."

Alex grabs Jade by an arm, pogo sticks in place on the couch, "I can, I can, what is it? Tell me! Tell me!"

"Okay," Night says, sighing, "I guess we'll have to show you. Get your shoes on, let's go.

On the porch she slips on her shoes, raises a foot, "Tie my laces."

"Oh, look at that, she can't tie her laces." Night shrugs. "We can't show her."

Alex moans in frustration, "I can't."

"Girls who can't tie their shoes can't take gymnastics." Jade says.

"Oh, all right!" Alex says, "I'll do it, wait for me."

They wait, and with a show of effort, she ties them. "I bet it's nothing, anyway. I bet you're just fooling me to get me out to walk."

"Are we, Jade?"

"You'll see."

"See what? Tell me, what?"

"Wait and see."

A block down, Night leads them up the walk to their house.

"Who lives here?" Alex says. "You know them?"

Jade looks to burst, "Can I tell her?"

"Go ahead."

"We're going to."

"Going to what?"

"Live here."

The way she says it sends a thrill through Night's stomach and into his throat. Ten years too late the dumb SOB becomes a father. Regret for years lost scalds his insides.

Alex follows into the house. "You are?" She looks at Night, "Why's it a secret?"

"It's not."

"But you're going to move?"

"When the work's done."

"How long?"

"A month, two maybe."

Her face falls back into the expression of apathy he hates. "Oh."

"We'll still see each other," Jade says.

"Sure we will."

Night can see she doesn't buy it. "Hey, you think you can find your way back?"

She nods.

"Then you can come visit anytime. As long as your mom says it's okay. So you going to come?"

A quick nod and a smile tugs at the corner of her mouth.

Night sees the light come back into her eyes. "Okay, then."

A quick look around and they head home. After her shower, Alex skips downstairs where she finds Night reading on the couch, Jade sprawled on the carpet with a book. Alex goes for the remote and Night clears his throat.

She freezes, "What?"

"Nothing, just thought you might have forgotten our deal."

Alex deflates, "Oh, yeah." She hurls it down on the couch, "No TV, you mean it?"

"I mean it."

She plops down on the couch, kicks her legs, stares. Three minutes pass by his watch.

"There's nothing to do."

"There's reading."

Chin on chest, she whines. "I don't have anything good."

"Jade has books."

Jade leads her upstairs. In what seems no time at all, they're back, a hardbound copy of *Black Beauty* dangling from Alex's hand. Night has to laugh when he sees it.

"Good choice."

"I like horses."

They settle in, Alex with the book propped up before her on the carpet. Night watches her. What he sees confirms his suspicion. She reads all right—like she tap dances. He lays his book aside, "Want me to read that to you?"

Instantly, she's up and beside him on the couch, thrusting the book into his hands. "I don't like reading by myself."

Translation—I don't read. He opens the book and begins reading. Face on the cushion, she watches. Surely as sun goes to ground her eyelids droop. As he reads, he feels her breathing slow. Five pages later she's gone.

Laying the book aside, he picks up his own and for the first time tonight, relaxes.

Can it be this easy?

He doubts it.

• • •

Night opens his eyes and nearly jumps out of his skin when he sees two pairs of eyes less then a foot away at the edge of the bed.

"Jesus." He squints through sandy eyes to see the time. "Are you nuts? It's six thirty. What the hell are you doing in here?"

"It's gymnaxtix day."

Rigid muscles relax, and he sinks back, eyes closing as he lets go a breath. "We've got time."

They bound on his bed, bunny-hopping over his legs. He is getting seasick. "Okay, okay, okay, I'm up, I'm up." He struggles erect, shielding his eyes with a cupped hand. "Did you ask your mom?"

"Not yet."

He starts to lean, threatening a fall back to warm sheets and they grab his arms to steady him. "Why not?"

"We were waiting for you."

He sighs, topples, pulling them, giggling and screaming, with him.

Jade shakes him. "Dad, come on, get up."

He schemes. "She up?"

"Not yet."

"Coffee made?"

"No."

He smiles into the pillow. "Wake me up when you're ready."

He hears them go out and lets go, tucking a fist clenching sheet and blanket under his chin.

Too soon they are back.

"She's up."

"Coffee's made."

He knows when he is beaten. "Okay, get out of here and let me get dressed."

Downstairs he finds them flanking the kitchen doorway. Lurking just out of Ceridwen's sight, they urge him on, Alex driving him on with two hands at the small of his back. At the table Ceridwen nurses a cup of coffee, paper before her. He takes a cup down from the cabinet. "You're up early."

She laughs, groans, holding her head in a hand. "Got me up and herded me downstairs like a couple border collies. I asked them what was so important. They wouldn't say, but they're up to something, I know that."

He pours his cup, glances back at the door to see them watching. "No good, probably." From the doorway they give him silent growls, showing teeth. He pulls up a chair opposite her, sits. A headline catches his eye and he reads upside down—SWEEPING NEW POWERS FOR DRUG WAR.

She follows his gaze. "Can you believe this?"

"What's it say?"

She reads. "'Governor calls for passage of SB 3498, a bill granting sweeping new powers to drug enforcement agencies in the war against drugs.'" She laughs without humor. "I feel safer already." She pushes it to him. "Here, I can't stand to read it again."

He tags a file in his mind, reminding himself to read through the article when he has time. "About the reason they got you up—I think I know what it is."

"You do?"

This is it. "I'm taking Jade to gymnastics this morning and Alex wanted me to ask if she could go."

He can see her eyes change as the meaning sinks in. "Oh, no, uh, uh. No."

He raises his hands. "It's not dangerous."

"Oh, sure." She rises, pours herself another cup of coffee. "Tell me about it."

"It's a beginning class, on mats. It's offered at Sheldon, part of the arts program. High school gymnasts teach it. You can call to check it out. They're great with the kids. They tumble, they do cartwheels, they balance on a beam six inches off the floor. It's for balance, strength, that's all. There are girls smaller than Alex there, little kids. Nobody gets hurt. Jade's never gotten hurt." No sooner is it out of his mouth than he regrets it.

"Alex isn't Jade."

Everything rides on her giving permission. She says no, all bets are off. Everything goes back to the way it was. "I know that." He takes a breath, starts over. "Look, I'll be there, I'll be watching every second. You can come, too, if you want."

"I don't."

He makes one last try. "Look, it's my treat. It's only an hour. One hour. We'll be back by eleven." He looks to see them peeking around the jam, on their bellies in the doorway.

"Get in here," Ceridwen says without bothering to turn.

Sheepish, they come out of hiding and Alex runs to hug her mother. "Please, Mom, please?"

She takes a deep breath, trains a deadly look at Night. The three of them hold their breath.

"Please?" Alex whines, sounding more like a little girl than he has ever heard.

In Ceridwen's face something gives. "You promise to be very careful?"

"We do, we do," they chorus, breaking for the door.

Girls gone, Night breathes a sigh, relieved, notices her eyes still on him. "I do."

The glare lingers, then breaks. "I'm trusting you."

"I know. You won't regret it."

"I'm going back to bed." She rises, flings her coffee into the sink, heads for the door. "See you at the emergency room."

• • •

By ten the gym is busy.

Timid, Alex sticks close behind Jade as she crosses the floor. Ready for disaster, Night registers her, writes a check for money he doesn't have, waits hunkered against the wall. He's not worried— tomorrow's pay day.

Alex lines up behind Jade, peeking at girls running and tumbling on the mat. Jade explains as they move up through the line, watching. Alex nods. She's next. Night dries sweaty hands on his jeans. How bad can she get hurt on the mat? How bad?

Her turn comes. She goes into the roll well, comes out of it and goes right down on her face. Heart clenched, Night comes to his feet. She rights herself, follows Jade around to rejoin the line. Teary eyed, she looks back. Her glance tells him she will stay in. He gives her a thumbs up and she smiles, wiping away tears.

This time she comes out of the roll on her feet and, like a laughing sprite, sprints around to the back of the queue. Watching her, he smiles behind his fist. He was right. It was what she needed. Moving up the line she looks nothing like the spoiled sleepy kid he's put up with for weeks. For the first time since he's met her she looks happy. Watching, he finds he doesn't dislike her nearly as much as he thought he did.

They're back by eleven, sun occasionally appearing with searing intensity in fissures between bloated cumulus meandering south. Car hot, girls chattering, Night pulls up the drive, finds Ceridwen weeding on her knees in the flower bed and a fire truck red BMW parked out front.

Out of the car before it comes to a stop, Alex sprints for her mother, throws herself into her arms, rocking her on her knees. "Mama, Mama, I tumbled, I walked on my hands, I did cartwheels!"

In her voice Night hears no artifice. Her excitement is 24 carat.

Over Alex's shoulder, Ceridwen watches him. "That's wonderful."

"We're going swimming." As fast as she came she pushes away, screams after Jade up the walk.

Ceridwen returns to her weeding. "So, she didn't get hurt?"

"Fell a couple times. I wouldn't be surprised if she's got a bruise or two. Nothing major."

She works at a stubborn rosette, twisting it round and round to sever the root. A jerk and it snaps. She tosses it into her pile, "Okay, so I baby her."

Beside her he hunkers, gathering purslane for a pull, succulent pads soft in his fingers. "I didn't say that."

"You don't have to say it. I know what you think."

What can he say? She's right.

"I'm not proud of it. But you haven't sat up with her nights when the pain was so bad the pills might have been sugar. You weren't there the night she woke screaming, handful of hair in each fist. You missed that. All you see is a brat with a smart mouth who won't mind, the mother too lily-livered to discipline."

She sits back, sighs, looking exhausted. "I'm no good at parenting, I know that."

He opens his mouth to protest and she raises a hand to stop him.

"Mama…" She breathes deep, lets it go. "Do you know she hasn't called me that in three years?"

"You should come next time. She'd like It."

"Maybe." She stands, stretches like a cat after a nap. "How about a barbecued burger and a swim? I've got the stuff."

He pretends to think about it, shrugs. "Okay. I've got an old malt mixer in a box in the closet. I'll bring it down and the girls can make their own malts."

She leads the way around to the back, through rhodies swollen with bloom. "Alex would love that."

No sooner are they inside than the doorbell bleats. He gets it. Outside waits a tall boy dressed in black leather, dog collar bristling with inch long spikes around his neck. Waiting in the VW at the curb is a girl in white pancake makeup and blood red lipstick. "Help you?"

"I…" Puzzled, his mouth drops in indecision. He looks back at the car. With an impatient nod, she urges him on. "Dr. Lawrence home?"

"Let me guess, forgot your book."

He smiles as if Night had just thrown him a life preserver. "Yeah."

"Just a minute."

Disgusted, he throws closed the door, passes her on his way out the back door. "For you."

Outside he lights charcoal, scrounges a few smaller pieces of oak from the wood-pile and lays it across flaming coals. Eyes on smoldering oak, he fumes. The whole damned thing stinks—him here standing by as she flaunts what he's stood for, lived for, risked his life for.

He feels her next to him, and looks up to see her looking guilty. Let her. She is.

"I'd better wash the grill." She stoops to pick it up and he takes it from her, tossing it onto the pyre where blackened grease sizzles as it contacts flame.

"Never scrub a grill."

"It's filthy."

What's filthy is a dealer with her face, with her class, with her voice, her body, her eyes. That's what's filthy. "It'll burn clean."

In silence they watch the grill burn as the girls yell and whoop around the corner in the pool.

"I hate washing the greasy thing, it always makes such a God awful mess."

Hypnotized by the flames, he doesn't bother to answer.

She goes, returns with a plate of patties. The grill is a light gray where the fire has cauterized it. Inside he's the same. No way will he let himself be drawn into caring about a woman like her. It sickens him he's come as close as he has. No further.

She watches him speculatively as he tosses the patties on the red hot grill. "You must be wondering about all the forgotten books."

"No."

Her eyes search his skin for a way in. He won't give her one. He keeps his eyes on the fire.

"You're not?"

"Uh, uh."

"You know, then."

He slaps raw meat on glowing steel. He knows he's a jerk for doing what he is. He knows they are both on borrowed time. "That's right."

"And?"

What can she expect him to say? He thinks it's swell she deals out of the house? "And what?"

"You want to move out, I'll give you back your money, all of it."

He'd love to, but he has nowhere to go. "Keep it, I'm not going anywhere." Not for three weeks he isn't.

"I understand if you don't want Jade around it."

Blood pools on the surface of the meat. He flips the patties and grease flares. Why is she telling him this? "I'm not crazy about it."

"It's just marijuana, nothing else. Just to some of my students, friends, friends of friends."

Why can't she just shut up? "I get it."

"I wouldn't sell anything else. Is that so wrong?"

He looks at her and sees her for the first time. "It's against the law."

"You don't smoke, then?"

"Not for twenty years, you?"

"Not since college."

Relief floods him. Why should he care? "Then, why do this?" Words said, he marvels at them. He doesn't do the why thing. His job is busting people like her, not asking why, not analyzing, not convincing—his job is taking away their dope.

"It's safer than alcohol or cigarettes either one. Making it illegal does more harm than good."

"Health food, huh?"

"What I sell is clean—no chemicals—old student of mine grows it outside Alvadore. Wouldn't use a pesticide to save his soul. If my students are going to smoke, I want them to know what they're smoking."

He smiles down at the coals. "Now I've heard it all."

Hand on hip, eyes hard, she watches him scoop up patties, tails him ·in. "Look, I'm a biologist. I know science. Not much else maybe, but I know that. And I can tell you that the crap you hear and read from NIDA is distorted."

He gets the feeling he should know what she is talking about. He doesn't. "NIDA?"

"National Institute on Drug Abuse. They're nothing but DEA's propaganda ministry. They'll fund anybody who promises to find harmful results for marijuana use."

From the fridge he gathers an armful of pickles, mayo, mustard. "You're saying they lie? Come off it, another government conspiracy? I don't buy it."

"Yes, they lie. Yes, another conspiracy. They ignore any results that find it harmless, exaggerate any claims of harm. Technically it may be selectivity of data, but when somebody does it consciously to deceive, I call it lying."

He's in way over his head. He's never spent his time pondering whether dope is harmful any more than when he gave tickets for speeding he spent his time analyzing speed limits. "I can't argue with you. I'm not a scientist. And I'm not about to chase my tail second-guessing the law until my head disappears up my backside. I can't find the catsup."

She finds it easily. "But you think smoking cannabis should be a crime?"

Easy questions he likes. "I do."

"Apparently most Oregonians disagree. Projections I've seen have Initiative 82 winning by ten percent. How do you explain that?"

Untroubled, he sets the table. "I don't."

Frustrated, she sighs, "Then tell me why it should be a crime."

Another easy one. Why does he get the feeling he's stepping into a noose? "To keep people from using it."

"Ah, deterrence." She smiles. "I can cite eight government studies since '69 that disagree with you." She ticks them off: "UK's Wooten Report, the Canadian Le Dain Commission Report, the Dutch Ben Commission, the US National Commission on Marijuana and Drug abuse, The National Academy of Sciences Report, the—"

"Okay." He raises a hand to stop her, "Okay, okay, I get it."

"By '78, all but eight states had reduced possession from a felony to a misdemeanor. Ten removed all criminal penalties for anything under an ounce. Carter was for legalizing less than that. Dan Quayle even recommended decriminalizing."

He was waiting for that. "And use went up."

This doesn't faze her. "Yes, it did."

He halts, afraid to misstep. "Well, there you go."

She slashes the air in evident frustration, "No you don't. Despite having the stiffest marijuana penalties in the western world, as many or more people smoke it here as they do anywhere else."

He opens his mouth and she cuts him off.

"Let me finish. Around the world cannabis use increased from 1960 through 1980—"

He pounces. "My point."

"But went down in the eighties."

"When we recriminalized."

"Yes, when we recriminalized. Captain Ray Gun took command in '80, and ever since we've been fighting The Drug War."

He doesn't see the flaw in his argument. "So where am I off?"

"In the nineties, use is up even though penalties for cannabis have been strengthened. Between 91 and 95, arrest rates increased 100%. In 95 alone 500 thousand people were arrested for Marijuana in the US."

"Sure, dealers are arrested." He doesn't get the problem.

"Almost nine of ten for simple possession. Our prisons are bursting with nonviolent marijuana users and sellers. And, here's the point—use is up."

He's not giving up that easily. "If it were legal more people would use it. If we didn't have DARE officers in the schools—

"Oh, please! There has never been a study of the DARE program which has shown any effect one way or the other. It simply has none."

"Maybe, but—"

"And what rebuts your argument is that in the 11 states that decriminalized in the late seventies there was no stampede to get loaded. What they always hold out there as this nightmare scenario just plain didn't happen."

Feeling cornered, he falls back to his keep. "It's against the law. Doesn't that matter to you?"

Her face tells him it does. "When the Brits ran the salt trade in India, it was against the law for Indians to make their own salt. Gandhi considered the law unjust and his followers broke it."

He laughs in frustration. "So now anybody with a finger bag is a mahatma?"

"I didn't say that."

Disgusted with this conversation and with his ignorance, he heads for the door, "I give up, you win. I'll call the kids."

She blocks his way, "One thing I've got to know—why do you care?"

He wants to grab her, shake her. Because I'm the one has to serve the warrant on you, I'm the one has to take your house. Because when you're cuffed face down on the carpet, pistol at the nape of your neck I'm going to have to look into your eyes. That's why. "Maybe I'm wrong, but don't people get in trouble for this? Don't they go to prison, lose their houses, their cars, stuff like that?"

She falters. "It happens I guess, but only if they're stupid about it."

Ah, yes, here we go. It only happens to somebody else. Every dealer thinks that—until their number comes up. "What's that mean, stupid?"

"Selling to people they don't know. Taking foolish chances. The police aren't going to come around here looking for a few ounces of marijuana. It isn't like I'm growing it in the garage."

If she only knew how wrong she is. "So you think because you live in a nice neighborhood, have a good job, drive a nice car, you're immune, that it? Police only bust people on the west side? I didn't know that."

"Look, I only sell small amounts to my students, to people I know. How is some narc going to entrap me? Huh, how? Who could do it?"

You're looking at him, honey-babe. He's sorely tempted to tell. It sticks in his throat like a seed.

"I don't take chances, I wouldn't with Alexis here."

This is a professor talking? He's known smarter tweakers. "Seems to me I've read about people losing their kids to SCF for selling drugs. You ever hear that?"

Her eyes are worried, "SCF?"

"Services to Children and Families." If she hasn't heard of them, she will.

For the first time fear comes into her eyes, and she moves away from the door. "I would never let that happen."

Her arrogance galls him. He'd like to see her try and stop it. "That's good, because I can see how much you love her."

He calls in the girls. Inside, the conversation hangs unfinished, a sheet of steaming dry ice between them. At the kitchen table, they sit. The girls sense something's up, get quiet. Three bites and Alexis shoves her plate away, "I'm ready for my malt."

He makes his face into a thoughtful mask. "They might give me a refund, I don't know."

She rolls her eyes, "I'm eating." She takes a Godzilla bite, "I'm eating, see?"

"Yeah, thanks," Night says, "I don't need to see that much."

Jade laughs, then they all do, and somehow the wall between them is gone. He can't stay mad at this woman. He should, but he can't. Not any more than he can jump up to cling to the ceiling by his toenails.

A dent in the wall over the kitchen table catches his eye, and he runs a hand over it. About the size of a palm, it looks as if something bounced off the wall.

Ceridwen smiles. "You noticed."

"What happened?"

"That's where I dropped the lasagna when my husband told me he wanted a divorce."

He looks again at the wall, at her. "Dropped it, huh?"

She nods. "Sure did."

He appraises her, impressed. "You've got an arm. Remind me never to get in the way when you drop something. You want it fixed, or is it a keeper?"

"Can you do that?" She laughs, waves her hand. "Of course you can. You keep doing things for me I'm going to owe you money at the end of the month." She sighs. "I've got some Spackle, I think."

"We'll need a piece of wallpaper, too."

"I've got some."

Finished with their burgers, the girls set the mixer to humming and whining. Malt ready, they split it. Melting chocolate moustache dripping, Alex comes to hug her mother around the waist. "It's so good, can we get a malt mixer? Can we, huh?"

"We'll see."

Out they run to the pool. Night follows Ceridwen into the garage, where she rummages through jammed shelves.

"Like hell we will. That's all we need. That was amazing, though. I haven't seen her eat all her dinner in longer than I can remember. Guess gymnaxtix did the trick."

He winces. "I know I have no right—"

"Are you kidding? It's exactly what she needs. I know I'm no good at it." She sighs. "She's got me trained, I'm afraid."

He spots the box, reaches past her up to the top shelf. Inside, the kitchen is quiet as he mixes the paste in a cup. From the kitchen window he nods at the BMW. "Nice car."

She skids the table out of his way. "Grant's home. He's out with friends, now."

"Nice to have him home, I bet."

She smiles wistfully. "I'm afraid he's got a lot more in common with his father than with me, right now. I don't really see him that much. This is just a place to drop off dirty laundry and catch a snack."

He nods at the mixer. "Split one?"

She looks torn, "I don't know."

"Nonfat frozen yogurt, skim milk, malt is all it is. So low in fat it actually has negative calories."

She laughs, giving in. "I'll make it while you patch."

He watches her move as he trims sheet rock. She reaches for the malt from a high cabinet and in his belly commences a familiar burning.

"You know," she says, "you don't always have to be working. You could relax some time."

With a thumb he crams the hole full of crumpled funny papers. "I'm lousy at sitting. Like to keep moving. This way I don't have to worry about entertaining anyone with my scintillating wit."

"I'm glad you don't try." She squeezes out a dollop of syrup. "I've had enough of wit." She contemplates the jar of malt. "How much?"

"Depends. Like it malty?"

She shrugs. "I'm not sure. Haven't had one since I was a kid."

He looks her over. "You seem a malty sort to me."

"That good or bad?"

He presses compound into the depression with a putty knife. "Good. Malt is sweet, alive, yeasty. Three teaspoons."

She spoons it in, sets the cup on the mixer, and it whines to life. "I don't feel like that very often."

He cleans his knife in the sink. "Smile."

She bares teeth as she might for a dentist.

"Mean it."

She smiles, turning away. "Happy?"

"See what I mean? Three tablespoons."

She watches the mixer, face coloring.

He drops the putty knife in the rack. "That's it until it dries."

While it mixes, they stand elbow to elbow at the sink watching the girls in the pool. Though the mixer drones, it is silence comfortable as a flannel shirt.

She peers in the cup. "How do you tell when it's done?"

He slaps the stainless glass, letting it spin with the force of the beater under his hand. On the steel is frost. "It's done."

She spoons half the malt into a glass, hands it to him. He sips, so thick he has to coax it out of the glass and into his mouth by tapping on the butt of the glass with the flat of his hand. Cold shocks his palate. "Now that's a malt. What do you think?"

"It's so thick, I can't get it to come out." Again she lifts the stainless tumbler, taps the bottom, and squeals. When she sets it down, malt covers her mouth, nose, cheek. "I'm such a slob!"

He hands her a towel, "I don't know, I think it looks pretty good on you."

"You're mean."

He fetches her a spoon. "Don't give up so easy. Some malts you drink. This one you eat."

He sets his glass in the sink, watches as she dries her face. "Listen, it's none of my business what you do, how you live your life. And I'm sure as hell not going to change your mind, I know that. I'd just hate to see anything happen to you because of it, that's all."

Arms braced on the sink, she turns to study his face. "We have a difference of opinion, I guess."

If it were only that. There's no use arguing about it. She knows ten times what he does about it, anyway. For all he knows her stats are right on the money. What he does know is, right or wrong, in spite of the arguments, the studies, the usage trends, in spite of all the research by all the pointy heads, very soon she is going to learn more about the war on drugs than she has any desire to.

"I guess you're right."

● ● ●

Ceridwen finds the girls waiting for her at the pool.

She lies on a cushioned chaise and they flank her, drawing close.

"Mom, isn't he nice?"

This from Alex after what happened at dinner. Enjoying the conspiratorial huddle, she glances behind them, lowers her voice to a whisper suitable for intrigue, "Yes, he is."

"And do you like him?"

Ceridwen keeps her face serious, her tone profound. "I do."

Alexis nods at Jade, passing the ball. "I knew it! Tell her, Jade, tell her."

"It's like this, my dad usually reads novels, mysteries and suspense, mostly, but since last week all he reads is books on biology and stuff like that. I couldn't figure it out until Alex told me you were a biologist, then it all made sense. He started reading those right after he found out you taught. He never said so, but I know that's why." She peers once more over her shoulder in the direction of the back door. "What could that mean? Only one thing."

Ceridwen nods anxiously, wearing her best conspirator's face. "And what's that?"

"Well… you know."

"I do?"

"Mom!" Alex moans through clenched teeth, "It means he's interested."

Feigning confusion, she frowns, "In biology?"

"No!" Disgusted with her obtuseness, Alex pounds the chaise with her fists. "In you."

Night slams out the back door, and with a final significant look as punctuation to their news, the conspirators run off to continue their game of Marco Polo.

Ceridwen watches as he finds a place on the rock, dangling his feet in the water. Not bad for a man of forty. She likes to see muscles in a man's arms and legs. Easy to see he doesn't sit all day.

He cocks his head. "What?"

"Nothing."

"You're staring. I have malt on my chin?"

"No, and I was not staring." She lies back, enjoying the heat, the air. Suddenly she is tired.

A car comes up the driveway. She opens her eyes and sees it is dusk. On the edge of the pool reading is Night. "That must be Grant."

The back gate opens hard enough to rock the post in the ground, and Grant struts in, friend in tow. Seeing Night, he hesitates, regains his stride. "Whoa, a party, huh, Mom?"

She laughs. "A wild one. Grant, this is Night. He and his daughter, Jade, rent the extra bedrooms."

Grant never takes his eyes off Night. "Renting my bedroom?"

More like distant relatives than mother and son since the divorce, never has she felt more a stranger. "That's right."

"Glad to meet you," he says to Night as if he's not.

"Your mom tells me you go to Davis? How you like it?"

"Fine. Hey mom, we're going out. I'll drop by later." His eyes return to Night. "We can talk then—if you'll be available."

Why is he being this way? "You know I will."

"See you." The gate slams behind them.

Ashamed of his rudeness, she decides to let it go. It's been a long time since they talked—about anything other than money and laundry, anyway. She looks forward to it.

"I think my pool privileges are about to be revoked," Night says.

The girls climb out, run inside to change.

"He's not usually rude. Don't let it bother you. Probably a girl." She hopes it is.

It's quiet. Water sloshes lazily under rocks set into the side of the pool as dusk settles about them. She lowers herself in, heated water only a slight shock as it soaks through her suit. She pushes off, turning onto her back, "Let's swim."

Side by side, Night lagging by a stroke, they glide through the water, her wet face cool in the night air. No pool light tonight, it's dark enough to turn the pool to ink. They swim, disembodied heads on black water.

Winded, he gasps. "Shall I turn on the pool light?"

"No," I like seeing the stars."

"In Eugene?"

"Okay, so I'm an optimist, leave it anyway."

The first laps they take in silence, then, she slows, rolls onto her back. "There, see? What's that star?"

"Venus, I think."

She laughs at herself. "I should have known, it's so bright."

She switches to the breast stroke, abandoning herself to the resistance of water against muscle. She does this every day, misses it intensely when she does not. Pushing off, she notices his eyes on her. "What are you looking at?" She rears, kicking off.

Doggedly, he trails. "You."

It's obvious he's winded. Obvious she could leave him behind. She holds back. "Don't."

"Why not?"

At the end of the pool she pushes off, passing him by, "It makes me nervous."

"Liar."

Incredulous, she watches him follow. Blood burning hot in her face, she realizes it's true, she is a liar. She groans into the water. The last thing she wants is more complexity in her life.

He stops, clinging to rock at the side, breathing heavily. "I can't do this."

She finishes her circuit, comes up behind him, the muscles of his arms and back drawing her eyes. When she comes to berth, she's close enough to feel the heat of his skin, of his breath. From so close she only has to whisper, "Yes you can."

He shakes his head no. "I don't do this every day like you do."

"Five more makes twenty." She shoves off and, grudgingly, he follows. Her speed she holds far below her threshold. To her chagrin, she realizes how much she enjoys his company in her daily ritual. Len would never do this—never. Couldn't is her guess. Yet Night plods after her, straining.

They finish, and he hoists himself out to lie on stone. Another two laps at full speed and she lies opposite him, head to head in the cool night air. Across sloshing black water she lets her eyes lose focus.

"What's so serious?" he asks.

Desolation washes over her like a wave. "Weekends."

"I don't follow."

Why is she telling him this? A man she hardly knows? Why can't she just shut up? Why is he so much easier to talk to than Len? "I hate them." The venom in her voice shocks her.

From inches away, he watches, "What's to hate?"

Too late to stop the words now, like a slide, once started, they come. "The time. The quiet. The house."

"You can't hate this house."

Empty she does. Before he and Jade came she did. She squints up at it. Now she's not sure. Cheek to warm stone, she chances a glance at him, "You're single, what do you do?" As soon as she says it, she wishes she hadn't. She doesn't want to know.

He shrugs, arms under his chin, their heads inches apart. So close she can smell onion on his breath. "Work. Read. Eat. Sleep—all the regular stuff."

Relieved, she smiles into her arm. "Wild you."

"Works for me."

She recognizes the routine. "Killing time."

"That's right. Until Jade came to live with me that's what I did. Anything to get through. You wouldn't know about that."

She cringes. "Believe me, I do."

He moves closer, giving her ample time to flee. To her wonder, she stays put. "You know what I'm going to do."

Fear takes her round the middle. "Don't."

"Why not?"

"I'm dating someone."

He inches closer. She trembles, thinks she could reach out with her tongue to lick the water dripping from his hair over his cheek. Trembling, she pushes the thought away. "Stop right there."

A smile threatens at the corners of his mouth. "I don't see you running."

"I'll slap you."

Now he does smile. "I might like that."

For the first time she is afraid. Serious, she pleads. "Don't ruin it."

Smile gone, he hesitates. "Ruin what?"

"What we have."

Returns the guile. "We have something, do we?"

He's being purposely simple and it galls her. "You know what I mean, you living here with Jade. You're a nice guy, don't ruin it like this."

"Maybe I'm not such a nice guy."

She could laugh. "You are."

"So how is this going to ruin it? Tell me that."

No way can she look away. It's as if she has lost the use of her muscles. "It will. You'll want to again." Or she will.

"I'll risk it."

"I won't. I can't."

He thinks it over, decides. "Okay, tell me you don't want me to and I won't."

She doesn't hesitate. "I don't want you to."

"What a terrible liar you are." Now so close they are two tines of a tuning fork vibrating in resonance. Beyond gentleness, he brushes her lips and she starts as if static sparks between them. She doesn't pull away.

He does—a millimeter.

"Deed done. Shall I move out, now?"

Unsure of her voice, she jerks her head no. She opens her eyes to see him watching her.

"I want you to know something."

She finds she's holding her breath, their faces close enough that down intermingles, clashes, sending jolts through her lips, her cheek. "Oh, God, what?"

"I didn't rent these rooms because I needed a place for Jade and I to live."

Suddenly she is afraid of what he will say. "Don't."

"I rented them—"

"Don't say it." She is pleading. "Stop."

"Because of you."

Involuntarily she loses the air in her lungs. She knows it, has always known it. From the moment he stopped on the stairs she had known it. Now she's afraid to say anything, afraid to respond at all. To make a sound would invite an avalanche of doubt about her life. Blindly, she flees, dives into dark water. Five furious laps later she emerges winded, chest heaving, to find a wet patch of stone where he had lain.

Thankful, she sags against the side, arms clutching rock worn smooth by years in a river. Cheek smeared against stone, she hugs it to her, breath coming ragged. Only a week ago, her life had been well-ordered, logical. Now it's as if he purposely tugs at the thread which will start it all raveling.

And knowing, she lets it happen.

• • •

Grant slams in at two a.m.

From deep in a chair Ceridwen looks up with bleary eyes. "You're late," she says, voice woolly with sleep.

He tosses his coat on the couch, a proprietary gesture. "So what's going on with this boarder, Mom?"

"What's going on? What's that mean, what's going on? He lives here, he and his daughter—that's what's going on. They pay rent and they live here. I need the money."

"You know that's not what I'm talking about."

She knows. What drives her to want to slap his face is that in his words she hears

Jeff prying, still after everything trying his best to control her, manipulate her. It isn't happening. "He's a friend, if that's what you mean."

"Dad tells me he's a garbage collector." He loads the words.

She pulls herself erect, bristling under his glare. Now just how had Jeff learned that? "Your point?"

"My point…" He perches on the edge of the couch, talking sense to a fool. "…is that I would hope you would have enough sense not to be—"

"Yes, Grant?" she says, voice dropping. "What exactly is it I should have enough sense not to be?"

He stands, snatching up his coat. "You know what I'm trying to say. I just thought you had more class than that, that's all." And he delivers the coup de grâce—"So did Dad."

"Did he?" She pushes up out of the chair, blood roaring in her ears, "And what would I be doing if I had class? Waiting around in an apron and slippers in case you drop in and want me to whip you up an angel food cake? Baking apple pies with my hair done up in a bun? Ironing your undershorts? Should I be growing old gracefully, Grant? Is that what a classy, sensible woman does when her husband shacks up with a girl half her age? Or maybe the classy thing to do would be to spend my days trying to figure out why I wasn't good enough to make your father want to stay. That's it, isn't it? Because it was my fault he left, wasn't it?"

He avoids her eyes. "That's not it at all."

"Oh, yes it is, but let me tell you something, you little shit. It was your father's choice to leave."

He watches the ceiling.

"Look at me—his choice. He's been gone two years. We are divorced. I know that's hard for you, but that's the way it is. Get over it—I have. Alex has." She breathes, drops her voice. "I'm not twenty any more. But you know what? I'm not dead, either. I'm alive. And if I can, I'm going to be happy. Your father should understand that. Why don't you try?" She grabs his hands. "You're my son. I'll always love you. That will never change. But don't tell me how to live. I'm thirty-nine years old and I'm single." She grabs his chin, turns him to face her. "And I'll live how I choose."

He tries to pull away, but she holds him, making a last appeal. "I like Night. He's decent. And he makes me happy. Is that so bad? Doesn't that make you happy, too?"

"What about Len?"

He would ask. She lets him go. "I haven't decided."

This hits him hard. "So what, you're doing two guys now?"

Her hand whips out so fast it surprises her nearly as much as it does him. Her palm cracks on the skin of his face hard enough to hurt her hand. What surprises her more is what she feels—nothing.

No more to say, she turns off the lights and climbs the stairs, leaving him alone in the dark.

• • •

Jo picks her way along the salad bar. "So, how's your boarder turning out? Discovered any deep dark secrets yet?"

"Secrets?"

"Yeah, you know, body parts in the freezer? Candle-lit rituals inside pentagrams?

Things like that?"

Ceridwen follows, rifling the lettuce for the least wilted iceberg, herding romaine to the other side of the bowl. "You're sick, you know that, Jo? You should see someone."

"Yes, do tell, how is your garbage man?" Pickering asks.

"He's not my garbage man." She will have to be careful what she says. They know her well. "His name's Night, he and his daughter each have a room."

Jo's eyes light with mischief, "And was he as nice as you thought he'd be?"

How should she answer? She can tell the truth. And what is that? "He's okay."

"Then why are you such a grouch?"

Ceridwen moans, exasperated, "All those credit card bills come today, and I don't know how I'm going to pay them, that's all. I hate even seeing them."

With tongs, Pickering examines cherry tomatoes for her salad as if they were tissue specimens, turning each this way and that to catch the light before setting them carefully on a plate piled high with carrot and celery. "You never should have let the bastard saddle you with those. I told you at the time to get councel."

Jo fishes for beets, "For all you know, you're paying for her lingerie."

Again they're going to beat her up over this. She's almost used to it. "Yeah, well, it may have been stupid, but I signed, and now I've got to manage somehow." Over her bowl Ceridwen sprinkles sunflower seeds, untangles a fork, "I just don't know how yet, is all."

Jo leads to a table by the front near the pie counter. "I'm so glad we came here. No more puck burgers for this kid."

"And what about Alex's treatments?" Pickering asks. "Jeff helping with those?"

Ceridwen grunts, mouth full, "Fat chance."

Jo pulls a face, "What a pencil neck."

"So far she's doing fine."

"And if she needs Sloan?"

"There isn't enough money."

Pickering shakes her head. "Million dollar mice. I don't trust any of them, the charlatans."

"Rattles and leeches, enemas and purges."

"Okay, I know it sounds way out there, but if it comes back, Doernbecher says there's nothing more they can do for her. What am I supposed to do, stock up at the magazine rack, pull up a chair and watch her die?"

Jo reaches out, "Relax, we're on your side."

Face hot, Ceridwen sighs, "I know, I know you are."

Jo's gaze wanders to the cold box. "Sweet Jesus, will you look at that pie? Look at that chocolate cream! I swear it's six inches tall. How can they do that?"

Pickering shakes salt on a tomato. "Easily, Jo, dear, they use lots and lots of fat. Whipped cream, butter, shortening—that's a pound staring you in the face, love. An inch right where you want it least."

Jo sighs, spears a beet. "Oh, I know. You're right. Why did we sit here, anyway?"

"Because you led us here," Ceridwen says.

"Oh, hell, I couldn't help it. My belly did it. Pig to the trough."

Pickering says, "Did you have any idea how much debt you were taking on at the time?"

"I thought maybe a few thousand at most. I had no idea it was as bad as it is."

Pickering wags a finger. "I'd have had a solicitor taking my part, watching out for me. You see what happens when you don't."

Jo leans forward, "How much did you say it was, fifty thousand?"

No longer hungry, Cer pushes her plate away. Talking about it is prodding the wound. "Not including first and second mortgage. So far I'm keeping up with the payments, but the interest is killing me. I owe more every month. Some of the cards are at twenty percent. I've had to mortgage the house for every kopeck, and I'm still only just treading water."

"Well, I think it stinks," Jo says. "After twenty years, he runs away with a cute young thing and leaves you holding the bag. What did he spend the money on, anyway?"

"Restaurants, motels, down payment on a Bug. Seen her in it two or three times around campus."

"Now you get to pay for it? The bastard." Jo hunches close. "Don't let him get away with it."

She wants to cry. "He already did."

"Have you thought of seeing an attorney now, at least?" Pickering says. "Maybe something could still be done."

Ceridwen shakes her head. "Can't afford to. Besides, what good can it do? I've already signed the papers. It's too late now."

"Well, at least your washer works," Jo says. "That's something. How was Saturday night?"

For an instant Ceridwen is puzzled, then in rushes guilt. "Len's a nice guy."

Jo wags a finger. "You know who's a nice guy, you know who's a real nice guy? Mr. Rogers. You wouldn't sleep with him, would you?"

Ceridwen gives her a cold glance.

"You know..." Pickering leans forward, punctuating her thoughts with a scallion. "Jo's got a point, Cer. Here you are, you've been dating Len for what, six months, year now? I don't think I've ever heard you say you love him. Do you?"

She can't believe she's asking her this. It's insulting. "Of course I love him."

Pickering nods. "Of course."

She must love him. "How could I not?"

Jo rises, slips a dollar bill under a glass with a smirk. "The lady doth protest too much, methinks."

They pay the check and start on the walk back to the college. Pickering sighs, "Next year, I'm taking summer session off."

"That's what you say every year," Jo says.

"Oh, that reminds me, you're both coming to my party on Saturday, aren't you? You're both to bring significant others."

Ceridwen stops, slips off her shoes to walk barefoot on damp lawn under maples. The possibility of another evening bored to tears is more than she can tolerate right now. Why can't everybody just leave her alone?

"I'll see."

• • •

On his knees, Night heels in tomatoes with an open hand.

June in Oregon. Foggy mornings, cool nights, clouds break over the Coast Range, flowing into the Willamette Valley like breakers over a sand castle wall. The house is still gutted, the pool still pea soup, but he gets the garden in now or he doesn't at all, so he wastes two precious hours of his Wednesday off rototilling horse manure and shavings into a small patch of soil. The raised mound, so soft he can plant by hand, cradles a dozen tomatoes. Those in, he can bide his time. Everything else can go in later, but tomatoes need every hour of sun they can scrounge to ripen fruit.

Sitting back on his haunches, he looks them over, satisfied with his work. He's felt a lack these three years with no garden of his own. Not much more than a king size bed, but good soil, his soil.

He hears a car pull into the driveway. Too early for Cer. Nobody else but Rita knows he's here, and she's working. The gate closes hard and Night is surprised to see Grant and friend head past the pool toward the house. "Here I am."

They stop, turn through the hemlock, ducking low branches, and head on back to the garden. Night's not sure he likes the look on Grant's face, but he stays on his knees, watching him come, friend from the other night dogging his heels. Night presses earth around a seedling up high so it will root along the stem. "How did you know I was here?"

Grant halts a pace away, sneakers crushing a tomato. "Saw your car. I want you out of my house."

Night looks up at him. Big kid. Six-three, maybe two-sixty, bullet head cropped short. No neck. Trapezius big deltas to the base of his skull. Straight out of the academy he couldn't have taken him bare handed. Twenty years later with a bad arm and stiff knees he doesn't want to try. The situation is more comic than anything else. "You're doing a Godzilla on my tomato."

Grant grinds it into the manure mulch and Night can't help but smile at the melodramatic quality of the gesture. What's next, kicking compost into his face?

"I want you out of there now...today."

For the first time Night feels worms of panic squirm through his insides. He's been beaten before. Never cared much for it. He reaches around him with his mind. He's in his shirt sleeves, nothing within reach except a small hoe. At the other end of the garden a spading fork is stuck upright where he left off turning under sod. Too far away. The friend Night's not sure about. He may have come to help or maybe just to watch. Not that it matters. Grant won't need help.

Halfway to school on her bike, Ceridwen realizes she's forgotten her wallet and turns back.

Nearly there, she sees Grant's car alongside Night's in the drive of the house on the corner. Coasting to a stop, she frowns. As long as she can remember an old couple have lived there. Odd.

Curious, and in no rush, she props her bike against a mailbox buried in ivy and climbs the walk to where she hears her son's voice. Without knowing why, she chooses not to go through the gate. Instead she cuts across the rhody bed, ducking under the last of the sagging blossoms to peer through a slatted fence. From here she can see Grant and his friend opposite a kneeling Night.

Suddenly worried, she barely breathes.

It looks to Night like he is in for an ass-kicking.

He can't afford one. Not now. He needs every day's pay he can lay his hands on. He takes a deep breath, reaches out for the short handled hoe, and propping himself up with it, rises to his haunches. "Look, I can see why you wouldn't want somebody living in your house."

"Get packing—now."

Night laughs, not sure how to explain the facts of life to a young man who has no interest in hearing them. "I'm sorry partner, but the nine hundred cleaned me out. It'll be a month before I go anywhere. Why not come on in? Let me fix you a tuna sandwich and we'll talk over what's got you so exercised. I don't plan on leaving any holes in the wall or cigarette burns in the carpet if that's it."

"It's not the carpet I'm worried about."

Now they're getting somewhere. "What then?"

"You know damned well."

He might at that. "I do?"

This seems to set him off. "I want you away from her!"

So that's it. "That might be hard. We do live in the same house."

"You know that's not what I mean." Grant sighs impatiently, waves him up with a sausage of a finger, "Come on, get up, I'm going to kick your ass."

Suddenly tired, Night sighs, "I don't want to fight you." Never has he wanted to fight anyone less.

Grant takes a step closer, so close Night can see the warp of his jeans, "Get up, garbage man."

It's his move. Night decides he won't make it easy. "I don't think so."

Grant hesitates, decides, steps back to kick him. Night brings the shaft of the hoe down across his shin with a crack like an axe biting grain. With a grunt, Grant stoops to hold his shin. Night takes up his right hand, bending the thumb back along the wrist and trapping it there with both thumbs. Grant reaches for him with his left and Night clamps down. With a groan, Grant opens his hand, signaling enough.

"It's hard to believe how much a shin can hurt and not be broken, I know." The friend takes a step and Night stops him with a voice grown very big, very hard, "You get into this, I'll not only break your arm, I'll have you taken to jail for assault. Now back off."

He does.

"Go on, right out the gate, wait in the car. Grant will be along in a minute. We need to talk."

He hesitates.

"Go on, Jason," Grant says.

Night watches him as he goes, smiles at Grant. "You're not so dumb."

Outside the fence, Ceridwen watches Jason go, sees him hesitate as he notices the bicycle. He doesn't see her. Turning back to the scene in the garden, She's torn between stopping it and letting it play out. Deciding Grant's in no danger, she stays where she is, giving in to curiosity intense as salt.

"Now we're alone, I've got to tell you something." Night's voice is velvet quiet. "First, you're going to buy me a new tomato. Can you handle that?"

Grant grunts.

"I asked if you can handle it?"

Groaning from the pressure Night puts on his thumb, he nods, head close to

Night's. "I can handle it."

"It was a Brandywine. They're not easy to find. They're antiques, thin-skinned, easily bruised—like me."

Grant reaches for Night's hands on his wrist.

"Uh, uh," Night says, and Grant lets his hand fall away. "Okay, now I want you to listen to me, you ready?"

"I'm ready."

"My name is Night, not Garbage Man. If you understand say 'Yes, Night, I understand.'"

He says it.

"That's good, I think you do. Something else I want you to understand. This is my house. I own it. I don't want you back here. And as for your mother's house, I live there, I have a lease. That means it's my legal domicile. My daughter lives here, too. I'm very protective of my daughter. Very protective. You'll understand that someday when you have kids of your own. What that means is that when you come to visit your mother, you knock and wait for us to let you in. And while you're there, you watch your manners. Still with me, Grant?"

"I'm with you."

"Do I hear impatience in your voice?"

"No."

"Good. Next thing you need to understand is that your mother and I are friends. That's all—friends. But whatever we are, or aren't, or become, or don't become, it's none of your business. When you come in my house—either of my houses, and legally they are both mine—you will be polite. I don't care what you're used to getting away with. That means polite to your mother, and to me, and to Jade, and to Alex. You aren't, I'll throw you out. Come on, let me hear it."

"I understand."

"Very good. I've got my daughter to think about, you understand? It's not that I don't like you, it's that I don't like spoiled brats, whether they're two or twenty-two, it's just a thing with me, you know? It's my age. You get older you'll understand that too."

"I understand."

"Good. What you did today was assault. I want to, I could have you picked up right now and taken to jail. Ever been to jail? "

"No."

"That's good. I have, many times. You wouldn't like it."

Grant raises his eyes to look at him, face close. "You have?"

"Sure. There's a low spring chair where they make you take off your shoes and socks. They give you orange coveralls to wear. You wouldn't like those, either. Not very stylish. Never been in a holding cell, either, have you?"

"No."

"Not your class of folks. For some people it's a way of life, jail, natural as evacuating their bowels. No sweat to them. Not for you, though, I think, huh?"

"No."

"Then for you it would be trouble. I don't think your dad would be too thrilled to have to bail you out and get you a shyster, do you?"

"No."

"Okay, now I understand why you wouldn't like me. I understand it would be tough to see somebody living in your room. I understand all that. Sometimes things are tough. Deal with it. Think you can do that?"

"Yeah."

"How's your leg?"

"It's okay."

"I'm going to let you up, now. We're going to get along okay, aren't we?"

"Yeah."

Night lets him go and he heads for the gate.

"Remember now, Brandywine."

An odd burning in her stomach, Ceridwen watches from her hiding place as her son backs down the drive and pulls away. What she has heard leaves her dazed. That Night could control her son so easily is something she never expected. She hasn't seen Grant do anything but what he wanted to do in a very long time. Feeling oddly traitorous, she is somehow glad it went the way it did.

Quietly, she slips to her bike, presses off down the hill. Jail—he said he'd been there. This puzzles her most of all. Everything she feels screams it can't be true. Can't be. But why would anyone lie about something like that? They wouldn't. There must be a part of him he hasn't revealed. Something ugly.

Pedaling through the mist of a June morning, she is suddenly flushed with fear. Obviously she is not the judge of people she assumed.

Who is she living with?

• • •

Tonight Ceridwen has a committee meeting.

A hot spell has driven temperatures up into the high eighties and she sweats on her ride home. Another summer here already. So much time on her hands. So much time to think about her life. It's six by the time she walks her bike up the drive to find Jade and Alex already in the pool.

"You don't have to worry about me, Mom, I ate with Jade."

She glances up from junk mail as she passes. "What did you have?"

"Dad barbecued New Yorks, corn and potatoes."

Ceridwen halts, puzzled. "I didn't think you liked steak, Alex."

"I don't usually, but these were good."

Another thing that makes no sense—these changes in Alex. "They were, huh?"

Alex bounds to the side of the pool waving her over, eyes bright with conspiratorial fervor. She stage whispers. "Night waited to eat with you."

"He did?"

"Yeah, He's keeping the coals hot. He said to tell you when you got home. "

She whispers back. "Thanks for the tip." On the way in she passes the grill. No lunch today, the smell coming off the coals weakens her knees. She showers, slips into a suit and a pair of shorts, taps at his door.

He opens up. "Ready to eat?"

First time she has seen his room since he moved in. What hits her are the books. Hundreds of them. Stacked on every horizontal surface. She slips past him. "These yours?"

At the door, he waits as if embarrassed. "They let just about anybody buy them, now."

She picks up a book, glances at the fly leaf, "Genetics?"

He shrugs. "Looked interesting."

She looks at him through new eyes, realizing she's underestimated him. "So what have you learned?"

He smiles, shaking his head. "Come on, professor, don't put me on the spot. I know when I'm out of my league."

"No, come on, tell me something, anything. I don't care what it is, something you've learned."

"Come on." He ushers her out the door. "I've got to get those steaks on before the coals are ash."

She follows him down, not willing to let him off the hook. "You don't get off that easy. I'm waiting."

He pours her iced tea. "Give me a minute to think of something, here, will you? I hope you don't mind Alex ate with us."

"You're kidding, right? No, I don't mind. Now you're making me feel guilty. It's me supposed to be feeding you."

He takes the plate of steaks out of the fridge and heads out, "Rare for you?"

"Medium rare." She follows him out into the heat. "Summer's here, at least for today." Will he tell her about today? She guesses not.

"Just glad I finally got the power turned on down the street so I could crank up the AC. The place was like a sweat box."

He slaps the steaks on and they hiss as flesh contacts hot iron. Smoke rises to sting her eyes and she turns away to clear them.

"Never guess who stopped by to see me today."

So she is wrong again. What's happening to her instinct about people? "Who?"

"Grant."

She works at feigning casual interest. "Oh, what did he say?"

He shrugs, shifting the meat, "Not much. Didn't stay long. We talked a little."

She keeps her voice nonchalant. "About what?"

"I think he was a little concerned." He shrugs. "Stranger sharing a house with his mom. It's natural. We got to know each other a little bit. I showed off my tomato patch."

She works hard to keep her mouth straight, "And was he impressed?"

"I wouldn't say that. Not the gardening type, is he. But by the time he left, I think we understood each other pretty well."

She looks away, nods, biting her lip to keep from smiling. "I'm glad you had a chance to visit."

When the steaks pool blood he takes them up and they head inside. At the table he reaches for her hands and for a moment it throws her. Gone blank, she reaches out before it occurs to her what he wants. "Oh, I forgot."

Her family had never said a blessing. Her parents both highly educated people themselves, she'd known she was agnostic before the training wheels had come off her tricycle. Listening to him say grace now, she's amazed by the sympathetic vibration it raises in her.

She likes the way he says it, for one thing—voice low and personal. She likes it that his eyes stay open and up and on her. The thought that God would want her to talk to him with her eyes shut, head bowed in cowering supplication has always rubbed her the wrong way.

Done, he smiles, "I've got it."

"Got what?"

"What I learned."

She laughs. "Go ahead."

"Something about Charlie Chaplin."

"I thought you were reading genetics."

"I am." He slashes the air impatiently, "Okay, a girlfriend of his... ex-girlfriend of his, very young, early teens—he liked them young—sued him for paternity. The three of them took blood tests— Chaplin, the girl, and the baby. New thing at the time, never been used before to demonstrate paternity in court."

This is interesting. She leans forward, "And?"

"And they found out Barry, the girl, had type A blood, the baby had type B, and Chaplin had type O."

The steak is good, very good. She watches him eat, likes what she sees. Not so prim as Len. Not sloppy either, but the right place between. Comfortable—the way he eats, the way he dresses, the way he is. Got a brain at least. That's something. And he reads. Like the flavor of remembered nightmare, his words come back—"Seen the inside of the jail? I have." She forces her thoughts back to the subject at hand. "He couldn't have been the father."

"No, but the jury didn't believe the tests and decided against him. He had to pay child support anyway."

What could he have possibly done? Something nonviolent she would bet her life. *Bet her life...* Her heart catches as she realizes by taking him as boarder she's already done preciesely that. "I didn't know that."

After dinner they move out by the pool to sit on the second step, water lapping at their chins. Light fading, the water takes on an opaque quality in the twilight. Jade on an air mattress in front of the diving board waits while Alex jumps off nearby, doing her best to capsize her. Jade gives her a big push toward the side, and a squealing Alex begins the cycle over again.

"Jade's so patient," Ceridwen says. "Most kids her age wouldn't be bothered."

He presses close, voice low, "Does Alex read?"

She's not surprised he's noticed. "Every word's a struggle. I've tried working with her, but it drives me batty. We'll sound out a word, and two minutes later she doesn't know it."

The girls get out, dry themselves, and with giggling and meaningful glances, go in.

"Her teacher wants to send her out for extra help, but I don't want her ostracized." She sighs, exasperation familiar as an old friend weighing on her. "I don't know what to do."

She pushes off and he follows in her wake. The feel of water flowing over skin is good, purifying. In it she can lose the guilt, the worry, the nagging anxiety over money. A glance at him tells her he's comfortable as she is with silence. It's good to have him there.

Laps done, they lie on sun-warmed stone, soaking up the heat as the evening breeze raises goose bumps along her arms. She has no business spending this much time with him. It's asking for trouble and that kind of trouble she does not need. It's all gotten away from her, somehow. Everything in her life is running out of control and she has the feeling there's nothing she can do to stop it.

"Heavy sigh," he says. "Must be serious."

She rises to her elbows, "I was thinking we probably shouldn't be seeing this much of each other."

He smiles, face on his arm. "I'll only buy three steaks from now on."

She is determined. "I mean it."

"And if I meet you in the hall, I'll pass without speaking."

What annoys her most is how easy it is for him to make her seem ridiculous. She slips back into the water. "Stop it."

In the center of the pool, she hangs with her toes barely touching bottom, interface of liquid and gas tickling her upper lip. As she watches he dives. With a mixture of disquiet and anticipation she waits for him to surface. This he does within arm's reach.

Mouths below the surface, words are out. Suddenly frightened of the man before her, she feels the need to back away, to swim for the side. She stays where she is, the field of his attraction holding her. In jail…he was in jail.

His eyes are impossible to read in the growing dark. What can he think? That she lured him back into the water? And isn't that what she's done? He moves closer. No way she can outdistance him now. Her speed won't help her this close; he'd have her before she were a stroke away. She pictures again his arms. No way she can fight him. She's known women who have been raped, seen how it changes their lives. She promises herself she'll fight. Somehow she will.

She hedges in the direction of the steps and as he pivots to follow waning light of dusk lets her read his eyes. Instantly she sees her error. Heart slowing, she giggles in the privacy of the water, bubbles clinging to the skin of her lip. Eyes like his don't lie. Nothing to fear in them. Hidden by the water she smiles, and when his eyes change she sees he knows.

How dare he laugh at her. She reaches out, shoves against a chest solid as the flank of a horse and his hands snatch hers, fingers entwining. He spreads his hands, reeling her in. He hadn't told her about Grant playing the ass. Neither had he mentioned the easy way he'd held him helpless. Why not? Len is always describing his karate meets, matches, whatever they are.

So close now she can see water beaded in his moustache, he releases her left hand and cups her cheek. Relieved not to have to fight a grope, she leans into it. Who is he? What is he, really?

A wall of ice solidifies under her ribs. She doesn't need to know. She has Len. End of story. Len, the decent. Len the boring. Len the reliable. Len, the physicist. There is no reason for her to care what kind of man Night is. He's a boarder, that's all. Her boarder who hauls garbage. Her boarder who can fix anything. Anything…

Desperate to escape, she pulls away, feeling a desolation as he lets her go. A pace away, she hovers, seeing in him an enemy, a subversive, a sapper tunneling under the carefully laid foundations of her life. She will not let him inside her. She will not let him confuse her. She will not.

In his eyes she sees he understands as well as if she had spoken. He backs away, hoists himself out of the pool, heads inside.

Standing alone in the quiet, in the dark, she knows she has won. She pulls to the end of the pool, shoves off, swims furiously for the far side. Expelling breath underwater, she yells as she does, eyes stinging from more than chlorine. Elation bitter as unripe persimmon smarting in her chest, she swims with fierce energy.

Lap after lap, one thought turns between her ribs, until at last, spent, she slumps, gasping at the side of the pool.

She has won.

• • •

Swing shift.

In the Squire it's dark, hazy with smoke. The air stinks of cigarettes and soured beer. As boob bars go, mid high end. In three years with INET Night has come to be a connoisseur of them. On his scale of class it comes in a 7. The toilets and the girls are clean, the owner, while a pig, doesn't pimp, and the bar serves a decent glass of OJ, concentrated but not canned. Something to milk and stay sharp.

Never been in one before he joined the task force. Three years later they no longer make him sweat. Neither do they excite him. But then, they never have. He's thought about why. All he can come up with is that it's all wrong—without the emotional connection as lascivious as a gynecological text. Boils down to one thing—boob bars are where deals are made. And where the deals are, they are.

"So what happened, man? I went over to the trailer and an old lady lives there now," Derek says. "You moved and you didn't tell me? What's going on with you? We strangers now or what?"

He wishes he'd never started the lies. He'll have to tell him something. "We're not strangers."

"Well, then where you living? What'd you do, move in with Sam?"

"I didn't move in with Sam." Trapped. Another lie coming. No easier, he's relieved to see. "I'm camping out at the house over on Fairmont. Easier that way to work on it."

"You're kidding, man, that place is like ground zero. Why not stay with me and Julie? The third bedroom is just sitting there waiting for you any time, man."

Derek's not making it any easier. "Sleep with my head on the Universal machine and my feet in the spa?"

"Hey, we can rustle you up a bed."

"That's all right, man, I need to get this thing done."

Lights up on stage. Music booms from speakers under the bar. Derek swivels on his stool. "You start hankering for a hot shower, come on by."

Night's least favorite dancer, Tanya, falls into her routine. He looks only long enough to note she's added maybe five pounds to her padding. Same slack-mouthed expression on her face. Meant to portray abandon, carnal ferocity maybe. All Night ever sees is piggishness.

Above them Tanya gyrates, handling herself, heels inches from Night's face. Impatient, he looks for patterns in the floating pulp of his juice. He shifts on his stool to look past her calves, and, relieved, elbows Derek, "There's our friend."

Compton has arrived. He scans the dark. Polyester western wear hangs off a lank frame. Compton might be a used car salesman. He might be an undertaker. What he is is just another tweaker on a dry spell. Night raises a hand, waves him over.

Night's never liked him. Typical crank addict. White trash, thinks he's a player. Pitiful in a way. Five kids by three different women. Dodging child support. IRS after him. Owns the clothes he wears, nothing else.

Compton slides onto the stool on the other side of Derek, eyes on the meat swinging overhead. "Hey, now that's just my kind of thing right there."

Night doesn't doubt it. He leans forward, "You're late. What do you have for us?"

Smirking, fairly ready to burst with self-importance, he leans forward to order a drink, milking the moment for all it's worth. Big shot. Big deal.

Tanya moves out of an overhead spot and Night notices Compton needs to floss. Night catches a hint of sour urine breath and turns away. Day or night, cranking or straight, it never changes. Mystery of medical pathology. Grateful for the seating arrangement, Night sips OJ, resigned to wait him out.

Compton raises his beer as if he's toasting the dancer, sips.

"So, what you got?" Derek says, tapping nails on the bar in time with the music.

"Bobtail of coke on its way down from the City of Roses."

Night leans close. "Bobtail?"

"Yeah, you know, one of them box vans."

Night is sure he has misunderstood. "A truckload of coke?"

"Damned straight."

Compton is strictly penny ante, his specialty tweakers selling out of the trunks of their cars. Night gives Derek a look.

"White dope, ton at least."

Night looks up from his juice to see if he's kidding. He is not.

Compton takes a business card out of his shirt pocket, lays it face down on the bar, keeps his hand on top of it. "I want fifteen points."

"Nine percent is it, man," Derek says.

Compton scowls, slowly pulls back the card. "I don't need this penny ante BS."

Derek traps the card under a finger, "We can ask, but that's all we can do. We don't make the rules. Now let's see what you got."

He thinks about it, lets Derek have the card. "Tomorrow morning ten a.m., corner of Seventh and Willamette. License on the card. White truck, Mrs. Somebody's Fish Sticks on the box." He drains his beer. "Don't screw it up, I got kids depend on me." He slides off the stool, casts a hungry look at the dancer and heads out.

Set over, the music dies to blessed quiet. "Pity them," Derek says, flipping the card. "This sound too good to be true or what?"

It has to Night from the first time he heard Compton bring it up. "A ton? That truck ten years ago with a false wall stopped on the eastern pipeline had what?"

"Hundred kilo."

"This would be ten times that."

"Hey, buddy, all this whoopdeedo about legalizing going on, we'd make the evening news."

Derek sounds excited. Night is not. "Oh boy."

Derek slides off his stool, "Man, you got to get a little more positive. This just may be our big break staring us in the face, here."

And it may be disaster. "I'll remember to think positively from now on. Thanks."

Derek slaps his shoulder, "That's better." He peers at the card, "Number looks right. I'll call it in and see what they come up with."

Night slumps. So, their lucky break has just arrived. He decides to head outside when the music comes back up, bass concussing the air. A petit blond moves along the runway to stop in front of him. He looks up, sees it's Sam, drops his face into his hands. Just what he needs, now.

Over him, Sam sways, bent at the waist, long hair cutting the air over his head. Through splayed fingers he watches her heels move in front of him. Such slender freckled ankles leading up toned calves to long Irish thighs.

The crowd howls, hoots. He reaches for his wallet, takes out a fifty, folds it three times. Good a time as any. Good for his image as a player. Head down, he crooks the fingers holding the bill, calling her close. Keeping his eyes down, he slips the folded bill under the ankle strap of her heel, skin like silk searing his hand. She moves on.

Derek slides back onto his stool, "Hey, big spender, you're missing the show."

"Yeah. What you come up with?"

Derek scowls. "You have turned into one cold fish, you know that?"

"The truck, what'd you get?"

Derek shrugs, gives up, goes back to watching Sam. "Clean. Title in the name of a holding company out of Alexandria V-A. What you think?"

Set over, Sam slips off stage. Night raises his eyes off his OJ, relieved. "I think we're at Seventh and Willamette tomorrow morning. You want to line up a cruiser or you want me to?"

"I will."

Sam comes out in worn jeans and a sweater, heads straight to Night. She leans in close, "Hey."

For the first time he looks at her, then to Derek. "Give us a minute." Taking her wrist, he draws her outside to his Lincoln. He opens the door, puts her in, slides in after. The car is warm and wonderfully quiet after the loud bar.

"You missed a good routine in there," she says in a voice dark as her hair is white. "It's a new one, I was kind of hoping you'd watch."

She sounds hurt, which burns him. He sighs, "You want to do it again sometime for me dressed a little more warmly, I'll be glad to watch. Meanwhile I've asked you not to do that."

"What, dance for you?" She slides close. "Make you nervous?"

Teeth clenched, he is determined not to repeat their last encounter. "Knock it off, Sam." He tilts her head back, thumb under the curve of a delicate jaw, works a penlight out of his jacket, shines it for an instant into each eye, releases her.

"Shit, you don't trust me?"

"I trust you."

"Sure you do. So what's the fifty for?"

"Thought you might need it. Registration for summer session is coming up next week."

She sighs, reaches for the door. "Not that again."

He reaches across her, slams a fist down on the button to lock it, "Okay, what's wrong?"

Arms folded across her breasts, face set, she sits erect. "Nothing."

"Yes there is, tell me."

"I'm on again at eleven, got to go."

"When you tell me."

Giving up, she turns on him, "I need some time off. I can't stand this! Bio's driving me up the wall, all that DNA, RNA stuff. They just look like a bunch of zippers to me. I can't do this, dammit. I'm not smart enough, get it? I'm a stripper, that's what I am."

He shakes his head. "That's what you do, not what you are." He leans near, an arm on the dash and one on the back of the seat. Now, right now, is when he needs to watch himself. Being near her is for him like being near a hard radiation source. He can feel the heat off her. "You cold? I can turn on the heater."

Exasperated, she lets out a long breath, "I'm not cold, Night. Will you stop mothering me? I'm tired is all."

He deserves the slap. "You know, I remember a girl I met a couple years ago. Coked out. Skin and bone. Tips going up her nose. Heading for the trade if she was lucky, a log aeration pond if not. Called in a few favors to get her into detox. Visited her every day. Took her apples. I'd set one on her tray and she wouldn't say a word. Just watch me. Eyes like a wild kitten. Two weeks it took her to decide she wanted to talk. Said she always wanted to be a nurse. Always. From the time she could remember."

Sam stares out the windshield, face set. "Things change."

"How long you got to go?"

Her eyes close. "Another year."

"Halfway there, and you're going to give up? You really that gutless?"

"I'm not gutless."

He likes her tough. "Show me. Stick it out. You need help with biology I know somebody can help you." He jots his number on a card. "Call me."

"I've got your number."

"New one, I moved."

"Moved? Out of the tin can?" She says it like she doesn't believe it. "Where?"

"Place out on Fairmont."

She whistles, slow and low, "You ripping off dealers, now?"

"Boarding. Jade's with me."

She smiles, nods, "Good for you."

Night watches her in the near dark, blond hair neon flashing on a night highway, promising comfort. Sweater doing little to hide the God-given assets that make her the most popular act at the Squire. Seven years older than Jade he reminds himself—seven.

She smiles. "I like the way you're looking at me, right now."

"Don't. What happened last time can't happen again."

"Why can't it?"

"Because it's best if it doesn't."

"Who says?"

"I say."

She moves close. "What if I say it isn't?"

He finds something to look at across the lot. "Do me a favor, wear a bra once in a while, will you? I hear support's good. You won't be nineteen forever."

"If you want me to." She watches the side of his face, clamping fingers in the hair at the nape of his neck until it hurts. "Why do you care if I make it? And why won't you give us another chance?"

He strains to turn his head to face her. "I'm giving you one."

"That's not what I meant. I know what I do to you. I know how much you want to look up at me in there. I feel it." She runs her tongue over his upper lip. Her breath is warm and smells of the cherry Lifesavers she lives on. "So, why cut me off, now?"

He keeps his hand on the back of the seat, her hair teasing the skin of his face. He will be damned if he knows. Stubbornness, maybe. A mule-headed need to do anything other than what would be easy. "Because a friend is what you need, and that is what I'm going to be from now on—a friend."

Her lips brush his as she speaks. "And what is it you need?"

Tough question. He knows what he wants, what he craves. And he knows how it makes him feel afterward. "I need a friend, too, Sam. Be one."

She slides away, but he can't interpret her face in the dark. "Oh, all right, you got one."

Derek shows up. "You two done out here?"

"We're done," she says, getting out. Leaning back in the window, she kisses him on the temple, lips cool, "See you, Night."

Night smooths the hair behind her ear, "Call me."

Sam backs away, card in hand, "I will."

Derek gets in, leans back at the door, watching him. "I don't believe it. You take Sam out to the car to talk to her? You really are one warped individual."

The feeling of nobility evaporates, leaving behind an empty ache.

It may be the right thing to do.

But that won't help him at two a.m.

Night starts the engine, "I know it."

THREE

Derek sees it first.

"There's the fish stick express, now."

The bobtail pulls to a stop at the light. On the side of the box is a smiling woman with a platter of fish sticks, lemon in the center torn and flapping. Night has had them—mostly flour and water. From the Fifth Street Market parking lot Night reads the plate through binoculars. "He's our boy."

"Eat them up, yum."

Night hits redial on his cellular and dispatch patches him through to the cruiser backing them up. Derek pulls them out onto Fifth. At the next light they see its left rear tail light is dark.

"There's our probable cause." Derek laughs, pounds the wheel like a conga, "Do we live right or what?"

Night's neck prickles. "I don't like it."

"What's not to like? This is as sweet as it gets. This time tomorrow we'll both be on the six o'clock news."

Night hopes he is wrong.

"Give me that." Derek takes the phone. "Let's do it."

Derek passes the truck, engine howling as behind them they see the cruiser's light bar flash to life. Now it all falls apart.

The truck locks up, tires smoking as it fishtails to a stop in the center lane. The tailing cruiser smacks into the back of the box. Fifty yards beyond, Derek stops them, rams the lever into reverse, desperate to close the distance before a car changes lanes, blocking them off. Through the back window they watch insanity unfold.

The driver swings down from the high cab, gun in hand. He saunters back to the cruiser, brings up the pistol as Derek slams the brake. The sound of double taps. Again. Again. Night pictures the two officers in the cruiser, dazed, deflated air bags in their laps, faces still numb from the concussions, taking rounds through the windshield, fish in a barrel, and his stomach contracts.

Derek and Night pile out, head back at a run and, as if on signal, the driver tosses away the gun, raises his hands to the cars passing as if on stage. Smiling, hands up, he reminds Night of a fighter after a winning bout. Moving up, front sight centered in his chest, Night is conscious of gawking witnesses behind him in cars blocked by the wreck, and is thankful for them, for the temptation they deny him.

Derek calls on the cellular for backup and an ambulance. Night comes up slowly on the suspect, finger tight on the Glock's double trigger, gun braced in both hands, mouth working from habit, voice booming up from his chest, ordering him to his knees. He watches his hands, keeps an eye on the cab of the truck.

Hands behind his head, the driver complies. Beyond him, in Night's line of fire, motorists rubberneck, feeling safe behind their windshield glass. Moving so the truck's behind the shooter, Night plants a foot in the small of his back and shoves. Down he goes and on his back Night drops hard with a knee, muzzle to the base of his skull. One hand he levers back, shoves the Glock in his jeans at his hip. He cuffs him, ratcheting them down viciously.

He yanks him to his feet by the cuffs, turns and slams him back to the box. Calm, dark eyes watch him serenely, unafraid. Night feels a cold nail trace its way up his spine. He's looking in the face of a man with no worries. He takes the pulse at his wrist and finds it hovering at sixty. He watches his face, incredulous. This is no panicked tweaker. This is a pro.

A siren howls, a second car pulls up and, ID held high, Night waits for them, unable to break the driver's gaze. The shooter smiles, unconcerned. To a uniform Night hands him off, goes back to check the cruiser. Traffic inches by. He leans in at the window, careful not to touch anything, as Derek, tears running down his face, administers CPR to a cop who has lost most of the back of his head. Night lays a finger against the jugular of the driver. Skin still warm, slick with blood. He is long gone. With thumb and forefinger he closes his eyes. Noticing the blood on his hand, Night looks for something to wipe it on, sees nothing.

Again he looks at the dead driver. Two in the forehead, one in the throat, one in the cheek. Looks like a .40. He's not sure. He glances back at the shooter, sees him watching through the window and wishes he'd shot him when he had the chance.

An EMT with Doublemint breath eases him out of the way. "Jesus!" she says. Seeing Night's hand, she clamps his wrist, "You hurt?"

"No."

"Sure?"

"Yeah." Night backs off, keeping an eye out for traffic, rubber-neckers the greatest danger, now. He circles to Derek, pulls him off the dead man he labors over so EMT's can reach him. In a tearful rage of frustration Derek lets himself be pulled away. "Son of a bitch!"

"Know him?"

"Name's Golden. We play poker. Owes me fifty bucks."

Night hears the back of the box rattle up on its rollers. "INET, you better get up here and see this!"

Still lightheaded from adrenalin, Night follows Derek to the box, squints up into the bright haze.

"Ever seen that much coke before?" the uniform asks.

Night reaches out, lays a hand on cool waxed paper, gives a push. Solid. He'd bet his life it goes all the way to the cab.

"Two, three tons, anyway," Derek says.

Night looks back at the cruiser, at the wall of coke, at the car where the shooter calmly waits, "I don't get this."

Derek, nose still running, sticks a knife in a packet, taps it into a vial, shakes it to mix the liquid, "What don't you get?"

"Why he shot them."

The uniform shrugs, "Didn't want to get caught with the coke, what else?"

"Uh, uh. This much money he would have made bail before we finished the paperwork."

Derek, hands bloody, raises the vial to show Night. It is pink and blue.

The officer peers closely, "Real?"

Derek pockets the kit. "Ain't fish sticks."

The rookie looks at Night, confused. "If he wasn't afraid of going to jail, then why?"

Blood pulls at the skin of his hand, shrinking as it dries. He works at it with his nails, nods to the suspect waiting in the cruiser. "Ask him."

Night leans back on the hood of the cruiser, unable to look away from the taut bundles towering over them. On each the stenciled silhouette of a bull's head in red spray paint, horns spread wide—the cartel logo. Marca registrada. On a hunch, Night takes his pocketknife and, with the short blade, unscrews the tail light cover, undamaged despite the collision. Inside he finds not a burnt out bulb, but an empty socket.

Numb, he slumps to sit on the buckled hood, still warm from the heat of the engine, the smell of leaking anti-freeze strong in the air.

Traffic crawls by and he thinks.

About a convenient tail light with no bulb.

About two tons of coca pura.

About Compton.

About a driver who throws in the towel as soon as he's made sure he'll be sent up for murder.

About two officers who won't go home.

About how it all looks like a set up.

About what it means if it is.

• • •

Classes over for the week, Ceridwen stops by George's office.

As usual, she finds his lizard skin boots propped up on the desk. Human Genetics in the air before him, he waves her in with a slim-fingered hand adorned with several turquoise rings and a Marlboro filter tip. "Howdy, stranger, where the hell you been hiding yourself?"

Tossing the journal down onto a messy desk, he drops his boots to the floor, clasps her to him. "Missed you, Babe. What'd you do, forget where my office was?" He clears clutter from a chair. "Have a seat, punkin. You haven't called me in a month."

Used to this line, she rolls her eyes. "I keep office hours the same way you do, George."

"Read this? They found the gene for basal cell carcinoma."

She nods. "Getting closer."

"What are we doing at this backwater teaching art majors? That should have been us." He tosses away the journal.

"I like teaching art majors."

He fans the air. "So, how's life been treating you?" His mouth under a bush of a moustache widens into a devilish grin. "More to the point, have you had any rip-roarin' sex lately?" He brays at his wit.

Accustomed to his teasing, she ignores him. She loves his drawl, his easy manner, his charm. He is the closest thing she has to a male friend, but that doesn't mean she can believe a word he says. Along with the southern drawl comes a facility for shaping the truth.

"That must mean no," he says, setting himself off again.

She sighs. "Ever think about anything else, George?"

"Is there anything else, darlin'?" He succumbs to a coughing fit.

"Been smoking grass again?"

"Me?" he says, offended. "Oh, you've cut me to the quick. I mean, how could you?" Act over, he smirks. "God, you are a goodie-two-shoes, aren't you. You're perfect for that nerd you service. What's his name, Clem? Clem Kadiddlehopper?" He laughs until he has trouble getting his breath.

She considers leaving, but keeps her seat, toe of her shoe tapping against the leg of his desk. "You can really be a jerk, you know that?"

His laugh dies. "I'm sorry, darlin'. I know you like him—what I can't figure out is why. Now, go ahead, tell me what's been going on. I want to hear all about it."

She takes a deep breath, annoyed, regretting the visit. "Why do I come to see you?"

He props his feet back up on the desk. "That's easy. You come because I'm the only man at this university who doesn't want to jump you, and you think I'm funny as hell. Am I right?"

She sighs, giving him a look. "You kill you, don't you, George?"

He points at her with his cigarette. "You do that just like my mother, you know that? God, I love it when you do that. That takes me right back. Do it again, sigh like that. She always sighed like that, at least when she wasn't passed out drunk."

She's heard this before. "George, I've got a problem."

"That's what I love about you, Cer, you've always got a problem." He raises a hand in her direction. "Here you are, cute as a button, free as a bumble bee in an alfalfa field, making, what, forty grand working eight months a year, surrounded by five thousand studs who would kick down a corral fence for a chance in the saddle, and you, poor thing, you're unhappy. If I were you, I'd be in heaven."

Why does she try to talk to him?

"But I'm doing all the talking. You've got a problem, you say, let's hear it."

She breathes deep, giving herself time. She doesn't trust him, but she's got no one else to talk to. She decides. "I've met someone."

"That's not a problem, honey. What that is is plain luck."

"No, it's not." She slashes the air with a hand. "I've got my life planned out. Len and I are doing fine."

He smirks at her over his cigarette, "Fine, huh?"

"Yes, fine. I know what's going to happen next. I know where I'm going. I like that—knowing what's coming, knowing what to expect."

The ash on the butt in his fingers he sculpts against the side of an overflowing ashtray. "And what's that?"

"Len is going to ask me to marry him. I don't need someone coming along and messing everything up, confusing everything."

"And when he does you'll pay off all your bills, get Alex her mouse therapy, and get a new Volvo, right?"

She glares, defiant. "That's right. And don't look at me like that. I'll do my best to make Len happy."

"Oh, God bless," he says, voice aspirated, hand over his heart. "You say that like a saint, but you know who does that, don't you, Sweetie, makes men happy in exchange for their money?"

His meaning dawning on her, she stands, grabs her purse.

"Whores, sweetness, whores do that."

"Dammit, George, I used to be able to talk to you."

He opens his arms easily, "You still can, darlin', but when you're wrong, you're wrong. I don't know who this guy is, but if he's got you squirmin' about this God-awful scheme of yours, I like him already."

Eyes tearing with frustration, she yanks open the door, "I give up. You be at Pickering's party tomorrow?"

Already back in his journal, he answers without glancing up. "Wouldn't miss it,

Sugar."

"See you there."

"See you, Darlin'."

The message waiting on her machine at her office makes her want to run and skip and scream all at the same time. Afraid to be seen doing any of them, she settles for a brisk walk to her car.

• • •

Ceridwen pulls into her drive feeling as if she could do a hundred laps without raising a sweat.

She opens the front door quietly, her secret making her giddy. In the kitchen she hears Alex and Night. Shoes in hand, she pads to the door. At the table facing away is Alex, a small book in her hands. Not *Cat in The Hat*. Not *Green Eggs and Ham*. Not any of the books they read together. Night is next to her, Jade at the counter doing homework. Jade looks up, but with a finger to her lips Ceridwen silences her.

"He sh... shut the d... door... in N... Nutkin's face." Alex laughs, pointing at the picture. "Look at that little door. Do squirrels really have doors like that? They don't, do they?"

"They might," Night says.

"Who builds them?"

"I don't know. Squirrel carpenters. Read it. I want to hear what happens."

Miraculously, she returns to her book. "P... I don't know this one."

"That's okay, sound it out. What's after P?"

"Pr... Pre... Present..." She peers up at him. "Present?"

"There's more. Keep going."

"Presently... Presently! It's presently! I got it!"

"Presently what?"

"Presently, a lit... little th... thr... threed?"

He frowns. "Threed? What's a threed?"

Alex giggles. "I don't know."

"I don't know either." He points to her collar. "What's that stuff holding your shirt together?"

She looks down. "Thread? You mean that's thread?"

"That's thread."

She points to the picture. "I don't see a thread."

"Well, keep reading and see what happens."

Alex laughs again, reveling in the attention.

"Okay. Presently a little thread of bl... blue sm... smo... smook." She looks up at him. "What's smook?"

"Alex, I keep telling you, these are words, real words. You know them. You've heard this word, and it's not smook. What is it?"

She turns back to the page. "Oh! Oh, now I get it, smoke. It's smoke, isn't it?"

He slaps his forehead dramatically with the heel of his hand. "Imagine that! Read it again."

She laughs. "You're silly. Okay, here goes. 'Presently, a little thread of blue smoke...' Hey, a little smoke was coming out, wasn't it?"

"Yes, it was. Go on."

"Presently, a little threed..."

He growls in her ear and she giggles. "A little thread of blue smoke from a woo... wood..." She looks up, triumphant. "Ha! See, I knew it must be wood because it was smoking. Pretty good, huh?"

"Yeah, that was fine, but will you get on with the story?"

"Oh, sure. Presently a little thread of blue smoke from a wood fire c... came up from the t... too... toop..."

He shakes his head in despair.

"Oh, top of the tr... tree, and Nutkin p... pee... peepee..." She covers her mouth. "He pee-peed."

Ceridwen bites her fist as her eyes fill. Alex has never read like this for her—never.

"No, he didn't. Look at him, what's he doing? He's not going pee pee is he? No, he's looking in the door."

"Oh, peeped, he peeped th... thr... throw... No. It's through. He peeped through the k... key... key-h..." She looks up for help.

"Where they put the key."

"Oh, he peeped through the key-hole and s... san... sang... he sang!" She looks up, frowning in puzzlement. "Why did he sing?"

"I don't know, we'll have to see. Now read the whole sentence again with no mistakes, and we'll have dinner."

"What's for dinner?"

"Macaroni and cheese."

"Who made it?"

"The maid made it."

She frowns, head canted in disbelief. "We don't have a maid."

"That's right, so who do you think made it, huh? Me." He taps the book with a finger. "Now, let's go."

"I'm tired." She whines, supporting her chin on a hand. "This is very hard for me. I have a learning disorder, you know."

"Oh, cut it out, you're breaking my heart."

"You wouldn't let me starve, would you? I'm a sick little girl." She cocks her head, scenting the air. "I smell it burning." She watches him slyly.

"Nice try, it's done. Going to read it or not?"

"I'm tired."

"Fine. Go take a nap. No sentence, no dinner. No dinner, no you know what."

She looks up, face stricken. "No gymnaxtics?"

He says nothing.

Defeated, she lifts the book. "Okay."

Ceridwen smiles, biting her lip to keep from laughing. Alex had used all her feminine guile and failed.

"'Presently a little thread of blue smoke from a wood fire came up from the top of the tree, and Nutkin peeped through the key-hole and sang.'" She jumps to her feet. "I did it! I did it! I read a whole page!"

She turns, sees Ceridwen standing behind her and throws herself into her arms. "Mommy, did you hear me? I read it!"

Petting her hair, Ceridwen does her best to keep her voice steady as, eyes on Night, she answers. "I heard you, Baby, I heard."

After dinner, they swim. By nine, light fades to dusk and the girls run in. She joins him on the second step, sitting so their arms brush under water. "Thanks for making dinner."

"Lasagna, macaroni and cheese, burgers—you've run the gamut of my culinary talent."

She looks at him, looks away, finds his hand underwater. In all the time she has known Len, he has never once spent any time with Alex. "I've never heard her read like that before. It must have been the attention from you. She's not used to a man's attention. Jeff was always too busy with his students." Seeing absurdity, she laughs. "Still is... And Len... Well, he's got a lot on his mind." Eyes shut, she takes a long breath. Why can't she stop babbling? "Anyway, thank you for that."

"No big deal." He squeezes her hand underwater. Above, in warm evening air, it's as if nothing has changed, as if her hand were not in his, as if every movement of his fingers did not thrill her. All at once she sees she is being stupid. Letting his hand go, she looks at him, eyes hard. "Tell me something?"

"Sure."

"Why are you doing this?"

"What am I doing?"

"Being good to us."

"Does there have to be a reason?"

She looks up at him, wondering how much of a fool he thinks she is. "Of course there does. You want something."

He laughs as if he wants nothing at all. "Why do you say that?"

"Everyone wants something. What do you want?"

"I think you know."

She pulls away. "I've got my life planned out. I'm just not the live-for-the-moment type. Some people are. I'm not. I'm sorry."

He stands, steps up onto stone and, dripping, throws his towel over his shoulder. "So you've said."

He heads for the kitchen door and she watches him go. "Night."

"Yeah."

"Tomorrow, there's a party. I was going with Len. He left a message saying he can't make it. Will you come with me?"

Back to her, he thinks it over. One breath, two. He turns, shaking his head as if in amazement, eyes hard on her. "I don't understand you. Am I supposed to make some kind of sense of this? Because if I am, I'm not doing a very good job."

Through his eyes she must appear mad. She sees that. It changes nothing—she still wants him there with her. "Will you come?"

"I'm not sure that would be such a good idea."

The thrill she had felt when she had listened to Len's message turns to vinegar. She hadn't considered the possibility of him refusing. "I'm asking you to come."

"Maybe it would be easier on both of us if you asked someone else."

Her jaw drops. It's not possible. She knows how he feels, she can feel it. He can't refuse. "You're telling me you won't?"

He heads inside. "I'm saying if I were smart, I wouldn't."

She swallows, breathing again, calls to his retreating back. "Good, we need to leave by nine."

• • •

At the fixer, Night forks the garden.

Tomatoes are doing fine. Already some fruit set. Still no replacement from Grant. Won't hold his breath on that one. The spading fork sinks to the shank with no effort. Here behind the rhodies, grass clippings and leaves were dumped for years and left to rot. Worms did the rest. The moment he stumbled on it he knew he had struck gold. The soil is soft, rich, veined with foot-long night crawlers which recede as exposed by his fork. Once he gets around to trimming a couple limbs off the spreading yew overhead to let sun in, it will be perfect.

He works the fork, turning things over in his mind as he turns humus. A dark smell, fecund and musty, wraps him up, buoys him. The smell of living earth. No matter what a mess his life becomes, this never changes.

He hears the girls come in the gate to find their spot under a rhody. This is their hideout. On the duff they set up as unseen, he watches. He could call out, but instead takes a break, guilt and curiosity wrestling under his ribs. He's found traces of their meetings, but never seen them at play. His guess is if they knew he were here, it would spoil it—and that he doesn't want.

"I'm the troll," Alex says.

"I'm Barbie," Jade says.

"My mom's the princess, and your dad's the goat."

"No, Dad's the lion."

Hearing her stick up for him, Night laughs silently into the back of his hand. Good old Booboo.

Alex sighs, put out. "Okay, then, the lion. You be Mom and I'll be your dad."

"Okay. Alex, time to eat," Jade says in a voice meant to be Ceridwen's.

Alex whines. "I'm not hungry."

Night presses the fork to earth and squats, recognizing the conversation from earlier this week.

"Alex," Alex says in her best baritone, "Your mother asked you to come in to dinner. I would appreciate it if you would do as she asks. Ha, ha, ha, I'll make her be a little slave just like Jade."

"I'm not a slave."

"Don't interrupt!" Back in character, she goes on in a small, pitiful whine. "Can't I just watch TV for a little while, not even PBS?" Then, in a voice low as she can manage, "Sure, go ahead, we'll miss you Sunday."

Now in her own sweet voice, "Mom! He can't tell me what to do, can he?"

"Alex, stop messing around."

"Oh, go ahead, then."

Jade takes Ceridwen's part. "He's not telling you what to do, Alex, he's just asking you to do what I told you, that's all. If you don't come now, you won't eat anything else tonight."

"Mom!" She puts her heart into the word. "It's not fair. He's not my father." Now she again takes his part. "I never said I was."

Night has to smile, teeth grating against tendons in the back of his hand. How she can pack so much venom into so few words is beyond him.

"You want to go to gymnaxtics with Jade, you're going to have to mind your mother. If you can't do that, you'll stay home. That's the deal." Again his evil laugh.

"Mom, he can't tell me I can't go, can he?" Her voice becomes Ceridwen's. "No, of course not, Baby. Take that, Mr. Hotshot!"

"Alex! Play right."

Night loses a breath through his nose. If adults could play like this, there would be fewer murders he is sure.

"You're no fun," Alex says.

Jade goes on, voice calm. "I'm afraid he can. Gymnastics was a deal between the two of you. I've got nothing to do with it. If you want to go, you'll have to do as you agreed. If it were up to me, you wouldn't be going at all."

"Mom! It's our house!"

"It doesn't matter whose house it is," Jade says. "Now are you going to come eat with us or are you going to go to your room and stay there for the rest of the evening?"

Hundred dollar sigh from Alex. "Oh, all right, if you're all going to gang up on me. But it's still not fair."

"Okay," Jade says, "let's pretend we're older."

"How much older?"

"You'll be fifteen, I'll be nineteen.

"Fifteen, wow!"

"We'll be in my bedroom and we'll be getting ready to go to the prom."

Night smiles behind his arm. This ought to be good.

"Oh, Alex, you look just like an angel in that dress."

"Sure I do. You look pretty all right yourself, Jade, baby."

"Who's your date tonight?"

"Oh, some guy with a nice car, I forget his name. How about you?"

"My date's name is Simon."

Alex says, "Knock, knock."

"Come in."

"Well, well, girls," Alex says, taking Night's part, "I see you're getting ready for the prom. You both look truly scrumptialicious."

"Thanks, Dad," Jade says. "It's nice of you to say that."

"And I just want each of you to know that I expect you to be back by seven o'clock or you'll be grounded until you're thirty."

"No, Dad," Jade says, "you must mean one, don't you? The dance doesn't start until nine."

"Oh, all right, then, one, but one second late and I'll be down there in my garbage truck to pick you up."

Jade sighs in exasperation. "Oh, my," she says in Ceridwen's voice, "just look at my two daughters, don't they look just like young ladies? Here are kisses for you both." Sound effects. "And one for you, Night."

Alex gags.

"It does make me proud to see them looking so nice, and both of them straight A students too. Isn't it swell, Night?"

"It's totally swell, Cer my little sugar dumpling," Alex says. "Sure makes me feel sorry for that old poop, Len. What do you hear from old Len these days, anywho?"

"He moved away to study atoms or something in the arctic. See 'em better up there in the cold. He writes once in awhile about the penguins, says he gets along pretty well with them."

They laugh.

"Ding dong!" Alex says.

"Oh, our dates are here and I still haven't done my hair!"

"I'll get it," says Alex as Night, "You two just finish getting gorgeous. I'll keep the boys busy." Sound effects of door opening. "Come in, men. I see you're two pretty handsome guys. I knew you would be. Sit down, I think we better have a talk man to man."

"Night," Jade whispers, "You'd better go easy on them or you'll scare them away."

"I know what I'm doing. Fathers know best about what to do at a time like this, you know. So, you're taking my two daughters out, huh?"

"Yes sir," Jade says.

"Well, I want to tell you that if you hurt one hair on their precious little heads, I'll cream you, I'll pound you into the sidewalk, I'll—"

"Night!"

"When I get done with you, you'll look like you've been through a food processor!"

"Alex, stop goofing around."

"Yes," Alex goes on, sedately, "as I was saying, you seem like two very nice boys and it just goes to show that our two beautiful, charming, straight A genius daughters would go out with someone like you. I want you two to know that their mother and I love them to pieces and if anything happens to them I'll come after you with a board with rusty nails in it."

"Now, Night," Jade smooths things over as Ceridwen, "you know you don't mean that."

"What I meant to say is that I'll be waiting for you at one o'clock…"

"Okay we're ready. Bye Mom, bye Dad."

"…with my gun."

"Alex!"

"Okay!"

"Bye! Have fun, Dears," Jade calls.

Night hears the door slam and a car roar away.

Jade sighs, "Our two girls, going to the prom. Why it seems only yesterday that they were just little girls playing with dolls in the backyard."

"Yes it does," Alex says in Night's voice. "Of course, I'll be worried sick until they return to our loving home, safe and sound. They're such precious little angels! Especially Alex. Why, to think I used to believe your lovely and talented daughter was just a rotten, spoiled brat. What could I have been thinking? What a complete jerk I was. Now that I know better, I have come to love and adore her just as I do my own daughter."

"Why that's so very peachy keen of you to say that, Darling Dearest," Jade says.

"Shall we just wait here by the fire and perhaps play a little Old Maid as we wait up for our little treasures, my love?"

Jade sighs. "You have read my mind, Puppy Feet."

For a moment there is nothing. Night wants to go back to spading, but decides to see it through.

"Alex?"

"Yeah?"

"Are you going to die?"

Night's stomach drops. He can't believe Jade asked.

It's a long moment before Alex answers, and when she does, her voice has changed. "Yeah."

Hair prickles on his scalp. How can she say it that way, as if it's already over, as if there's nothing to be done?

"Are you afraid?"

Again, hesitation. Through the base of spreading rhododendrons, Night sees her, head bowed, combing the hair of a kewpie with her hand, "A little."

"I've thought about dying," Jade says, "about what it must be like."

Night listens with interest. Never has Jade spoken of it.

"I think it must be like going to sleep."

"Uh, uh," Alex says, voice dark. "I know kids who died at Doernbecher."

"You do?"

She nods. "It hurts—the pills don't help much."

"Do you hurt a lot?"

"Sometimes I do."

"Where?"

"My stomach, my legs, too."

"But they can help you, can't they?"

"No."

"But your mom told Dad—"

"That's just some stuff they say. It doesn't really work."

"But…you're in remission, that means you're better."

"No, it doesn't. It just means it's resting. When it's ready it'll be back. That's what the kids told me, the ones who died." Alex rises, brushes off. "I'm thirsty, let's go home."

As Night hunkers, frozen by what he's heard, they gather their things and go.

And he's been telling her how to live her life.

Even more absurd, this ancient child has played along, toying with him, letting him think he knows anything worth knowing.

Humbled numb by an eight-year-old, he returns to his spading.

• • •

Jade watches as Night fixes her dinner.

He reaches into the oven for her chicken pie, burns himself on the rack. "Shit—sorry, Baby." He sucks on his thumb.

"Dad—relax. Am I watching Alex while you're at the party?"

"If you can handle it."

"Sure, will you be late?"

Will he be late? How should he know. He has never known a woman more mercurial. "Don't know yet." He tips the steaming pie out of its tin onto a plate, adds a dollop of cottage cheese.

"Goy food," Jade says.

"What?"

"Goy food, that's what Ray calls it."

"Well, you tell him it's the secret of our success." He gets a glass, pours her milk, drops into a chair across from her. "Long time since I've been to a party."

"You'll do fine."

He watches her eat, envying her night at home.

"Want some?"

"Just one bite."

Concern crosses Jade's face. "What are you wearing?"

"Hadn't thought about it."

"You're going to be meeting her friends from the university. You can't show up in that stuff you usually wear."

He looks down at himself. "Jeans. Tee shirt. Sneakers. Classic American slob wear. What's wrong with what I wear?"

She gives him one of her God-but-you're-dumb looks that places him somewhere below the mollusks for raw reasoning ability. It's been a while since he's gotten one. She's getting better at it. "What's right about it?"

"It's...comfortable."

The same look again only she ups the voltage. "It looks it." She trots up to his room, Night following. On the bed she lays a print buttondown and clean jeans. "There, now at least they won't be able to tell what kind of fast food you ate on your last bust." She eyes him sternly. "Look, Dad, these people may be total geeks, but they're her friends. What they think of you matters to her. Try to get along, okay?"

He smiles at the role reversal. "Think I should?"

"I think you should."

He wraps her in a head lock, draws her to him, pressing her face to his chest. She speaks, lips against his sternum, "I wish you didn't have to say you were a garbage collector."

The breath drops out of him like a stone down a well and he lets her go. "I do too, kid."

"Dad..."

This is going to be a tough one. He can feel it.

"Those guys, her students, the ones who are always coming to the door..."

He's not surprised she asks. She is no fool. "Yeah."

"They're not here for books, are they."

He drops onto the bed, leans back on an elbow. "No, Booboo, they're not."

"Are they here for what I think they are?"

Twelve years old and she knows. Of course she does. It's everywhere. "What's that?"

"Dope?"

Both relieved and saddened, he nods.

Deep in thought, she watches him as if he's transparent as a cave fish. He's been as blind, thinking he could keep this from her. What now? Tell all?

"How did you find this place?"

Never any beating about the bush with Jade. Straight to the aorta. "What a shyster you'll make."

"Was it to bust her?"

And he thought Derek was sharp. He waits, watching her mind work behind shrewd eyes. No reason to say anything. She's doing fine without his help.

"It was, wasn't it?" She frowns. "But you didn't."

Getting warm. He feels like a rat at one end of a tunnel. At the other, the weasel works its nose.

"Because you liked her..." Understanding widens her eyes. "Derek doesn't know, does he."

Her questions aren't. He smiles, lips tight, teeth clenched. Almost there.

"You're taking a big chance, aren't you?"

So much for his big secret. "It isn't that I don't trust you, you know that."

"I know." She sits, eyes troubled. "You like her that much? To take a risk like this?"

What can he do? He can't lie, not to her. "Some jerk, huh?"

Her eyes brim. "No." Something hits her. "No wonder you're nervous about tonight."

"Nervous?" He gathers clothes, heads for the shower, running his knuckles over her scalp as he passes. "Who, me?"

She watches him, unimpressed, "Nice try, Dad."

At the door he looks back at all he has in the world.

"Love you, Booboo."

• • •

Ceridwen drives the Volvo.

Night sits back, arm out the window, watching Seventh Avenue pass by as daylight slips into night. The way she jackrabbits light to light tells him she's as nervous as he is. "You know, nobody this century has hit every light red all the way down Seventh. You planning to be the first?"

She laughs, eases off the accelerator. "Pickering's parties are talk and more talk. Be prepared to be bored."

He dries his palms against the legs of his jeans, wondering which of them she is trying to reassure. "I may not have much to say."

"You don't have to. With this group, the hard part's getting a word in."

She takes them up the hill behind LCC—Rita's Neighborhood.

"My ex lives not too far from here."

Ceridwen looks at him, surprised. Of course she is. Garbage collectors don't live in neighborhoods like this one. Neither do cops.

"Amazing, isn't it?" she asks.

"What?"

"I was just thinking how this city's changing so fast. Those two cops shot over near the Hult—unbelievable."

He sees again a bullet-pocked windshield, the officers inside, the driver as he tosses away the pistol. "Yeah, unbelievable."

"They said it was a drug bust, a big one. It seems like there's nowhere you can go to get away from it."

He doesn't follow. "What, exactly?"

"The killing, the drugs, all of it."

If he couldn't still feel the blood on his hand he might have laughed. The green dope dealer decries the world going to pot because of drugs. For an instant he hates her.

"Here we are."

A dozen telephone poles bristle from the flower bed at odd angles, ends sharpened and painted to look like colored pencils. "Your friend an artist?"

"Her husband is. She's head of Life Sciences."

They head up the walk to the door as he puts pieces together. "She's your boss."

She nods, flashing a wavering smile. "That's right."

Then she is nervous, too. Good. He counts twenty cars along the street. "Popular place."

She rings the bell, "Pickering's parties are always a success—her open bar makes sure of that."

He can hear voices through the door. He slips three fingers inside the collar of his shirt to adjust a vest that isn't there. Waiting, he feels heat build up in his face. SWAT entries are a cinch compared to this. "I can't do this."

"What do you mean, you can't? It's just a party."

He's growing desperate, familiar panic rising. "I can't, that's all."

Ceridwen looks him over, realizes it's the first time she's seen him nervous. "Can't what?"

"Mingle. I always feel like I forgot my pants."

She takes his hand, hiding a smile. Nice to know something makes him nervous. "I'll be here."

Pickering greets them at the door and her eyes light. "So, you're Night. Come in."

Pickering leads the way through a crowded living room, draws Ceridwen away. "The bar's that way, we'll just be a minute."

Ceridwen looks back, doing her best to reassure him as Pickering leads her to the kitchen where Jo bleeds a glass of chablis from a box.

Pickering sets out more ice. "You never said he was that attractive."

Jo leans over the counter to peek. "That's him? the tenant you didn't notice the looks of?"

Though she scowls, Ceridwen is pleased by her reaction. "That's him."

Jo takes another long look. "Does Len know you're here with him?"

An icy hand clamps Ceridwen's heart and she fights to cast it off. How would he react if he did? She's not sure. "I said I'd probably not be coming."

Pickering fills a bucket with ice, sending cubes skittering across the floor. "And you think he won't find out, with this bunch?"

Ceridwen takes a long sip of wine. "I'm not worried about it."

Both women consider her with interest. Jo takes another peek out the door, "Oh, oh, look who George has got his claws into."

With regret, Night watches her go. He orders an orange juice at the bar and takes a look around. He would rather be anywhere else. Someone takes his elbow. He turns to see a man with a large moustache and eyes aglitter with alcohol, mischief or both.

"I'll bet you're the one Cer was talking about." He offers a soft hand. "I'm George."

"Night."

The eyes sparkle. "Night?"

He is used to people reacting to his name. "As in day."

"I like it." George looks him over. "You look as if you are going to be sick, Night."

The remark Night might resent from someone else. From George he doesn't, he's not sure why. The laughter in his eyes, maybe. "Parties aren't my thing."

George regards him with amused eyes. "Then why come?"

"She asked me."

"Smitten, are you?"

Night's not so sure he likes the smile. "You a friend of hers?"

"We talk."

Now Night is curious. "You say she mentioned me?"

"Not by name." George lights his next cigarette with the butt of his last. "She said she'd met a man that was upsetting her plans." He sends a cloud of smoke pluming toward the ceiling, points at Night with a turquoise-ringed finger. "That would be you."

Night turns to see her at the kitchen counter flanked by Pickering and a younger woman. She seems vaguely worried and he wonders why. "I wish I thought that were true."

George motions extravagantly, "I know how stubborn she is. She thinks her only way out of the mess she's in is to marry that geek." He lays an arm around Night's shoulder. "Maybe we can change her mind."

Night permits the embrace though he's not sure why. Something about the guy he likes. George is gay, he senses that. What it means is they are not competitors. "Why would you want to do that?"

George uses his beer bottle for an ashtray. "I like her, I'd like to see her happy."

"Why not with Len?"

His eyes smile playfully. "You haven't met her beau, then. Stick around, things may get interesting."

Night opens his mouth to ask why, but before he can Ceridwen takes his arm. "What stories are you telling now, George?"

"Me? Just passing the time of day." He waves across the room at a young man just arriving. "Talk to you later." With a wink at Night, he drifts away.

She frowns. "What was that about?"

"I'm not sure."

Her eyes narrow playfully. "I sense a conspiracy."

He turns, startled to hear in her voice what he feels himself. He would bet his life George is up to something.

"C'mon, I'll take you around."

She leads him to two men squared off opposite a woman, discussing heatedly. The people he spends his days and nights with care about drugs, about money, about sex—not too much else. He is curious to know what it is these people care enough about to argue over.

The man with the beard chops the air. "I can't believe you're suggesting including Kipling. *White Man's Burden?* You can't be serious."

A tall man in a jean jacket chips in. "We've got a responsibility to be sensitive to the feelings of students of color, and that means not including racists like Kipling. And London—no way should he be on the syllabus. *Valley of the Moon* drips with venom. White supremacist garbage is all it is. Try to find it in a library. No one but Nazi bookclubs even sell it anymore."

The target of their barrage, a slight woman with glasses seems eager to placate. "It was just a suggestion. I just..."

"Ah, Cer," says the man in jeans, "tell us, what do you think?"

She raises her hands in surrender, "I'm staying out of this one. I want you to meet a friend of mine. Night Hume, this is Jerry Pitcairn, Lydia Cray, and Kirk Mohr of the English department.

The men nod, hands conveniently occupied with drinks. Lydia offers her hand and he takes it.

"So, Night," says Mohr, "what do you think? London, Kipling, and their ilk, best allowed to molder quietly away as a part of an unenlightened Eurocentric past?"

Night's stomach ignites. Not a question. Meant to establish their superiority and garner quick ascension. Not today, pointy heads. "In whose favor?"

The two men exchange looks.

Kirk says, "Better writers."

Night doesn't like them. "That doesn't tell me much."

Beard laughs, speaks as if he's talking to somebody whose IQ barely breaks two digits. "Oates, Isherwood, Allende, Gordimer, Quindlen, Morrison, Angelou, the possibilities are endless, really."

The other nods agreement.

"You're sure you want my opinion?"

Again, the beard laughs, "Assuming you have one. What is it you do, by the way?"

Night smiles, looks them in the eye, "I collect garbage."

The three stare. Mohr's mouth falls open. "Garbage?"

"Yeah, you know, the stuff we want to get rid of, stuff that's no good for anything, stuff that hurts people. I clean it up. Somebody's got to, right Jerry, right Kirk?"

"Yeah, sure."

"Right."

Night's conscious of Cer nearby, knows she must be suffering and doesn't care. She invited him. People he knows, you talk to a guy like this you're apt to get a Buck knife thumbed open in your face. If she expects him to take their condescension with a smile she is mistaken.

Jerry turns away, "Well, then, don't worry about it." The kiss off.

"I do have an opinion... if you want to hear it."

The two shrug in a way that strikes Night as comical. They don't know what to think about this slob they can neither intimidate nor shame into silence.

"Sure."

Night speaks to Lydia. "You're right."

The two men laugh in amazement. "Oh, then you've read *Valley of the Moon*, and found no racism?"

This is really supposed to shut him down. "You thought it was racist?"

"Of course it is."

Night frowns, scratches his head, "I didn't get that." He meets the woman's eye, winking at her quickly. "True, the hero is a salmon fisherman saddened to see the influx of immigrants into California, but he praises their use of the land, too. To show you what an insensitive bastard I am, I thought it was a damned good yarn."

Lydia, face brightening, speaks up at last. "And Kipling?"

"Kipling packed more truth into a single poem than most authors today can squeeze into a five hundred page novel. And he made it rhyme."

This is too much for Jerry. "You are suggesting we read the author of *White Man's Burden* in a 21st Century lit class? Don't you think that would be just a bit insensitive?"

Night thinks it over. "You can't expect an author writing a century ago not to offend someone in a world where everyone walks around bristling with raw nerve endings. Kipling wrote from a white man's point of view, a soldier's point of view—neither very popular just now."

Pitcairn guffaws. "Neither very applicable, either, just now."

Night ignores him. "Kipling wrote plain words in a time when convolution was the rage, and has been snubbed by English and American literati ever since."

Ceridwen drags him by the arm before they can respond. "Bye, now, got to be going." And into his ear, "We are sitting down."

He turns to call back as she leads him away. "And the protagonist in *Valley of the Moon* is a boxer, not a fisherman. You never know... you might even want to read it sometime."

As they go she flashes him a bewildered glance. Under her breath, she whispers, "You always carry that soapbox around with you?"

"They asked."

"Maybe, but try to stay off it the rest of the night, will you? They're used to giving the lectures."

The rest of her introductions are short. She drags him on before he can get in trouble. In five minutes he has met most of the guests—and forgets them as quickly. She finds them a seat on a sofa close by Pickering, Jo, George, and several others and they wedge themselves in.

He smiles, whispers in her ear, hair tickling his lip, "I think you're enjoying this about as much as I am." Her eyes tell him he's right. "How about if I catch a bus home?"

In answer she locks up his hand in hers, whispers in his ear, "You're staying right here."

He presses her hand to his thigh and stays where he is. Knowing how stupid he is being does nothing to lessen the way it makes him feel.

"Such waste," Jo says. "Two men dead and for what?"

From a silver case, Pickering selects a joint. "We've been discussing whether or not the Drug War is working."

Night is sorry to see Jerry slump on the couch opposite. "Isn't it obvious? It's not."

Pickering lights the joint carefully. "Last year a half million people were arrested for marijuana. Nine of ten of them for possession. Ten million in the last twenty years. That's four percent of the nation—four percent. Forty percent of the beds in prisons are filled with drug offenders.

Jo takes the doobie from Pickering. "What do you think, Night?"

Ceridwen looks at him as if the gods conspire against her. Knowing how she feels, he can only smile.

Ceridwen sits forward, "Jo, I don't think…"

"Oh, come on," George says, "he must have an opinion."

Jo dashes ash into a tray on the table before her, "You're a sanitation worker, Cer tells us."

"I'm a garbage collector."

Unsuccessfully hiding a smile, George taps his cigarette into the mouth of a beer bottle on his lap. "I'd be interested to know what he thinks. Most of my colleagues here…" He picks a bit of leaf off the tip of his tongue with long-nailed fingers, "are convinced dope ought to be legal. Every one of them plans to vote for 82."

Pickering sips wine, annoyed. "Let's move on to something else."

"No, no, no," George says, long fingers fluttering. "I want to hear what he thinks."

Night finds himself the object of the group's attention. He isn't happy about it. "I clean up other people's messes, what do you want from me?"

"Your opinion," George says. "I can look at a sanitary landfill and tell you it's a boil on the ass of the earth. That's my opinion. It doesn't mean I know anything about recycling or compaction or anything else."

Night looks around, feeling a tightness in his chest. He should never have come.

"Come on." Jo cants her head, cropped hair bobbing at the corners of a tight mouth, "Tell us what you think."

Cornered, he gives in. "If I were a cop I'd say it isn't my job to second guess the law, it's my job to enforce it."

"But you're not a cop," Pickering says.

It's obvious he has no allies here. Outnumbered, he relies on the same arguments he has for twenty years. "Marijuana is a gateway drug. It's what everybody starts with. Maybe it isn't deadly itself. It's what comes next."

"I've heard that, too." Cer releases his hand to take the roach from Jo, "But I've read the studies. There is no pharmacological basis for the gateway effect. It's hype, it's propaganda, that's all. Less than one marijuana smoker in a hundred uses cocaine." Eyes defiantly on his, she takes a short hit before passing it on.

He's not beaten yet. "Okay, you're saying that even though we've been doing what we can to fight it, it's still here. Well, what if we had done nothing? It might be ten times as prevalent as it is now."

"Actually, no," Pickering says. "Before 1980 several states had decriminalized anything less than an ounce—Oregon was one. Use was no higher in any of them."

Mohr smirks. "Shoots hell out of the argument that if it were legal everybody would do it, doesn't it?"

Another of Night's pet arguments evaporates. If it weren't for the fact that he'd look and feel as if he were running out on a fight, he'd walk. He eyes the front door feeling an intense desire to be gone, and in strides a man in white oxford and black slacks. He feels Cer stiffen as she lets go his hand. George pats his knee, "You walked right into that one, old buddy."

Cer hands Night the joint with trembling hands and he sees worry in her face. He passes it to George, who takes it in the same hand as his Marlboro, between his ring and middle finger. Night watches the recent arrival move closer, his eyes on Cer's and knows who he must be. Night feels the urge to laugh. So typical, this. He should never have come. Why the hell did he? Still, he isn't willing to concede just yet. "I've got a daughter. You're telling me you'd want your kids smoking pot?"

"Rather than drinking or smoking cigarettes, I would," Pickering says.

"You've never seen the nobody home smile? never felt like you're talking to yourself when you're talking to a head? I have, and uh, uh. Not for me, not for my kid."

Pickering leans forward, intent. "That's it, that's the big lie. No studies have ever proven a loss in long term memory, or a reduction in reasoning ability in habitual smokers."

Night smiles, following Cer's gaze across the room to where her geek Romeo lurks. He doesn't need studies. He's conducted his own two-decade long study on the street. He can spot a heavy user the same way he can spot an alcoholic, and he's never needed a million dollar grant to do it. "If it's a choice between studies and what I see, I'll go with my eyes."

Jo says, "A half million people a year die from cigarettes. Alcohol kills maybe a third as many if you throw in drunk driving accidents. Yet they're both legal. Nobody has ever died from marijuana—not one person in 60 years—and it's the one that's illegal—why? Tell me."

Night has heard this one before. It's never impressed him. He can feel Ceridwen's eyes on Len and doesn't care. Looking up, he sees him hanging across the room, drink in hand, looking as if in desperate need of sleep, a change of clothes, something. "I know about drugs. You've given me a lot of reasons why it's no worse than drugs that destroy hundreds of thousands of lives every year. And your answer is that we need more of the same? That's your best case for legalization? If so, it's pretty goddam weak."

Pickering raises a cigarette, lets go a lungful of smoke upward, "There, I'm legal." She lights up. "I think our point is that keeping it illegal is worse than legalizing even assuming a few more people try it as a result, which I'm not at all certain about anyway."

Mohr laughs. "So, if your daughter came home drunk she would get in less trouble than if she smelled of marijuana, that right?"

Night doesn't like him talking about Jade. "Either way we're going to talk."

"Know what I think, Night?" George says. "I think you're right on the money. When we find something eases the pain, we're on it quick as a duck on a June bug. Jesus knows I can't quit. I could say I can, but I've tried, I know. I can't."

Pickering rolls her eyes. "Oh, come on, George. It's not addictive."

Ceridwen reaches over to pat his knee. "George, you want to quit, you can."

"Sweetheart Darlin', I know that, and I'm still scared. You see, I don't want to. It's a filthy habit, smoking anything, makes you smell like you rolled around in moldy hay. If I could stop I would. I sure don't want to go to jail or lose my job. But I'm not so sure we should give those little airheads out there with pierced tongues and god only knows what else the benediction of legality to get stoned. Maybe it's better the way it is. Maybe it's better to keep them looking over their shoulder, I don't know. I just don't know."

Ceridwen rises, goes to meet Len. Intending to introduce himself, Night leans forward to rise and George lays a restraining hand on his thigh, "I'd stay here if I were you, the man's a black belt."

"In what?"

"In something painful."

Len takes her arm, leads her to the door. She wrenches away and they go into a whispered huddle. Len is not happy—that he and everybody else watching the show can see.

"Here we go," George says.

"What's that mean?" Night asks him.

"You'll see."

A second time Len attempts to guide her to the door but she isn't having any. For a moment Night thinks he may blow up. He doesn't. What he does is head for the door. She follows.

"Don't give up so easy, Lenny boy," George says sotto voce.

At the door she takes his arm, attempting to draw him back. He throws off her hand, spits something with a hard consonant, bitch maybe, Night can't tell.

"Len," her voice rises in the quieting room, "I thought you were sick, I—"

The slap comes out of nowhere. She almost falls. At once the room is silent. "I'll just bet you did."

She catches herself, hand pressed to her mouth, "Len!"

Len takes in the room, sees all pretense at privacy gone. "Shut up, get your stuff, we're going."

"Len, please—"

He jerks her around violently by an arm, gives her a shove toward the kitchen, "I said we're going. Now get your goddam purse."

Night's hand presses his shirt pocket, finds it empty. "Give me your pen," Night says to George, voice low.

George hands it over. "Taking notes?"

Eyes running, Ceridwen staggers as she passes, going for her things. The room couldn't be any quieter if it were under water.

"Len," George says, "you are one fourteen carat horse's ass."

Len covers the distance between them in three strides. "Get up, faggot, and I'll kick your sissy ass."

Seeing no better time for it, Night rises. "Len, I'm Night, Cer's told me all about you."

Len turns on him warily.

"My daughter and I board with Ceridwen." Night sees comprehension dawn in his eyes—but no friendliness. Night offers a hand, "How you doing, man?"

For an instant Night is afraid he may refuse. Succumbing to convention, Len offers his hand. Relieved, Night smiles a genuine smile as he clamps Len's hand between his own, pen trapped over the gap between Len's carpal and radius. He bears down with his thumbs and Len yelps, dropping to his knees. Mouth to his ear, he says, "You're going to jail, partner." To George, Night says, "Call 911."

Instantly, George is up and on his way, "I'd love to."

"Sit down, George. Let me go, you prick."

"I don't think so."

Ceridwen is there at his elbow, "Let him go, you're hurting him."

"Am I hurting you, Len?"

Face turned away, flushed with humiliation, he strains to rise, but the pinched nerve keeps him on his knees. "Let me up…" Voice breathy, more of a whisper than speech, he gulps air. "I'll go."

"Oh, I will, and you will. Just not yet."

"They're sending somebody," George says.

Party ruined, guests rise to make awkward goodbyes, filter out.

Ceridwen, trembling, whispers at his ear, "I'm asking you… please… let him up."

Battered woman syndrome, must be. Though he expects it, the reaction never fails to amaze him. Too late to stop now, anyway. "Embarrassed, huh? That's okay, be embarrassed. Embarrassment is good. Being embarrassed is better than being dead. Embarrassment means you're seeing things with new eyes." He nods at Len. "Take a good look—this is the man that hit you right here. Like what you see?" A drop of blood puddles at her chin, falls to his bare arm. "You're bleeding on me."

Jo guides her to the bathroom to clean up.

"So, Len, old buddy, I hear you're a black belt, is that just with women and children or what?"

"Goddamit!" He lunges for Night with his free hand. Night bears down on the pen and he goes down, cringing, pinched nerve respecting no martial degree.

Ceridwen returns, towel pressed to her lip, "Night…" she says, pleading.

He motions to the wall mirror, "Take a look, Babe. What do you see? An independent woman? A smart woman? That what you see?"

"When you let me go, you'd better run," Len says. "Hard."

Night bears down and Len groans. "And you'd better keep quiet, Einstein."

The house is mostly empty, now, Jo, Pickering and George all that remain. George drops into a chair, lights a joint, draws deeply. "Face it, Cer, he's a creep."

"Shut up, faggot!"

Night's hands are beginning to sweat. He eases up, Len could slip free. If he does, he has no doubt he can kick his ass all over the room. There's a knock at the door. "You might want to flush that, George."

George runs for the bathroom with the joint, fanning air as he goes.

"I won't press charges," Ceridwen says, defiant.

Night can't resist smiling. How many times has he heard that? "Doesn't matter, your friend here's going to see the inside of Lane County Jail."

Night knows the cop. Name is Hoppe. Night was his training officer. He knows he won't give him away, isn't worried about it. "Glad you could make it so soon, I'm getting kind of tired of holding his hand."

Hoppe sniffs, "Smells like a party. What happened?"

Pickering speaks up, "This ass hole just slapped my friend, is what happened."

"I did no such thing."

"Be quiet." Hoppe says. "Who saw it?"

"Half the staff of U of O saw it," Pickering says. "I can give you names, if you like."

Hoppe flips open a clipboard, "And your name, sir?"

"Night Hume."

"You one of the partiers?"

"Yeah."

Hoppe gives him an amused glance, "Been holding him ever since it happened?"

Night gives him a look, "Just a passing fling."

George guffaws. Hoppe turns to look at him and he catches himself.

Hoppe snaps a cuff around Len's free hand, "You can let him go now. From this bad boy's eyes, I'd say he's had a little too much nose candy." He pats Len down, "Any weapons I should know about, any needles?"

"No." Len keeps a steady gaze on Night, "I'll get you, you—"

Hoppe sets him down on the couch, "What you'll get is put in the car if you don't keep quiet."

Hoppe turns back to speak to Jo. and Len bounces to his feet. Hands behind him, flat footed he kicks, catching Night square in the mush between nose and lip.

Before Night can react, it's over. White cotton floods his head as blood pulses out his nose, "Goddamit."

Hoppe hustles Len out as Night looks for something to stanch the blood gushing out between his fingers.

Over his shoulder Len shouts. "You haven't seen a thing, yet, prick, not a thing!"

"You shit!" Pickering calls after him, tosses Night a towel. "Don't you ever come back in my house!"

Through bleary eyes, he snatches it, feeling stupid for not seeing it coming. "Sorry about the rug," he says, sounding like a man with a cold. "I'll clean it."

Pickering sits him down, looks him over, "Screw the rug. How's the beak?"

"I'll live."

Ceridwen bolts for the door. Pickering calls after her. Running, head back, Night catches her at her car. "Where you going?"

She unlocks the door, glaring, "To bail Len out."

Figures. He was wrong about her. About as wrong as he's ever been about anything. "What's the rush?" He leans against the hood, coughs, spits blood. "He'll be there when you get there."

She looks at him, worry on her face, and something else, maybe desperation. "You okay?"

"I'm fine."

"Why did you have to stick your nose in?"

"I'm beginning to wonder that myself."

She starts the car. "It was nothing. He was mad, that's all. He's never touched me before."

By her door, he hunkers down in the street, resting an arm in her window to steady himself. "You know something?" Even though he knows he's wasting his breath he needs to say it. "There are people so frightened they might not get what they want, they'll do anything to make sure they don't."

She looks at him with the most magnificent puzzled eyes he's ever seen. "That makes no sense."

Of course she wouldn't see it. It had taken him years of dealing with losers to understand all truth is contradiction. "Yes, it does."

"You think that's what I'm doing, making sure I don't get what I want?"

"Go on." Disgusted with her, with himself, he pushes himself erect, waves her on, "I don't think anything. Go on, get going, your boyfriend's waiting."

She stays where she is, watching him. He won't look her square in those eyes. Not now. "You should have stayed out of it."

It really is hopeless. How he ever could have hoped for anything between him and this magnificent screwed-up woman is beyond believing. He nods, "You're right."

She pulls away and he watches her go. Hoppe stops by on his way back in to get statements. "You run with a pretty fast crowd."

Night glances back at the house to see if anyone's watching. No one is. Len waits in the cruiser, but he isn't worried about him. He can't hear anything. "Real fast."

"This an undercover thing or what?"

Dread bubbles up inside him, an artesian spring. This will get around. Never guess where I ran into Night last night... Had to happen. Inevitable. "Here with a friend."

"Yeah," Hoppe says, looking in the direction Ceridwen had gone. "Not bad, but you might want to have a talk with her about her choice in boyfriends."

"She won't press charges."

"So she said. That's no problem, I'll book him on a DC. Training officer I had once taught me that. If the vic won't press charges for assault, get them on disorderly conduct. Cagey old bastard, he was."

Night looks him over, for the moment forgetting the mess he's in. "Did a good job on you, didn't I?"

Hoppe starts back inside. "That you did. Watch yourself, Hume."

Night stands on the curb, unsure whether to start walking or call a cab. A hand on his shoulder scares the breath out of him. He spins, guard up, sees it's only George.

"Offer you a ride there, cowboy?"

"No, thanks anyway."

George smiles, "I'm not going to make a pass."

Night laughs. "Never for a minute dreamed you would."

George's eyes watch him in the dark. "A lot of men live in dread of the possibility."

"Somehow, too, I manage to struggle through life despite the very real possibility a vacuum cleaner salesman should knock on my door. No, thanks has never failed me yet."

Slowly, George smiles. "I like it. Come on, let's go, my car's right here."

Night thinks of the walk home, follows. "Why not."

George raises a hand after Ceridwen. "Where's she headed in such a hurry?"

Night slides in. "To post bail."

George growls in disgust. "Guess I shouldn't be surprised. She's been under his thumb since she met him. Damned if I know why. Sad to see, though." He watches Night from the corner of his eye. "Very sad."

Streets slide by, wind cool on Night's face. "Known her long?"

George draws on his Marlboro, glowing red in the dark, "Since she came on staff fifteen years ago. Something about her makes her put up with some of the worst men."

Night thinks about her on her way to bail Len out with blood still wet on her face. "I've known a lot of women who put up with that, but they're not usually college professors."

"She thinks if she marries him he'll pony up for Alex's treatments."

It all falls together in Night's mind. "She mentioned something about mouse serum."

"Latest poop down the pike. Long shot, but when its your kid you don't analize odds, you grab straws."

"But it works."

In the light of a passing streetlight Night sees George cast him a sour smile. "I've read a little about it. Who knows, maybe they've got something. At least they're trying. Desperate people will try anything. And want to know the saddest part? Len's not even faithful. He's nailing half the split-tails in the department. Wouldn't think so, would you, wing tips and the whole bit? Every female grad student with looks earns a special appointment in his office. I hear he bats about 500, excuse the pun. So far they've kept it quiet."

In front of the house, George pulls up, cuts the engine, leans back against his door. His eyes reflect the glowing cigarette as he drags it to life behind the car's lighter. "You care about her, I can see you do."

Uncomfortable with the veer of the conversation, Night opens the door for fresh air, braces his foot at the hinge.

George rolls down the window, blows smoke, watches him through liquid, laughing eyes. "Nobody else at our gathering of illuminati would have lifted a finger to stop him. You did. Why?"

"In my circle you don't sip your Miller and take in the show."

George laughs. "And what circle is that?"

"I told you—"

"Yeah, yeah, I know, you're a garbage collector. And I'm your fairy godmother."

Night laughs. He is starting to like this guy. "So how many wishes I get?"

"I'm serious, what are you really? Come on, you can trust Uncle Georgie."

Night guesses he can. That doesn't mean he will.

"Okay, be that way. I'll tell you something, then. She likes you so much it scares her stiff. You've got her on the run, plans crashing down about her ears—and that's with her convinced you're a trash man."

Night gets out. George makes him feel as if he has neon on his forehead flashing his thoughts. It's an uncomfortable feeling. He slams the door, leans in at the window, suddenly curious. "You know what beats hell out of me, George?"

"What's that?"

"How did Len know? Somebody had to tell him I was there with her. Who you think it was? Any ideas?"

George takes a long drag. "Now, that…" He flicks the butt out the window. "Is one hell of a good question." He smiles and Night sees he has no intention of answering. "How's the mouth?"

Night reaches up to feel his lip, finds it numb. Teeth a little wobbly, but still there. A week and he'll know if they made it. Root severed, they turn a dull gray. He hopes they won't. A bridge he doesn't want. "May have to give up popcorn balls for a few days."

"That could be hard." George laughs, starts the car, calls after him. "And, Night…"

Night turns.

"Don't give up on her, not yet."

Night keeps walking.

He might.

If he had a choice, he might.

• • •

Downtown, Ceridwen posts bail.

Then she heads west to the jail. Across the lobby of LCJ she paces. Night said he'd been here. What had he done? She looks around her. Orange. Chairs, carpeting, walls—all orange. Who but the government would buy orange?

Electric doors rumble open slowly and Len tears through, passes her by on his way out to the street. "I can't believe this. It'll be all over the physics department tomorrow. What am I saying? It'll be all over the university."

She follows into cool midnight air, watching him curiously. This is the man she's slept with for a wasted year of her life. "Len."

"Let's go."

"Len, we need to talk."

"We can talk later." He tries her door, finds it locked, "Toss me the keys, I'll drive."

She stays where she is, arms folded across her chest, "No, Len, you won't."

He leans forward, arms outstretched over the roof of the car," What's that mean? Give me the goddam keys."

Oddly, she is not afraid. She doesn't worry about what may happen tomorrow. She doesn't worry about anything. It's a wonderful feeling, a freeing feeling. Later she can worry. Right now she's had enough. She runs her tongue over the cut on the inside of her lip. "No."

Looking like he'd love to hit her again, his gaze rises to take in the jail looming behind her and he sighs. "What is it now? I've just been in jail for the first time in my life, and I want to get home to shower the stink off me, so tell me, what? What is it?"

"This is it, Len, I don't know why I put up with you as long as I did, but this is it. I bailed you out. I'm not pressing charges. That's it. I'm done."

Mouth hanging, he says nothing, only moves aside as she crosses to the driver's door, slides in, shuts the door, rolls down the window.

"You're kidding."

"No, I'm not."

"I'll miss you."

She laughs, grimacing at the sickness she feels under her breastbone. "No, you won't. You really think I don't know what you are? Everybody knows, Len, everybody. I chose not to see, that's all."

He looks up Fifth, no cars in sight, "What am I supposed to do, now?"

She braces for the guilt—nothing comes. "I don't care. Just stay away from me, far away. And if you ever think about hurting Night, I'll go to the Board of Regents about you, I swear I will."

He smiles at her and she feels suddenly filthy. "What would that make you?"

"A fool. I would look just like a fool. You don't think I will, just try me."

She pulls away, watches him fade in the mirror and, so great is the feeling of lightness about her, she feels like screaming. She stops at a light, closes her eyes, waiting for her heart to slow.

Free—she is free.

She did it.

She has absolutely no idea how she will get through if Alex relapses, but somehow they will make it. In front of her runs the path she has always feared. Night said it. There is something she wants. She may not get it, but she won't spend her time running from it either. Not any more.

From right now her life starts over.

Empty streets fly by as she heads home, anticipating dawn.

• • •

School is out.

Grateful he has no one to shuttle, Night is up and out before he has to worry about running into Ceridwen. On the way downtown he broods. It's a good day for it—the sky is dark as the inside of an overturned kettle. By seven he sits across a booth from Derek.

"What the hell happened to you?" Derek asks, admiring the cut on his lip Len left with his size 13 wingtip.

Night fingers it gingerly, winces. "Jade and I were playing basketball."

Derek frowns. "And what, you ran into the pole?"

"No, it was an elbow thing."

Derek reaches out, points. "There's a line there."

"Yeah, it was her bracelet… caught me…" Night knows what a terrible job of lying he is doing and doesn't much care. "When she swung around."

"Bracelet? On her elbow?"

Night is too tired to argue. "I don't know, we were scrambling for the ball, maybe it was an anklet and she kicked me. Anyway, she got me and it hurts like hell—okay?"

Derek shrugs. "Okay. Looks like hell. One mean basketball player, huh?"

"Yeah, she's good."

The waitress slides pancakes the size of dinner plates in front of them and Night finds he isn't hungry. He watches Derek eat.

"Ever wonder just what the hell we're doing this for?"

Derek swamps his hotcakes in syrup. "Nope."

"I mean, here's a guy, garage full of grow lamps, too stupid to know we'll notice he's using enough kilowatts to run an office building. We do a low crawl, find the garage, get the warrant, go in, and shut him down. It's about as exciting as raiding the library to take down the reference librarian."

Derek motions with a fork bearing a skewered wedge of griddle cake, mouth full, "There was that librarian, remember?"

He does. "We take him to jail, he bails out. We take his house, which if he's smart he's got all the equity out of, then what?"

"Good guys win again. The world's a safer place, amen."

Night takes a bite of hotcake. "Noticed any dearth of green dope?"

Derek shakes his head no.

"We're wasting our time."

Derek points a black finger. "You said that, not me."

"Aren't we?"

"You think too much, man. Eat your hotcakes."

"I'm asking you. We do all this over and over and over. What changes?"

Derek shrugs. "Another day, another dollar."

"And that's okay with you?"

"What we do sends a message."

"To whom?"

"To all the lazy butts out there want to beat the system, to the guys who want to coast not paying taxes. We're pulling their weight. They're living high, and we're carrying them and their kids, too."

"And are they getting it, this message we're so busy sending?"

Derek watches him, sighs, tosses down a ten, "Come on, we don't get going we won't make briefing."

• • •

In the briefing room Night waits for it.

Herrera bustles in with a sheaf of printouts thick as the raised glazed doughnut on top of it. When he gets to Night and Derek, he flips impatiently through his sheets. "I don't see anything here about our professor. She retire to Belize, or what?"

Derek looks to Night, shrugs, "We've been giving her time. We'll drop by again, see what she says."

"Think she made you? Want somebody else to try?"

Night raises his hands as if this doesn't matter, as if this isn't the nexus of his life. "Still nothing, what can I tell you? We'll get it when we get it."

Herrera fixes him with pig eyes. If Night didn't know Herrera could barely find his parking place he might worry. "Two days." He makes a note. "Get off your thumb on this one. Professor pushing green dope to the little kiddies at U of O while INET does squat? That would make a real catchy headline in Sunday's *Guard*, wouldn't it? They catch wind of this, somebody's career's down the toilet, and it ain't going to be mine. I want her shut down, and I want it done yesterday."

In the lot, Derek waits for him to open the door. "Well, what about it, man, you ready to move on her?"

Night slides in, unlocks the door, "Don't want to rush her." He knows how lame that sounds.

"Rush her? It's been two weeks. Let's drop by, see what she says."

Night's hands go numb on the wheel. "Let's not queer things by getting too anxious."

Derek gapes. "Were you in that briefing with me or did I imagine it? Come on, man, we're close. Here we are, Villard, turn."

As he makes the corner Night's mind runs wide open searching for something to stave off disaster. Nothing comes. He parks across the street, sits frozen behind the wheel.

"Well?" Derek watches him. "Go ahead."

Nothing he can do. Nothing he can say.

Derek reaches for the door, "Want me to?"

"No." He can't let him go. She might sell to him. Probably would. Night gets out, starts up the walk to the door, praying the girls don't see him out the window. He glances at his watch. Ten a.m. Jade will be up. If she answers, what then?

Halfway up he hears them out in the pool. So far so good. He pretends to press the bell, stands back, waits, sweating though it's seventy. Ten more seconds and he's home.

Just as he's ready to turn away, Ceridwen passes by the front window in her suit and sees him. That's it. He is screwed. They both are.

She opens the door, face swollen after last night. "What are you doing standing out there?"

What does he say, now? "I..."

She frowns, confused, "You what?"

"I wanted..." It's a moment that calls for a lie and all he can think of is the truth. "I wanted to say that... it's none of my business what you do. Whether or not you stay with Len or anybody else. I said some things I shouldn't have."

She looks down to see the car waiting at the curb. "You took off work to tell me that?"

"My partner and I are on break."

She seems to buy it. "You told the truth last night, that's all. I liked it that you did what you did."

His stomach floods with scalding warmth. "You liked it?"

"Yeah." She looks down at Derek waiting in the car, "You want to invite your friend in, I can make some iced tea."

"I uh...I've got to go."

She nods, "We can talk about it later. We are talking again, aren't we?"

"We're talking." He backs away, "I've got to get back."

From her the hint of a smile. "See you."

On his way down the walk his elbow vibrates as if a current passes through it. He massages his hand to bring back feeling. Derek watches him like he's sizing him up. Night doesn't like it much. "All that and you come back with nothing? What were you doing, discussing the weather?"

He pulls away from the curb. "I don't rush, you know that."

This Derek accepts. "So?"

So far his luck's good. "Friday."

Derek's open hand bangs loud as a gunshot on the roof of the Lincoln, "What's with her? You suggest she might want to contact another supplier?"

"Sure didn't."

"Well, maybe you should have. I'm tired of that bantyweight Herrera breathing down our necks on this one." A block goes by and Night is starting to relax when Derek slaps the dash. "I don't think she trusts you."

"She trusts me."

"You mention the name?"

Night can't think of it. He asks him and the game's over. "I mentioned it."

Derek taps a gold-capped incisor with a nail the way he does when he thinks. He decides. "Take me back, I want to give it a try. She may have a soft spot for colored boys."

Night yanks the car to the curb, kills the engine. "Look, she may have the hots for Sidney Poitier for all I know, she's still out of product."

Night sees suspicion spark. Derek has never looked at him this way. "What harm can it do?"

"What harm? You think she didn't see you in the car? How will it look to have you show up ten minutes later?"

"She saw me?"

The truth will set you free. "She asked about you."

"Shee-it." Derek thinks it over. "Forget it, then."

"Hey, you want to blow the whole thing, go right ahead, I'll take you back right now." Night starts the car.

Derek considers as Night holds his breath.

Again he slaps the roof of the Lincoln with the sound of a bass drum. "We wait for Friday."

Night fills his lungs, pulls away.

• • •

Night would rather be anywhere else.

Today he doesn't feel like he's doing anything for the world. He's going through the motions, that's all. Three hours he spends with a three hundred pound black woman with a baritone voice and a condescending manner in a back office at Pacific Power looking for a sudden spike in KWH. When he finds it he groans.

This means a low crawl tonight. Swell. Another night away from Jade. For what? To keep the price up on dope coming up from Calexico? There is more on the street every day. More every year since the eighties when Reagan began targeting domestic growers. It's almost as if the Mexicans are calling the shots with DEA. What could be any better for business?

He heads in to the office and is finishing up a report when Derek comes in and slams the door to the briefing room behind him.

Night keeps his eyes on his report. "What's up, buddy?"

Derek pulls up a chair, straddles it, says nothing. Night sees his face and his heart drops. He knows. It's over. He clicks the button of his pen with his thumb, seating the point, sets it down on the table parallel to the top of the report. This is it. "You don't look happy."

"I'm not happy."

Night feels guilt snap open, a switchblade in his gut. He doesn't want to be here for what comes next. "Want to tell me why?"

"Yeah, I'll tell you." Derek looks at him hard. "Guess who I ran into last night at the Squire."

Night doesn't know where he gets off being angry, but he's getting that way. "You got something to say, say it."

"Linda. And you'll never guess what she told me. She told me your friend the professor's got enough bud to stuff a mattress. She told me she's not out of dope. She told me she's never been out of dope."

Night wonders how much worse it can get.

"And you know what else? She told me she ran into a couple of her students that told her the professor's got a new boarder."

Night's stomach feels like he's swallowed liquid nitrogen. "Yeah?"

"That's what she said. You know what I told her? I told her she was full of it. I told her my partner wouldn't lie to me. I told her if Night tells me she's out of dope, she's out of goddam dope. That's it. How you like that?"

Shame hits him like a slap. He takes a breath, lets it go. "Derek, I—"

"What a horse's ass I am, huh? What a gullible jerk. That's what you're thinking, isn't it?"

"No."

"What a fool!" He kicks his chair into the corner where it caroms off the plexiglass front of the candy machine and skids to rest. "To think a guy I trust with my life wouldn't lie to me. To think a guy I've known since I was a kid wouldn't lead me down the path."

"If anybody's a fool, it's me."

A rap at the door, "You guys okay in there?"

It's Hererra. All Derek has to do is call him in and Night's career is over. Derek watches him, whites of his eyes antique ivory against caramel. "We're fine." To Night, voice lower, "With me so far?"

He's still not ready to throw him to the dogs. What Night doesn't understand is why. "I'm with you."

"Okay, good, that's good. Then merrily I go on my ignorant ass way, right? One dumb, happy colored boy, that's me. Then this morning who should I run into but Hoppe down at the station weight room."

Night feels yet another sandbag of dread settle onto his neck.

"You'll never guess what he tells me. It's very interesting."

Night is sick. "I know what he told you."

"No, no, don't interrupt, this is good. You got to hear this. He says last Saturday night somebody I know is at the scene of a battering at a party at some prof's house on Powell. He says this foxy professor gets her lip bloodied by her boyfriend, and some undercover cop saves the day. Then he tells me this guy gets kicked in the mouth by this jerk after he's in cuffs cause the guy's some kind of Jackie Chan or something. Now I think that's pretty goddam funny, because you see, my partner—by an incredible coincidence—had his lip cut in a game of basketball with his daughter on the same day. Is that wild or what?"

"Let me explain."

"Now, I is one stupid ass nigger, but by now even I start to get the idea that maybe something ain't right, so I run up to check at the trailer park where my good old buddy, where my partner, used to live, and what do you think he left as his forwarding address? Huh? What?"

"Derek…"

"That's right!" He slaps the table. "The foxy professor's house. You remember her, don't you? The foxy professor that's supposed to be out of dope, the professor he's been saving from her no good boyfriend, the professor we were supposed to bust for selling out of her home to all the little dreamy love children at U of O? I know you must remember her."

"Will you let me explain?"

"Oh?" He laughs. "You can explain? That's good, I want to hear this, because you know what it looks like to me? It looks like my good buddy is in some deep doodoo, and I'll tell you something, I ain't getting drug in after him."

Voice low, Night speaks from the pit of a stomach turned to heavy metal. "I was wrong, I know that. I was wrong to lie to you."

Derek turns on him. "To me? I'm not the only one you lied to. What about Herrera? You lied to him, too. Hell, I lied to him! Goddam it, you may want to throw it all away, but I need this job! I'm not going down with you!" He throws open the door so that it bangs back against the water cooler, setting it burbling. Hutto passes by, eyes straight ahead. "Let's go see him right now."

Night stands, shuts the door quietly, locks it, "You still haven't heard my side."

Derek laughs, a bark, "Your side?" He is yelling now. "What side is that? The conspiracy side? The obstruction of justice side? The hindering prosecution side? What side? Tell me, man, what side is that?"

"You're not willing to hear me out?" Past caring, Night's voice is calm, low. "After twenty years you don't owe me that much?"

Derek hesitates, still standing. Face bitter, he thinks it over.

"Not even that?" To Derek's lack of response he nods, moves for the door. "Okay then, let's go."

"Wait." Derek drags over his chair, slams it down, drops into it, "I'm listening."

Night sits across the table, takes a deep breath. Inside, he's empty. The job's gone. That he accepts. Making Derek understand is all that's important, now. "When I went in to make the buy, I meant to do it. There was no question in my mind. I meant to do precisely what we've done a thousand times."

Derek turns away, tip of his tongue probing white teeth.

"I know you don't believe that. I wouldn't either, but it's true. I've gone over it and over it in my mind. I didn't plan what happened in there."

Derek turns back, face hard, "What did?"

Night presses an aching head in the vice of his hands, "I don't know."

Derek aspirates a chest full of air. "Well, something must have. She's not the first good looking split tail you've run across. She must have done something, said something to make you shit can everything."

Night places both hands flat on the table, watches them as if the answer might be tattooed on them. "I go in and she thinks I'm there to rent a room in her house. I try to tell her, I drop the informant's names, but she's so hyped about renting the room she won't let me get a word in. I figure, okay, I'll play it, see how it goes. Not force things, you know? Next thing we're upstairs and she's telling me how nice the room is—"

Derek lets his head loll back. "And you're overcome by a tidal wave of passion."

"No."

"Well? What, then?"

"Nothing, I don't know, it's not like anything big happened. No flash of light, no fireworks. I'm following her down and I just think, Christ, I'm watching her and I think, man, you've got to rent these rooms." Night sees his face change. "Listen, I know how this sounds. I wouldn't believe me, how can I expect you to? But it happens to be the truth."

Derek nods irritably and Night continues. "I just think, if you rent this room Jade can live with you. If you rent these rooms you can start to get something going in your life besides low crawls and boob bars. You can be something besides a maggot. You can be a father."

Self consciously Night smiles, half expecting Derek to laugh. He doesn't. "Stupid, I know. I write her a check, and I don't even have the money in the account to cover it. I have to go down and shuffle money around so it doesn't bounce, but I don't care. Why? I don't know. Why do we do any of the stupid things we do? A feeling, maybe. I just knew I had to, that's all."

Derek's eyes are on the floor now. On the oak table top brown fingers beat a cadence.

"She's thrilled. She fixes us tea to seal the deal. At that point I don't know, maybe

I still intended to ask her about the bag, but her kid comes home, and I'm not going to do it in front of her.

"So?"

"So I come out."

"And tell me she's got nothing."

"What was I supposed to say? Hey, Derek, guess what, I'm nuts about a pot dealer? So nuts about her I rented a couple rooms in her house? That what I'm supposed to say?"

"So, you going to tell me she's clean, now?"

He dearly wishes he could. "No, I'm not going to tell you that."

"Then we got a problem." Derek stands, eyes hard, cold. "She's dirty, man. Now you're dirty—that makes me dirty."

Night nods. This can only go one way.

"The question is…" Derek paces. "What are we going to do about it?"

Hererra's office waits across the hall. Fifteen minutes from now he'll be out the door. "It's your call. You say go, we go. I got no answers."

"Well you better find some. I want to know, what are you going to do about it?"

Night can't believe what he's hearing. Is this a chance? He knows he heard wrong. "What I should have done in the first place—put her out of business."

Derek looks at him the way Night's seen him look at lying informants. He decides to take it to Hererra, he won't blame him.   "You asking what I think you're asking?"

Night nods.

"This a line to keep from going to Hererra?"

Night meets his eye, sees wariness there, "No."

"If you're jacking me around—"

"I'm not." Night breathes. Can it be he still has a job? a life?

"What about our warrant? We've got no buy."

"I'll write the affidavit. I've seen sales since I've been there."

Derek considers, "Do it, then." He heads for the door.

"Hey, man, I—"

Derek cuts him off with a raised hand, "Save it. We're still partners a week from now, say it then." At the door, Derek turns, "Okay, tomorrow night you're out with the new guy. What's his name, Ron?"

"Yeah."

"We'll leave that alone. Show him around a little. How about Saturday?"

"Saturday will work."

Derek nods, "I'll line it up."

Saturday. His home will be gone in four days. Her home will be gone in four days. And with it any chance he has of ever being more than her boarder. Not that he ever had any.

Derek's eyes narrow as if he's read his thoughts, "You live with that?"

"I can live with it."

Night watches him go. Her or his job. Not much of a choice. After Jade his job comes next. He can't see himself doing anything else. Ceridwen never was an option anyway.

Not really.

Three days and she will lose everything—house, child, job, car, freedom.

He heads out to the Lincoln and, with a pang, thinks of Alex in foster care.

Just one of the things she should have thought about before she started dealing.

• • •

Sky clouding over, threatening rain.

New guy on the team, Ron rides with Night down Willamette not long after sundown. Night looks him over as he drives. Twenty-five, in pressed chinos and oxford he looks more college-man than INET maggot. Still a bit gun-shy. Month ago at an all night gas station he killed a man who drew on him. Took it hard.

Tonight Night shows him around. Ease him into the routine. On their way to a serve a warrant. Strictly jumbo peanuts. Good bust to pop his cherry. They both wear vests and raid jackets, flaps hiding POLICE in lemon block letters chest and back to keep them from being shot by other cops.

"You're telling me you go home, pick up your kid from school, cook her dinner, spend time with her, tuck her in bed, then come back in?"

Night smiles, "That's it."

"I don't think I'd like a shift spread out over eighteen hours."

"I never thought I would either. Right now it fits."

They spot him at the same time. A Mexican Night has seen before leans on the hood of a tricked out Chevy. Ron brushes a finger under his nose. The Mexican tilts his head signing affirmative.

Frantic, Ron opens an empty wallet. "You got any money, man? They haven't given me my buy money yet."

"Yeah, sure, what you want?"

"A twenty, give me a twenty, come on, come on, pull over."

"Don't be so goddam eager. It may be your first buy, it won't be your last."

Frantic, he examines his reflection in the rear view. "I look okay?"

Night looks him over, zips up his raid jacket to conceal the vest. He hands him a twenty. "You're fine."

"Okay, here I go."

Night clamps his arm, "Remember, breathe in, breathe out."

"Yeah, I'm okay."

Night follows, keeping out of sight. The dealer draws Ron around behind a semi parked along the curb. Night comes around the back side, waiting for the signal from Ron once he has the balloon of coke. Before he can, the dealer senses him, turns, bolts down an alley. They chase, Night calling after him in his best lousy Spanish. *"Policia, Alta! En sus rodillas!"* Which seems very optimistic considering the last thing on this Mexican's mind is stopping long enough to get on his knees.

Coke he throws one way, money the other as he sprints down the alley, Night struggling to keep up. Less than a block and his body already complains. Too many burgers, too much vending machine junk. Not enough time for the laps in the pool to do anything. As he pumps, revulsion for himself and for the life he leads wells up inside him.

A block later, Night realizes he's left Ron behind him somewhere. He knows what happened. Ron faded on him—caved and left him with nobody watching his back— in Night's world, the ultimate infidelity. The kid disappears around a corner and Night realizes he hasn't the slightest idea where he is.

Around the corner he flies at a dead run, mouth open, lungs full to call out a warning when he sees the Mexican plastered to the wall like a lizard in shadow. Too late Night sees the gun come up. Three shots, very loud, very fast, three solid line drive swings to his spine just above the tailbone.

Down he goes. Hand numb, he loses his Glock. In the silence after the noise, he hears the Mexican's shoes grate gravel as he comes up on where he lies. Night watches him come, left hand working to unzip the pocket to get at the backup Walther. He's trying to hurry but the zipper won't cooperate.

The kid mumbles in Spanish, too fast and slurred for Night to pick up. Not sure of the words, he gets the drift. He's going to finish him, and his vest won't do a damned thing about it. The zipper won't come, and he's out of time.

Over him the Mexican towers, Beretta dangling from his right hand. This time it won't be a torso shot. It'll be to the head. The kid smiles like he's going to enjoy it. If Night could move his legs he could trip him up, but he can't. All he can do is watch it come.

Desperate, he stretches and the zipper gives. The kid lets the nine hang over his face, barely a foot away from Night's nose, so close he could reach up and grab it. Night's fingers burrow into his pocket, close on the PPK. Watching as the kid's finger tightens on the cocked trigger, Night extricates the little pistol from the tangle of his jacket and empties it upward. The nine goes off once, sending a spray of gravel into Night's cheek and the kid falls heavily on his legs, face on Night's sternum. Brown eyes open, he looks surprised as hot, arterial blood soaks down through Night's jeans and onto his groin.

Night can smell perfumed hair oil, can feel the kid's breath on his chest through his shirt. Right hand still buzzing and useless, Night lays his left hand onto curly hair, feeling the pulse at his temple fade. Lying under him, too weak to move, Night watches him die. In the sudden quiet he can hear him mumble something, and though he doesn't catch a word, he understands. Too late they speak the same language. Night feels him relax and knows it's over.

He wants out from under but with one good arm and no legs he is going nowhere. It takes a while, but at last he works his cellular out of his right pocket, presses the preset for station dispatch.

"Eugene emergency dispatch." It's Tammy, the little blonde.

"King three, down in an alley near Twelfth and Willamette."

"King three, say again."

Frustration erupts out his throat in a breath and he answers louder than he intended. "King three, suspect and officer down." His back feels like the vest failed. His guess is a cracked vertebra. He tries and finds he still can't move his legs. No. No way he's going to end up in a goddam wheelchair.

"Copy, King Three." Copy comes across a breathy aspirated "—pee," the first half of the word lost in the delay of a voice activated mike. He can hear he's irked her and regrets it. She's good at her job, a hell of a lot better than the sergeant that spells her on breaks.

"Adam Three, King Three, units and an ambulance on route, stand by King Three."

So quick, so cool. She's good. "Thanks, Tam." Against regs to use her name but right now he needs to say her name, needs to talk to somebody with a name.

Like a slap her answer comes back, "Copy, King Three."

Okay, so it was stupid. He tries to worm his way out from under the kid who seems heavier now. "Son of a bitch!" he says at the top of his voice to an empty alley.

"Hang on, Night."

Through the pain he smiles, regaining the breath panic had robbed. Through an open mouth he pants to keep the pain at bay. "I'm hanging, Tam, I'm hanging."

"—py King Three. Two minutes."

He drops the cellular to push at the kid's shoulder but his right hand is still no good and his legs are gone. He gives up. He'll have to buy Tammy a box of Girl Scout cookies. The mint ones are her favorites.

A flash of lightning illuminates the alley, thunder fast on its heels rattling his ribs. Night looks up to see rain spark as it falls past an orange streetlight at the mouth of the alley. He thinks about Ron and wishes he would find him so he could tell him what he thinks of a cop who ditches his partner.

He looks down at the Mexican, still pinning his legs. His first shooting in twenty years. Does he feel the crushing guilt he's heard so much about? He feels around inside himself, like feeling for something dropped in the dark. Nothing there. What he feels is glad to be alive.

Over the open phone a new voice crackles making him jump. "King Three, Adam Eleven, at the corner of Willamette and Twelfth.

"East, go east... an alley, you'll see my car. Ron should be there somewhere."

"King Three, Adam Three, is a second officer down?"

Eyes tearing with frustration, Night laughs. "Not yet, he isn't."

"Adam Eleven, King Three, we see him."

It isn't long and he sees their lights. Night works to get his legs free and the pain spikes unbearably. He settles for propping himself up on an elbow and has to give that up, too. He needs to do something to show he's still alive. He sees lights at the mouth of the alley and waves his one good arm. "I see you. I'm north of you."

They want to put him in the ambulance but he isn't going for it. Ron takes him in the Lincoln. Night, still angry, won't talk. Ron's smart enough not to try. At the hospital he brings him his keys, drops them into his hand on the gurney. "I'll catch a ride."

He turns to go but Night calls him back. Looking into his eyes Night sees a man haunted and the anger he felt drains away. Night offers a hand and Ron takes it.

"Sorry, man."

"Ron, do me, do yourself a favor. Find something else to do."

• • •

Mind a block of ice, Cer floors her Volvo, flashing down Franklin much too fast on the way to Sacred Heart. By the door Jade rocks herself, arms wrapped tightly around knees.

Ceridwen watches her, thinking, needing to ask, needing to know. "Your dad isn't what he said he is, is he?"

Mutely, Jade shakes her head.

A tabby streaks across the street, a shadow under streetlights, and, hands tense on the wheel, Ceridwen holds the car steady, eases off the accelerator. It makes the sidewalk as she flashes by. How stupid she's been. How blind. "He's a cop, isn't he?"

"He made me promise not to tell. Ever since I was little I had to lie." She rocks on the seat, cheek to knee. "I'm sorry."

She reaches to pet her hair, "It's okay."

Hands white on the wheel, she slows to check a cross street, runs the red, accelerator to the floor. Why is she afraid? Why does she feel at risk? It's Jade who stands to lose a father. It's Jade should be worried, not her.

This late, they find a space in the parking lot near the front door. Night's room they find with no trouble. Jade rushes to cling to him, pressing her ear under his chin as Ceridwen, unsure he would want her here, hangs out of the halo of light cast by a sconce over the bed. She hears his voice and an unbearable weight is taken from her.

"I'm okay, Booboo, I'm okay."

Chin on his chest, Jade peers up at him. "Oh, Daddy, did it make a hole?"

"You can't put holes in the Pillsbury doughboy." The intensity of his stare over Jade's shoulder makes Ceridwen believe he can see her even here in the relative dark. "Do something for me? Ask the nurse if I can have another happy pill, will you?"

With a quick glance back at Ceridwen, she stands. "Okay, be right back."

From the bed by the window there comes a muffled snoring. Night's eyes remain on her. The silence between them presses against her ribs, making it hard to breathe. She backs until her hand closes on the cold stainless of a door handle. "I can wait outside."

"Stay."

Hesitantly, she leaves the cover of the dark. "Who are you? Who are you really?"

"You know who I am."

"What are you then?"

"A cop, but you already know that, don't you. Disappointed?"

She feels the need to laugh. "That you're not a garbage collector?"

"The way some feel people feel about cops, it's a step down."

"I don't feel that way."

"Some of your friends might. Len for one."

She ignores the dig, convinced she's close to seeing something she should have seen long ago. "What kind of a cop looks the way you do?"

His mouth turns up into a tired half smile. "Think about it, it'll come to you."

In a rush, she sees, and her mind sputters.

"Thought you'd get it. You've heard of INET."

She has the feeling she should know what that means. She doesn't. "INET?"

"Interagency Narcotics Enforcement Task force."

The pieces fall together in her mind, cold and ugly. She doesn't like the picture they make. "You weren't looking for a rental. You never even saw my ad, did you."

"I did try to tell you, but you were so excited, I didn't have the heart. I just figured I'd let you show me the room, and make the buy later."

Her spine crawls. "The buy you needed to bust me."

"That's right."

"Then…" She is more puzzled now than ever. "Why'd you take the rooms?"

He looks away. "That part I'm still trying to figure out."

"Are you…" Desperately, she searches for the right question. "Are you supposed to do things like that, rent rooms from people like me?"

Chin on chest, he laughs silently until the pain in his back stops him.

Outrage rises in her, hot and acrid. "Is that the way you work? Living in people's homes? Spying on them?"

He shakes his head, looking sick. "No."

She thinks, scrambling to fill in the blanks. "The other day, when you came by during work. You were supposed to make another try at a buy, weren't you? That's why you were so nervous, wasn't it?"

His look tells her she's right.

As her thoughts snake she sees no end to it. It just keeps going and going. "But you didn't." He opens his mouth to speak and she stops him with an upraised hand. "No, wait a minute—you don't need a buy. You've seen me sell, you've had more than enough time. It's been weeks and nothing's happened. Why not? Why aren't I in jail? What are you waiting for?"

Responding to her rising voice, the man in the next bed mumbles in his sleep. Together they wait for him to resume snoring. When he does, Night answers, voice low. "I don't know."

His eyes say he does.

She moves to sit in a low chair at the side of the bed, suddenly chilled. "Tell me." He closes his eyes, breathes as if it's his first breath in a while. She can see he is hurting and she takes a cruel thrill in it. "I said tell me."

"You want to know?"

She is through pretending, through being anything but what she is. "Yes, I want to know."

"It was you."

His answer leaves her confused and frightened. It was not what she expected. Not at all. "Me?"

"It was a feeling I had about you. I guess I was wrong."

It hurts to hear him say it. "And if you'd been right? What then?"

For a long moment he watches her. "Things might have been different."

"Different?" In frustration she slaps the arms of her chair. "I don't know what you're talking about.

"Yes, you do."

"Different how?" She has to know and at the same time is afraid to.

"Don't make me say it." His look changes as tension seems to drain out of him. "God, you look good."

She reaches to smooth her hair. "I look like hell, I was in bed."

He smiles, eyes closing. "I know."

She reaches out to take his hand and he clamps hers, eyes closed.

"Are you hurt bad?"

"It's a pain in the ass, but I'll live."

She laughs at him. Pain plain in his face, he plays the tough guy. He intertwines his fingers with hers, eyes open now and on her face. It's as sexual a feeling as any she's known. The force of it scares her. "I…should go."

He tightens his grip, "Not yet."

She sinks back, relieved to be able to justify staying and he pins her with his eyes. "Will you get out of it? out of the business?"

Feeling hunted, she looks away. "I can't."

The pressure of his hand increases. "You can."

She needs to be away from him, out of this room. "You don't know, you just don't know, okay?"

"What don't I know?"

She looks to the door, "Where's that nurse?"

He reels her in, drawing her close despite her attempt to pull away. "Tell me."

Feeling trapped, she faces him, trembling, "You want to know why? I'll tell you why," she says soto voce, afraid to wake the patient in the next bed. "I need the money!"

His face goes blank. "But your salary—"

"Is not enough."

In his face she sees growing enlightenment. "You mean for the treatments."

In bustles the nurse sweeping aside the curtain, metal loops rattling. "Need something to help us sleep, do we?"

Embarrassed, Ceridwen breaks free, backs away, "I'll wait for Jade downstairs." Outside, she passes Jade without breaking stride.

She hurries away down the corridor, whole body atremble.

She told him. Why did she tell him?

• • •

Downstairs she runs into the man she remembers having seen waiting in Night's car.

He seems to expect her. "Professor Lawrence, right? You and me got to talk."

"Why is that?"

He flashes a badge. "Because we do, that's why." He takes her elbow.

Resenting it, she jerks free. "Not unless you can give me a good reason."

His glare metamorphoses to smile of grudging respect. "Tough, huh? Good. The topic is our mutual friend. If you would be so good as to spare me a few moments of your valuable time I should be greatly in your debt. That better?"

She finds a couple vacant chairs in Emergency across from an obese woman with a swollen face. "Who are you?"

"I'm Night's partner. You here to see him?"

She looks away, disgust welling like bile. "No, I'm here to do a little drug pushing."

He laughs. "Hey, that's good. My Mama always said a sense of humor will get you through anything." His smile vanishes. "How is he?"

"He's okay. Jade's with him."

He nods.

"You're the friend in the car. You're INET, too?"

"Guessed that, huh? I guess it's no surprise, you must be smart to be a professor."

Hearing the contempt in his voice, she decides she's heard enough. "Look, I—"

"Then you're smart enough to know what he's risking by not taking you down."

She hesitates. "Suppose you tell me."

"He lied to me about you. That's what kind of a fool he is. That's how naive he is. He thinks he can change somebody like you."

A strange alloy of joy and anger spar in her stomach. "Finished?"

He sits back, "Sure, go ahead, go home and curl up with your charm boy. From what I've heard you deserve each other."

She rises.

He waves her on with long black fingers, "Go on, he's waiting." He punches air, clowning, "Probably doing a little work out right now, warming up for you."

She drops back into the chair, "You despise me, don't you?"

He smiles, chin on palm, "Damn right, I do."

Why does she care? "Because I sell?"

He straightens, leans close enough for her to smell his after shave, voice low, "Because you got Night to lie for you. Because you drove a wedge between me and my partner. Because you're ruining a good cop."

She looks away, world gone bleary, hating herself for her weakness. "I want to stop. Don't you think I want to?"

"Then do it."

Rabbit in a snare, her voice is a low hiss. "I can't."

The intensity of her words draws the attention of the woman across the aisle. In embarrassment, Ceridwen turns away.

He smiles, "You know how many times I've heard that? Hundreds, thousands, millions, maybe. And you know who from? From people down so low they got nothing left to lose. No families, no homes, no nothing. They're the ones I feel for, not you." He sits back, raises a hand, "Look at you. What's there to feel sorry for? So what if you've got a dick for a boyfriend? You've got it all. You shouldn't be anywhere near this business. Why are you?"

She opens her mouth to answer.

"And don't give me the line about how good it is for you compared to booze and tobacco, either. It's against the law. And let me tell you something else. You will lose that castle of yours. And your kids."

The second time she's heard this. The second strike of a trip hammer, it knocks the breath out of her. "Alex?"

"SCF will have her out of there so fast it'll make your head swim."

"I..." Fear prodding her, she stands, "I've got to go." She heads for the door.

"Sure, go on," he calls after her, "probably got some customers waiting on your doorstep right now."

• • •

The nurse, Night sends away with her pills. He doesn't want to sleep. He doesn't want to forget what a mess his life is. He wants to remember, to roll in it the way dogs roll in dung. He may not have long left as a cop, and he wants to savor every stinking minute.

The door opens again and he's glad to see Jade peek in. "She coming back?"

"I don't think so."

"Oh." She sits. "Feel sleepy yet?"

"Not yet. Thanks, though."

"I saw the nurse come in. They take time to work, I guess, huh?"

What a gift she is. He reaches out to take her hand. "Yeah, that's right."

She studies the floor. "I took my time getting the nurse so you could have a chance to talk."

He's not surprised. "Pretty sneaky, there, Booboo."

She looks up, "Did it help?"

Why can't she ask something easy? He sighs. "Don't know."

"Yes, you do, you just won't tell me."

"Smart kid."

She nods. "It's funny, you guys get along so good, and yet it doesn't seem like things ever work out."

He shakes his head, not trusting himself to speak. "You better go, kiddo. I'll be fine. They're just keeping me overnight. See you tomorrow."

She looks at him as if she's afraid to ask what's on her mind.

"Go ahead, ask."

"The person who shot you? What will happen to him?"

She doesn't know any easy ones, this kid. He should have figured that out by now. He wants to say this right. "Well, you see, Booboo…"

"Nothing's going to happen to him," Derek says from the door. "It already done happened. Your daddy took him out."

She looks up, eyes wide, "Took him out, you mean killed him?"

Goddamn him. Night strains to sit, gives up when his back spikes him, sinks back. "You ever knock?"

"Nobody knocks in here. Not even when you're buck naked." Derek drags over a chair from the other bed, legs scudding on tile. The man in bed A coughs. "Deader than a door. Seven in the kill zone. Your daddy's good. Not as good as me, but good."

Jade's eyes search his face. "You did, Dad, you really did?"

"I had no choice, Baby."

She squeezes his hand. "Wow." Her voice is breathy, solemn, awed.

"Now if it'd been me, I would have shot him before he'd got me, but your daddy's not as fast a draw as I am, or as good a shot, so that was the best he could do. Isn't that right, Big Daddy?"

"Kiss me goodbye, kiddo, it's late. Cer's waiting for you downstairs."

She hugs him long and hard. "I love you so much."

"I…" His throat is not cooperating. "I love you too."

When she's gone, he glares at Derek, "What did you tell her that for?"

"You don't want her to know?"

"She's a sensitive kid, for chrissake."

He leans back in the chair, lifts his hands, "Sensitive or not, the truth's the truth. You want her to find out by reading the paper? Did you see the look on her face? She was proud of her old man."

He saw and it makes him ashamed. He's not proud and he doesn't want her to be. "I wanted to tell her myself."

"Well excuse me all over the place." Derek props his feet up on the bed, "So, where's this leave us on the thing with your girlfriend?"

Where does it leave him with anything? It leaves him nowhere. "She's not my girlfriend."

"Whatever."

"Nothing's changed. It comes off."

"With your back?"

"I won't be wrestling her."

Slow smile. "I hear some sour grapes?"

Night ignores him. "It comes off."

Derek claps hands. "Hoping you'd say that. Everything's set for Saturday." For the first time, Derek looks directly at him, "So, you all right?"

"I'm peachy."

"Don't look it. Saw Ron on the way out. Looked worse than you. What happened?"

"Ask Ron."

Derek nods. "Thought so. You tell him he might want to look elsewhere for employment?"

"Something like that."

He notices Derek's expression. "What?"

"Nothing."

He's got something to say. He always does when he puts on that guess-who-just-ate-the-canary look. Night just wishes he'd say it. "Goddam it, what?"

"Ran into your significant other downstairs."

Night is too tired, too sore to argue nomenclature. "And…"

"Not too bad from up close." Night can see the smile start around the eyes. The old smile. The look that says they're partners. Despite it all, still partners. "You know, for a white woman."

"Get out of here before I climb out of this bed and kick your lilly-white ass."

"Anytime." The smile fades as he rises. "Maybe after it's all over… I mean, who knows?"

Night knows. No chance she'll ever speak two words to him after the bust. No chance at all. "Yeah, maybe."

Derek slaps a foot under thin covers, "Hey, could happen."

He likes that about Derek—that he has a sense of humor. "Yeah, sure. Now will you get the hell out of here? I'm going home in three hours. I want to get some sleep."

• • •

First light glows dull gray in the east as Ceridwen drives Jade home.

"What was Derek talking to you about?"

"About what I've been doing wrong in my life."

"That's all?"

She laughs and it comes out an exhale, "Big topic."

"About Daddy?"

Ceridwen's breath catches as she realizes what Jade means. "You know, of course you know." She feels so stupid. "Yes, about your dad."

Ceridwen can feel Jade forming her next question and anticipates it as she does a dentist's prodding.

"You like my dad, don't you?"

"Yes."

"Then, why—"

Gasoline on a hot griddle, her patience evaporates. "Things aren't that simple, that's why. They're complicated, they're hard. That's why."

She sees her draw back. "Oh."

Goddam it, what's wrong with her? "Jade…" She gives herself time to breathe. "I'm sorry."

"It's all right. I'm sorry I lied to you about him being a junk man. I wanted to tell. I only did it because he made me promise. I guess it's because you sell dope, huh?"

Ceridwen flinches. "I guess so." She uses the pause to brace herself for the next volley. A glance at her face in the light of a passing street lamp tells her it's on its way.

"Why do you do it?"

"Because I don't think it hurts anybody and I need the money."

"Would you want Alex to smoke it?"

Ceridwen thinks of the people she's known who smoke every day, who stink of it. "Of course not."

"Why not?"

"She's too young."

Terrier worrying rat, Jade won't let go. "What about when she's 18?"

"Stop it, will you? just stop it. I've got a lot to think about right now." Ceridwen nearly laughs, thinking how true are her words. More than true, understatement. She has too much to think about.

The rest of the drive they endure in silence, Ceridwen fighting the black certainty of ruin rising within her.

• • •

Night is home by noon.

In the kitchen he finds Ceridwen at the table, checkbook and bills arrayed before her. He is prepared for her to ignore him.

"You're home." Her eyes make it plain she's glad about it. She rises, hesitates. "You need to be in bed?"

"Not now."

Want to sit?"

He makes it to the counter, leans across it, easing his back, "This is good."

"Does it hurt?"

"It's the backache from hell."

She moves as if to touch him, then catches herself, sits. He wonders why she seems so nervous. "They dropped off your car last night. How'd you get here?"

"Derek."

"You should have called. I'd have come."

"Thought you'd be at work."

"I've got a few days before summer session."

He listens, hears nothing. "Where are the kids?"

"At your house, I think. They took the doll bag."

Remembering the play he eavesdropped, he laughs despite the pain. "I think we'd all be better off if we had a doll bag and somebody to playact with." He notices a chicken thawing in the sink. "Have any plans for this?"

"I haven't thought of anything, yet."

"Okay if I cook?"

"Now? with your back?"

"I'm okay. It's something to do…take my mind off it."

"If you want to, sure."

He takes down an iron skillet, glad to be busy, sets it on a low fire. "After that hospital breakfast, all I could think of was food. It's easier to get out of jail than it is that place." He takes a boning knife from the block. A few strokes with a steel and he parts out the bird.

She moans, head in hands.

"Sinus again?"

"No, it's nothing."

"I know that to a woman nothing means everything. I learned it young from my mother." He cracks several cloves of garlic, finds the olive oil, pours some into the pan to heat, braces his arms on the counter. "Look, my back is too sore to beat a confession out of you, and I forgot my sap in the trunk anyway. You going to tell me or not?"

"No," she says, voice barely more than a whisper. "It's my problem."

Fresh cut garlic watering his mouth, he nods, "None of my business. Got it."

She looks back, "No, no, no. I don't want to bore you with it."

The chicken spits and sizzles as he drops it with minced garlic in hot oil to brown. "Bore me. The way my life has been going I could use a little boredom."

She turns, "It's a small thing. Very unoriginal."

"So tell me."

She sighs. "I ran out of money before I ran out of month." Her laugh comes with breathy desperation. "Trite, huh?"

He doesn't get it. He raises his voice to be heard over spattering chicken, "My rent, your dealing, and your salary, how can you be broke? Tell me you're not a plastic junkie."

"No."

"You blew it on Lotto?"

She exhales through an open mouth. "It's Jeff's." She rises to pace. "From before the divorce. I signed an agreement saying that along with taking title to the house I would be responsible for all debts. It was dumb, I know, but I didn't have any idea how much there was. Now, I can't even make the minimum payments, not and pay the power and sewer, and buy gas for the car and food, and…oh, God!" She drops her head. "I'm drowning."

He turns the chicken. "They were his cards? In his name?"

She nods. "He bought gifts, meals, motels, even a down payment on a car. Now I get to pay for it all."

She rises to pace. Watching her, he sees a caged leopard.

"I'll have to get another loan on the house—if they'll give me one. There's no other way."

He thinks as he adds pineapple juice, wine mustard, tarragon. She comes to snoop, "Whatever it is, it smells good."

"Trust Jade to watch Alexis for an hour?"

She looks up, curious. "Yeah, why?"

"There's someone I want you to see." He covers the pan, turns the fire down low. "Let's go. This has to simmer an hour. You'll need a copy of the agreement. Get it and I'll call to make sure he's home."

• • •

Ray answers the door in his robe.

"Jade's not here." He laughs, strikes palm against forehead. "What am I saying? You know that."

Behind Ray, the ball game blares.

"This how you shysters make your millions?"

Ray's eyes rove over Ceridwen. "Court's canceled. Judges get sick, too. Thought I'd do some research."

"So I hear. Watching the game with a law book on your lap is worth two-fifty an hour, now?"

He closes the door behind them. "Five hundred, come on in, I've got Sunday's game on tape. Your friend take a beer?"

Night introduces them and she offers her hand.

"My friend's got a problem."

Ray blanks the screen, takes her hand, holds it, "Your taste in friends is improving. Sorry Rita's out, she'd want to meet you." Reluctantly, it seems to Night, he lets go her hand, falls back onto the couch, props slippered feet on inch thick plate glass.

"What's so important you interrupt my research?"

She hands Ray the agreement, and he fishes bifocals out of his robe pocket, reads, motions them to sit.

In a living room with a ceiling twenty feet high, they watch him read. Night has always wondered how they change the bulbs.

"Uh, huh. Uh, huh. Oh, that's great." He chuckles. "Oh, marvelous." He peers up at them over his glasses, looking a Benjamin Franklin with out of place toupee. The paper he taps with a nail. "They saw you coming, this is really a beaut. Rita should see this! She'd get a kick out of it. So you agreed to pay off all your ex's debts so you could get the house." Ray says this as if it were a great joke. Noticing their eyes on the top of his head, he reaches up, flings off the toupee, "Rita insists I wear the damned thing."

Night meets Ceridwen's eye, sees her suppress a smile.

"So what do you think, Ray, anything she can do?"

"I'll tell you what you can do—don't pay." He snarls, disgusted, tosses the document onto the table as if it were junk mail. "The agreement's invalid, unenforceable. They're his debts. You're divorced. How can they force you to pay them? They can't. It's the oldest, dirtiest trick in the book." He runs a hand over a bald pate. "I assume you saved money by not hiring an attorney?"

She nods.

"Your first mistake. Hey, I know we're evil, but we're a necessary one. And you've been paying these debts, whatever they are?"

She nods. "Two years."

"Don't pay another nickel. I'll write him and his attorney tomorrow to let them know you're done being a patsy. I'll have Rita file legal notice in the *Guard*." He picks up a dictating recorder, scoops up the agreement. "Okay if I keep this?"

She nods.

Into the recorder he mumbles, leafing through the agreement. When he has finished, he sets it aside, levels a finger at Ceridwen. "Not another cent, you understand? If it doesn't have your name on it, mark it return to sender." He walks them to the door. "I'll take care of it tomorrow, send you a copy along with your originals."

Again she offers her hand. "Thanks, Ray. I don't believe it, but thanks. Send me the bill, okay?"

He laughs. "Don't worry about it. Night's family." He clamps a big hand on Night's shoulder, "Night's going to frame me my new gazebo, aren't you, Night, old buddy."

Night can't dislike anybody that direct. "I am?"

"Sure you are, thought I told you."

"Send the plans over with Jade. I've got next weekend off. Materials be here?"

"Waiting back there now. Hey, you guys want to catch the end of the game? It's a close one. I've got Oregon ale in the fridge." Seeing their hesitation he opens the door. "Of course you don't. Now remember, not another cent. And kiss Jade for me."

• • •

On the ride back, Ceridwen stares numbly out the windshield.

So much has happened so quickly. "I can't believe it." She looks at Night. "It's really over?"

"Looks that way."

Suddenly she thinks of something and reels, feeling rich. "I didn't mail the checks yet."

"Good timing."

They pull up outside the house and he kills the engine. Neither of them makes a move to get out. The Lincoln ticks as it cools.

"I want to pay you what I owe you for those washer parts."

"Sure."

It is maddening the way he gives in and doesn't really budge at all. "I mean it."

"I'll find the receipt, I've got it somewhere."

She doesn't buy it. "And now this." How does she repay him for this? Impossible.

He faces her, one arm on the wheel, one on the back of the seat. "I didn't do anything."

She watches him, thinks she sees sadness. "You are the strangest person I've ever known. You keep doing things for me—for us—why?"

He throws open his door. "Let's walk, you want to do that, you want to walk?"

"You don't need to lie down?"

"No." He gets out, careful about how he moves, "I need a walk. It helps."

They walk up Villard to Fairmount as it meanders under drooping oak and maple before quiet homes. Night savors what may be their last time together. After the warrant service she'll want nothing more to do with him.

Cresting the hill in silence, he spots a pair of gray squirrels on an expanse of sloping lawn and reaches out to alert her. Larger sprints after smaller, who waits coyly for her pursuer. Night whispers in her ear, "Catch that come-hither look?"

"A don't-you-dare look is what that is."

The male leaps to clasp her from behind.

"There he goes misinterpreting."

"Typical male."

Night watches as the female disengages, bounds up a leaning big leaf maple. "Now what's that about?"

"Regained her senses."

"Guess not, she's waiting."

"Run, you fool," she says. "Now, while you can."

"Too late."

She sighs, "So much heartache just to insure the exchange of genetic material. There must be an easier way."

"Name one."

She cants her head, "How about a lottery."

Night doesn't follow. "A lottery?"

"Yeah, everybody sends in a sample of DNA and the postal service sends them back out in random distribution."

He can't help grinning, "The postal service?"

"Why not? Think of all the misunderstandings, all the hurt feelings, all the cruelty we could sidestep."

"I'll stick with what I know. Thanks anyway."

She laughs under her breath. "That was fast."

"Exceptionally high strung mammals, squirrels."

She gives him a cynical look. "Irksome personal experience has revealed the contrary."

Understanding, Night suppresses a smile. "You're associating with the wrong mammals."

They move on, Night following the pair's overhead retreat. "And there they go, hunting for a cheap studio."

"Oh, sure, he stays with her now. What about when there are six mewling little bundles of joy in a cramped little hole with no bath high over the street. What then?"

"Maybe he's smart enough to hang around, bring home the nuts, spend nights spooning mama squirrel."

"And maybe not."

The rest of the block they walk in silence.

She is first to speak. "What's it like being a narc?"

He should have known it was coming. Next come the jokes about doughnuts. "It's a job."

"That's all it is, a job?"

"No." He doesn't mind telling her. "It's more than that. It's a chance to clean up some of the mess out there, to fight for truth, justice, and the American way."

She gives him an austere look. "Don't make fun. You're serious about it, aren't you."

He reaches back to massage his lower back, wishing he'd brought the Vicoden with him. It is beginning to get bad. "Yeah. I'm serious."

"You ever question what you do?"

Easy answer—used to be anyway. Recently he's not so sure. "Never."

Her face drops. He can tell this isn't the answer she hoped for. "Oh."

He doesn't know if he can make her understand, but he can try. "Look, every dealer isn't a college professor. They're not all like you. As a matter of fact I've never met one anywhere close. Most of them are smart enough to play the game, but not all. Out there you spend your time debating pros and cons of drug legalization and you'll get popped. I leave laws to politicians. I'm a grunt. I do what I have to. The other night I ran across a thirty-year-old Salvadorian dealer from L.A. with a 14-year-old girl. He had everything—scale, baggies, all of it. Everything but the dope."

He has her attention.

"The girl's panty hose were wadded in a ball on the floor of the car. We knew where the dope was."

She looks at him, eyes narrowed. "You mean…"

"Yeah. Him we took in. Her we cut loose. Did we do any good?" He shakes his head, the hopelessness of that night rushing back. "She's probably with him right now."

"And did you ever ask yourself—if he couldn't make any money selling the stuff, would she be with him?"

He feels his heart take off. "I'm through arguing legalization. For all I know your interpretation of the facts is right and we've all been fed a pack of lies. I'm not a scientist. Right now, I don't care if it's the greatest thing since tofu. It's against the law. You think it's so great, then change it."

"We can't. There's too much stacked against us. Everybody—CIA, cartels, politicians, police, DEA, prisons—they'd all lose money. So what happens? They feed distorted data to a lazy and gullible media who regurgitate it on command. This to scare us into giving them another twenty billion to keep the carnival on the road for another year."

"Look…" He stops, "I give up. You may be right, I don't know. I just do my job, okay, that's all I do. I don't pretend to be able to argue with you intelligently. I may be a dupe, me and a lot of other decent cops, but don't assume we're part of some conspiracy, okay? We're not. They legalize tomorrow, I'll go back to patrol in a New York minute. I don't do this for kicks. I do it because it's what the law says. The law—you know, the rules we're all supposed to live by."

"I get the point."

"Good, that's good." He walks on and she says to his back, "That doesn't mean it's always right."

He turns on her. "No, it doesn't, but I'll tell you what it does mean. It means that you defy it you'd better be ready to pay the price." Suddenly they're not talking in the abstract any more. He can see in her eyes she understands. "Are you?"

She doesn't answer. The walk home they pass in silence. At the house they find the girls in the pool.

She stops him at the gate, "Look, can we agree to disagree?"

With the raid two days away, Night doesn't see it much matters what they do. "Why not?"

She offers her hand. "Truce?"

As he takes it he fights off the urge to warn her, to give it all away, to betray Derek a second time. That he can feel it repulses him. "Truce."

They go in and the girls swarm him.

"You're back!" Alex runs small hands carefully over his spine. "I don't feel any holes."

Jade makes a face, "Of course there aren't. He was wearing his vest."

"You mean the bullets bounce off, just like Superman?"

"Not quite. You don't want bullets bouncing around where they could hit somebody. You want them to stick."

She frowns. "Like a mouse on a glue trap?"

"Yeah, like that."

"Can I see one?"

"I'll bring you one."

"Neat!" And off she runs.

After dinner they swim alone. The pool is calm. In his suit, he sits on the second step, water pleasantly warm in an evening already turning chill.

Ceridwen reaches out to examine his back, "My God, you're bruised. I never knew getting shot with a vest on bruised you so bad. You never hear that. Somehow you always just assume it's like wearing a raincoat in the rain. She runs cold fingers lightly over his back. "They look like someone hit you."

"Someone did." With three hollow points traveling at over 1400 feet per second. If the timing had been different, if he hadn't been on his way to a raid and wearing his vest… "The doc says I may have to have a skin graft."

"A graft, why?"

He reaches back to find the spot, guides her hand. "There. Right there."

"The dark spot?"

"Skin's dead. I can't feel your fingers."

"My God, I thought the vest protected you."

"Oh, it does. But it's still about like getting hit by a fast ball, so they say." He slips into the water. "I can't sit too long. Let's swim."

She holds back. "Can you?"

He won't know until he tries. "Sure, come on."

The first laps come hard. Back bothering him, he drags, finally struggling to hold position half a lap behind her. No talk. No wind to spare for it.

He trails at the lip of her wake, stretching out his bad elbow, ache in his back nagging. Seventeen laps later he crosses to the side, winded, resting forehead against stone. Nearly dark, he closes his eyes, letting sloshing water lull him relaxed.

Behind him he feels her. Cool hands press against his chest. Bare skin glides against his back. An electric tingle passes through him as he realizes she's ditched her suit.

"Am I hurting you?"

More than she knows. "I'm fine. What are you doing?"

"What I've wanted to do for a long time."

He turns and she wraps herself around him. He touches her, that's it—game over. His hands he keeps on rock. It's the only chance he's got. His throat burns like he's bolted a tenth of Scotch. "Put your suit on." He has trouble breathing. "Put it on."

Her eyes go stark with hurt and she pushes away to pull herself out. She snatches up her towel and, without a word, runs in, bare feet slapping. Night looks up at the house. How much will Linda get for it? Fifteen grand is his guess. All of which will go right back into her veins, her lungs, her nose. Ceridwen loses her home. The department gets her car, her house. Linda her commission. Everything tied up in a neat parcel. It makes a convoluted sort of sense. And what does he get?

Exhausted by the effort at self control, he basks in the miserable comfort of denial.

It's a dry pleasure—dry and hard.

Nothing like the feel of her body against his.

But it's what he's got.

It's all he's got.

FOUR

Lying abed, Night hears the rumble of a Mustang in need of a muffler pull up outside.

Sensing disaster, he rises, glances at the clock, sees it is not yet seven, slips into jeans and a pullover. The cement of the walk is cold against his bare feet as he goes to meet an overawed Sam. "Hey."

She gazes open-mouthed at drooping oaks and the house beyond. "You live here?"

"You're early."

"Am I?" She lifts a hand to gawk at a watch on the inside of a painfully delicate wrist. "Oh, god, I'm sorry, I can come back. I've got a class at ten is all, and I thought…"

He takes her hand, finds it icy, leads her up to the house, chafing it between his. "It's all right, come on in, have some breakfast." He bends to look into her face, "You look tired."

"I look like the dead, is what I look like. Been up all night studying this crap and I still don't get it."

"Christ, Sam, you're shaking like a leaf," A thought hits him, scalding his stomach.

"I'm clean," she says, offended. If he knows her at all she's telling the truth. "Goddam it, Night, you don't trust me?"

"I trust you," he says, drawing her in under his arm, "I trust everybody, and I count the money. Come on."

She stops dead, twisting free. "If you regret telling me to come, say so. I know what I am. I know what I look like. You got something good going here, I won't screw it up for you."

He sighs, guilt coiling in his stomach. "Sam, will you stop it? Come on in, meet the professor."

She holds back, "You sure?"

He looks her over. Blonde with boyish hips in worn-through jeans and sweater three sizes too big. What will Ceridwen think? He knows exactly what she'll think. And she'll be wrong. Mostly anyway. "I'm sure. Come on in."

She allows him to lead her. "What are you doing in a joint like this?"

"I rent a room."

At the door she hesitates, eyes wide, "Sure your professor wants to be bothered tutoring an air head like me?"

He can't help smiling at her. So naive and so worldly, this child he pulled from the brink, tried to love and failed. "I'm sure. Now will you get in here?"

• • •

Amazed, Ceridwen watches Night usher a blond in the front door.

Feeling herself clench up, she opens the waffle iron, "First one up, Alex!"

Night follows her in, "Where's Jade?"

Ceridwen shrugs, "Not up yet."

[148]

"I'll get her." At the door he turns, "Cer, this is Sam. Be right back."

Sam alights on a kitchen chair as if it's made of spun sugar. Ceridwen senses her unease, and despite her hostility feels a surge of compassion. What if she is his squeeze? She's just a kid, she'd guess her at half Night's age.

"You the cook?"

Ceridwen smiles, drizzling batter over a hot waffle grid, "Chief cook and bottle washer, maid, chauffeur—that's me."

Sam sighs with relief, "What kind of guy is this professor, anyway?"

Ceridwen adds to the batter, measuring flour, "She's not."

Sam wrinkles her nose, "The prof's a she?"

Ceridwen is enjoying this. "Why shouldn't she be?"

Sam shrugs, "No reason, I guess. Crabby old bag, I bet, huh?"

Ceridwen measures baking powder, conscious of Sam's eyes on her. "Can be."

Sam nods knowingly, "Thought so. Smart people…" she wrinkles a freckled nose. "Hard to get along with." She brays, "Guess that's why I'm so easy."

Ceridwen smiles with her, wishing her easier to dislike. Looking down, she notices the light has gone out on the iron. "Looks like this one's yours. Want milk with it?"

"If you've got no-fat." She laughs, pats a flat stomach, "Got to watch it."

Ceridwen looks her over, shakes her head as she fetches the milk. Was she ever that silly—or that thin? "I'll just bet you do."

"I do, really, especially in my line of work. You should have seen me at sixteen." There's that goofy laugh again. "I was the Goodyear Blimp."

Ceridwen smiles, unable to picture the freckled sprite as anything but anorexic. "What is it you do?" She thinks fitness trainer or aerobics instructor. Something that doesn't demand too much education.

"I dance at The Squire." She says it as if she's proud.

Ceridwen has heard of it, passed it on her way downtown, wondered what sort of woman would dance nude in front of a room full of strange men. Now she knows. "Like it?"

Sam shrugs, "Not so much any more."

Fascinated, Ceridwen sits, chin propped on her hand, unwilling to feel the smallest tinge of disappointment. So this is the kind of woman Night wants. What kind of jerk dates a child half his age, whatever she does for a living? A burning kindles in the pit of her stomach. What gall to bring his stripper honey here, to her home, to Alex's home. "Oh? Why's that?"

"I'm tired all the time. I get up at six to go to school, then dance from ten to one."

"School?"

"Yeah." She sighs. "Lane Community College."

This she hadn't expected. "What are you studying?"

Sam kicks a bare foot, chases her sandal around with a pink toenail. "Nursing. Halfway done and it seems like I've been doing it forever."

Ceridwen is curious despite herself. "Why nursing?"

"Well…" Sam stuffs a bite into her mouth and syrup traces a path down her chin. She wipes it away with a finger, sucks it off, finger smacking, smiles like a kid. Ceridwen finds herself clenching her teeth. Night really is slime, using a girl this young, this dumb.

"I always wanted to be a nurse ever since my mother was sick when I was five. That a hoot or what? Me a nurse, can you see that?" She lifts the syrup jug. "This is good, but it don't taste right. What is it?"

"It's maple."

"Tastes different, watered down or something."

"That's because it's the real thing."

Sam frowns, "Real? What have I been eating all my life?"

"Corn syrup, flavorings, preservatives."

She raises a lip. "Yuk, then what's this?

Ceridwen is enjoying this. "Tree sap."

"Huh?"

"Boiled down forty to one, the sap of the sugar maple tree."

Sam squints at the jug and Ceridwen guesses she needs glasses to read. How perfect. She would. She doesn't feel jealous any more. A little sorry for her is all. Sorry for Night, too, that this is who he would pick.

"Sap, huh? Sounds sick." She pushes the plate away. "You get a deal on it or something? Most people want real maple syrup. You could get in trouble if that crabapple professor catches you serving her sap instead of syrup. Ever think of that?"

Ceridwen hides a smile behind her hand. "I'll be careful. Want another waffle, plain this time?"

"Okay, sure." Sam looks the room over.

Ceridwen stands over the iron, waiting for the light to wink out, "Need something?"

"A cigarette is what I need, but Night made me promise not to smoke. I'm climbing the walls."

Doggedly, unwilling to pass up the chance to hear more, Ceridwen brings her back, "How did you two meet?"

"Night and me? I always crack up when I think about it. Couple years ago—"

She's interrupted by Alex and Jade crashing into chairs at the table.

Alex peers through drooping eyes. "Who are you?"

"I'm Sam. Who are you?"

"I'm Alex and that's Jade."

"I know Jade. Are you the professor's daughter?"

Alex looks at her mother, frowns, looks back at Sam as Ceridwen slides a plate in front of her. "Yeah."

Alex drizzles on syrup and Sam leans close, "I wouldn't do that."

"Why not?"

Sam whispers. "It's sap."

"So? It's good."

"If you say so. But aren't you afraid you'll sprout buds or something?"

Alex smiles, looks up at her mother, "She's funny." Then to Sam, "You're funny."

Night comes in, pours milk for the girls.

"I'm not so sure we ought to be doing this," Sam tells him.

Ceridwen looks up from the iron, curious, "Doing what?"

Night groans, presses his eyes with thumb and forefinger. "Dammit, I forgot to ask."

"Don't cuss!" Alex says.

"Sorry."

"Night!" Sam says, slamming down her fork. "You mean she doesn't even know I'm here?"

He looks to Ceridwen. "Look—I meant to ask—Sam's having trouble in biology and I told her you might be willing to help her out. What do you say?"

Now it dawns on Ceridwen what he wants. Oh, he is a prince. Now she can pay him back for his help by tutoring his sweet thing. She slams the waffle iron closed, sets the batter bowl in the sink, fires him a look that Sam can't see. She won't do it. She looks at Sam, sees the eyes of a deer ready to bolt. She dishes the last waffle, sets it in front of Jade. As she does the anger drops from her and she deflates with a sigh. "My first meeting isn't 'til ten. I've got an hour."

She notices Sam staring as she dries her hands on a dishtowel and feels guilty for the satisfaction it gives her.

Tentatively, Sam rises. "I better go."

Hands on her shoulders, Night presses her down. "You'll be okay. Come on, girls, get your stuff, Rita's waiting. See you, later, Sam. Thanks for this, Cer."

Alone in a kitchen suddenly silent they sit across the table from one another. Seeing her discomfort, Ceridwen smiles. "So here we are, the crabby professor and the stripper."

Sam closes her eyes, head in her hands, "Oh, God, I'm such a dupe." She rises, gathers her books. "I'm sorry, I really am. I better get going."

"Will you sit down? Don't worry about it." Ceridwen is beginning to like her. "I'm the jerk, I should have said. It was rude not to."

"I just assumed somebody who lived in a place like this would have a cook. It's just like a castle, you know that? Oh," she sighs, "there I go again, of course you know, you live here."

Ceridwen reaches out to press her hand, "Relax, okay?"

"But, you're Night's friend, I don't want to ball things up for him. He's been good to me."

She is sure he has, the bum. "You won't."

"Oh, yes, I will." To Ceridwen's astonishment, tears well in her eyes. "I always do. And Night...he's just about the best friend I've got."

Ceridwen can imagine what a good friend he is. "Is he?"

She nods, "He's the one started me going to LCC, started me on my way to being a nurse. He's the one kicks my butt and keeps me going when I want to quit."

Ceridwen watches her, stomach roiling. For him to take advantage of a girl this naive.... How she could ever have thought he was decent is beyond her. "He's a great guy, all right."

Straight faced, through running mascara, Sam nods. "He is. Did you know that when he busted me, he's the one pulled strings to get me a place in detox? There was a line four states long, but he got me in. I thought I was dying. And when I was puking and shaking and down to eighty-five pounds, he came to see me every day. He was the only one who did. I didn't get why."

Ceridwen does. Wanting to tell her to shut up, she clears dishes. "Did he?"

"Yeah, and you know what else? When the manager at the Squire started handling me, Night had a talk with him."

Ceridwen scrubs dried batter off plastic with her thumbnail. She might just puke. "How very decent of him."

"Night can be pretty persuasive when he wants to be. Comes from being a cop, I guess, huh?"

Ceridwen slams plates in the washer. That she can agree with.

"Keep that up and you're bound to break something."

Ceridwen turns to see concern in her face and, arms braced on the sink, has to laugh. "You're right."

"I know what you're thinking and you're wrong. He's a friend, that's all he is. A real one. I've had a lot of the other kind." She looks over painted nails. "I know you don't believe me. Nobody does. They all think we've got something going, and I don't think either of us minds that too much. I'm always kidding him about it, but no. Uh, uh."

Ceridwen straightens her back, numbed by what she hears. "You're telling me you aren't an item?"

"A what?"

"A couple."

Sam brays, freckled nose wrinkled, "That's what I'm telling you. I know it seems strange. Anybody does that much for somebody you would think they wanted something, right? Not him. When he comes in the Squire I always come over, you know, dance for him. But he's so cute. He won't look up. It's like he's afraid of me or something." She laughs. "Me, imagine that. A guy like him afraid of me. That's a good one, isn't it?" Ceridwen thinks she says it a little sadly. "You sure you don't have to go?

"I'm sure, let's see what you're having trouble with."

Sam opens her book, then looks back at her, head tilted. "What about you?"

Ceridwen raises her guard, "What about me?"

"You like him, don't you?"

Suddenly she is uncomfortable. "I like him all right."

She appraises Ceridwen with a glance, "You're more his type, yeah, I'll bet he likes you." She slaps her knee, "Now isn't that just like him. He had to know what you'd think about me, about us, and he brings me in here." She laughs, "What a goof."

Thoroughly confused, Ceridwen points to the book, "We don't have much time. You want to go over this, we need to get started."

• • •

Derek waits for Night at a booth far from the door.

Night eases into the seat, careful of his back, waves at a waitress for coffee and a tall, bony woman lumbers over. Night watches the homemade tattoo of a cross on the web of her thumb as she pours. When she goes away he speaks. "Order yet?"

"Yeah." Derek gives him the once over. "You look like death warmed over."

Night adds sugar to his cup, "You're no prize yourself. What's on for today?"

"Sure you're up to this?"

The ache in his back is bad, but it won't stop him. The coffee is hot and strong and sweet enough to make his molars ache. "I'm sure."

Derek shrugs, "When will you have that affidavit?"

The words sting. "Today, I'll finish it today."

"Got it on the board for tomorrow night. You be ready?"

Will he be ready to deconstruct four lives? "I'll be ready."

Derek nods, smiles, "That's what I like to hear." He punches him playfully in the shoulder, "Hey, you know it isn't exactly like you're Bogart in the *The Maltese Falcon*. She won't be going away for twenty years."

Night knows he is right. With no record she won't do time. Maybe a fine.

"Spade got to strip search her before he sent her up the river." Derek laughs. "Can't help you out there, but I'll bet Sam would be more than happy to stand in."

[152]

Night casts him a quick glance as he sips coffee. "That's over."

"Sure it is." Derek straightens, smile fading, "That professor's really got your goat, hasn't she?"

It's not that he doesn't want to tell him. It's that there is no reason to. By tomorrow there won't be anything to tell, anyway. "What'd I miss yesterday?"

"While you were at home with your feet up, we crime fighters were out here saving society from heinous evildoers and keeping the devil weed from rotting the brains of impressionable youtes."

Their eggs come and Night asks for a glass of skim. "Besides that, I mean."

"Compton left a message. Something about a crank lab out Alvadore way. He should be by any time."

Night's sorry to hear it. "The Compton whose last tip left two cops dead? He's been a busy boy."

"Hasn't he?"

"How's he come up with this stuff?"

"Damned if I know. Only place I ever see him is warming a stool in the Squire."

"He's a wonder, all right. So, what's the plan?"

"I've got the entry team on standby for tonight at ten. Compton was late…" He turns his wrist to see the time. "…fifteen minutes ago." Derek taps his nails on the counter in a vaguely military tattoo. "So, tell me, what's it like living with the foxy professor?"

Night doesn't want to talk about her. "We don't see much of each other."

"Oh, give me a break, your toothbrushes nestle side by side in tranquil domesticity, and you're telling me you never see her? Just tell me one thing, how's she look when she rolls out of bed in the morning? Like a sea hag, I'll bet, huh? Eyes all baggy, hair like a squirrel's nest, bony knees and varicose veins, am I right? Come on, tell me I'm right."

Night pictures her and his stomach burns as if he's just bolted his coffee. If only she did. "She's a mess, all right."

"That's what I thought." Derek nods at the door, "We've got company."

Compton takes a seat beside Night, raises a hand for the waitress, "Another one of whatever they got." Coffee he waves away. "So, how are things?"

"What you got for us?"

"Something you'll like." Compton slides over a paper folded to the size of a half dollar, glances apprehensively over his shoulder at the door.

Night follows his glance. "Tax man tailing you again?"

"Between them and some woman, there's always somebody on my ass. So, you guys ready for another big one?"

Night watches him, unamused. "Why didn't you say anything about the driver being a psycho?"

He holds up both hands, "I look like a shrink? How am I supposed to know? These dudes are crazy, man."

Night senses he is hiding something.

Derek unfolds the paper, "I've got an address here."

"Tonight's good. They'll be cooking. All there—three, four guys out of Portland. Cost me fifty bucks in whiskey sours to get that out of him. Which reminds me, you got a check for me? I got kids depend on me, you know."

"For what?" Night says. "All they ever going to get they got the night they were conceived."

Compton half rises off his stool, "What the hell's that supposed to mean?"

Derek clamps his shoulder. "Sit down." He does. "Ever send child support?"

"And have their mothers' boyfriends party it away? Hell, no. I visit them, take them stuff they can use, give it to them myself. Got to make sure it's something their mothers can't sell."

Night shakes his head, repulsed, "Your ex's sound like some classy female flesh,"

Compton chuckles, showing tar-stained teeth, "Picking good women's never been my strong point, if you get my drift."

Night turns his face away. Compton's breath is no better in the morning. No longer hungry, Night pushes away his plate.

"About that check…"

Derek slides an envelope across and Compton slips it off the table, glancing at the check inside, "Yeah, baby, come to papa."

"Nine percent of a quarter million, twenty-two, five," Derek says, looking disgusted.

Compton smiles, "What a country, huh?"

Night's curious. "How long did you work for that?"

Compton frowns, "What you mean how long? Guy I ran into at the Squire had a few too many and did some bragging to prove what a big man he was. How he was growing fifty plants in his garage. Wasn't no work."

Night looks at Derek, "Beautiful system, ain't it?"

Derek raises a hand to stop him. "I'm not going there."

Night points to the check, "How you cash that? You can't have a bank account, they'd seize it."

Compton stashes it in an inside pocket of his jacket. "Check cashing place over on Seventh."

"What do they stick you for?"

"Five points."

Derek makes an incredulous face, "A thousand bucks?"

Compton shrugs, "Cost of doing business, man."

Derek smiles, "Hey, partner, you're a highly paid professional law enforcement officer. How much you got on you? Maybe we can save him the trip."

Night feels his pockets, "Damn, left the wad at home. Next time."

Compton sneers, "Yeah, sure." With a final glance at the door, he slides out of the booth. "It's been swell."

"Hey," Derek says, "you got a short stack coming."

Compton backs away. "Don't eat breakfast. Already drank mine." He smiles, waves at the door. Night calls for a check, hands the girl his plate. "That is one worried maggot."

Derek frowns. "Worried? About what? I just handed him a check for more than we make in a month of Sundays."

"I don't know." Night shrugs, "Something on his mind."

A different waitress this time, little sprite with rings on each childlike finger, three in each ear and two in her nose brings Compton's order, "Where'd he go?"

"Had an appointment," Derek says. "We'll take it."

Compton gone, Night regains his appetite, takes a stick of bacon.

Mouth full, Derek says, "So, what do you think?"

"I don't like it. You notice he didn't ask when he'd get his cut of this one?"

"Or how much it would be? I noticed."

"That's got to be a first. My guess is he's not planning on being here to collect. What I want to know is—why not?"

"IRS could have a tail on him, hoping to snag the check before he can cash it."

Night doesn't think so. He waves over their waitress, "This milk is doing a pretty fair impression of cottage cheese."

"Is it gone off?" She takes it, goes to check the carton in the cold box, makes a face, disappears in the back.

"Teach you right for drinking that chalk water anyway. You ought to stick with good old all American homo like me."

She comes back, apologetic, crosses off the charge for his breakfast. "On the house."

In the car, Night tries to shrug off the sour taste in his mouth, "You notice his hands?"

Derek works at his teeth with a pick. "Shaking?"

"Like a tuning fork."

"That's par."

"He's bad scared."

"He better be," Derek says, "He isn't exactly in a triple A rated occupation."

"No, he was more nervous than usual."

Derek shrugs. "Whatever. Everybody has problems. We're on for tonight at ten. You coming?"

Night drives, unable to shake the feeling that something isn't right. His gut tells him there's a connection with the two officers gunned down on Willamette. If he can't name it, he can feel it.

And it feels wrong.

It feels very wrong.

He takes them onto the street. "I'll be there."

· · ·

On the way home, Night sees Jade roller blading down Franklin.

He whips over to pick her up, watches her in the rear view mirror as she skates for him. A guy in a Mercedes flashes past, gives him a dirty look for daring to exist. Night reaches to massage his sore back. When did it happen? When did the job become a chore? Did the job change, or did he?

She climbs in, breathless, "Hey, Dad, thanks for the ride."

He pulls back into traffic, turns off the main drag and up Villard. "Dangerous place to skate."

She gives him a look, "Dad, I'm twelve years old."

He looks at her, starts to tell her what a joke that is, wisely decides to clamp his jaw.

"You're acting funny, Dad. Something wrong?"

Wrong? What could be wrong? That the search tonight makes the back of his neck prickle with dread? That tomorrow he'll be serving a warrant on his own house? "No, babe, nothing's wrong, why?"

"I don't know. Are you and Alex's mom getting along?"

Getting along… An interesting choice of words. He doesn't get along with the dealers he busts. He doesn't try. "We're getting along fine."

"Did you tell her that you and Sam are only friends?"

Here it comes. Does this kid ever miss anything? "I didn't have time."

She frowns, disappointed, "Dad!"

"Hey, look, kiddo, I know what you and Alex scheme about, and I gave it my best shot, but you know sometimes things just don't work out."

"Yeah, but that doesn't mean you just ruin it. What's she supposed to think about Sam? You know what everybody thinks."

Guilt rises in his throat, bitter as bile. How do you tell your kid you're not Sir Gawain. How do you tell your daughter you're weak? that you make mistakes? that you do things you are ashamed of? "When you get to be my age, you don't have to care what everybody thinks."

Giving up, she sighs.

At home, Alex waits on the front lawn, cat on her lap. She greets them with a weary smile, "I'm hungry."

Night hunkers down, strokes the cat, "You mean you haven't raided the fridge yet? You're slipping, kid."

"I waited." She speaks slowly, as if half asleep. "Something smells good, what's for dinner?"

"Soup."

Her face crumples, "Soup?" Remembering, she rolls her eyes, "I mean, oh boy, soup!"

Night reaches out to smooth her hair, notices the blank look in her eyes, "Don't overdo it, kid. Come on in, you look like you could use some blood sugar. I'll pour you some OJ."

Ceridwen comes in as he ladles. "Something smells good." She follows her nose to the crock, peers at him, "You made this?" He opens his mouth to answer and she stops him with a raised hand, "Of course you did." She pours herself a glass of tea, "I don't know why I should be surprised. Sorry I was late, Alex, got tied up at a meeting.

"That's all right," Alex says, voice dull.

Night sets bowls of soup on the table, goes for spoons. Alex stands, chair skidding, and hurries out, leaving Jade at the table alone.

Ceridwen looks up from her mail. "Everything okay?"

Night shrugs, "Far as I know. She looked a little pale when we came home, said she hadn't eaten."

Ceridwen's glass hits the counter hard as she chases after her. Seeing her go Night feels a fool for not understanding sooner.

"Is she okay?" Jade asks.

"I don't know, Babe." He plants a kiss on the crown of her head, thankful for what he has. "I don't know."

• • •

Ceridwen finds her in the bathroom.

Worry gnawing her insides, she calls through the door, "Alex?"

Nothing.

"Alex, you okay?" She knows what it is. She knows precisely what it is. It's back. It's back and this time it'll kill her. Panic takes hold of her and shakes. "Alex!"

"What, mom? What?"

"Can I come in?"

"It's not locked."

She finds her sitting fully clothed on the toilet, bent over, hands hugging aching shins. Face wet with tears, she looks up, fearful, caught in the act. Ceridwen's fear confirmed, she slams the door behind her, panic surfacing as anger. "Dammit, you've been hiding it! How long have you had pain in your legs?"

Alex's eyes flash. "What difference does it make?"

"What difference? It makes a lot of difference. Don't you understand what this means?"

Alex speaks, face between her knees, voice dead, "More chemo."

"That's right. It means Sloan Kettering and high dose chemo, and cold antibodies—"

"And bone marrow harvest." Alex recites. "And hot antibodies and MIVG."

"That's right, and you've been hiding it. Are you out of your mind?" Ceridwen is yelling. Spurred by fear she can't stop. "Are you?"

Alex, small arms hugging herself, doubled over, face chalky, answers in a small voice. "I'm not doing it."

Stupidly, Ceridwen watches her in the mirror. What do you say when told up is down, darkness light? What answer is there? "What's that mean, you're not doing it?" The words feel foreign in her mouth.

Alex gives herself up to the pain as another wave washes over her. Moaning through clenched teeth, she endures it. When it subsides she answers. "You know what I mean."

Of course she does. They told her chemo was brutal on children. Brutal was only another word to her then. Hours of misery and sweat, terror and vomit had redefined it for her. The night she held Alex as she vomited her stomach lining into the toilet bowl had taught her brutal. "That's not your choice, Alex, you know that."

Alex bolts past her and down the hall. Ceridwen follows. "Alex!"

At her door she turns at bay, "What are you going to do, hold me down?"

Will she fight to keep everything she has in the world? "If that's what it takes, you bet I will."

Alex slides down the jam, surging brightness of pain slapping her down. In her voice is searing desperation. "So I don't get to decide. Who's decision is it, then, huh, whose? Yours?"

On her knees, Ceridwen reaches out. "Ally…"

Viciously, Alex shoves her hand away. "Why? Because you're my mother? Because if I die it'll mean you failed?"

Alex's words knock the breath out of her. Her hand swipes Alex across the face and instantly anger crystallizes to regret. Ceridwen knows she's made a mistake, done the one worst possible thing she might have.

Alex doesn't cry, doesn't flinch. "I won't take any more poison, I don't care what you say. You try and make me and I'll run away. I swear I will."

At the mention Ceridwen goes chill.

"I won't do it!" She screams loud enough to make Ceridwen jump.

In her eyes Ceridwen sees certainty, a self-confidence she wishes she felt herself. She feels suddenly exhausted, beaten. "You're willing to die to get your way?"

The cynicism in her child's eyes takes her breath. "I'm dying now, we both know that. No more pretending, all right? No more. I'm not stupid. Do you think I'm stupid?"

Ceridwen, weighed down by hopelessness, presses the heels of her hands to her eyes. She has lost—she knows that. "I don't think you're stupid. I've never thought that."

"You think I didn't talk to the kids at Doernbecher? You think I don't know what my chances are?"

Ceridwen shakes her head slowly. Inside her plumes respect for this pale girl, this stubborn, tough kid who has been on intimate terms with so much pain. She reaches to press a palm to Alex's cheek. "I'm sorry I hit you."

Storm blown, Alex looks dazed. "It's okay." Legs up, arms hugging them tightly to her, Alex rocks as she rides the ache to another crest. Holding her breath like a diver, she waits it out. Rising for a quick breath, she looks to her mother, face indignant, eyes tearing. "Mama, why aren't you hugging me?"

Laughing through a running nose, Ceridwen presses her face over Alex's heart, feels it against her cheek, hears it surge at her ear. The one heart in the world that is welded to hers, that anchors her in the world.

"Dear, God…"

Alex clamped hard in her arms, she speaks the words in her mind, not sure she knows how to pray, not even sure if that is what she intends.

"Dear God, please…"

• • •

Night drives to meet the team.

Humid and warm, a layer of cloud does little to cool things off after a rare June day topping out above the century mark. He reaches to his neck to tug at his vest and shrugs like a lizard shedding a skin to bring it down where it doesn't rub. That Alex was sick he knew, but that was all. To hear what he heard makes neuroblastoma more than a word. Alex's illness is one more factor in the equation, a factor he has not considered. Thank God Jade will be taking Alex with her tomorrow to Rita's. He doesn't want either of them there when the warrant is served.

Twilight settles fast under the layer of cloud as Night pulls into the parking lot. In the briefing room Hererra waits at the marker board. Jenaro stands, legs splayed by the window. Frank and Ron loll on the beat up couch. Sid and Jean straddle straight back chairs. Derek lies on the other couch. "Nice you could make it."

He dumps Derek's feet to the floor, drops into the couch. "Good thing I didn't miss anything important."

"As I was saying," Herrera continues, "this one will be a piece of cake." On the board is the house, showing doors, front and back. "Ron is new man on this one. Glad to have you along."

Night worries the nap of the couch with his nails. It has always irritated him the way Hererra talks as if it will be him going in when what he'll be doing is warming a chair in the office. Night glances at Ron, finds him busy taking notes. So he has decided to tough it out. Maybe he'll be okay.

"Jenaro is first man in, then Frank, Ron, Sid, Jean, then Night. Derek covers the back."

Derek's mouth falls wide. "Say, what? The back? This was our bust, now I'm out parking cars?"

"That's your assignment."

"Yeah, it stinks, too."

Night raises a hand. "You forget I'm number three?"

"I didn't forget." Herrera smiles, yellow teeth white against coffee skin. "You're late, you're last."

A slow burn ignites in his bowel. They are being spanked for not coming up with anything on Ceridwen. Night reaches up to tug the vest away from his throat, "Three years I been doing this and you put a newby in third? You nuts?"

Herrera's smile vanishes. "You're last in." He looks to Derek. "And you are watching the back." He tosses down his marker. "Now let's get to it."

The team filters out. Night stands to confront Herrera. He opens his mouth and Derek drops a hand on his shoulder, hustles him out. "Got it, we got it, don't we partner? We got it."

Outside Sid and Jenaro wait, barely keeping their faces straight. "Hey, man..." Jenaro clamps Night's shoulder with a big hand. "Things get too hot out there..." Here he comes close to losing it. "You call for backup, you hear me? We don't want any dead heroes."

Night pushes his hand away. "Yeah, yeah, get out of my way, I got a job to do."

This starts the big Mexican guffawing as they load into the van. Night rides packed into the back with the rest of the team. Derek sits up front. Jenaro drives.

It's hot and dark in the van, which has been sitting out in the sun all day. In his jacket and vest Night swelters.

Fifty yards from the farmhouse Jenaro pulls over and when the back doors open Night breathes in the cooling night air, heavy with the odors of summer night. He looks around him to see a house like any of hundreds amid rich hayfields on the west side of the Willamette Valley. If there is anybody within a mile he would be surprised.

"You sure this is the place?" Sid asks Jenaro.

"I'm sure."

About them crickets chirr. In a culvert under the road a frog sends out a tentative croak. Ron whispers as if hesitant to disturb the night. "Quiet."

Derek elbows him in the ribs, "I seen that movie. This is where I say, yeah, too quiet."

"Vacant's more like it." Frank yawns, stretches long arms. "We'll be falling all over each other in that cracker box."

Jenaro groans, cracking the action of his Remington to see brass. "I think your snitch is jacking us around on this one."

But for the unease coiling in the pit of his stomach, Night would agree. Ron passes, careful not to meet his eye, and Night feels a pang of empathy. "Do good, man," he calls to his receding back.

"Thanks."

Derek is last to cross. "Our bust and I'm stuck out here. Is this chicken or what?" He takes his arm. "I don't like it."

"I don't like it either. We should be going inside."

"No, I mean the way it feels."

"Aw, come on, don't start with that feeling stuff. Dr. Laura's very down on that. Let's get this over with."

Massaging the ache in his back, Night follows. The house waits, dark, silent. Nobody home. Nothing, no cars, no dog, no cooking smells, no garbage cans. If ever Night has seen a house with nobody home, this is it. Good.

Beside him, Derek trods lawn under an inch of water. "Damn! What's up with the pond? My feet getting wet. Damn!"

Night watches, listens—nothing. "Nobody home."

"You got that right. We been toyed with."

Beginning to doubt his intuition, Night's skin tingles with rising anger at Compton—and with relief—none of which he allows into his voice. "Sure looks that way."

On the porch the team waits, poised for entry.

Jenaro raises a hand impatiently, and Night steps up, nods to show he's ready."

Jenaro raises one finger, two, counting down. Just then comes a car, and he raises an open hand as a sign to wait for it to pass.

It slows.

Night watches as, incredibly, the car pulls up to stop behind the van. Impossible. No one knows where they are but Hererra and Compton. Blinded by headlight glare, Night can see nothing of the car. Jenaro signals to him to go check on it and, gun out, he moves as fast as the throbbing in his back will let him.

Gun at his thigh, he approaches from the passenger side, trigger finger crooked along the Glock's frame, dark his only cover. The driver's door opens just as he recognizes the car. "Cer?"

She runs to him. "Thank God I found you!" She wears shorts over a damp one piece. Holstering his pistol at his thigh, he puts her in the passenger side, ducks in after her, cuts the lights. "What are you doing here? You can't come to a warrant service. "

"I had to warn you."

Night scrabbles to catch up. "Warn me? How did you know where we were?"

"Sam called, frantic. She ran into Condon, Comdon, something...."

"Compton?"

"That's it, Compton, at the Squire. Bragging about screwing over INET. Promising you would be in the headlines tomorrow. Saying Sam could dance at your funeral."

In his chest fear blossoms, bears heavy fruit. He gropes for the door handle. "I've got to get back out there, go home."

She grabs him. "You can't."

He glances across the street, sees Jenaro raise a hand to signal ready. "Go home." He opens the door and she jumps astride him, locking arms around his neck, "I won't let you."

He tries to pry her off, but can do nothing without hurting her. Stymied, he sighs in frustration, "Cer, dammit! I've got to go, will you let me go? You'll get me fired, that what you want?"

He hears them bust the door without him, hears them yell "Police!" He's missed it. Straining his legs, he does his best to buck her. In her face he sees commitment. "Goddam it, will you get off of me?"

"I won't. I believe Sam, I believe what she said. I won't."

He understands it all, now. Why Compton didn't dicker about his percentage. There wouldn't be one. "Cer, you don't understand any of this. You can't believe what guys like Compton say. He's a zero."

Ceridwen has just opened her mouth to answer when inside firing explodes, a cacophony of drum rudiments. Under it all an ominously familiar sound that raises the hair on the back of Night's neck—the sibilant muffler sound of suppressed MP-5's. It's not a song you forget. The entry team's .40's and 12 gauges boom over the deadly hiss, then, much too quickly, fall silent.

"You see?" She lets him go. "You see?"

Sliding out from under her, he bolts through the dark across the road toward the farmhouse, Glock a toy in his hand. Only one reason the team is not firing back. They are down. In only a few seconds all of them are down. Clearing macadam, he sprints across wet lawn, boots slipping in muck. In the dark he slams into Derek and goes down sprawling, losing his gun. Derek grabs him. Night struggles to break free. "What are you doing?"

"Keeping you alive."

"We've got to get in there."

Now come single shots sounding like the burst of air from a released air coupling. In the near dark he finds Derek's eyes. In them he sees they share the same thought. No one on the team carries anything suppressed. That means one thing—they are passing out coups de grâce.

Jenaro.

Jean.

Frank.

Each time he hears the sound Night flinches as if it were he that takes the slug. Derek yanks him to his feet. "Let's go!"

Scooping his Glock out of muck, Night holds back.

Ron.

"Goddam it, let's go!"

"They're dying in there."

Sid.

"Not anymore, they're not." Derek drags him on, "We're next if you don't get your ass moving, now come on!"

The two of them cross the road as headlights wink on at the back of the house. On high beam, they turn, reach across the road, pinning them in blinding glare. The van catches the first burst just as they reach it. It lists on its springs as the front tire flattens. Night runs on to the Volvo, scrabbles up embankment gravel, pulls himself behind the wheel. As his hand contacts the key in the ignition, the side window shatters, turning glass to shrapnel. Ceridwen goes down across the seat and, unsure if she's been hit, he keeps her down with a hand on her head.

The back door slams as Derek dives in. "Go."

Night whips them around and away from 9mm swarming thick as hornets about them.

"Jesus Christ!" Derek says to nobody in particular from low in the back seat. Night hears him punch at his cellular. "This is King Seven on East Airport. Five officers down, shots fired, we need SWAT and ambulances out here."

Behind them, Night sees headlights pull onto the road. He guns it and as he watches the mirror, they stop, slew into a U, heading back the other way, taillights fading. On impulse he romps the brakes, whips around to follow.

Derek peeks over the seat. "What the hell you doing?"

"They're running."

"Let them run."

Ceridwen climbs up his thigh, "See? You see, now?"

He looks back at the road, finds the taillights gone. "I see. You all right?"

She is.

Warily, he pulls into the yard to see smoke billow. He slams it in park, bolts out the door, leaving it swinging. Halfway to the house Ceridwen jumps him, nails in his arms, dragging him back, "No, Night, no!"

A muffled ignition from inside the house and windows shatter inward as the fire draws oxygen. Inside a rising glow. Inside, the men he's worked with, depended on, lying unable to move as fire consumes them. Night drags her closer as whips of flame follow superheated volatiles out windows and up. "We've got to get them out."

"Night," Derek calls from the idling car.

Ceridwen's hands shackle him. "You can't help them."

"We can't leave them in there."

"Night!" Derek says, voice urgent as ball peen on anvil.

Night turns and headlights flare. He's been suckered. Ceridwen he propels ahead of him to the car. He slams the door, reaches for the gear lever and the windshield opaques. No sonic crack. No report. Only bullets impacting glass. It's eerie. As if someone on the roof smacks the window with a hammer.

Night slams the lever into drive and slews the car around on wet lawn. Derek fires. The wind captures the blast, funnels it inside the car, setting Night's ears ringing. Derek reloads, empties a second magazine at the glare. "Empty!" He must be yelling, but with the ringing in Night's ears he sounds tinny, far away.

Steering with his left hand as headlights gain in the mirror, Night digs in his jacket for two magazines, slaps them on the back of the seat where Derek grabs them. Night ducks under the high beams in the rear view mirror, trying to see the road. "Damn, those things are bright."

Derek seats a magazine, releases the slide, stripping a round, "Write them a ticket, they'll be here in a second."

A fast look in the mirror tells him it's true. Night floors the pedal and they widen their lead. The instant he's starting to feel happy about it the mirror goes black. Coasting, he watches tail lights wane for the second time.

Night pulls over, letting the engine idle, heart beating 150 somewhere near his throat. Cat and mouse. He reaches out to check Ceridwen on the seat, running a hand over her head, her hair, her neck, hoping to find her whole. "Okay?"

"The glass down my suit isn't very comfortable. Is it over?"

"Not yet. Derek?"

Facing rearward, he answers. "Those like any meth dealers you ever met?"

With gloved hands Night opens a hole in the windshield as Ceridwen watches.

"They were shooting at us, weren't they? They were trying to kill us."

Night reaches across her, strapping her in, feels her warm breath on his neck. "That they were."

She watches him, eyes wide, neck and arms glowing white in dash glow. "What are you doing? We're waiting for the police, aren't we? Aren't we waiting?"

Night pulls out onto the road in pursuit, milking the Volvo for everything it has.

"That's what I thought," Derek says.

"Be ready to lie down if I tell you."

She laughs breathlessly, a little hysterically. "You're such a romantic." She stops smiling. "You're kidding, right?"

"He better be," Derek says.

"I'm going after them."

"You can't."

"She's right, partner, we can't, not with her in the car."

Ceridwen turns to face Derek, "This is my car. You're not dumping me off. I'm not going anywhere."

"You don't mind?" Night asks her.

"Mind? Why should I mind? I think it's a great idea." She watches as the speedometer stutters up to seventy. "I do have one question, though. What do we do if we catch them?"

As they sweep past the burning house, Derek leans forward over the seat. "Good question, professor." And to Night, "Shouldn't we be securing the scene?"

The fleeing van turns right and Night blows through the intersection against the light to follow. "You remember what we all said when we talked about it? When we talked over what we wanted when we were dying? Whether we wanted somebody to stop and hold our hand our catch the bad guys? We all said the same thing. You remember what it was?"

"I remember, but—"

"Well, I'm going after them. That's what they wanted, that's what they're going to get."

Hair whipping her face through the blown out windshield,   C e r i d w e n takes the curves eyes locked on Night's face, hand in a vise grip on his thigh. "You're nuts, you do know that?"

Tires howl as he accelerates around a turn. Ceridwen hums involuntarily with fear, laughs when they clear the curve. "I didn't know my car could go this fast."

A second curve and he begins to wonder if he will have to have her hand surgically removed from the muscle of his thigh.

She yelps. "Stop sign."

He taps the brakes and on the perpendicular he glimpses the van waiting. Ceridwen's head he slams to his lap as headlights glare.

"Here we go." Derek says into his ear.

Rounds spark off the hood. Night romps the accelerator as bullets hammer like a mad tinker along fenders and trunk.

Derek yelps.

"What?" Night cranes his neck to look back and can see nothing.

From the back seat floor a groan in crescendo. "Shitshitshit!"

"What is it?"

"Caught one in the vest."

Night keeps their speed up, staying as low as he can. "That's the way we like it."

"Not this time." His voice is a breathy grunt. "Punched through."

A chill takes Night's spine in its fist. "It what?"

"I'm bleeding, man. It cut right through the goddam vest!"

Night hears him curse and hiss with frustration as he shrugs out of the vest. He winces, the pain all too easy to imagine. "Bad?"

"Ain't good."

The firing falls off and Night notices the engine missing. Ceridwen shakes her hair, ear cocked. "What's wrong? The car doesn't sound right."

"What you run in this thing?"

"Cheapest stop and rob I can get."

Night slaps the mirror to get the glare out of his face, plays with the accelerator. It doesn't help. Worry gnaws and he talks to the car, cajoling, "Come on, come on, don't die on me, now." Scanning the dash he notices the temperature gauge in red and understands. "They got the radiator."

Through the shattered back window, Ceridwen watches. "Here they come."

The engine convulses, sputtering.

"That's just great," Derek says, "I'm bleeding all over the upholstery and I've only got one magazine left. Can we call time out?"

"They won't come after us." Night says, hoping he's right. "They know we can outrun them."

Ceridwen laughs. "They think we can."

"Well?" Derek says from the seat, "Say something. They coming?"

Ceridwen watches, peeking over the back of the seat, "Yeah, no…wait…they're turning…they're going." She slumps, head lolling. "They're going."

Night pulls over, is amazed to find the dome light unbroken. The interior of the car looks like it's been worked over by a dozen gang bangers with ice picks. Foam bulges out so many holes in gray leather, he's amazed they weren't all hit. He leans over the seat back. "Let me see it."

Derek looks at him, pain in his eyes, "It's all right."

Night reaches back to open his jacket as Derek turns away, eyes shut tight. "Sure it is." In the brown skin of his shoulder just below the swell of clavicle he finds a hole the size of his little finger dark with clotted blood. On the back of his shoulder a dime-sized exit hole. Bleeding is not too bad, he is glad to see. "Damn!"

Derek opens one eye. "What? What do you see?"

"Danged if you don't bleed the same color as white folks. Went through, missed the bone. You are one lucky colored boy."

"Want it?" Derek grimaces, "You can have it."

"No thanks." Night searches the car for something to make a compress, is about to peel off his jacket when Ceridwen slips out of her shorts, shakes out glass, puts them warm into his hand.

Night presses it over the wound, "Take this and hang on."

Derek looks up, eyes wide. "Hang on? What do you mean, hang on?"

Night belts himself back in, kills the light, whips them back onto the road, Volvo lurching.

Ceridwen hugs her knees to her, "Night…"

"What you following them for, man? Let SWAT take over, we did our bit. Call in, man, come on."

Night concentrates on the road. "They are not getting away."

"They've got to be heading Beltline to 5," Derek says. "It's that or the airport."

Night notices the temp gauge pegged. How long before the engine freezes?

Derek sniffs, "What's that smell?"

"That's my car."

The tail lights turn right on old 99, then right again onto a side road. Lights off, engine knocking, Night follows. Two hundred yards ahead, he sees them. "There they are." He pulls over, cuts the engine.

"Where are we?" Derek asks.

"Culvert plant on old 99."

"What are they doing out here?" Ceridwen asks.

"Sitting."

"Don't make any sense." Derek's breath whistles through clenched teeth. "They want to be out of here."

From behind the wheel, Night watches, thinking. He should know what comes next. "Wait a minute." He turns to Derek. "What was that you said before?"

"About what?"

"About heading for Beltline."

"That they'd head for Beltline or the airport?" He moans, fighting the pain. "So I was wrong."

Ceridwen leans forward, points up into the night sky, "What's that?"

Night sees it, now. No airport for these soldiers—their ride comes to them. A spotlight, unbearably bright, stabs down. Night starts the car, forces the lever into reverse, cajoles the accelerator to keep it idling just in case they have to back away.

Ceridwen watches entranced, spot from above lighting her face, "A helicopter, now? Who are these guys?"

Night watches it drop. "That's what I want to know."

It sets down, the light winks out. Something tells Night it's time to move. He floors the accelerator and, sounding like a demolition derby junker, the Volvo revs on half its cylinders. Night backs them around a corner of chain link piled high with culvert just as a spot cuts the dark. Along the street the chopper sweeps toward them at treetop level.

"They see us, we're dog food," Derek says.

Ceridwen's neck clamped in his hand, Night pulls her down onto his lap and drops over her as it roars overhead and away.

The engine dies and the only sound is hissing and ticking from the block.

Ceridwen gapes. "Look at that!"

Night glances out as fire erupts from the windows of the van.   Night reaches back. "Still got the cellular?"

Derek speaks as if he's got enough to do to keep astride of the pain, "I don't know." He feels around the seat, passes it up.

Night tells the dispatcher where they are, asks for an ambulance.

"I don't need a goddam ambulance!"

Night slips the phone away. "For once in your life, do something the easy way."

Derek manages a grimace, "Look who's talking."

Ceridwen combs glass out of her hair with her fingers, "They burned their van. Why did they do that?"

A black and white, bar strobing, turns behind them, comes up fast. Night holds his badge out the window.

Derek breathes like a cross country runner. "It works, that's why."

Night thinks about that as they await the ambulance.

Pros ambush their team out in the middle of a hayfield and are spirited away. Why?

Nothing he has seen in twenty years as a cop gives him a clue.

The more he thinks about it, the less sense he makes of it.

• • •

They ride in the ambulance with Derek.

Left in a hallway Derek mumbles, drunk from loss of blood. Night sticks by him, flashes his badge whenever someone tries to split them up. Leaving somebody you care about in a hospital without someone to watch over them is some kind of dumb. He isn't about to.

When at last they get to him, Night lets himself be edged out, hovers just outside their reach. Once he's sure Derek won't be shunted to the side and forgotten, he heads out into the night and fresh air.

Ceridwen waits outside in the pool car left for him. On the seat she shivers in her one piece. Sliding in, he shrugs out of his coat, drapes it around her. "You okay?"

Her eyes are red. In the suit she looks incredibly frail. "How is he?"

He heads home. "He's all right. I'll check on him in the morning. Sorry about your car."

"It doesn't matter."

"Insured?"

"Ha. Just liability."

He was afraid of that. "It may take a while, but I'll replace it."

"No you won't."

"I will."

She watches him, face by turns revealed and hidden as they sweep under streetlights. She looks to him like she might be in shock. "I don't get it…" Her voice is breathy. "…how you can do that day after day."

He has to smile as he reaches to brush a bit of glass from her scalp. "It's not usually like that."

"Then I'm just lucky, huh?"

"We're both lucky."

Home at last, all he wants is a shower. He strips, piling clothes caked with mud and powdered glass. Under spray hot as he can stand, he sags, head hanging, eyes shut, hands flat against cold tile. Water hammers him, running in a stream off nose and chin. Breath coming ragged, he sees Jenaro, hand raised on the dark porch and can't breathe. Stomach cramping, he wraps his face in his arms.

The sound coming out of his mouth starts down in his gut and forces its way out through his lungs. Letting it go is painful. He does only because keeping it would hurt more.

He should have been there. He should have gone in. Jaw clamped shut, he howls into his forearm, smothering the sound, smothering the evidence of what he cannot stop under the sound of the shower. It lasts until he is empty. When there is no more he lets his arms fall leaden to his sides, presses his face to cold tile and works at breathing again.

The sliding door opens behind him and cold air strikes him in a frigid wave. Without looking he knows it's her and his heart stutters. Her skin is bone cold against him. She turns him to face her with icy hands. Eyes shut tight, he doesn't fight her.

Hair plastered to their heads, water courses between them, scalding, peppering. He opens his eyes and water floods his vision. She pulls his arms down and he lets her, knowing it can't last, this balancing on a knife edge, a wrenching magnetism held at bay. He can't stand it—it would kill him.

He clears his eyes by pinching them with his fingers and when he opens them sees her eyes on him. At the same instant each gropes for the other. Madly, blindly, frantically they slam together.

No room in his mind for guilt, for questions, for consequences.

No room for tomorrow.

Room only for now, for need.

• • •

Night reaches for her and comes up with cold sheet.

He finds her at the kitchen table, his tea waiting.

"Made you a cup."

He sits, unsure of what to say. "See that, thanks."

After last night he aches to talk. About anything, it doesn't matter what. Because it's something people do, something ordinary. "A lot happened last night."

She tosses the paper. "It made the front page."

He sips tea, letting it scald his tongue, glad for the pain, for the proof he's alive. He thinks of the shower and after. It should never have happened. It can't again. As soon as Derek's back on his feet he will serve her. He gave Derek his word, and he will keep it.

Her eyes get the look, the one he will think of when this is all over. It's a look raw as Sam's but with the cayenne of intellect. The combination is potent.

"We didn't get much of a chance to talk last night." She watches her hand on the table. "Not much. Want to?"

He wants to, needs to. But it's much too hard. The ache in his gut is not to share.

She moves to slosh her tea in the sink. "Forget it."

He traps her against the counter. Her hands hard against his chest hold them apart.

"Let me go."

"It's not easy."

She strains her neck turning away. "I understand, now can I go?"

"He pins her wrists to her sides, pulls her to him, "Dammit, Cer."

She turns away, exposing her neck. He presses his mouth to its heat, feels her pulse with his lips. The scent grabs him hard.

"I said let me go." No longer does she fight. He releases her wrists, presses her to him. "You were there. You know."

Hesitantly, her hands press his back. When she lets him go he fetches their cups. They lean on opposite counters regarding each other warily.

"That was a gutsy thing you did last night."

She looks at the floor, "I didn't do anything."

"If you hadn't driven out, Derek and I would have made seven."

"Sam seemed worried. I thought you should know, that's all."

Night watches her and remembers the feel of her, the smell of her, the urgency, the solemnity of their coupling. Wrong it may have been. That does nothing to devalue it. He thinks of Alex. "How is she?"

"Better." She watches him with worried eyes. "It comes and goes. I've got an appointment to get her some stronger pain meds."

It hits him like a sand bag. Will SCF take her? put her into a foster home? Will she die there?

This is what he is, now? This is what he does? Leading children to slaughter? He busts Ceridwen and Alex gets a death sentence? For what? To prop up a system hollow with decay?

Derek, he's got to see Derek. He sets down his cup, snatches up his jacket, heads for the door as if pursued. "I've got to go."

Under her puzzled glare he skulks out.

He ought to wear a bell.

Judas goats wear bells.

• • •

At Sacred Heart, Night finds Derek watching CNN.

"Hey, Buddy, 'bout time."

Same expression, same kewpie doll hair. It's good to see him. Night tosses him a paper bag. "Dare to keep cops off doughnuts."

Derek looks inside. "Jelly, cinnamon twists, buttermilk, and from the Hmong place downtown. I may cry. You shouldn't have."

Night reaches for the bag. "You're right."

Derek snatches it back. "Drop it, I may have to shoot you."

"Give me a twist."

Derek hands one over, takes a jelly for himself.

Night takes a bite, sets his on the table. "Didn't we just do this?"

"I liked last time better." Derek thumbs up the volume on the TV. "Seen this?"

"Eugene Miller, deputy director of the FBI, is in Portland, Oregon, today to address the Fraternal Order of Police, where he will call for passage of SB 3498, a bill written by senate Republicans granting sweeping new powers to drug enforcement agents in the war against drugs. He cites yesterday's deadly raid on a meth lab—as well as confiscation of five tons of cocaine and the recent shooting of two officers only a few days before—as ample proof of the need to get serious about the drug war."

A man's face fills the screen and Derek points. "Here he is."

"'Our agents are outgunned in the field by drug smugglers and drug peddlers. Yesterday, seven INET agents were killed in the line of duty. This comes on the heels of the shooting death of two patrolmen in a stop of a truck carrying more than a half billion dollars in cocaine. It's high time we get serious about getting drugs and guns off America's streets.'"

Night feels the world close in. Can he have heard right?

"The director also calls for defeat of Oregon's initiative 82 which would decriminalize possession of marijuana by adults. Though favored by more than two to one by Oregon voters, in the light of this week's tragedies in Oregon, Miller predicts 82's defeat in November. For CNN news, this is Erica—"

Derek switches it off, "Don't waste any time, do they?" He tosses the remote across the bed, "Vultures."

Still reeling, Night drops into a chair. Could Derek not have noticed? "You catch that?"

"What? I heard same as you did."

A buzzing tingle starts in the bottom of Night's spine, rises up his back, "How many agents did he say?"

Derek thinks, canting his head, "Seven?"

"That's what he said."

Derek frowns, "So? That's right. Five last night and two on Willamette."

"Nonono, he mentioned the two cops, he said seven from last night."

"So?" Derek shrugs. "He made a mistake."

"Did he?" The more he thinks about it, the less he likes it. "Why seven? Why not eight? Why not nine? Why seven? When every paper in the country says five, why seven? Why? Think about it."

Derek throws up hands, one of which is tethered by an IV drip. "I give up, why?"

"Maybe because the speech was written before it happened. Maybe because seven is how many of us were scheduled to go in with the entry team, and it wasn't in the plan to have any of us make it out."

Derek searches his face, waves him away, "Get out of here. Don't give me that conspiracy crap. You'll have me seeing KKK under the bed next. It's a mistake, that's all it is."

"If you say so."

Derek thinks. "How would they have known?"

Night says nothing. In Derek's eyes he sees his own thoughts mirrored.

"They would have had to look at the scheduling board," Derek says. "Or have somebody tell them what was on it."

There is nothing Night can say. Either possibility is unthinkable. Either means they've been sold out.

"You don't believe that."

"A year ago I wouldn't have." Needing air, he opens the window, takes a deep breath, turns back, leaning against the radiator.

"What are you saying, that now you do?"

"I'm not saying anything. So how you doing, anyway?"

"They're supposed to cut me loose tomorrow. That won't be soon enough for me. You tasted the food in here? Breakfast, lunch, dinner, main course, dessert—I swear they cook it all in the same pot."

Night smiles, knowing precisely what he means. "Julie been in?"

Derek's face lights up. "Here and gone, be back after work."

Night slaps his foot. "Well, then I guess you'll get by somehow, huh?"

"That I will. You caught any hell yet?"

Night shakes his head, "Haven't been in to see anybody."

"They track down that helicopter?"

"That my cue to laugh?" Night drops into a chair, toys with the I.V. drip, "What's this, MD 20-20?"

"I wish. Bug killer."

Night twines the tube between his fingers, thinking—about Ceridwen, about Alex, about what he wants to do, what he has to do.

Derek watches his face, "Can't do it, can you."

Night looks up, stunned. It's as if Derek has seen into his mind. "Can't do what?"

He laughs through gold teeth. "You know what. You think I can't read you like a DC comic?"

Night lets his head fall back against the back of the chair, eyes closed, relief flooding through him. It's been said. What he came to tell is in the open. "I thought I could. I can't"

"I knew it." Derek watches him speculatively, "She the one?"

He's asked himself that so many times and come up with nothing. "I don't know. I don't know anything anymore."

"Must be close, anyway. I've thought about it a lot the last few days."

"What?"

"If it were Julie, could I do it?"

Night waits for his answer. "Well?"

"No way."

Night's been dreading this part. Afraid to ask. Afraid not to. "What now?"

"Not up to me. I'm going to have to go to Herrera."

Night nods, heart leaden. So it's over. "I wanted to tell you where I stood. I'm glad I did."

For a moment neither speaks.

"She's got a kid, right?"

"A girl, Alex." Night debates whether to tell him, decides it can't make any difference now. "She's sick."

"Sick, what do you mean, sick?"

"Cancer."

"Christ."

"She's got her scheduled at Sloan Kettering in a couple weeks. SCF takes her now, it's a death sentence."

"Damn." Derek watches him, habitually jovial eyes turning grim.

"It's not your problem. I just needed to tell somebody."

Derek sighs, laughs, "And I'm the lucky one, huh?"

"Yeah."

"Tell you what, man, I'll tell Herrera we've got nothing. He goes after her or not is up to him, but it won't be us. Sound fair?"

Weighed down with a burden of gratitude, Night struggles to speak. "Can you live with that?"

Derek shrugs, "I'm a hero. The guy you better worry about is sitting in that chair."

Night looks inside, sees void. Every day he cares less whether or not he works the Net. Every day he spends more time wondering if he hasn't been a maggot long enough. Choice made, he feels only relief. Being fired from INET he can live with. Only now does he see what a swollen festering thing was his anxiety.

"Thanks, man."

• • •

Next morning.

A screaming Jade and Alex run to flop onto Night's bed and land on Ceridwen.

Looking embarrassed, but still giggling, Jade backs off, drawing Alex after her, "Sorry, we didn't know, sorry."

Nude, Ceridwen clings to him under the covers. From the way she sinks her talons in his arm he can guess her mortification. Night sits, pulls on a tee shirt. "Sit down, guys, we got to talk."

Under the covers, head in his lap, he can feel her shake her head frantically no.

Timidly they perch on the end of the bed, all eyes.

"Come out, Cer."

She sits, tightlipped, sheet wrapped tightly about her.

"Hi, Mom."

"Hi."

Night sighs. What do you say at a time like this?

"Dad, you don't have to say anything. We shouldn't have come in."

"Knocking is nice, but you're here, now, and I want you to know some things."

"This isn't going to be one of those talks, is it?" Alex says.

"No, it's not going to be one of those talks. Will you just listen?" He looks at Ceridwen and sees she will be no help. He takes her hand. "I want you girls to know that this is not fun and games." He looks at Alex and sees through the cynicism. "I want you to know, Alex, that I care very much about your mother."

Alex raises her eyebrows expectantly. "And?"

"And… she saved my life the other night. We're friends, we're good friends." Too far out on the limb to go on, he looks to Ceridwen for help.

"And…" Jade says.

"And," Ceridwen continues, "we want you to know that we care deeply about each other."

"Very deeply," Night echoes, feeling foolish. The girls nod expectantly, straining to draw him on. The problem is he has nowhere to go. "And…that's what we wanted you both to know."

Alex looks at Jade, shakes her head, disgusted. "Oh, that was such a good talk." She pushes herself to her feet. "That was so very reassuring, wasn't it, Jade?" She sighs, tugs Jade up and out. "Well, I'm having breakfast, now. See you. " They close the door behind them.

Night looks at Ceridwen and she starts to smile. He surprises himself by laughing. Then she starts. They laugh until their eyes water.

"God." He buries his head in his hands, face burning. "I didn't know what the hell to say."

"Neither did I." Her shoulders sag. "Oh, God, what a lousy mother I am."

He pulls her to him. "No, you're not. What you are is human and flawed and decent."

Her smile vanishes. "Flawed? what do you mean, flawed?"

The doorbell rings. Knowing well who it will be, neither moves.

Then again. Night can see in her face she's been dreading this. "It's for you."

She dives back under the covers. "No, it's not."

He snags her wrist, hauls her out. "Answer it."

She yanks away, "You."

He wraps her in her robe, tows her downstairs by the belt, her arguing all the way to the front door. "Open it."

It rings again and she waits, frozen. "I don't want to."

"Get it over with."

With a hateful look she flings the door wide. On the walk wait two students. At the curb their lowered car waits, sub-woofers rattling windows and the air in their lungs.

"Dr. Lawrence, we forgot our book in biology the other day and—"

"I don't have it."

"Sure you do, you remember—our book. I took this one by mistake."

"I don't have any book for you."

She reaches for the door and the largest steps in, stops the door with an arm and a foot, "Aren't you Dr. Lawrence?"

"Yes, I am, and I'm telling you I don't sell any more. Do you understand? I don't sell dope any more."

"Come on, Doc, you can make an exception for us, just this once."

Ceridwen struggles to shut the door. "Will you please let me close the door?"

"Sure, Doc, just as soon as you get my book. Here's yours."

"Goddammit, I told you! I flushed what I had."

Night motions her away from the door, flings it open, holds his ID in front of the kid's face, "INET, heard of it, Maggot?"

He looks up, face blanching, "You're a narc."

"You're here in ten seconds and you get a tour of Lane County Jail."

They back off, bolt down the walk. Their toy-wheeled car makes surprising time down the street.

He turns to see her looking at him with disgust. "That was subtle."

"Little late to worry about subtle, isn't it? Should get the word around, anyway." He throws the door to.

In the kitchen she sits, watches him make tea.

"I blew that upstairs, didn't I?"

She tries a smile, lets it go. "I wasn't any help."

He waits for the kettle, stomach clenched. "What could I say?"

"Don't worry about it. They'll survive."

In sweats and shorts, the girls gallop downstairs. When Ceridwen sees them, her mouth falls open, "Oh, no you don't."

Alex looks up, ready to fire back, then looks at Night, frustrated, "I can't argue, so what am I supposed to say?"

Night raises hands to keep them apart. "Didn't we already go through this? And didn't she survive?"

Ceridwen slams her teacup into the sink, making the girls jump and sending bits of crockery skittering across tile, "She's scheduled to start treatment in New York in two weeks and I won't have her throwing herself around on a hard gym floor where she could break something."

"Oh, sure," Alex says, sneering, "tumbling is too dangerous, but drinking poison's okay?"

Eyes deadly, Ceridwen levels a finger. "Don't you even start."

Night moves between them. He leads her by the sleeve of her robe out onto the back patio, shuts the door behind them. His voice he keeps low. "What harm can it do to let her go?"

"What harm?" She seethes. "What harm? Haven't you been listening? We're leaving for New York in a little over ten days. What if she breaks a leg?"

The woman can be a mule. "She won't."

"What if she does? Do you know how hard it is to get into Sloan? Do you? What am I supposed to say? Sorry, she broke her leg, can we reschedule in two months? She doesn't have two months."

He has to know. "Can they do something for her?"

She sighs and her voice comes down. "They're the best. If anybody can, they can. They treat Neuroblastoma aggressively and they treat every kid individually, not according to a universal protocol like everybody else. It's the only chance she's got."

"The mouse antibody thing?"

She paces on a short track. "It's the whole thing. It takes a year. First is chemo, 25% hotter than what she got in Portland. Then come antibodies. Then they take some of her marrow, freeze it, and give her more antibodies, this time tagged with an isotope. The idea is the antibodies take it right to the malignant cells and the radiation kills them. While this is going on she has no white blood cells at all, none. She's open to any infection she picks up. When that's done they put her own marrow back." She wipes hair from her face. "She breaks a leg now they might not take her."

Night swallows, for the first time understanding. "Jesus."

"It's a dangerous time."

"This works?"

"They claim 70 percent." She shrugs. "I don't know."

"Only that?"

"It's the only game in town, we've got to try it. I'm not letting a broken bone screw it up."

She starts back inside, but he stops her. "Look…" He won't give up. "Don't take this away from her." He's not sure why this matters so much, but it does. "Out there on the mat was the first time I've seen her smile, laugh, act like a kid. It was the first time I've seen her eyes wide open." Her eyes tell him he's not getting through. "Tell me you didn't notice something, tell me."

She looks away.

"Don't take that away. Don't take away something she loves. That's not protecting her from anything. You want her to live, give her something to live for."

She glares up at him. "A reason to live? She has that, she has her whole life."

"She's a kid. She can't see that far. Look…" He decides to put his cards on the table. " This is why she kicked the tube."

"What?"

"This is why she reads with us. Why she helps in the kitchen, why she eats dinner instead of playing with it. That's how much she wants it. I gave her my word. Don't make me a liar." Words barely out of his mouth he regrets them.

Contempt is in the look she sends him, "Would I be doing that?"

He lets his head drop, " Okay, I deserve that." When he raises his gaze he can tell she is about to drop a bomb on him.

"And you can save the lecture for Alex."

He's lost again. "What does that mean?"

"She refuses chemo, that's what it means! She says she knows she's dying, and won't go through it all again."

Why can't he see these freight trains coming? "Why didn't you tell me?"

She rubs at her face roughly as if ashamed of her tears, "I didn't tell anybody."

He decides to push it. "Come today, come watch her."

She moves for the door. "I haven't said I would let her yet."

"But you will."

She stops at the door, turns to cast him a bitter glare, "You assume one hell of a lot."

Seeing her face, he lets go the breath he's been holding.

She goes inside and he follows, knowing he's won.

• • •

The gym echoes with the voices of a hundred girls.

It smells—of wood, of mats, of female sweat. Ceridwen stands at Night's elbow, back to the wall. Alex and Jade join the others in line to await their turns on the mat.

"I had no idea gymnastics was so big."

"Rita got Jade into it. I don't know why they love it so much, but they do. It's not a horse, but it runs a close second."

Hand to mouth, Ceridwen radiates tension. Alex is up next. Night watches, jaw achingly tight. After all he's done to get her here, please don't let her get hurt. "There she goes."

Ceridwen moans under her hand as Alex throws herself forward. She does a shoulder roll, comes out of it a little too far forward and goes down. Ceridwen starts to her and Night catches her arm. "Wait."

She regains her feet, springs round to rejoin the line, waves, face alight. Night breathes. "She's okay."

Sagging back against the wall, Ceridwen shakes her head in dazed wonder. "I don't know if I can take this."

"You can take it."

They watch as she works her way up to go again. This time there is no mishap.

Ceridwen sighs and it ends up a sorrowful laugh. "She loves it, doesn't she? Look at her face, it's rapturous."

Aware of the childishness of the remark that comes to his mind, he says it anyway. "Told you so."

She smiles, grudgingly, it seems to him. "So you did. So you did."

On the way home Night watches Alex in the mirror as he drives. Her face glows with an unnatural brightness. He pictures a bulb's last flash before going dark, pushes the thought away.

At the house, the girls run in to change. Ceridwen notices he hasn't shut off the engine, gives him a curious look, crosses to lean in at his window. "It's your day off, isn't it?"

"Going to see Derek, be back in an hour." She searches his face, says nothing. In her eyes he sees she doesn't believe him. "Couple hours, tops."

Nodding, with doubting eyes, she starts to pull away, but he catches her with a hand at the back of her head and draws her mouth down to his. He lips are cool, dry.

Too soon she pulls away. "See you when you get back."

He backs down the drive, regretting the lie.

• • •

Night passes Sacred Heart.

Knowing where he's heading but not willing to admit it, not willing to admit what it means, he drives. Off Thirteenth he parks in front of a two-story craftsman sectioned off into apartments. Potted plants cluster at the sides of the stairway leading up to the second floor, a wandering jew spreading across the treads crushed from passing traffic. On a wide porch, sway-back couches squat. On one of these lounges a young man, face obscured by a thatch of hair. Deep in drug induced reverie, he fondles a tenth of Thunderbird at his crotch absently as Night mounts sagging steps dodging bicycles hanging from the rafters.

With a bare knuckle Night raps dirty door glass. From behind a haze of curtain a face materializes purple-black, bearded, overloaded with dreadlocks. The Jamaican glares through the glass. Rumored to sell the most potent bud in Eugene, he answers the door, pistol in hand. The Jamaican is on the scheduling board for next week. And here Night is at his door. The synchronicity makes Night want to laugh.

"Hey, man, need some bud."

Eyes look him up and down with evident repugnance. "I don't know you." The curtain drops and through the fabric Night sees him move in his crablike way back to a blaring TV. Night raps again harder this time and he returns, movements exaggerated with anger. "Off my stairs, muh-fugah."

A hundred dollar bill Night presses to the glass, raises five fingers. The going price is twenty. Night would pay twice that right now, but he offers more it will only queer the deal.

The Jamaican eyes the bill, and with a last probing look at Night, lets the curtain fall. Night hears tumblers turn, and the man inside flings the door wide. The pistol at his thigh he doesn't bother to conceal. Night flinches before stench pushing out the door solid as paste from a tube—hemp, curry, garlic, over it all the sour tang of sweat.

"Wait." He limps to a back room, emerges, tosses zip locks onto a table caked with lentils or rat turds. He snaps his fingers, extends his hand. "See the money."

Night hands him the note. He holds it up to the light to see the bill fluoresce. Satisfied, he slips it into the pocket of his silk shirt open to show gold chains lying heavy against a bony chest.

Night takes a quick glance at a bag, tosses it back down, ire rising. "I said bud." Night is conscious of the nine tucked into the waistband of the dealer's jeans. "I ain't buying your trash, give me back my money."

The Jamaican smiles. "This ain't no K-mart, we don't give no refunds."

Night stays where he is, watching the man's right hand. "I said give me back my money."

The Jamaican is less than worried. He calls over his shoulder a word Night doesn't catch and a black with arms the size of Farmer John hams comes to lean against the jam. "Get your dope, muh-fugah, and get out."

Night would like to do just that, but the stem and leaf in the bags is no good to him, and he's not walking away from his bill either. He hadn't wanted it to go this far, but now it has, there is only one way to get what he needs. "Okay, I'll tell you what I'll do." He reaches into the inner pocket of his jacket, draws out the .40, centers the front sight on the Jamaican's heart. With one hand he points at the big man in the doorway. "You stay right there where I can see you." He looks to the skinny man. "You, with your left hand, put that nine on the table. That's right, now step away. There. Now I'll give you ten seconds to get either my bud or my money back on the goddam table, muh-fugah."

The thin Jamaican takes a step back as if to go into the back room. No way Night is letting him out of his sight. "Stay right there. You got five seconds."

The Jamaican grabs for the gun and he'll have to kill him. The big man in the doorway pushes away from the wall with a shrug of his lats, gives him a look that says he'd love to get his hands on him. That much muscle mass he can empty the Glock into him and still have problems.

"Keep those arms crossed. All I want is the dope I paid for. If this is all you got, just give me my money and I'm gone."

In the little guy's eyes, he sees a thought flicker. Could be bad news—for both of them. "You think this is your lucky day, skin, I'm here to tell you it's not."

Keeping his eyes on Night, he backs to a cigar box on the couch, tosses bags onto the table. "Now get out."

"A glance tells Night it's the real thing. THC beads on plastic like dew, buds green, convoluted scarabs. With his left hand he stuffs them in his jacket, backs to the door. He has never gone down stairs so fast in his life. On the couch T-Bird man doesn't even look up as he passes.

In the car he slumps, waiting for his heart to slow. Numbly, he stares out a window pocked with rain.

He doesn't like breaking laws he's enforced most his life.

It's not as if he has a choice.

• • •

Night walks into Derek's room with his heart in his throat.

When he sees Derek is okay, he shuts his eyes for a moment, letting out a long breath. With what he heard on the way over, he wasn't sure he would be.

Derek notices him and switches off the TV. "Hey, partner, what you doing here?"

Night tosses him a bag, sets a capped cup of coffee on the table.

"Bring chocolate-chocolate this time?"

Night shakes his head, feigning disgust. "You darkies are all the same."

Derek peeks inside, a slow smile widening his mouth. "Oh, now you are precious—for a white boy." He picks one, offers Night the bag. "Tomorrow I'm out of here."

Worried, Night waves away the doughnuts, drops into a chair.

"You don't look too happy to hear it."

"Caught the news?"

Mouth full, he shakes his head. "I have been researching my dissertation on the decline and fall of western civilization as reflected in the societal mirror of the soap o-pera. Have you seen what they let them do on TV these days? Disgusting." When Night doesn't smile, Derek drops it. "What?"

"They found a sixth body in the house."

Derek pushes himself erect, "Six? They got one? Good for them." He notices Night's face, drops the remains of a chocolate-chocolate into the bag, tosses it aside. "Okay, I take it it wasn't good news. So what else they say? You going to tell me or do I have to guess?"

"That we walked into a working meth lab. You smell anything cooking?"

"I didn't smell nothing."

"Me, neither. They said it was a shootout with the Devil's Disciples."

Derek's eyes narrow. "Bikers?"

"From south Douglas County, near Canyonville."

"They said it was bikers?" Derek searches his face for a sign this is a joke, sees none. "Well, they got it wrong, that's all."

Night raises a hand to stop him. "You don't have to convince me."

Derek's eyes turn inward. When he speaks, his voice is breathy, almost a whisper. "What's going on, man?"

Night feels sick and, for the first time since the farmhouse, scared. "I don't know."

"They found the van?"

Night shrugs. "Frame, seat springs, wire from the radials, tranny a puddle of aluminum in the sand, that'll be it."

"We've got your prof's car doing a good imitation of Swiss cheese. We've got a dead perp. We've got two trained law enforcement officers as witnesses. We'll tell them what we saw. They can't ignore both of us."

This starts Night thinking. What he comes up with forms a knot in his gut. "You know, that's another thing. Where are the reporters? This thing is the biggest thing to happen since that oil tanker ran aground. What was it..."

"New Carissa."

"That's right. Let a kid get suspended from middle school for taking a knife to class and they're thick as ticks in high grass. Where are they now? Anybody called you?"

Derek shakes his head. "You?"

"Not call one. I'm not saying Herrera wouldn't give them the brush off. But these guys know their way around. They want a guy's number, they can get it. Since when don't they try for a story?"

Derek stares at his feet, not seeing. "Okay, so what have we got?"

Night isn't sure he wants to hear it. He does and it will make it real. And this he doesn't want to be real.

"We've got a van, house out in the middle of nowhere. Now we get a tip from Compton on a meth lab that doesn't exist. We go out, it looks empty, and we run into a team of what, five, seven guys?"

Night shrugs. Four maybe, no less.

"We've got suppressed HK's with AP 9mm. We've got a blacked out helicopter." Derek looks up from ticking off dark fingers. "And we've got a story blaming bikers."

"That's about it."

Derek makes a try at a laugh. "It's like some bad movie made so cheap they be shaking their guns around and then dubbing shots on the soundtrack. Who would go to all that trouble to kill a few cops? It makes no sense."

If only it didn't. "I just want you to answer a question for me. Last night went perfect for them—whoever they are—except for three things. You tell me what they are?"

Night sees he can, but doesn't want to. "Aw, now, come on—"

"Can you?"

Derek holds his eyes, speaking slowly. "You would be talking about yourself, me, and the professor, wouldn't you?"

For one timeless moment his scalp prickles. He can tell Derek reacts the same way. All that's missing is the run down the wind chimes. "That's right."

Night decides, fishes his compact Glock out of his pocket, slips it under the covers near Derek's hand.

"What's this for?"

"You."

He raises his hands, looks around. "I'm in a hospital, I don't need that."

"You might."

"For what, sex-starved night nurses?" He offers the gun back. "I met them already and, trust me, I'm safe."

Night ignores the gun, reaches for the remote, surfs until he sees a hospital scene, tosses it onto Derek's lap. "There they are, now."

"Really, man, I don't need it."

Night glances at his watch, does some fast figuring. "Give me a couple hours to get something in my stomach and catch a shower and I'll be back."

"What are you talking about?"

Night sits, leans forward close enough to whisper. "What do I look like?"

Derek snorts, "Want me to tell you?"

"Exactly. Nobody asked me who I was on my way up. I just walked right in here."

"So what?"

"So, you are one of three witnesses to one of the biggest drug related crimes in U.S. history. We both are. Our names made the wires. The lies are flying fast and heavy as turds at a cow pie throwing contest. And you and I—we can call them liars."

Derek rolls his eyes. "Don't start with that conspiracy sh—"

"You know who would raise a stink if you choked to death on a doughnut up here tonight?"

"Julie would."

"Besides her."

"Who?"

"Nobody. Nobody but me, and I may not be around to do it." Night sees he has his attention. "Now you keep that thing where you can get at it and stay off the Vicoden until I get back. What'll it be, Scrabble or chess?"

Derek's mouth drops open as understanding dawns. "You can't spend the night here."

Night turns on his way out. "See you in an hour."

• • •

Night walks in on a silent house.

Jade he finds in the kitchen. Her expression tells him something's wrong.

"She's sick."

"Where is she?"

"Upstairs. Ceridwen's with her. They were both sleeping when I went by."

He considers his options, decides he has time. From his jacket he pulls one of the bags of bud. Conscious of Jade's eyes on his back he crumbles it into the big mixer on the counter.

"Dad?" Her voice is laden with worry. "Is that what I think it is?"

At the sink he soaps sticky resin off his hands. "Yeah, kiddo, it is."

In the pantry he pulls down Betty Crocker, finds a recipe for brownies. Chewy, that's what he wants. Mouth already watering, he laughs at himself. He won't be eating any.

Jade peers into the mixer, "I can't believe this."

He fetches eggs, cocoa, flour, sugar, oil. "Believe it."

"But…"

Egg poised over the edge of the stainless mixing bowl, he hesitates, waiting for her. It shouldn't take her long. Not if he knows her at all.

She exhales hard. "It's for Alex, isn't it."

"That's right." He cracks an egg, holds it poised over the bowl. It would be an expensive batch to burn. "Hope I'm up to this."

"Can I help?"

He was hoping she would ask. "Can you help? I thought I raised you not to ask stupid questions." He draws her to him for a quick clinch. "See if you can find the vanilla."

• • •

Upstairs, he finds Alex in Ceridwen's bed, looking so wan she scares him.

He checks, sees she's awake. "Hey, kid."

"Hey," Alex says, voice stretched thin as a latex balloon.

Ceridwen looks up from the easy chair wiping her eyes. "What smells good?"

By her he hunkers to whisper into an ear. "Jade did some baking. What's going on?"

Her look is accusation, indictment, trial, verdict. Her voice is a whisper. "Her legs hurt. We have her on some stronger pain meds. They knock her out."

Knowing how useless words are, he asks anyway. "Was it—"

She answers with a shake of her head. "The tumors are growing again."

"Mom?"

Ceridwen goes to her, "What, baby?"

"When can I go swimming with Jade?" Her voice is weak and Night can tell it's no act.

"Maybe tomorrow, we've got to get you rested for your treatments, don't we?"

"No, we don't."

Ceridwen's smile looks as if it may shatter as she reaches to smooth Alex's hair. "Aren't you the stubborn one?"

Alex shoves her hand away, "Don't treat me like a baby. I won't do it, I won't take any more of that stuff."

Night sees Ceridwen work to stay in control. She rises stiffly, makes for the door. As she passes, her eyes look to him in silent appeal. When she has gone, Night sits on the edge of the bed, runs his nails through Alex's hair. Her eyes droop. She sags, a rag doll. "That feels good, keep doing it."

"If you'll listen to what I've got to say."

Her eyes stay blissfully closed, "I won't do it."

No more than he expected. "Alex, you know how to kill a werewolf?"

She squints through one eye, "What?"

"Do you?"

She snorts. "Everybody does."

"Oh, yeah? How?"

"Garlic."

"Nope."

"A cross?"

"Uh, uh."

"Wooden stake?"

"That's vampires. For werewolves you need a silver bullet." He holds up a small foil wrapped cube still warm from the oven. "This is chemo's."

She reaches for it and he holds it just out of reach.

"Let me see."

He unwraps an inch square block of chocolate brownie, "You can smell, that's all."

She sniffs, "Smells like chocolate."

"It is."

"What's a brownie supposed to do?"

"It's supposed to keep chemo from making you sick."

She casts him a cynical glare. "Nah."

Night nods. "Oh, yeah."

"If it's so good, why don't doctors use it?"

Because the laws are made for the convenience of those who make and enforce them and not those who must live under them, that's why. "They've got their reasons."

"How's it work?"

This is a topic he'd rather avoid. But he won't try to kid her. She's too smart. "It's got THC in it, that's how."

"THC?" Her face changes, eyes searching his face. Behind them her mind works. "There's dope in there?"

He's not surprised she would know. Probably picked it up in DARE. Our tax dollars at work. "That's right."

She sighs, "And that's supposed to do something?"

"It works. I can get you the literature if you want to read up on it."

She smiles a sickly smile. "That's okay. Will I get high?"

"You might get a little sleepy."

Head tilted, she glares at him as if she's sick to death of lies, of pain. "I won't puke my guts out?"

He prays he is telling her the truth. "You won't puke your guts out."

Gray eyes narrow, "Cross your heart?"

He does.

"Hope to die, stick a needle in your eye?"

"That, too."

Her hand rises, poised to strike. "I'd do it."

He has to smile. "Don't I know it."

Face stricken, she squeezes her eyes shut, breath coming ragged from a shuddering chest. When words come, they come from deep in her chest, low and breathy. "I don't want to die."

Hand behind her head, he presses her hard to him, "Nobody does, kiddo, nobody."

She pulls away, small hand icy on his wrist, "You're a cop, what are you doing with dope?"

Naturally, she'd ask. "That's my worry."

"What if they catch you?"

"They won't." Now where has he heard that before? Here comes the hard part. "Now, here's the deal."

She moans, falls back. "Everything with you is a deal."

"You betcha. Now let's say I get it for you as long as you need it. What then?"

On her face awareness dawns with disappointment. "You mean will I do chemo?"

"That's what I mean."

She considers. "It depends."

Now what? "On what?"

"On you."

Why with this kid does he always seem to be struggling to keep his balance? "How's that?"

Her eyes become cagey, "You like my mom, don't you?"

"I like a lot of people."

She rolls her eyes. "I mean you like her."

This is one tough cookie. "What makes it your business?"

"She's my Mom, that's what makes it my business."

Defeated, he drops his chin to his chest. Why does he feel as if he's talking to another cop? "Okay, it's your business. And, yes, I like her."

"She likes you, too."

He's had enough. "Look, kid, I was young once. I know how simple it seems. People like each other, maybe they love each other, they should live happily ever after, right? It's not that easy."

Her hands drop to lie flat. "Why not?"

He shakes his head, feeling the same hopelessness he felt as a child, "It just isn't."

She snatches his hand, brings it to her head, starts it moving, "Scratch."

He resumes, fingers moist with perspiration from her scalp.

"Harder."

"I'm scratching, I'm scratching."

Later, head drooping, she whispers something as she nears sleep. He bends close to hear, "Say again."

"I'll do it."

Letting his head rest on her chest as his heart quakes, he strokes her scalp. Ceridwen returns silently. Night motions her over, rises and she replaces him, her hand taking the place of his on her scalp.

Without opening her eyes, Alex moans. "Mama?"

Ceridwen looks up to see Night gone.

Why does she get the feeling the two of them share a secret? Illogical though it may be, she doesn't like it. "I'm here, Baby." She takes icy hands between hers, chafing them warm. So small, these hands, so big the eyes looking up at her. She won't let her die. She will spend a year holding her down herself if that's what it takes, but she will take the treatment. She will live.

"Mama?"

"I'm listening."

"I'll do it."

Ceridwen hears and it is as if the tumor is not in Alex at all, but in Ceridwen's own throat. Her daughter crushed against her, she whispers against Alex's chest. "You are going to live, you hear me, goddam it? You're going to live."

• • •

In the briefing room Night stands at the window awaiting Herrera.

With him wait Derek and the other five men remaining in INET. Outside in a courtyard below a Judas tree bows under its burden of violet bloom. Night watches it sway. He does not want to be here.

No talk today. No banter, No jokes. Five desks stand empty around the circle.

Hutto, a husky blond across the circle from Night, speaks to his back. "So what happened?" Unspoken, the accusation is there stinking like a thing dead.

"Yeah, Night, tell us." Tall, sporting an earring, eyes those of a dog a generation too close to wolf, Blaze glares. "Since when does a warrant team go in with only five men?"

Night keeps silent. It's that or let what he feels out, and he doesn't trust himself to do that.

"You weren't there, I was," Derek says. "We had a civilian outside, Night was keeping her out of the way."

Blaze laughs. "I'll bet he was."

Derek leans forward, "Where were you while we were getting shot at, huh? Parked eating a taco burger? We don't need any armchair quarterbacking from you, pretty boy."

Night keeps his eyes on the tree. He won't get drawn in. He knows what they feel. He would feel the same. "We were out of our league." They laugh when they hear this. Considering the news, he is not surprised.

Blaze looks at him with contempt. "What I want to know is why you didn't even try to get them out."

Night won't look at him.

"That's enough, Blaze." Herrera struts in looking plump as a capon in an over-filled suit. "Just got the FP's report from Salem. Some of us might be relieved to know that they were dead when the fire started."

The words fall like a sandbag.

Hutto loses air. "Dead? They had vests, helmets. They all did."

Herrera reads. "They all took multiple hits to the torso, and at least one head shot."

Hutto's eyes widen, "Head shots?"

Herrera nods and Hutto brings a big fist down on the desktop, hissing a favorite Saxon verb. The men around the circle sit in stunned silence.

Night doesn't bother to turn. "They were executed."

An angry Herrera barks. "When I need your editorial services, Night, I'll let you know, how will that be?"

Night clamps his jaw.

Hutto shrugs. "So what else does it say?"

"Perp was found in a back room."

Night opens the window, craving air.

"The perp you know."

Night turns, confused to see Herrera gloat.

"It was a Richard Compton."

Expletives of disbelief spread around the circle.

Derek sneers. "Compton wouldn't know a cartridge from a suppository."

Hutto agrees. "Compton take out five of our guys? Not in a million years."

Herrera ignores them. "Dental records showed a positive ID. Shot himself through the mouth before the fire got to him."

Night can listen to no more. "That's BS and you know it."

"You got a problem, Night?"

He swallows his disgust only to have it come back up, burning like bile. "Didn't you read my report?"

"I read it."

Night can feel their eyes on him. Can feel, too, the hostility displaced by something else. "It was a shooting gallery in there. You telling me they never touched him?"

Herrera shrugs, leafing through. "Autopsy doesn't mention it."

For a long moment no one speaks. Then, Bryce, a blond with a fireplug build and a bandana tied over long hair, grunts. "What did they find on him?"

Herrera skims, finds it. "Uzi modified for full auto and a dozen magazines."

Hutto shakes his head. "Compton with an Uzi take out Jenaro, Sid? five guys? Cut me some slack, here."

Bryce again. "They recover any of the bullets?"

Hutto sighs in exasperation, "They would be 9mm, wouldn't they?"

Herrera leafs through the report, "Here it is." Herrera frowns. "Ballistics says it was 9mm AP."

Night meets Derek's eye, gets the message to shut up and listen.

A low whistle from across the room. "Armour piercing?"

Bryce nods, mind made up. "Whole thing's bogus."

Herrera sighs, irritated. "This is going to go awful damn slow if we've got to stop every five words. What's that supposed to mean?"

Night has never heard Bryce say something he couldn't back up. "Why do you say that?"

"No way an Uzi will chamber conical AP, that's why."

Night's mind races.

Bryce goes on. "Armor piercing ammunition has a distinctive cone shape. The French stuff is pointed, American is truncated at the tip. Both make weapon selection a consideration. They won't all feed it. Pick the wrong gun and you have misfeeds."

"Hey!" Herrera says.

Hutto ignores him, leans toward Bryce, "What are you saying?"

"I'm saying, Hutto," he says as if speaking to a child, "that a conical bullet hangs up on the feed ramp. Uzi's were designed in the fifties to feed ball, not a round that didn't even exist at the time. Get it?"

"Where would Compton get hold of that much AP, anyway?"

"He wouldn't," Bryce says. "Very hard to get."

Derek sits forward. "We don't use it. What about SWAT?"

Hutto shakes a shaggy head. "Nope, hollow point plus P plus."

"Then who does?" Derek asks.

Bryce sits back, "The alphabet soup agencies—DEA, DOJ, FBI, ATF. None of them dick around with Uzi's any more. They use MP-5's. Whoever set this up is assuming they're dealing with a bunch of yokels."

"Which they are," Night says. "The media doesn't know. Research is expensive. Easier to regurgitate. The public doesn't know. They depend on the media." He laughs.

"And anybody that does know," Bryce says, "knows enough to keep their mouth shut."

"So where does that leave us?" Derek asks.

Bryce shrugs big shoulders. "S-O-L."

Herrera looks ready to explode. "This isn't a goddam debating society."

Night senses a change in the atmosphere of the room. Gone is animosity toward him, toward Derek. In its place, tension that prickles and sparks like socks fresh out of the drier.

Derek questions Herrera. "Footprints?"

"Volunteer fire company got there first. The yard was under three inches of water by the time they got the fire out. Had to tow the tanker out of the mud."

"What about the car?"

"In impound."

"Damn," Bryce says, "you were in that Volvo when it took all those hits? Remind me to have you pick my Lotto number next time."

Night ignores him. "What about the van? Get a VIN?"

Herrera leafs through the inch-thick report. "Stolen that night. No prints. Happens every day. Juvi's mostly."

Bryce leans forward in a desk that creaks under his 240 pounds, looks at Night. "So, why don't you tell us what happened?"

Herrera's hand comes down on a stack of paper. "Report's right here."

Hutto answers, "That's a load and you know it."

"We're not FP's and this isn't Quantico," Herrera says. "We're not here to speculate. This is how it is."

"I want to hear what Night has to say."

Herrera will not give up. "Richard Compton was the shooter and the morgue has remains to prove it. We've got the weapon. We've got the FP report. We've got ballistics. That's it. The fat lady has sung. You want to hatch some wacko theories, do it on your own time." Herrera opens the roster on top of the report. "Now... what you got going, Night?"

Night looks at Herrera, torn between smashing his face and walking out. "You know, to show you how naive, how stupid I am... I always thought that no matter how hot the politics got, no matter how much the pressure, when our guys went down we'd do what it took to get the guys that did it. Now five men die and you don't even have the balls to ask what really happened?"

Herrera's eyes flash. His hand comes down hard on the report, "This right here… this is what happened."

"I was there. Derek took a bullet. They shot up Professor Lawrence's car. We've got the van. We've got the AP they were shooting. There must be casings by the hundred scattered from that house to 99. The airport's got to have a record of the helicopter. You're telling me we're going to shut our eyes and swallow?"

Herrera's eyes hold Night's. "That's what I'm saying." His voice grows ominous. "Now, I asked you what you have going, Night."

Night looks around the circle. Bryce leans back, arms crossed, looking disgusted. Derek watches Herrera, mouth open in what might be surprise. The others examine patterns in the linoleum as if it has suddenly become fascinating. Night waits for them to speak. They keep silent. "Why is Salem covering for these guys? Why are you?"

Herrera rises, barrel chest out, "I'm not covering for anybody. I'm doing my job. If you'd done yours instead of making the beast with two backs in the backseat they might be alive right now."

Night goes for him. Hutto beats him there, holds him off.

"This is the best you can do? Compton with an Uzi? One shooter? Something we've drilled a thousand times? He kills them all and they never graze him? Then he finishes them off, sprays another five magazines into Cer's car, goes back inside, sets the fire, and bites the barrel? That's it? that's the story? That's the one you're going with?"

Herrera looks around him, sees the absurdity of his position, storms out. "In my office, Hume."

Amused, Night watches him go.

At the door, Herrera stops, bellows. "That's an order, Hume. Now!"

Night has to laugh. "How about this, Herrera, how about you stick that report, huh?" He heads for the door. "The whole thing stinks. I'm out of here."

Herrera lets him pass, yells after him, voice straining. "You walk out of here you won't be back."

Behind Night the door slams. The sound reminds him of a book slamming shut— the book containing the last twenty years of his life. Outside he sits on the trunk of the Lincoln, boots on the bumper. It's worse than he thought. That Salem would issue a report so full of holes leaves him numb. He knows they're not that stupid. What then? As he works his way through the possibilities, he grows more worried still.

Derek leans on the trunk, head down. "What the hell was that? You been watching Dirty Harry movies again? Can't you be a little more original?"

"I'll do better next time."

"I'm staying to see what else I can pick up. Where will you be?"

Night tries, but can't seem to think, "I don't know, call me."

FIVE

Night finds Ceridwen sitting alone on the porch.

Before he's halfway up the walk he can tell something is very wrong.

"We need to talk."

Not a good beginning. He drops beside her. "Okay."

"Got a letter today.

"I like letters."

"You wouldn't like this one. They're taking my house."

He looks at her, sees it's true. "Let me see."

She fishes it out of a pocket and hands it to him folded twice and warm from her skin. A glance at the return address tells him all he needs to know. He reads it anyway and learns nothing. He lays it on her folded knees, "Start packing."

"They write me a letter and they take my house? In America? How can they?"

He breathes, eyes closed. "They need probable cause. They've got it, had it when I showed up. To beat it you need a preponderance of evidence proving your home is innocent."

She stares, face blank. "Innocent? My house? What does that mean? How can a house be guilty?"

He sighs, not wanting to talk about it. Three years he's lived and breathed this. Today it's all coming down around his ears. "In rem. It means against the thing. English Common law. They used it to take smugglers' ships. It's the way forfeiture works."

"But…"

He can guess what's coming next.

"I haven't been convicted of anything."

"You don't have to be. You don't have to be charged."

"And they can take my house?"

Night thinks of the night in front of the farmhouse. When she showed up he was a half second from following them in. He is only alive now because she came. "They can, and they will."

She's incensed, but then they always are. "Without proving I'm guilty of anything."

"That's right." He meets her eyes, "But you are, aren't you?"

"According to them, I am." She turns to the street, hunches over as if cramped, moans, "It's not right."

"It may or may not be, but it's the law. It's been around two hundred years and it's here to stay."

She thinks. He can feel her grasping, can guess what she'll say.

"What about the Constitution, what about due process?"

He's heard this so many times. He smiles, numbed to the heart, "A common misconception about forfeiture. The Constitution doesn't protect the rights of things. It's your house being accused here, not you."

Her mouth gapes, "You're telling me…my house… is being charged with selling dope? And I'm not?"

She does a better job than most of making it sound ridiculous. "That's exactly right."

"And there's nothing I can do?"

"Not a thing."

Again, she moans, "My house, they're taking my house. It's all we've got. There's nothing here any more. I threw it all out a week ago."

He knows she is telling the truth. "I know."

"They can check."

She doesn't understand, and for the first time, he's not sure he does either. "It doesn't matter."

"Then what does?"

"That they got an informant to say they bought some dope here once. That's all it takes. It's happened to people who have inherited houses. They get their probable cause and before the heir knows what hit them it's over. The informant gets his nine percent and the department gets the proceeds from the sale to buy equipment and training. Everybody lives happily ever after."

"Except the heir."

"Except him."

Eyes alight, she looks up at him, "I'll fight it."

"Go ahead. You'll lose. The house is tainted, dirty. And you did it. Even if you didn't, you'd lose, but you did. You broke the law." How empty the words sound.

"If I wanted to fight it... what could I do?"

He raises his hands in a gesture of futility. "Post bond."

"I don't have it."

"Good, save your money."

He can feel her taking a strong hold on herself. He gets the feeling she's going to ask him something and he dreads hearing what it will be.

She looks up, eyes fierce. "Was it you?"

He can't blame her for asking. That would have been his guess. "What do you think?"

"Answer me!" In her voice is panic, despair, maybe hate. She breathes deeply, forces herself calm. "I want to hear you say it."

"Why?"

"Just..." Her eyes close as she works at mastering her emotions. "Just tell me."

"It wasn't me." Even as he says it he knows, were their roles reversed, he would not believe him.

"And I'm supposed to believe you?"

He laughs. It's nuts. "Do or don't." He starts to rise and she grabs his bad arm and draws him back down.

"Then who did?"

He thinks of Carla, dismisses the thought. She is Derek's. No way. She knows better than to go over his head to Herrera. "I don't know."

"Will I ever know?"

"Probably not."

She sags, cheek on his thigh. "What do I do now?"

"Find an apartment."

"How long do I have?"

"Three weeks...a little less, maybe."

"Three weeks... I guess I shouldn't care. I owe more on the house than it's worth."

He has to know. "Where'd the money go?"

"You know where."

"Alex?"

"Every dime." She sighs long and hard. "I've really messed everything up, haven't I?"

He's never agreed with anything more.

Her eyes probe. "You've done this sort of thing before, haven't you?"

"Yes."

"You've taken houses?"

"Three houses on three different Hawaiian islands once. Cars, boats, planes. I've got a list here I'll sell you—buy a Ferrari for a dollar."

"You're kidding."

"Yeah. Even took a motor home once."

"How did it make you feel?"

He shrugs. "Part of the job. Do I bleed for the dealers? No."

"Because we're scum."

He won't group her with them. "Because they live off us. Don't pay taxes. Don't pay SSI. They just take."

He combs fingers through her hair and feels her mind work under his hand. He has never been with a woman half as smart. Or half as dumb.

"You won't... do anything..."

He feels her stiffen and knows what she is trying to ask is costing her. He wishes that somehow he could save her the effort.

"...to help us."

Not a question. More of an observation. Not that it matters. "It's too late."

"If you could, would you?"

Hopelessness pressing him like a vice, his voice drops to a whisper. "I can't."

She sits up, pulls away and he misses the warmth of her skin against him. "I understand." She rocks, arms hugging her knees.

"Where will you go?"

She surprises him with a breathy laugh. "Timing's propitious at least. In two weeks we'll be in New York."

He had forgotten. "Where will you stay?"

"Ronald McDonald House. They're incredible, really so kind. If it weren't for them, I couldn't afford to go with her."

"What about money?"

She smiles a tightlipped smile, eyes upturned to an overcast sky. "Money I refuse to worry about. The treatment she has to have. When insurance runs out...it runs out. I'll work somewhere. We'll eat somehow. We'll live somehow."

"I gave Ray a call about that. I hope you don't mind."

She didn't look up. "Mind? No, I don't mind."

"He said he would look into it."

She didn't laugh, but she might have. "That's nice. Anyway... It doesn't matter. None of it does." She rises, heading inside. The screen door spring prangs as she swings it wide. "Alex has to live. That's all that matters."

She lets it swing to behind her and wood claps to frame with a bang that makes him jump where he sits. For the first time since he has known her she has not softened its closing.

• • •

Ceridwen arrives at her office just in time to grab her notes and make her ten o'clock lecture.

At noon she meets Jo and Pickering at the department office. Instantly Pickering reads her face. "What happened?"

Faced with such perspicacity her resolve disintegrates. "You going to lunch? Let's walk."

They move beneath maples as fine mist wafts down through a cotton sky.

"I knew it," Jo says. "You're pregnant by the garbage man."

Ceridwen sighs, exasperated with her tabloid view of life. "I'm not pregnant, Jo, for crissake."

"You've found out he's not really what he says he is."

"Shut up, Jo," Pickering says.

Ceridwen stops dead still.

Seeing her face, Jo laughs. "I'm right, I knew it! Look at her, I'm right!"

"How did you know?"

Pickering sputters. "What?" She looks from one to the other, confused. "What does she know?"

"What is he, a spy? a writer? a rich business man? What?"

"Jo's right?"

"He's a cop."

Pickering's mouth hangs slack, "A cop?"

Jo nods smugly. "I knew it, undercover, right?" She walks on. "I knew it."

Pickering hurries to catch up, "That's why you look the way you do?"

"No."

Sagely, Jo nods. "There's something else, isn't there."

Pickering frowns down her nose, "Jo, for goodness sake, this isn't one of your talk shows."

Ceridwen needs to tell it, to share it. She checks for passersby, sees none. "I've lost my house." She barely gets it out and her nose is running. "They took my house."

"Lost your house? How?" Pickering asks.

"It's that, isn't it." Eyes sympathetic, Jo gnaws a thumbnail.

"Will you shut up and let her tell us?"

Ceridwen sees her mind work behind green eyes. "You knew?"

"About you selling?" Jo shrugs. "I've heard."

Ceridwen's stomach gives a lurch. "You mean everybody knows?"

Pickering takes her arm, draws her on down the street toward Fifth Street Market, "You can't very well keep that sort of thing secret. Not when you're selling to half the department."

She sees it's true, sees how stupid she's been. It gives her an ache in the gut to know. Her face flushes with embarrassment. "I'm such a jerk."

"You say they've taken your house? Have they charged you?"

They push through the glass door into the Market, grilled lamb and simmering curry strong on the air.

"Not yet."

"There must be something you can do," Jo says.

"No."

Pickering's eyes narrow. "Was it him? It was, wasn't it."

"He tells me it wasn't."

Jo is aghast. "And you believe him?"

Ceridwen thinks. "I guess I do."

"So gullible! You are so gullible!"

Pickering sighs, "It's her life, she knows him better than we do. And anyway, from what I saw at my house, there's more than professional interest on his part."

They take a place in line along a stove laden with simmering lentils and eggplant.

Jo gasps. "You mean it's gone just like that? the house, everything you got out of the settlement?"

"What equity there is, which isn't much to worry about."

They order from a goateed man in a soiled apron who ladles their portions of hummus, tabouli, cucumber salad with yogurt. On a plate he stacks their pocket bread, still steaming from the grill. Ceridwen pays and Pickering leads the way to a table. "Is there no way to fight it?"

"Night says it would be a waste of money. I'd have to come up with a five thousand dollar bond. I don't have it. What I have I need for our trip to New York."

Jo fetches their food, and Ceridwen, chin propped in her hand, watches as they eat. Only now is it coming home to her that she has lost her home, that she will drive by and see strangers moving behind the windows. She can see the future, and it leaves her feeling as if she has swallowed liquid nitrogen. "I never thought it would happen to me. I thought, you know, I wasn't hurting anybody, I was just in business. I only did it so we could keep the house. Funny, huh?"

Pickering's eyes are concerned. "What will you do?"

The question reaches her in a strange dialect. Though she knows the words, the meaning eludes her. What will she do? She struggles for an answer and finds none. It's as if, nose six inches from a wall, she's asked what lies beyond. In her chest lies leaden emptiness. "We'll go to Sloan, and Alex will get better. We'll deal with the rest when we come to it." Remembering, she panics. "I'll need a sabbatical, Jean. Will I get it?"

Pickering's eyes cloud over as she kneads hummus with a plastic fork. "Ceridwen…"

At once she understands how bad things are.

"If you weren't tenured, they wouldn't have renewed your contract for next year. Will they help you to go when what you intend is to come back in a year?" She shrugs.

Ceridwen flushes with shame. "I see."

"But, then… it's all in how you present it, isn't it? If I give the committee a choice between your staying and your having a year off to look for another position back east…" She shrugs, eyes foxy.

In her heart hope blooms shockingly bright. "You would do that?"

"It's the truth, isn't it? Of course, if you don't find anything…" She lifts painted eyebrows, taking a bite of falafel and pepper sauce.

Overcome with a surge of gratitude, Ceridwen squeezes her hand. "Thanks, Jean."

• • •

In the kitchen Night runs into Jade.

He needs to tell her and he dreads it. He knows what she'll think. "You're up early."

"Couldn't sleep."

"Why not?"

Face wooden, she paddles the dregs of milk in her cereal bowl with a spoon. "I'm going back with Mom, aren't I?"

"No." He sits, leans forward. "Why do you say that?"

"Because Ceridwen's losing her house."

He is not surprised she knows. "Alex tell you?"

She nods. "We're going to have to move out, aren't we?"

One step ahead of him again. "Yes we are."

The hurt on her face slashes him like a razor.

He takes her hand. "This isn't about us. We're going to move in the corner house. I'm going to have it ready in a week, most of it. We'll be okay. We can eat out for a couple weeks until the kitchen's done. We can make it. We would have to move anyway with them going to Sloan."

"That cancer place?" She looks over at him, confused, "They'll be there a year?"

"That's right."

"Where will they go after?"

Always the million dollar questions with this kid. She doesn't know any other kind. "I don't know."

She squints as if trying to make out the truth, "Will you see her?"

He has to laugh, so futile, so predictable, "I don't know. Look, I've got to meet Derek. I'm late."

"I know, I won't see you tonight, will I?"

He pecks her forehead, "Maybe not, don't—"

"I know, don't wait up."

He's at the door when she calls.

"Dad, I don't care where we live as long as we're a family."

It's suddenly impossible for him not to empty his lungs. He returns to crush her to him.

"We'll always be that, kiddo."

• • •

Night palms his way through the door to the shoe repair shop, bell clanging behind him.

Past the woman with her perpetually dour expression he strides, one of her many girlfriends swinging legs dangling flip-flops from her perch on the workbench. For the thousandth time he marvels that this sallow-faced amazon can lure the procession of sweet things she does into her shop. At the back he punches a code on the keypad of a door marked PRIVATE.

Herrera looks up from the sports section with a bleak stare, "What you doing here? Your professor got the curse?"

Night slaps the paper out of his hand, "This isn't Florida. You can't take a woman's house without even doing a search."

As maggots surface in corrupting flesh, a smile appears on Herrera's face. "Watch me."

"It may be the way you do it down in Bubbaville, but up here we charge somebody before we take everything they've got."

Herrera scoops the paper off the floor with a grunt, belt cutting into his gut. "I don't care how hot that little jabañero professor of yours is. That house is ours. Now, back off and stay out of it."

"It's not right."

Herrera leers. "Read your law and wise up."

"She's clean, has been for weeks."

"Oh, you reforming them, now?" His smile sours. "I don't care if she's clean enough to eat off of. You know she's been selling. We know it. She knows it. Half the goddam U of O knows it. You think I'm going to let that go? Why? because one of my agents likes the scent under her tail? Come off it. Down in Volusia we took in over eight million off drivers southbound on 95." He raises three fingers. "That was in three years. Seventy-five percent of them we never even charged."

Night knew he came from Florida, but has never heard this. "Nobody fought?"

Herrera shrugs, "Sure. Four we lost. The rest got most their money back, but only after they promised not to sue. It still added up to quite a pot of gold."

The man revolts him. "It's guys like you give us a dirty name."

He shrugs. "We had probable cause. We had dogs go over the cars."

"And they found what, their cash stank of coke? You know as well as I do ninety-five percent of the bills in circulation do."

Herrera sits, and, hands woven behind his head, leans back, reminiscing fondly, "One boy had five thousand in his sea bag. He fought it. Got half of it back after a donation to the widow and orphan's fund."

"Like I said, this isn't Florida. We always verify an informant with a search. You do that, you'd find out she's clean."

"And what about when we first sent an INET officer out? Was she clean, then?"

A point for Herrera. "So why do it now? You knew we had her on the board for a warrant service. Why jump the gun?"

Herrera grins smug. "We got a tip."

Night's ears prick. "Who snitched her off?" It wasn't Carla. She works for Derek.

"What's it matter who? She was fingered." He smiles. "Quite an image, isn't it?"

Night works to stay in control. In INET he's history. He slams Herrera's face in, he can kiss his job and a pension goodbye along with it. "Who? I want to know."

"Don't get your panties in a bunch. You're out, remember? By the way, I want that ID."

"I asked who it was."

Herrera tosses him a file. "Look it up yourself."

What Night sees he doesn't believe.

"That's right, her own son. What do you think about that? Some taste in women, huh? Teenage strippers and women whose own sons turn them in for peddling drugs." He laughs. "And you lecture me on integrity? What a joke."

Night tosses the file into Herrera's lap, "I don't like your kind of cop."

"Do me a favor, hot shot, don't tell me the way it should be." Rising, in Night's chest he jabs a thick finger. "You think you're hot stuff because you've worked SWAT. Let me tell you something, you wouldn't know beans with the bag open. Forfeiture is federal law. She wants her day in court, she'll get it. She'll lose."

He is right and Night knows it. "We'll go to the *Guard*, raise a stink."

"We?" He smiles, "We, now, huh? Go ahead. You're not the first to go native. You just tell your professor girlfriend something for me. You tell her she's wasting her time fighting it. She just may as well start packing her lingerie right now. That house is ours."

Fists cracking with tension, knowing it's hopeless, knowing that if he stays he'll end up going for him, Night heads out.

"Your ID."

Night stops, turns, fishes it out of his wallet, flings it at Herrera. It caroms off his chest and across the room. So much for three years of his life. He moves for the door as Herrera's voice pursues him down the hall.

"Nice working with you. And tell your babe she'd better look for a cheap apartment. You tell her that."

• • •

Night picks Derek up at home.

They end up out on Airport. Derek takes an envelope off the dash, and photos tumble out onto his lap, "What's this?"

Night hasn't noticed it before. "You tell me."

Derek leafs through in silence, face blanching.

Night sees his face and is curious. "What?"

"The families, wives, kids…"

"Whose?"

Derek looks at him with suspicious eyes. "Our entry team." He frowns up at Night. "Where'd you get these?"

Slowly, the world constricts around him. "I didn't."

Derek checks the envelope, finds nothing, "Then who did?"

At the scene of Friday's raid, Night stops, kills the Lincoln. The cooling engine metronomes. Derek taps a tooth with a nail in time, considering. "Something stinks in Denmark."

Fighting off a chill, Night kicks open the door and slides out to look around. Tatters of yellow police tape hang limp from overgrown juniper under a warm sun. Derek peers down into the blackened pit that was the basement. "Not much left."

Night turns, trying in vain to recapture the feeling of Friday night. In bright sunlight, house gone, it's not easy. "Okay, let's go through it."

Derek sighs, "Oh, come on, man, what for? There's nothing left but a hole in the ground. What could they have missed?" Derek walks away, shoes sucking in drying mud.

Sun warm on his back, Night hesitates. He knows they are missing something. "I don't know. Let's just go through it, can we do that?"

Derek raises arms wide in surrender. "Go ahead."

Night takes a moment to clear his mind. "We were parked there.

Impatiently, Derek tilts his face up to a cloudless sky, "Yeah, yeah."

"You were back here, and I was by the van with Cer."

"We know that."

"Just humor me, okay? The shooting started… What did you do?"

"I kicked the back door, almost broke my ankle. Must have been boarded over."

Night nods, trying hard to see it again. "I came running across the road for the front door. That's when you ran into me." Night searches the muddy lawn for a sign and sees only deep ruts from fire trucks. Night pivots, doing his best to picture the farmhouse in the darkness. "Right about here it must have been."

"Then the van's lights came on back by the barn."

Night heads back behind the house, bends to examine a confusion of tracks in gravel.

Derek follows, looking bored. "What you after? You figure maybe one of the shooters dropped his Penney's charge card?"

Night comes up empty. He forces himself to think. "Didn't we catch some fire from the front, too?"

Derek shrugs, "Might have. No muzzle flash to see, they were suppressed. I couldn't tell where it was coming from."

Near the blackened front porch Night squats, combing silken mud with his fingers. Derek finds shade under a redwood seared rust from the radiant heat of the fire. "Done playing in the mud, let me know. You won't find anything. They've been over this place with teasers and x-ray machines."

Disappointed, Night gives up, rises. The area must have been scoured clean.

"Whatever you find, Salem's got it already. It won't change their minds. Let's get some breakfast."

He is not ready to leave. "When we came back and found the house on fire they were waiting for us."

"You betcha."

"Where?"

Bored, Derek considers, points to the far end of a circle drive in the shade of overgrown rhodies, "There."

Night's stomach burns with hope. If he's right, they might have missed this. Hunkered in gravel and rotting leaves, still surprisingly cool in the shade, he searches, sifting leaf mold with mud-caked fingers. There in moist black duff he finds what he came for. A quick glance at the casings tells him Bryce was right, that Salem's report is a lie, that something has gone terribly awry.

In the cool shade he considers the last two days. It can't be as bad as it seems. They've missed it, that is all. Cover-ups, conspiracies—the stuff of B movies and supermarket book racks. This is real life. Here there are no dark conspiracies, no media complicity. Here people tell the truth unless they have a reason not to. In 20 years he's never seen anything like this. Investigators make mistakes, they miss things, but not this. If Herrera is too stubborn to think for himself…

He knows what he has to do.

He slips the brass into his pocket. Back at the car in the warm sun, he feels the need to scan the flat grassland around them. He sees only man-tall seed heads waving lazily in the breeze. Paranoia. Who would care what they found? Nobody. Still, his skin crawls with the feeling they are somewhere they should not be. "Let's go."

Derek sighs, slides in, "About time. I'm starving."

Night pulls them out onto the road, takes them back to Beltline and east to the interstate. He may not be able to change anything but he has to try. "Breakfast can wait."

· · ·

Derek watches as they pass the IHOP doing 75 north on the freeway.

"Where we going?"

Night opens his cellular, dials Oregon State Police. Two minutes later they have an appointment.

"Salem? We're going all the way to Salem?" Derek groans. "Now? I'm a wounded man. I'm starving, here. I need my strength."

"Got us in to see the man in charge of the investigation."

"Oh, man." Derek looks unhappy, "You sure you want to do this?"

Night wants to believe they're going to get somewhere, accomplish something, get someone to believe them. "You don't think it's a good idea?"

Derek watches gouged mountainside glide past, "I don't know, man. I just don't know."

In Salem they turn onto Capitol, park below Public Services. Tension ripening, they make their way through underground parking. In sour silence they await the elevator. Derek moans, reaches to press the hole in his shoulder, "I don't know about this."

They ride the elevator to the fourth floor. As they rise a small humming starts at the base of Night's spine. Before he's ready, the doors slide wide. He steps out, turns to see Derek hang back. The door closes and Night reaches out to stop it, "What are you waiting for?"

"Changed my mind."

"Get out here."

A secretary takes her place by Derek in the car, waits, eyes on vacant space.

"I don't think this is too smart."

Night blocks the door a second time. The woman gives him a look. "We're here, let's go in."

Derek glances at the secretary, "What we doing here, huh? They wanted to know what happened, they would have asked us. They didn't."

Night doesn't want to think that. Not now. "Let's find out."

The idiot door runs into his arm again, buzzes angrily on the third try.

The woman turns eyes the color of Bahamas water on Night, "If you're the officers from Eugene, they're waiting for you."

Derek backs away from her the way he might from a chittering rattlesnake. Night takes his arm, hustles him through the door. A secretary with pinched eyes shows them to a room marked CONFERENCE. Inside wait three funeral-faced detectives. One sits, two perch on the edge of a table, faces closed. They introduce themselves, motion them to chairs.

Night forgets the names as soon as he hears them. Chilly is their welcome. No camaraderie, nothing to suggest they're on the same side. Only ice. Not a good start.

The sitter speaks. "We understand you have something to add to the investigation."

This was a mistake, a waste of time. Night can see that now. "No." Night says, "We've got nothing to add."

Derek frowns, puzzled. Confused looks among the three. "Then why are you here?"

"I thought you might want to know what happened." Night takes in their faces one after another, finds suspicion. "From one member of the law enforcement fraternity to another. You know, in the spirit of colleagiality." His jest meets their hostile stares. "You don't, do you?"

The sitter, the one in charge, bridles. "We've taken statements from everyone involved."

In amazement, Night smiles, "Everyone involved? Just who was that? We were there. He took a bullet. Everybody else on our side was wasted. What am I missing here?"

In lowered voices they confer. Night had assumed the sitter was the boss. Now he's not so sure.

Derek speaks, voice low. "Maybe they had a chat with our friends in the van."

The same man turns back to them, taps a pen on the table top carelessly, "Isn't it true, Detective Hume, that you have a history of alcoholism?"

Night is a blank slate. "Alcoholism?"

He leafs through a file, "According to statements we have, you were intoxicated at the time of the incident."

Derek whispers in Night's ear. "What'd I tell you?"

Night's still playing catch up. "Who told you that?"

The leaners gloat. Sitter leans back in his chair, "We have eyewitness accounts that place you at the Squire nightclub drinking on duty."

Derek shakes his head slowly. "Don't waste your breath, man."

"We have information that leads us to believe that you were in fact derelict in your duties in not accompanying the entry team inside."

"Yeah, you would have preferred that, wouldn't you?" Derek says.

Night can't believe this is really it. That they would choose something so banal to smear him. "What about Derek? Why didn't you ask him what went on? Was he drunk, too?"

Derek raises his hands, backs to the door, "Hey, this boy didn't see nothing."

Sitter regards them with cagey eyes, "Wounded, delirious with pain, how can we expect him to recall events accurately?" He raises his hands palm up, "I'm just playing devil's advocate here."

Derek looks as if he may spit. "Sure, you are."

He has come this far. He decides to show his cards. "And Professor Lawrence? What about her? There a reason she can't be believed?" Even as he says the words, Night guesses their answer.

Sitter opens a second file, "A dealer? I hardly think her testimony would be credible in front of a jury. Do you?"

Derek takes his arm, "Come on, man, let's get out of here. I need some fresh air."

Night rises. The chair he sat in calls to him, crying out to be thrown over the table. His palms itch to do it. So trite, so predictable. Intimidation by contract agents, government operating like mafia. It happens—in Washington. This is Salem. This is where he lives. It's different here. It has to be.

He spreads his arms wide, taking in the office, the three, the entire Oregon State Police floor, sense of futility strong as vinegar in the air, "That's it? You write off five good cops?"

The agent in charge shuts the file, slides it away, signaling the interview is over.

Derek tugs Night back, and he wrests free, heat geysering into his throat. He takes a step nearer the table. "You aren't cops. If you ever were, you aren't now. You're suits, that's all. You don't give a rat's ass whether cops get killed as long as you draw your pension."

Sitter looks up, tapping his pen, "If I were you, Officer Hume…"

Night snatches it and hurls it at the wall of glass where it caroms harmlessly. "You're not me."

The sitter ignores him, pushes on. "If I were you, I would just sit back, thank God you're alive and let it go. Just…let it go."

"Let it go?"

"That's right."

Night searches the eyes of the seated man for something human. "Do what you got to do, but don't risk that check." He digs the envelope out of his pocket, empties the photos into his hand, holds them up. "This is Alicia, Jenaro's wife. This is Lupe and Sabrina, twins. This is Tamara, Sid's wife, due in September with their third."

He holds the photos like a hand of cards. "Take a good look. A week ago, they had fathers, husbands. Take a real good look, and remember. Remember them while you're traveling around in your land yachts waiting out your coronaries."

Derek takes his arm, "Time to go."

"I don't know whose shit you're burying, and I don't care, but I'll tell you this, you are some bent sons of mongrel bitches."

In whisks the secretary with a pink box of what Night sees are doughnuts. As she passes, he swipes them from her grasp. Through the door he puts them, box gaping mid-flight. Glazed, jelly, powdered sugar doughnuts scatter, sending the three at the table dodging. "Hope you choke."

Derek hauls him through the door and to the elevator.

The door closes them inside and, eyes tearing with frustration, Night slams a palm against polished stainless.

Derek leans against the wall and sighs, shaking his head as they drop to the parking garage. "Why'd you have to go and do that? Why'd you have to go shaking the hornet's nest?"

Night looks at him, sees a stranger. "Why? You have to ask me that? Nobody believes in honest cops any more, and now there are five less of us to believe in. That's why."

"Yeah, well, they didn't want to hear it. So I guess we get an E for effort then, don't we. Now maybe we better just do what the man said and let it go."

Inside Night something solidifies.

That is the one thing he will not do.

• • •

The trip home they pass in silence.

Sense of impending disaster heavy on them both, they stop in to talk to Sam. After her set she finds their table, slips into a chair, presses an icy hand into Night's. In her eyes he sees fear.

"Couple guys been in here, watching me."

Derek says, "I don't know how to break this too you, honey, but a lot of guys come in here to watch you."

She sighs impatiently, "I think they may have taken my picture."

Alarms going off in his head, Night scans the dark room around them, "How you getting home?"

"With Kelly, why?"

"Get Roy to walk you out."

She gives him a cynical grimace. "Oh, yeah, what'll Roy do? Can't you drive us?"

He sees no reason for anyone to target her. "You're on your own, tonight. Got that Beretta I gave you?"

She nods.

"See them again, call."

In the lot, Night waits behind the wheel, making no move to start the engine.

Derek watches him, unwraps a piece of gum, rolls it into his mouth. "What you thinking, man?"

"About the way Herrera was so eager to believe that garbage out of Salem."

Derek laughs. "Eager to believe it? I guess so. Where you think they got half that shit?"

Night thinks about it, realizes it must be true.

Derek sighs, stares straight ahead into the dark, "What'd you fir d out there today? you never showed me."

Night drops a casing into his hand.

"Shit, oh dear." Derek turns it in his fingers under the light in the glove box. "Fluted chamber markings." He hands it back. "HK all right."

"Kid could tell the difference."

"We both know Compton wasn't the shooter. So what's going on?"

Night turns to look at him, Derek's dark face invisible in the dim. "I don't know, but the bobtail has to be part of it."

Derek laughs a bitter laugh, "They can't think that report would fool anybody."

"All they have do is fool the media, and that's not hard."

Derek slaps the dash, "Oh, come on, man, I'll tell you what. You got to give that a rest. Everybody be rolling their eyes when you start with that conspiracy stuff."

Night turns to him in the dark, "You were there. What did it look like to you?"

"Come on, start this thing. Let's get going."

"No, tell me. The week after a bobtail of cocaine gets two officers gunned down we walk into an ambush? In a city where it makes the front page every time we bust a jerk with a few grow-tubes in a closet? That feel right to you?"

Across the lot two sedans with darkened headlights pull out of adjacent spaces and head their way.

Derek sighs.

"Does it?"

"I ain't getting into this, so you just might as well start the car."

Giving up, Night starts the engine, waits for them to pass before pulling out. "Fine, you're right. We'll stick our heads in the sand and it'll all go away."

"Ostriches don't stick their heads in the sand. Don't you read *National Geographic?* That's just something your ignorant lily white assed stupid sharecropper ancestors dreamed up."

Night watches as the two cars cross the lot and fights the feeling there is something he should notice. "My ancestors, how you know it wasn't your jungle bunny spear-chucker ancestors with their massive male members?"

"Sheeit, none of us be dumb enough to make up something like that. The birds graze, man. Africa ain't sand anyway, man. It's clay. You'd have to have post hole digger to make a hole in that."

In front of them the two cars brake, blocking them in.

"What the hell's this, now?" Derek says.

Two men pour out, one moving to each of their windows to level a suppressed carbine from a position just behind the doorpost. A third, face masked in a balaclava, nails them from an open door. Derek reaches for his SIG. Night stops his hand, "You got a death wish?"

Derek loses air through his teeth with the sound of a leaking balloon, "Who'd we piss off now?"

Night fights the urge to reach for the muzzle inches from the nape of his neck. Hands open and in sight, Night looks them over. "Military."

"Shut up," the hood at Night's side says.

Derek ignores him, "You saying what I think you're saying?"

Night notices index fingers lying along gun frames. It takes training to get muscle memory like that. "That's what I'm saying."

"Jesus," Derek says, voice a breath. "Got an application for the John Birch Society on you?"

"I'll drop by a copy of the *New American* tomorrow morning."

"They take Negroes?"

"They let me join."

"Oh, well, then, I guess they take anybody."

"I said shut up."

Night looks in his eyes. Young, dark eyes. Derek he asks, "Why are we still breathing?"

Derek looks up into the gunman's face, "Either they just slow, or they want something."

"We ain't slow, Jack."

A forth man, this one a suit, slides out of the passenger side of the second sedan, ambles over, leans down to peer into the window on Night's side. "How are Night and Derek this evening?"

"Little nervous just now," Night says.

He seems to notice the carbines for the first time, chortles, "Ah, don't pay them any mind. It's me you need to worry about."

"Why doesn't that make me all warm and fuzzy inside?" Derek says.

The suit smiles. "I'll only take a moment of your time, gentlemen. The unfortunate incident out on Airport Road the other day—my employers are satisfied with the investigation's conclusions. They would prefer no one question the data presented therein. They hear someone is, they'll be peeved. When they're peeved, they nag, and I don't like being nagged."

From a vest pocket he takes a tablet, slips in a disk. "I love a good photo, don't you? You got the prints we left on your dash, I see. I have some more for you." He lights the screen, holds up the tablet for them both to see. Julie stands at the kitchen counter. "This one's for Derek. Notice where she is. Such a happy domestic scene."

Derek grabs for him, "You son of a—"

Night holds him as a gloved thumb snicks off the safety on a carbine at his ear.

The suit smiles, waits. "These are for you, Night. Oh, lucky man, you have three. I'm impressed. First this one..."

Night's back ices when he sees it. It's Jade riding her bike, turned half away, looking back. The suit presses a stud and the second is Sam on stage doing her number. The last is Ceridwen. Taken from out in front of the house, she's just sliding out of the Volvo, skirt riding up a toned thigh. They've got him. They've got them both. "Who are you?"

He seems to find the question entertaining. "That doesn't matter. What does is that life is precious. You see enough death in your jobs to know that. Don't throw it away."

"You son of a bitch, you whacked seven of our guys," Derek says, spitting consonants, "seven good cops."

Night keeps a hand on Derek's chest over his gun.

"I see you have drawn conclusions about the incident on Willamette. Observant of you." He shrugs. "This is business. In business there is competition. There are winners, losers—people get hurt. Their families will be taken care of."

"Is that supposed to make it up to Jenaro's twins for growing up without a father?"

The man pauses, seems to consider, then a hard face gets harder. "He knew there were risks when he took the job. So did you. So do the wives. Their numbers came up, that's all. The miracle is we're having this conversation at all. What you should be thinking of is the people in those pictures. What do you say?"

Night keeps his eyes on the guy in the back seat of the sedan, muzzle leveled at his face. At 900 rounds per second, he would be no pleasure for Rita to iD.

"You want to know what I say?" Derek says. "I say kiss my lilly white ass."

The man at the window sighs, a tired sigh. "A kid trick what you pulled this afternoon in Salem. You won't make any difference, you know. Maybe you aren't smart enough to be afraid. More is the pity."

The two at the doors shield their carbines from view as two men pass, heels crunching gravel. The suit leans against an elbow on the roof of the Lincoln, lights a slender cigar, "Nasty habit, this, infantile form of satisfaction. Trying to quit. Not easy, though."

Night watches him, intrigued. What he wants to know is why he bothers with them.

Witnesses gone, the guns rise. The suit goes on. "I'm the only reason you're both not dead already. My superiors are impatient men. When it got back to them what you were up to..." He shrugs, drags, empties his lungs through his mouth. "But you know, you impressed me."

Night is not sure what to think of this. "How's that?"

"I mean, to take us on the way you did, the two of you with a woman in that wagon. Audi was it?"

"Volvo."

"Feisty. I could tell there was a cool head behind those headlights. Your colleagues died well, went out the way we all hope to. I wanted you to know that." He muses, eyes skyward. "Big one, blond, looks up at me, actually reaches for his pistol. I step on his wrist and with the suppressor at his ear, eyes on mine, he tells me what I can do." He drags long, smiles up at the sky, "That was a warrior."

"Sid," Derek says, "his name was Sid."

"Men like I work for..." He shakes his head, disgusted. "They don't understand that." Now he looks directly at Night. "Crying shame to waste good men like that. I didn't want to kill two more without at least trying." He leans in the window, flicks the cigar away, "You two I like. You've got guts. The question is, do you have brains?" Another sigh as he slips a card onto the dash. "Any questions, call this number. Ask for Simon. I'll get back to you. You get the urge to be a hero..." He ejects the disk, tosses it onto Derek's lap. "Take another look at what you have to lose."

He goes to the car and is followed by the two at the windows. Night and Derek watch the sedans slip out of the lot and into the ebb of late night traffic.

"No plates," Derek says.

In something close to a trance, Night realizes that was what he noticed before.

"Damn." Derek slumps. "What do we do now?"

Night raises a hand to silence him, pulls out.

"Where we going?"

"Dinner."

Outside the Electric Station he parks.

"You're hungry?"

Night motions him to follow.

Inside, they are shown to a table.

"What are we doing here? I'm not hungry."

"Neither am I."

"Then why—"

"Because we never come here, that's why."

Derek thinks. "You think the car's wired?"

Night smiles at his simplicity.

Derek lifts his arms, "What about us?"

"Don't think so."

Derek lays the disk on the table, "Goddam them."

Night understands. It's a lousy feeling being so exposed.

"Okay, so what do we do?"

So like Derek to think there must be an answer, a right thing to do. Over Night there weighs a sea of hopelessness. He can barely muster the energy to answer. "We keep quiet. Isn't that what you said?"

"That was before this." Derek prods the disk.

"That changes something?"

Derek stares at him as if he is insane. "Hell, yes it does. They came to our homes to get this."

Night shrugs, "What you want to do?"

"Where do we stand? We've got the shooter from the bobtail, we've got the professor's car full of government agency AP."

Night smiles, raises a hand for the cocktail waitress, "Do we?"

Derek gives him a puzzled look as he orders an OJ. Derek asks for the same.

"No beer?"

Derek shrugs, "Julie."

"Cold turkey?"

He makes a face. "Juice and skim milk."

Head hanging, Night chuckles.

"Go on, laugh, you won't be single forever. So what do you mean—do we?"

"With them here to tie up loose ends, what you want to bet by tomorrow morning the Volvo is a two by two cube on a flat car of sheet steel headed to Portland?"

"Okay, forget the car, we've got Sam."

"An X-tweaker? A stripper? She's found raped and strangled tomorrow in her bath tub, who does more than click their tongue? Nobody."

"Your professor, then."

"A dealer, I don't think so."

Derek thinks, "We've got the air traffic data transcription. We weren't a stone's throw from the airport."

Night shakes his head. "Called this morning. A glitch wiped six hours of tape. Guess which six and win a carob energy bar."

Derek slaps the table with a hand, and a family across the aisle turns to stare. Derek smiles his Richard Pryor smile, waves, "Just one of my spells, over now." When they turn away, he leans close, voice low, "Okay, then the controllers. I talked to them yesterday and they remembered warning them out of the air lanes."

Night slides his phone across the table.

Derek rolls his wrist, glances, "Too late."

Night smiles, amused. He can see he already knows what he'll find. "Wake them up."

Reluctantly, Derek takes the phone, punches them up, "This is detective Peterson, is this Marty? I know it's late, I…son of a gun." He redials, looks up at Night, "Hung up on me. We just talked yesterday. "Yeah, Marty, you remember me, we—" He slams down the phone, glares.

Night is enjoying this. For as long as he's studied history he's understood it is more planning than chance. Yet somehow the view, however logical, brands proponents fanatics. Here in front of them the onion sheds its layers. "Get it yet?"

In Derek's eyes Night sees understanding dawn, and maybe a hint of panic. "Just a minute." Derek finds a number, punches it in. "Carol, this is Detective Peterson, you remember we spoke this—"

Night watches his eyes and can guess what he's hearing. Who said people were dumb? They see danger, they back off. In his book that's a pretty good definition of smart. He's not so sure either of them qualifies.

Derek waits for his chance to speak, "Listen, yesterday you said you would. Who got to you?" More from the other end. "You know we can subpoena you. Hey!" He jerks the phone away from his ear, slides it across, blows air.

"That convinced her, I bet."

Derek notices the father across the way staring, waves. "It's okay, took my meds." Voice low, face grim, to Night he says, "Okay, I get it."

"So…" Night leans back in the booth, sips OJ. "What have we got? We got you and we got me. Me—a cop living with a dealer he's supposed to be investigating. And you—"

Derek nods. "They'll tar me with it, too."

Night nods, seeing it's true.

"It don't make no never mind. We saw tonight how hard we'd be to fix." Derek thinks, shakes his finger at him, "Let's not forget the truck and the cocaine."

Night nudges the phone across the table with a finger.

Derek reads the look in his eye, calls, speaks quietly into it the way Night remembers him speaking into his epaulet mike on his portable radio when they were in uniform. Long ago, it seems now. Across the table he sees Derek's expression change as he reacts to what he hears.

"What? What the hell you mean, you think so?"

Disgusted, he disconnects.

Night knows what he's going to hear. "Tell me."

"DEA checked the truck out of impound and the coke out of evidence storage this morning."

"The driver, at least we've still got him."

A dark certainty falls heavy as dew about them. In Derek's eyes Night sees he feels the same. "Do we?"

"This guy killed a couple cops in broad daylight if front of fifty witnesses. You telling me they're going to let him walk? I don't think so."

Night hopes he's right, but a black bruise deep in his insides tells him he's not. "We're not even a block away, let's check."

They call their waitress, tell her to hold their order, walk the short block to Lane County Jail. At the door from the lobby to the annex they wait, ID's raised to the monitor over the door. It opens slowly on motorized rollers.

"Who you?"

Invisible behind inch thick plastic, Elaine sits with flashing monitors in a dark room from which she controls every remote door in the jail.

Derek pounds the glass with his fists, pressing his face against the glass, "I want candy or I'm breaking this wall down, woman."

"What candy? Get off my window, you! What you talking about, candy?"

Night loves her Korean accent. "He's just an impetuous Negro, ma'am, if you don't get us our candy, I may not be able to control him."

They hear her laugh from the dark. "Oh, I recognize you now. You not slime balls, you Derek and Night, my mistake. You need haircut bad, Night. Get fleas with hair like that."

Night preens, running fingers through tangled hair. "You're just jealous."

"You want candy, huh?" Through the trough under the glass she pushes a spray bottle of ammonia and the sports page, "First clean my glass."

"Derek backs off, "Don't do no windows."

Night scrubs the glass, "I'm always cleaning up after you."

"What you think God made white folks for? It's in the Bible, I can show you if you want. Deuteronomy, something, something."

"Yeah, right." Night sprays the glass again, "What you been eating, man? There's a quart of grease here."

"What you think I been eating? Baby back ribs and collards, what else us darkies eat?."

"You wish." Night makes the glass squeak, passes the bottle back through.

"That better, here your Lifesavers."

Derek snatches his up before Night can get it.

"You got my cherry again. I hate lime."

Derek waits at the door to parking. "Tough luck white boy, cherry's mine."

The door to parking rumbles open and they lock their guns in the small safes in the wall, taking the keys. Inside, they wait at the door to booking.

"Elaine," Night appeals to the camera over the door, "Do you think it's fair that whenever you give us candy, he always grabs the cherry? Do you?"

Her voice comes over the speaker, "He fast boy."

"I sho is, and I can dance."

Inside at a long desk, Linda smiles. Skin tan, hair streaked down the center of her scalp with silver, she has the longest nails Night's seen on a woman. It's always fascinated him watching her type.

Her eyes flash at the glass wall of the holding room. "Should you be here?"

Not long ago Night would have worried about being recognized. Not now. "Just a quick visit."

She looks them over. "You guys look like something my cat leaves me on the back porch."

Night leans over the counter, feeling secure here. "You know what you just did to our self-esteem? You know what this means?"

Derek shakes his head, sadly. "Another five years of therapy and a lawsuit from the NAACP."

Linda ignores them. "Where are those doughnuts you owe me?"

The standing joke is anybody books three or more in one night he owes the staff doughnuts. Night is behind. Way behind.   "Next time."

"I've heard that before." She leans forward, face serious. A taloned hand she presses on one of theirs. "Heard about you guys. I want you to know we been thinking of you down here. You going to the funerals?"

Night realizes he hasn't thought about funerals. Of course there will be funerals. Seven funerals for seven cops. All in less than a week. If Ceridwen hadn't driven up when she did there would be two more. "We'll be there."

"So, what can I do you for?"

"Checking up on our cop killer."

She frowns at him. "Rigo?"

The name means nothing to him.

"The truckload of coke, right?"

Derek says, "That's him."

She frowns, curious. "You're a little late."

Night sees in Derek's eyes the dread he feels himself. "What do you mean, late?"

"Didn't you hear? He hung himself this afternoon."

The words hit Night a blow to the solar plexus. With two hands he grips the lip of the counter. "You're sure?"

She pops her bubble gum. "Saw them take him out."

Night sees again the face of the man he cuffed at the truck. The smile. The eyes. "See his face?"

She shakes her head, "He was bagged, why?"

Night thinks of something. "Do me a favor, look him up for us."

She shrugs, punches it in. "Here he is."

She turns the monitor and Night sees a face he doesn't know.

Derek says, "That's not him."

She runs blood red nails through her hair, scrolls up. "Sure, it is. See, it says so right—"

"No, no, no." Derek shakes his head. "That's not the guy, that's somebody else."

Her eyes narrow. "Derek, I saw his picture on the news. Trust me, this is the guy."

Night thinks. "You book him in?"

"I was off, but, let me see…" She frowns, fingers working keys, eyes intent on the screen.

"You check the booking log?" Derek suggests.

"Keep your pants on, that's what I'm doing. Ah, Doug was on." She calls a deputy over. Night has seen him, short man, mustache, barrel chest. "Doug, you book the cop killer?"

He nods, "I did the maggot. How about that, huh? Saved the state a lot of time and money."

Night's beginning to worry. How many more people is he drawing into this?

Linda waves him close to look at the screen. "Rigo, right?"

He leans over the counter and love handles fight to escape the confines of his belt. The man is so ordinary, so matter of fact, Night can't help but be reassured. He must be wrong. Things like this don't happen in Doug's world.

"That ain't him."

Night's hope for normalcy crumbles as fast as it came. Another deputy is drawn to the commotion. Doug spots him. "Mike, you helped haul Rigo out, right?"

"I cut him down."

"That him?"

He looks. "That's him." He turns away to greet a new arrival.

"I'll be damned." Doug speaks in a whisper. "They brought one in, took another one out." His boyish face strains with thought. "I don't get it."

Linda searches their faces. "It's got to be a mixup, that's all."

Fear caustic at the base of his spine, Night decides. "I changed my mind, Linda. Never mind."

Derek slaps him with a look. He ignores it. Night doesn't blame him for thinking he is nuts. That he can live with—having more good people hurt he can't. She keeps working at the keyboard. "Linda, look at me."

She glances up, then back to the screen, involved in her search. "Yeah?"

"You listening?"

Puzzled by the intensity of this voice, she looks up. "I'm listening."

"I want you to forget it."

She laughs, "Forget it? Why? It's a mistake, it's—"

"Because I say so."

Seeing the look on his face, her smile fades. In its place comes a worried frown, "That's no reason. It's got to be straightened out."

Doug leans over to reach her keyboard and she slaps his hand away, "Hands off."

"Hey, you called me over, remember?" Arms up, he stalks off.

Night sighs, worry heavy as a lead vest. "You want a reason? Because everybody that comes within a mile of this thing gets hurt."

Her eyes show she begins to understand. Warily, she glances at the woman in the booking chair, and back at him. "You don't think it's a mixup."

He shakes his head.

As it sinks in he can see her eyes change. "If you say so."

"I say so. Clear the screen, get his name out of there."

She does, looks up, face concerned. Voice barely above a whisper, she says, "What you messing with, Night?"

Heart sick, he nearly laughs. "You don't want to know. I don't want to know." He shoves away from the counter, "We'll see you."

They wait for the door to open to the outside. Neither speaks. Night looks up at the monitor, knowing Elaine can see him, knowing he must look sick. He feels sick. She has to notice. She always notices. The eyes, nerves, brain of the jail, she misses nothing.

She pegged him the day he learned Rita dumped him. Caught the expression on his face and emerged from her sanctum to lead him inside. There, in darkness broken only by strobing security cameras, she heard him out and sent him on his way with a pat and a Lifesaver. He's never forgotten it.

"You okay, Night?" Her voice comes over the speaker in the ceiling. "You want talk?"

He smiles at the black glass to his right, wishing he could tell her, wishing he could tell everybody. "Can't this time. Thanks, though."

"Okay, see you guys."

The door rumbles ponderously on its rails. "Hey…"

Over the speaker comes her sharp-voiced benediction.

"You be careful out there."

• • •

Back at the Electric Station the waitress sets two slabs of prime rib in front of them.

Derek saws off a bite-size plank, holds it aloft on his fork, "Julie smells meat on my breath, she'll skin me."

Night enjoys his struggle.

Longingly, Derek regards the bite of rare beef, "God, I miss it."

"Go on, she'll never know."

Derek is shocked, "What are you, the little white devil sits on my shoulder and prompts me to evil?"

"That's me."

Derek thinks about it, inhales, moans, recovers, "Nah." He drops the fork, slides the plate away. "I could have my teeth cleaned and she'd know. She's like a geisha, can smell it on my skin. I'd be sleeping in the den for a week. Not worth it."

The pink beef on Night's plate might as well be wax. Through frustration, fear, futility there is no room for hunger. Night sets his plate on top of Derek's. The waitress checks on them, and Night has her bag them both.

Derek sighs. "Neat, having him hang himself. He couldn't just disappear. Now they've got a body. Everything sewn up tight. Wonder who he was."

"Never seen him. Some junkie sleeping under the overpass, wrong place, wrong time."

Derek nods. "So we got no perp. Where's that leave us?"

"Right where we started."

"Nowhere."

Night nods.

Derek stares across the emptying restaurant. "Seven men… eight counting Compton."

"Let's not."

"Seven then."

"They're dead, we're alive."

Derek leans close, whispers. "We could go to the *Register-Guard*."

Head hanging, heart a stone under his ribs, Night has a long quiet laugh. "You still don't get it."

"*The Oregonian,* then."

Night lets the laugh die, "And do what?" he snaps with more bitterness than he intended.

"Tell the truth."

"The truth?" His hands he clasps in front of his forehead hard enough to set his knuckles popping. When he can speak he looks up. "Give them a song and dance about a government conspiracy? What did you think about conspiracies a couple hours ago? Look at us. We couldn't get their attention if Sam did her routine on their desk. Can't you guess how it would go? They'd call to verify our credentials and they'd get what we got in Salem.

"Within 24 hours some Peruvian illegal maid would find the four of us in a room at The Blue Moon. I can see it now—two drug cops, stripper and dealer in kinky sex melange found overdosed in motel. Even dead we'd be lucky to make "A" section. Don't you get it? These are the guys you never want to meet, the guys JFK pissed off before Dallas. They don't lose. And the beautiful thing, the sweet thing is, nobody believes in them. Is that perfect, or what?"

"We could line up SWAT, set up a meet."

Night watches him, incredulous. "You're suggesting we murder them? This is coming out of your mouth?"

Derek leans forward, "They threaten Julie? They threaten Jade? I'm suggesting we take them, let them decide how. They start something, we finish it."

Night thinks it over. "First we'd never get the go ahead to call them out. I don't know anybody over there any more, do you?"

"Hutto does."

"Second, if they were out-gunned, they'd throw in the towel and walk away. They'd fade into the woodwork just like Rigo or whatever his name is."

Derek looks at him with contempt. "You saying we roll over? You saying we let them get away with it? I can't believe you, man."

Night lifts a finger, sights over it at Derek, "Hey, don't give me that. This isn't some grocery rack detective yarn where the spunky old lady and her cat solve the murders sharing her recipes for lasagna along the way. This is that ugly place where Jack is crushed by the giant. This is real life, buddy. And if you think we're going to take on these guys and come out smelling like roses, I'm here to tell you you're sadly mistaken." Night gives himself a minute to calm.

The waitress takes away his Visa. They brood.

Feeling the placidity that comes of fatigue, Night muses. "Makes you wonder, doesn't it? Busting white trash bikers peddling meth... Taking down growers with a few grow lights in their garage... Arresting people who sell pot to their friends... For what? So these guys can bring in a bobtail of white dope any time they want? What are we, their stooges? their price support system? Strong arm men they use to elimi- nate the competition? Is that what we are, now?"

Derek shakes his head, looking sick. "I'm no Nietzsche. You want to do the why- are-we-here thing, you're going to have to do it by yourself. What I want to know is why us? Hundred thirty thousand people? Eugene's a pimple on the ass of a real city. Why are they bothering with us?"

Night pays and they head home through a downtown deserted.

He has been wondering the same thing.

• • •

At four a.m. Night gives up on sleep.

Bare footed, OR scrubs he sleeps in hanging off his hips, he pads into a dark kitchen, feeling his way, unwilling to turn on a light. It's a useless gesture, he knows. They can see him just as well in the dark. For the hundredth time he feels how vulnerable he is, how vulnerable are all the people with lives and jobs to lose.

He fills a cup with water, sets it in the microwave. As he waits, he runs a hand over his belly. The last few weeks he's dropped some weight. It feels good. Watching the cup turn in its irradiated stage behind the glass, he wonders if he could fit into his uniforms. He guesses he might—just.

A chip beeps and he retrieves his cup, yo-yos a tea bag over it, too impatient to let it steep. He pinches the scalding bag between his fingers and drops it on the counter. Feeling claustrophobic in the kitchen, he heads out the front door. On the porch stoop he nearly trips over Ceridwen. "Jesus, what are you doing out here?"

"Couldn't sleep. You?"

He takes a place beside her on the stair. "Uh, uh."

A meteor zips across a clear sky and is gone, leaving a fading ghost trail.

"See that?"

For some reason it's passing saddens him, "Ever wonder where they come from, where they go?"

"Sure."

"Like rocks on a pond." He looks at her, "You're a biologist, what do you think? Anybody out there?"

She laughs quietly, turns a face resting on folded knees in his direction. "I like not knowing."

"Nobody knows. What do you think?"

She laughs warily. "About what?"

"About everything, about all of it."

"You mean the biggie? The what-does-it-all-mean biggie?"

He smiles at her, finds himself wishing she weren't going to disappear from his life in only a few days. "That one."

She breathes, lets it go slowly. "I like the idea that we're here to learn, that we're here again and again until we get it right."

"The wheel." He rests his head in his hands, "God, that's discouraging."

"On the road to Benares." She laughs. "It may be a while." She watches him through the half light. "The men that were killed—you haven't talked about it."

As he might pull away from a finger prodding an open wound he feels himself close off. "What's to say?"

"You don't believe in talking about feelings?"

"Talking doesn't change anything."

"Maybe not, but it helps."

He feels a drawing at his intestines. The ache in his gut he holds back. He lets it come, he may not be able to stop it.

"I'm listening."

She lays a cold hand on his and it all crumbles, all his resolve, all his will melting like wave-washed sand. He slumps to rest his head in the warmth of her lap and her hands roam his face, his hair, his back. Eyes shut, lids fluttering, images in negative flash. The farmhouse. The bobtail. Her Volvo. Flames billowing from shattered house windows. "I heard them die. I was right there, right outside, and I ran."

She pets him, cool hand soothing. "If you had stayed, would you have been able to help?"

Ashamed, he squeezes his eyes shut tight. The answer is easy. Saying it isn't.

"You would have died. That's true, isn't it?"

Ear crushed to the warm luxury of her lap, he says nothing.

"Then you did the right thing."

She doesn't understand. In his intestines guilt worms its way. "We were right outside. We should have done something."

"You did do something—you lived." The certainty in her voice is ice on a burn—his burn. "The news said they found the man that did it in the house. They said it was Compton, that he killed himself. I just don't see how one man could have—"

"Compton was the fall guy. They left him there for us."

Her hand halts in its path along his aching spine. "But, the news said—"

"The news is wrong. It's a lie, all a lie."

"How do you know?"

How much should he tell her?

"Tell me."

He decides she has the right. "Couple nights ago we met them."

"You met them?"

"They met us. In the lot outside the Squire. They came to talk."

"Talk? The same men that tried to kill us on the road? About what?"

"About how we shouldn't raise a stink. They gave us a photo disk."

He feels her stiffen.

"Derek got one of Julie taken through their window at home."

"What about you?" Her voice is laden with dread. "What did you get?"

"I got one of Jade. One of Sam. One of you."

A tremor passes over her. "Jesus, where?"

"Here."

"They know where we live?"

Where we live—in any other context it would have a nice sound. "They know."

"What kind of dealers are they?"

"They're not."

"What, then?"

"Don't know yet."

"But you suspect."

She's done it, found the head of the infection, the boil crying out for the lance. "I suspect." But he doesn't know. And if he ever wants to sleep again, ever wants to stop hearing the voices of the five as they died, he has to. Who. More importantly, why.

Now he sees. As precipitate coalesces in solution, an idea forms in his mind. Obvious, elegantly simple, uncomplicated, perhaps deadly—it is the only way, he is sure. From her lap he pushes upright, fishes the card from his jacket pocket. By the light off his cell phone pad he reads it.

"Who you calling?"

"Them."

"You're calling them? Are you crazy?"

Too fast it rings. He fights the urge to disconnect. "Probably."

The voice at the other end repeats the number he called—why doesn't that surprise him? Stomach panging with regret, he forces himself to speak. "I want to talk to Simon."

"You are?"

"Night Hume."

"He'll get back to you."

"My num—"

The line goes dead and, ribbon of cold sidling down his back, he puts the phone into his pocket.

"Well?"

"They'll get back to me."

"That's reassuring. What are you going to do?"

"Set up a meet."

"Why?"

It's not something he's sure he can voice, not something he's sure won't sound ridiculous if he tries. What he needs is to get started, to move, to make it happen. He stands. "I'm not going to let them get away with it."

She exhales, glaring up at him. "You think you can stop them?"

"I can try. And I can find out why."

In the growing haze of dawn, amid mist lazing down from a pewter sky, she moves close. "They'll kill you."

Inside he is dull and catchy as if he's bolted half a watermelon on an empty stomach. "They might and they might not. There may be a way to do it." The closer she gets the more her influence on him grows. This close all he can think of is reasons to stay alive. Cup of tea forgotten, he heads inside.

"Will I see you again?"

He thinks over his chances. "When it's over you might."

• • •

The third floor of the parking garage still radiates the heat of day.

Beside Night, Derek leans back, boot propped on the dash. He reaches over to flick a finger at the hula dancer on the dash, sending skirted hips swinging.

"They all in?"

Derek laughs. "When I told them who you were meeting? You kidding me? Three guys from SWAT are in, too. Couldn't keep them out."

Doubt itches at the back of his mind. "Can we trust them?"

"If Hutto says we can trust them, we can trust them."

"Where are they now?"

"At Hutto's."

"What about Herrera?"

"What about him?"

"He know?"

Derek laughs through his nose. "As far as anybody knows we've got a poker game going at Hutto's. By the way, I talked to a guy I know at the DA's office. He talked with the district attorney. He told him that if we have the eyeballs we say we do, he'll make sure Rigo doesn't get lost in the shuffle twice."

"Well, then we'll just have to get him, won't we?"

Derek nods.

Night's stomach growls and Derek smiles at him, "Hungry?"

"Nerves. How about weapons? There could be eight, ten of them."

Derek sighs, rolls his head on the back of the seat. "Will you relax? Bryce works SWAT. We'll be ready."

Night is worried. "But with no AP."

"But no AP." Derek looks at his watch. "When Simon say he'd call?"

"Fifteen minutes ago."

Derek watches him. "Maybe he got cold feet."

Night's cellular hums and they both jump. Night takes a long breath, raises a hand to quiet Derek, listens. "I'll be there."

"We on?"

"Skinner Butte parking lot, thirty minutes."

Derek smiles. "Perfect."

Night thinks about what they are about to do and his stomach clenches. "Yeah. We've got them right where they want us."

"Will you stop worrying?" Derek reaches for Night's cellular.

Night slips it away. "Use a land line." He nods to a telephone by the elevator.

Derek frowns. "Let's not be paranoid about this."

"Nobody ever died of paranoia."

In less than a minute Derek is back. He leans in at the window, "They'll be set. Hutto wants you by the wall."

Night nods, starts the car. "Better get going."

Derek stays where he is. "Got your piece?"

Night tugs at the neck of his vest. "Got it." The compact Glock .40 rides in a belly band just under his belt. Not that he expects to keep it long.

"Cuffs?"

"In the trunk." Night needs to move. He sits there he may suffocate. "Got to go."
"I ought to be there."

Night is ready for this. "You will be—right where I need you. This part I do alone."

Derek grimaces. "Go ahead, be a cowboy, I ain't ID'n you."

"If it goes that way I won't need any company."

Derek pushes off the door, heads for his car. "You is one stubborn white boy."

Night pulls away. "Be seeing you."

Derek turns. "I hope you're right about that. I surely do."

• • •

Top of Skinner Butte.

Night paces alone the low stone wall overlooking Eugene. On his right, a drop down a rocky slope, brushy with teasel and broom. To his left, his Lincoln. Across the lot a van waits with the hood up, to all appearances abandoned. Below him the lights of downtown spread out, muted by fog, glowing dim as if submerged.

Night speaks to the air. "Hello out there in radio land." He paces some more. Years of bad luck with wires gives him doubts. "If you can hear me give me a light."

Across the lot the van's brake lights flash once.

Below, he sees two sedans turn up the long winding drive. "Here we go." Suddenly nervous, he glances around him into the dark. Beyond the van a hillock and two century old fir. What will those old men see this morning? Nothing they haven't already, he would guess.

The cars wind their way up the hill. Headlights round a curve below him, rise along the winding road to the lot. Feeling a naked jaywalker in downtown noon traffic, he watches them come. He considers dropping over the wall, losing himself in blackberry bramble. He peers over, decides it's not too far down. Might break a leg but he would live.

But he wouldn't know why and it wouldn't be over. They could get to him through Jade any time they chose. He is here for her, and for the seven who will be buried tomorrow. If he plays his cards right, this will be an end to it. One way or another—an end.

Headlights darken as they glide behind his Lincoln, blocking it in. Doors spring wide and four ninjas from the first sedan come for him. Three sight over suppressors as a fourth motions him down. From the second sedan three move to secure the lot. Seven not counting Simon.

The wall, high ground, his last advantage. Once he steps down, lost. He remembers Jade the last time he saw her, he remembers they know who she is, raises his hands to the top of his head and drops to the macadam. The forward man reaches for him. All Night can see are their eyes—it's enough.

"How you been, Rigo?"

Rigo hesitates, then with an arm on his back propels him to the hood of his Lincoln. Night's boots he kicks apart, and as Night waits, hands on cold steel hood, pats him down. He is not gentle. Keys he takes from his jacket and tosses to clang on the trunk lid.

"Easy on the paint, huh? This is a classic here."

His forty Rigo finds easily. It, too, goes on the trunk. The transmitter in his vest Rigo misses. He spins Night roughly, and muzzle to Night's sternum, smiles. With a gloved finger he taps at Night's vest just under the wire, "Think that's going to do you any good?"

"Creature of habit."

"Take it off."

"Why?"

He backs up to cover him. "Off, toss it on the car."

Night does as he is told.

"Shirt up, pants down." He waits for Night to comply. "Now turn around." When he has, Rigo signals to the waiting sedan, tosses him his vest. "Leave the vest, get dressed, wait there."

Night dresses.

Rigo checks the car, opens the trunk, tosses in Night's Glock, slams the lid, goes to speak into a window of the second sedan. Simon emerges, two shadows at his heels. Taking Night's arm, he leads him to the wall, where they look out over downtown. "The cuffs in the trunk?"

"Picked them up at a yard sale."

"Planning on arresting somebody?"

"Care to be the first?"

Simon chuckles, "Thank you, anyway. You called."

Night isn't sure where to begin. What he wants to do is to lift him by the lapels and drop him over the side of the bluff. He doubts he'd make it three steps. "Who are you?"

"Me? personally?"

"You..." Night lifts a hand, taking in the five gunmen behind them. "Impersonally."

He smiles and Night wants a shower. "I think you know. Am I wrong?"

"I know who you'd have to be to do what you do and get away with it, yeah."

"What did I tell you?"

"Why? tell me that, then. Why seven good cops?"

"You're forgetting our Mr. Compton."

"I'm not asking about Compton.

Simon breathes deeply, surveys the lights stretching out below. "Nice town."

"You going to tell me or are we going to admire the sights?"

"Like I said before, they knew the risks."

Night grabs him, pulls him close enough to spit words into his face.

Amused, Simon raises an arm to hold off the men around him.

"They knew the risks—of busting bikers cooking crank, not of running into you guys. Tell me why we're out here busting our butts bringing in dealers when you're driving semi's loaded with the stuff. Tell me that."

Simon pries Night's hands off his jacket, goes to stand at the overlook. "I'm surprised you haven't figured this out yourself. You'll never stop drugs. Even a dumb cop like you must know that. Drugs have been around forever. Elephants will eat fermented fruit to get a buzz, monkeys, too. Man has been licking frogs and chewing shrooms for a hundred thousand years. You think cocaine is a modern invention? We got it from the Indians. Been south of the border?"

"No farther than TJ."

"Drugs are like gravity down there, like air. Without drug money there wouldn't be any. Anybody—and I mean anybody—with anything on the ball at all is busy giving the gringo what he wants."

Night looks for a fit with what he knows, finds none. "Governments fight narco-traffickers. Their armies wipe out coca fields, destroy processing facilities, I've seen it."

Simon shakes his head, tutor dismayed by an obtuse pupil. "Come on, Hume, you're bursting my bubbles here. I thought you guys were sharp. It's a shell game. Kid along Uncle Sam and get the money, get the certification. When the show's over everybody goes back to work."

A cold feeling spreads inside him. He knows the truth when he hears it. This is it. "They may be playing games, we're not. Here we bust our butts doing the job."

Simon smiles. "What you're doing is supporting prices. One way only you'll ever put the cartels out of business. One thing they're afraid of. Prove you're not a dupe. Tell me, what is it?"

The answer Night finds waiting. A few weeks ago it wouldn't have been. Now it's obvious as a horsefly on angel food. "Legalize."

Simon claps hands three times slowly. "See? you're not so dumb."

A thought, dark, ugly. "The initiative up for vote this fall…" Dammit, what was it? He can't remember.

"Eighty-two," Simon finishes his thought for him.

That Simon knows of it confirms his fears. "A week ago the polls were sixty-forty in favor."

Simon smirks. "Not now."

Thrill coursing his scalp, Night makes the connection. "That's what this is about? That's why the show? That's why eight men died?"

"Who says doughnuts make you stupid?"

A sense of injustice rises to choke him. "We're supposed to be on the same side!"

Half shrug. "We are. But, we're realists, too. We have to be. Somebody does."

Night's mind careens. "All the lip-service about a drug war, all the money, all those touching ads by The Partnership For A Drug Free America, the speeches…"

Simon laughs and it sounds more like a cough, "Come on, now, you're playing dumb again." He raises an arm, sweeps it out over the city below, "That's for them, all those poor stupid working slobs out there who believe what they see, hear, read. We give them what they want. What's wrong with that?"

Night forgets the wire, forgets the team waiting about them, the snipers sighting in on them from the dark. He forgets it all. In his mind there is room only for Simon's words. They leave his insides cauterized. "Then it's all a lie."

"That's a strong word, don't you think? I prefer therapy."

"Therapy?"

"Sure. Everybody out there knows somebody hurt by drugs—a brother, a sister, a mother, a father. What do you think they want? Legalization? You think they want to hear that it was little Johnny's fault he ended up aspirating his own puke? No. What they want is something to blame."

"When Dick Q. Public gets mugged, broken into, has his car stolen, you think judges, lawyers, lawmakers want them mulling over a ninety percent recidivism rate? Hell no. They want them thinking reefer madness. They want them convinced drugs did it. They want them envisioning a world without the evil powders and leaves that lure so many to perdition." He offers his open palm. "More taxes, please."

"And your job is to make sure it stays that way."

"You think we like what we do? We're just the errand boys. You ask, why? Ask the slime you put in office. Running D.C. like they're still wading hip deep in Dixie

Mafia. Anybody care?" He shrugs. "Nobody."

Night turns, looks out over the city where he's worked for twenty years. He's been a fool and he knows it—it hurts. "Tell me something. How can scuttling one lousy initiative legalizing pot in a state like Oregon be worth so many lives?"

Simon glares, contempt plain in his face, "I was wrong about you, you're not smart. It's bad precedent, that's how. Oregon may be small, but you're cutting edge. This thing passes, people all over the US are going to be watching to see what happens. And not just the NORML crew, either."

Night stops him. "Those jerks?"

"You bet those jerks—National Organization for the Reform of Marijuana Laws. They may have the facts on their side—we've got the money. But if eighty-two passes, America will be watching. The same way they watched after the right to die thing. When pot-crazed maniacs aren't hacking their neighbors up with hedging shears or writhing in an orgiastic stupor on front lawns, when, in fact, nothing has changed except for a decline in burglaries and robberies, people might start asking themselves why we fought the drug war at all. Can't have that, can we."

Disgusted, Night looks away, "And there goes your job."

"And yours, pal. Get it yet? With drugs illegal everybody's happy. Congressmen get to save us by passing more laws and raising taxes to pay for them. Cops get laws granting admissibility of improperly seized evidence. Bureaucrats get more power. Lawyers get more business. Prison workers get job security. Cartels get higher prices. Juan in Cartagena gets a job. Police departments get millions in forfeited property. And Mr. and Mrs. America get to feel safe in their beds at night." He shrugs, "Does it get any sweeter?"

Night sees it, sees it all, and doesn't much like it. "But they're not safe, are they?"

"Oh, I'm devil's advocate, now? Sure, I'll play." Simon smiles. "Of course, they're not. Not from addicts, not from gangs financed by drugs, not from a government that slices and dices the Constitution to fight a war it has no intention of winning, not from police departments tempted by the lure of easy money from forfeitures. That about cover it?"

Night has heard enough. It's time to wind this up. "You going to let me walk away after telling me this?"

Simon smiles, "What have I told you? Nothing anybody couldn't find out at any public library. I like you, Night. That's why you're alive now. Keep it to yourself and you'll live to draw a pension. Any more questions, or can we go home now?"

Night looks to the watchful hooded men about them and wonders if Simon will be quite as fond of him after he's told him what he has to say. "Just one." Night swallows. The muscles in his throat function perfectly. His heart beats. He is alive. He wants nothing so much as to stay that way. "Will you please put your hands on your head? You are under arrest."

Simon laughs, then his smile falls away. His look is at least as menacing as the smg's aimed at Night's gut. "Tell me you're not that stupid."

"Have your men put their guns down."

Simon's hand slips into his overcoat pocket. "You're bluffing."

Feeling suddenly naked before the pistol he knows is in Simon's hand, Night tries another swallow and finds his throat too dry. "I am a lot of things. I am naive enough to believe in America. My partner tells me I am stubborn. I am a lousy father. And right now I am scared. But there is one thing I am not, Simon, if that's even your name, and that is bluffing."

Simon's manner changes. "You know what this means. It means you're dead."

"I may be. But if I am, so are you. Right now a .308 is trained on the dome of your aristocratic forehead. Every word we have said is on digital audio tape. So let me tell you the way it's going to be. You are going to jail."

Simon glares. "What do you think you'll accomplish with this? We'll be out before you've finished the paperwork."

Night smiles. He had guessed that was coming. "Sure you will, all but Rigo. He stays. For him we've got eyewitnesses every step of the way. He won't slip out twice. We'll have your faces and your prints, and a DAT of our little chat."

"Which in your dreams buys you what?"

"The knowledge that in future you and your ninjas will be playing somewhere else. The moment anything happens to Derek, to me, to our families, or to anyone else in this department, a packet with everything we have goes out to every wire service, every net news service, every network, every cable news network in the continental U.S. And you start getting recognized on the street."

Simon looks from one end of the dark lot to the other, considers, smiles. Night can see he's made up his mind. It's almost over. He can go home. Simon shifts his weight and Night sees he has misinterpreted. Fear geysers up his spine. With it comes compassion for the man that has twice spared his life. "Don't. Don't do it."

Simon brings a pistol trailing a long suppressor out of his pocket and lets it hang by his thigh.

Night's stomach flip-flops as if he's swallowed a live fish. "We can all go down off the butte together. Nobody has to die tonight."

"You bet wrong, cowboy." Simon raises the pistol and Night sees the muzzle gape before his face. The slug will enter at the bridge of his nose. It's a .45. He won't suffer.

The sonic crack of the .308 as it impacts Simon is as loud as a shotgun fired at Night's ear. The force of the sound effects him as a physical impact. Bone sprays, stinging his face, his ear. He drops to the pavement alongside Simon.

Simon's team sprints for the cars, firing as they go. From cover rifles crack, echoing across downtown. Each time they speak one man falls. Four of Simon's team make the first sedan and head for the road down. Night hugs asphalt as subsonic switches the air overhead, chipping stone behind him. A ricochet swats him in the back of the thigh and frantically, he feels to find no damage done.

Over the hissing of the carbines he hears bursts of 10mm smack the windows of the fleeing car. Before it reaches the exit Night sees it isn't going to make it. Instead, it veers right to pile into the cut in the hillside. From the back seat, two emerge, empty hands reaching high. Night, mouth chalky, ears ringing, snatches up Simon's pistol and, teeth rattling as if with chills, covers them as they wait to be cuffed.

At the top of his voice he orders them down and can barely hear himself. By now cruisers block both roads, bars strobing, headlights illuminating the lot. As uniforms come up, pistols drawn, Night tosses Simon's gun down on the lid of the trunk, raises his ID.

Shielding his eyes, he checks on Simon. With a free hand he presses Simon's neck and finds what he knew he would.

Feeling an odd itch at his ear he reaches up to feel something sticky and warm. Holding his hand up to the light he sees it's blood. He makes the trunk of the Continental and, bracing a hand on a tail fin, vomits.

• • •

Outside a darkened bank, Derek whips his black and white close enough to Night's to mingle dust on the side view mirrors.

Driver's side to driver's side, they cut their lights.

"Quiet night."

Night nods. "That's the way I like it. How you doing?"

"Like riding a bike, you never lose it." He points at Night's bandage. "How's the ear?"

"Better."

He raises two fingers. "Simon had been just this much faster…."

Night reaches up to press the wound gingerly. "Didn't even feel it."

"Fear will do that." Derek offers Night a bag. "Jelly, twist?"

"Julie know you're eating that stuff?"

"Brush my teeth before I go home."

"Sneaky." Night takes a twist. "What about those bars Julie sends to work with you?"

Derek shudders, rolls down the passenger window, tosses them out. "Hate those damned things."

"I'm telling."

"You ain't telling nobody nothing or you can give me back my twist."

Night takes a bite. "Hear anything about Rigo?"

"Name's Holman, Henry. Lost some small intestine. They tell me he'll make it. DA has him under guard twenty-four/seven. He'll do time. I went to see Golden's wife. I told her that."

Night comes up blank. "Golden?"

"The uniform in the cruiser."

Night remembers. "What about the others?"

"The three Hutto didn't reach out and touch bailed this morning." Derek shrugs. "I say let them go. Just kids doing what they were told. Had nothing on them anyway."

The signal on the corner makes three cycles as they sit in the dark,

"Then it's over."

"That's up to them. I bought Julie a .38, took her to the range on Saturday. She's not bad, either. How about you?"

Night thinks about that. "They want to find me they know where I am. I explained things to the ones we cut loose. Sent a copy of the tape with them."

"And you think that'll do it?"

"We'll see."

Derek shakes his head, laughs.

Night searches his face. "What?"

"Just thinking…" He raises dark hands. "Here we are again."

Night smiles, knowing what he means. Twenty years later they're back in prowl cars—broken down old men fighting to keep a gut off and counting the years till retirement. "I'm okay with it. How about you?"

Derek shrugs. "Give the hot shots their turn." Derek cocks his thumb at Night, "Six years, three months, five days."

"Five years, ten months…" Night counts. "Twelve days."

Derek moans, "You're slipping."

Arm to arm, they look opposite ways, comfortable with silence broken only by radio prattle they hear without hearing.

"Heard about Herrera seizing her house. Sorry, man."

Night feels nothing and finds it a relief after the last couple weeks.

"You still friends?"

Night thinks of the strained silence, the awkward meals since forfeiture and says nothing.

Derek grimaces, "That bad?"

"That bad."

"Turned out lousy all around, then."

Night won't argue. "She's leaving in a few days anyway. Taking Alex to New York."

"She blame you?"

Night shrugs. "I don't think so. I just think the whole thing left a bad taste in her mouth."

For a long moment neither speaks.

"Hey," Derek prods him, "come on, first night back at it. We need some excitement. Bingo's on down at the Church of God. They let out at ten. How about ticketing some grandmas?"

Night shrugs off the joke, "They want me to fight crime tonight, they're going to have to give me something."

Defeated, Derek sighs. "You still at her place?"

"Not for long. Sprayed the last coat of interior on my place yesterday, be dry by tonight. Carpet will be in tomorrow. Glue's got to set for 24 hours. We'll be in by the weekend."

"You don't sound very happy about it. That's what you always wanted, isn't it?"

He nods. Then why does it feel like somebody died?

"Ah, come on, don't let her get you down, man, she's not worth it."

Though there is nothing funny, Night smiles a tight-lipped smile. "You're wrong about that. Not that it matters, now, but... yeah, she is."

Derek raises his hands in surrender. "Okay, okay, you win. Far be it from me to get in the way of a man that serious about his wallowing. Live it up, man."

A call comes for a stolen bike at an apartment complex. Derek beats him to the mike, takes it, slams the shift into drive. "Evildoers beware, I is back." Bar strobing, siren whooping, Derek tears away.

Night follows, accelerator to the floor, hits the horn, runs a yellow to stay in sight of him. Mike to his mouth to let dispatch know he's on his way, he catches himself smiling. The old rush. Back to stolen bikes. So it's small time. At least here he can tell the bad guys when he sees them.

They find the apartment. Inside is the man who called. Homeless, he's about to eat pizza at a friend's. They run him through dispatch, find he's got a warrant for vagrancy, missed court date. Gently, Derek cuffs him, puts him in Night's cruiser.

"Next time, partner, eat the pizza before you call us." And to Night, "Take him in for me, I've got to take care of something. Catch you for dinner at Spring Garden at ten."

Puzzled, Night watches him go.

• • •

At the jail he boxes his gun, spray, baton. From the control room behind dark glass comes Elaine's voice. "Night? that you?"

"It's me, Sweetheart."

"Hair all gone, huh? No more maggot."

"No more."

In the booking alcove he clears the wino's pockets, takes his belt, checks him for weapons he knows he doesn't have. Inside the jail Night is greeted with hoots and whistles. His ribbing he takes with a smile, knowing he'll only have to do it once. He doesn't mind. Sibling stuff. Lets him know he's one of them again. It feels good. He sits the old man in the low booking chair. Welded on a suspension spring, it can take the best the berserkers can dish out. The old man waits in a Thunderbird haze.

Linda's at her place behind the counter, talons hot pink today. "Hey, where's our doughnuts?"

"I gave them up. Just say no, right? That's all it takes."

She pops him a raspberry with plum lips. "Yeah, right."

He passes her the forms and she enters them, nails flashing across the keyboard.

"Love the nails."

She glances up. "Love the hair. What'd you do with it, stuff a mattress?"

"Passed it out to my girlfriends one lock at a time."

She laughs without looking up. "Lucky them."

"Might have one left."

"I'm touched." She passes him a form. "New one this year."

Night fills it out while he waits for them to return his cuffs. From the corner of his eye he watches the old man take off his shoes. Doug backs off and stench hits Night like a wall. From a safe distance Doug encourages the old man's efforts. Socks strip slowly down varicose calves, weave and woof of thread welded to the skin of his feet as if glued. Somehow the smell rises thicker.

"Jesus," Doug says, grimacing as he backs away. A nurse appears from the psych wing and, without hesitation, takes a foot in her hand. Impressed, Night watches her work. Giving like that he respects. Not flashy, not anything they'll ever make a movie about, give out awards for, but it takes guts. He couldn't do it. On her way to fetch supplies, she whispers to Night. "Trench foot. Never take their shoes off. Weeks, months in wet socks, happens all the time."

Back on her knees before the prisoner, she examines his feet as Night breathes through his mouth. With cotton gauze and alcohol she daubs them. Rising, she lays a hand on his stooped shoulder, "We'll get you a shower and some clean dry socks, huh? How would that be?"

A grunt is her answer and her thanks. Humbled by kindness that real, Night takes back his cuffs and heads out.

As the door to the lot rumbles aside, the speaker over his head carries Elaine's voice: "Hey, Night!"

He stops, thinking he may have forgotten something.

"Be careful out there, hear me?"

• • •

Derek checks in with dispatch, asks for a break, gets it.

He turns south off Franklin past the pharmacy, heads up the hill. He parks the black and white across the street, climbs the slope under big trees, envious. Why is it a dealer can afford a house in a neighborhood like this and he can't? He rings the bell.

Ceridwen opens it to the chain. When she recognizes him her eyes set. "How's the shoulder?"

"Sore."

She waits for him to tell her why he's here. When he doesn't, she takes a long irritated breath. "What do you want?"

Seeing her again, he understands why Night's down. He understands, too, why she would be less than thrilled to see him. "Nice to see you too, Professor."

"Yeah. Look, my daughter's asleep. If this is about the house, I'll be out Monday."

"It's not about the house."

She thinks about that. "Night can tell you I'm not dealing."

"Not about that either."

She frowns, "What, then?"

"You going to ask me in, or is us niggers supposed to use the back?"

Wearily, she unlocks the chain, opens the door. Derek smiles, heads for the kitchen. "Works every time. Liberal white guilt—better than a battering ram. Never fails on anybody been to college."

Arms folded protectively over her breasts she sighs, "So I fell for it, now what? And save the jokes for somebody who appreciates them, all right?"

He leans against the counter, drops the smile. The woman is so sure of herself. He has to remind himself she's just lost her home. And with a daughter dying of cancer, too. Nothing cowed about her. He wonders if he would handle it as well. "I want to ask you something."

She glares, cynical smile on unpainted lips. He's got to admit it, they're nice lips. Derek's guess is she could earn more tips in a night than Sam if she were of the inclination.

She sighs impatiently, "So ask."

"How's it feel?"

"How does what feel?"

"Knowing Night gave up INET for you?"

She frowns, "I don't understand."

"You knew he was INET?"

"I knew."

"Then you knew he quit."

"Quit." She says it like she's never heard the word before.

"Yeah, you know, voluntary termination of employment? He threw his ID in Herrera's face the day he went to try and get your house back for you. He didn't tell me that, I had to ask around, piece it together, but that's what happened. You didn't know?"

Her smile is gone, now. Derek notices her confidence sag. "I didn't know."

Seeing her weaken, he presses his attack. "And I want you to know that when he came here, it was to set you up for a warrant."

"He told me."

"Did he tell you that I was pushing him to go through with it? Did he tell you that he kept stringing me along and that when it came right down to it he couldn't do it? He tell you that too?"

Her look is his answer.

"Didn't think so." Message given, he is suddenly uncomfortable with this beautiful woman in her lost house. He backs to the door. "A good cop dropped out of INET because of you. I just wanted you to know."

She follows him down the hall, "And you?"

"What about me?"

She raises a hand indicating the uniform. "Why'd you quit?"

He doesn't like having the tables turned on him. "I had my reasons." He reaches for the door and she holds it shut.

"You mean the whole time he was living here he was planning to bust me?"

"No. I mean the whole time he lived here I was planning to bust you. He was making sure it kept getting put off." He looks her over, sees nothing but class. "I tried to convince him you weren't worth it." He laughs, looks away. "I'm still trying. For some reason he thinks you are."

She takes her hand off the door and he leaves her standing on the stoop as he heads down the walk, thinking he had underestimated her. She is nothing like what he had expected her to be. He thinks of something, turns. "Oh, and by the way, thanks for showing up out there."

She leans, hip to porch post. "Sure. Tell me something—who turned me in?"

"You mean who went to Herrera? I saw his name..." He thinks, tongue pressed between lips. "Grady, no...Grant, that's it, Grant something. Didn't catch the last name."

Without waiting to see her reaction he heads for his car.

• • •

Night comes off shift at one a.m.

First night back and the high point of the evening was the stolen bicycle vagrant warrant. Still he is tired. He doesn't bother to turn on lights as he feels his way toward shower and bed. He has one foot on the stairs when he hears her voice.

"We need to talk."

He can see nothing. "Cer?"

"Here."

Her words are slurred. "You're drinking?"

"Undeniably true."

He feels his way to the wall switch.

"No lights."

Curtains drawn, the living room is dark as the inside of his head. He gropes his way to the couch, hoping Alex hasn't left her skates lying in his way.

He makes it, finds her hands, warms them in his. "You're cold."

"We haven't talked a lot lately, have we."

What does he say to that? "I've been busy, I know you have been... with New York so close."

"Don't make excuses. I've been hating you, part of me has anyway. Losing this place is harder than I thought it would be." She reaches to find his face. "I don't want to hate you." Her hand stops when it reaches his chin. "You shaved." As the hands of the blind move so moves her hand to his neck, then up over his scalp. "My God."

He smiles into the dark.

"Is it you?"

"It's somebody else."

"Someone I don't have to hate."

"That's right. No more narc. Just a cop."

"Why didn't you tell me?"

He notices the gravity in her voice and thinks it odd. "You'd see me soon enough."

"I mean about Grant."

He hadn't seen that coming. "I didn't know if I should."

She takes her hands away and he wants them back. "Didn't know? You didn't know?"

"Maybe I should have."

"You're damned right, you should have."

"I'm sorry." He is shocked by her laugh. "What?"

"You are the only man I've ever known who could say that at the drop of a hat…and mean it."

"Practice makes perfect."

Her hand returns to his face and, eyes closed, he leans into it. "Why did you cut it?"

"In uniform I'd look kind of funny with it, don't you think?"

Her hand moves to his chest to feel for a uniform.

"I don't wear it home. It's in my locker."

"With your gun."

"With my service pistol. "He guides her hand to his hip. "I wear my own. Why, you want me to shoot somebody?"

"Me."

"Not funny."

She sags against him and he lets her in under his arm. "Derek stopped by to-night."

He must have misunderstood. "Who?"

"Your partner, Derek. Remember him?"

Anger flares. He knows precisely when. "Why?"

"To set me straight."

She reaches for her glass and ice clinks. He takes it, sets it out of reach.

"Gimme."

He pulls her back. "Uh, uh. What did he tell you? besides about Grant?"

"He told me you quit INET. He said you went to Herrera about my house. He said you were the reason I wasn't busted before, the reason I didn't lose Alex." She pulls away from him and though he can't see her, he can sense her looking at him from only inches away. "It's true, isn't it—all of it."

When he answers he does it quietly. "It's true."

She lays back against him, snuggles close under his arm. "Sorry you quit?"

"No." As he says it he realizes it's true.

"Going to tell me why?"

"I'd had enough."

"Of what?"

"Of being a maggot, of everything."

"So you're back on a beat."

He smiles. "A beat is a foot patrol. I'm back in a cruiser."

"Ah, the latest in community policing."

"That's it."

"That what you want?"

He thinks that over. Funny she should ask. After three years as a maggot does he want to spend his days in creased navy blue gabardine? "I guess it is."

She snuggles close. "Then I'm happy for you, Officer Hume."

After a while her breathing slows. He carries her to his bed and after a shower slips in behind her. Moaning, she finds his hand and guides it between her breasts just over her heart. Face in her hair he inhales the scent of her and presses her to him. As sure as he has ever been of anything he is sure about her now.

Now it's too late, he is sure.

• • •

The doorbell jars Night awake.

Back aching, he slides out of bed and pads barefoot through a silent house. He opens the door to find a vexed Rita on the porch. Dumbfounded, he stares, able to think of no reason why she would be here. He squints in bright morning light. "Rita?"

"You might have called."

"Called? About what?"

"To say you were all right. We've been out of town, just got back last night. The papers didn't mention anything about you, but the house burned, so I thought…" She peers beyond him, "You intend to let me stand out here?"

Reluctant, he moves aside. In the kitchen, he leans on the counter as she snoops. "I had to know…for Jade's sake." Having seen all she can see from the kitchen, she crosses well-fleshed arms. "Not bad."

Though he wishes she hadn't come, oddly enough he's glad for her approval. "We like it." He sees no reason to tell her they'll be moving in less than a week.

"I have some good news for you." She lays an envelope on the counter in front of him.

He has never liked envelopes. Night fills a kettle, sets it on the burner. "What is it, Rita? Just tell me."

"I think you should read it."

He turns it with a finger, finds it imprinted with Ray's firm, and fear floods him white hot. He should have known better than to trust a shyster. "I don't believe this. What now?"

"Just open it."

No way can he afford to fight Ray in court. He'll spend everything he's got and lose Jade, too. "The custody thing, is that it? Jesus Christ, Rita, what do we have to fight about?"

She smiles and that angers him more. "Will you just read it?"

He rips off the end, taking the letter's edge with it. The letter is from Ray's office. It says he's entitled to $358 a month child support. That's all it says. Ray signed it. A P.S. is scrawled at the bottom—*Where's that gazebo? Beer's on ice.*

She smirks at him. "You see?"

He sees. It's as if a car has just been jacked off his chest. He won't lose Jade. "This Ray's idea?" He can't imagine it's Rita's. She enjoys the things money buys too much.

She sighs, "He loves her, you know that."

Fear surprises him with how easily it turns to anger. He throws down the letter. "I don't want his money."

"It's Jade's money. You know how he is. He's worried about her. He pictures her living in a dump somewhere."

"Well, you tell him for me…" As quickly as it comes, his rage drains away. Trying to hate Ray is like trying to hum along to Mark Isham—more trouble than it's worth. "You tell him if I need help, I'll ask."

She makes a show of looking around. "I'll tell him he doesn't have to worry." Rita jangles keys, diamond flashing. "So you're boarding here, that it?"

Just how much does he have to put up with to get her to the door? "That's it."

"Night?" Ceridwen sleepwalks in in a long tee shirt, voice fuzzy as kiwi. She sees Rita, freezes, backs out, "Sorry."

He clamps her wrist, draws her back, "Rita, this is Ceridwen."

Awkwardly, they face each other, Rita's eyes wide with surprise. He can't help it, he enjoys it. Ceridwen with rat's nest hair and eyes sticky with sleep face to face with his ex as he watches. Between them there is no contest.

Ceridwen rubs at her eyes. "Night's told me a lot about you."

"Oh?" Rita says with a meaningful look at Night, "Wish I could say the same." She smiles archly. "I've got to run, just stopped by to deliver the letter. I'll let you get back to...whatever it was you were doing. Make sure and have Jade home early next week, we've got a trip to the coast planned. Chinook's running and we've got to get an early start if we want to beat the other boats up the Coquille. Nice meeting you...Ceridwen was it? Nice to know Night's in... good hands." Her last look is one Night does his best to ignore.

Sighing with relief, he shuts the door, leans against it. From behind the blind Ceridwen watches her go. "Cute Mercedes."

"Rita and her Mercedes. She would have married the devil for one."

"Tell me that diamond wasn't real."

He wraps arms around her, feeling pleasantly conspiratorial spying with her from behind the blind, "Two point three two carats, color seven, clarity nine. She's very proud of that diamond."

"I could tell. She almost blinded me with it. And she came all the way over to deliver a letter? Sounds ominous."

He leads the way to the kitchen. "They want to give me child support."

"You're kidding, that's great."

"Ray's pushing for it. That's the kind of guy he is." He raises a hand, "Hell, you know, you met him."

"What'd you say?"

"No, thanks."

Back to the counter, she gapes. "You're crazy."

He goes out the back to pick peppermint. The walk is cold on his bare feet. In the sink he rinses off aphids and stuffs the pot. Menthol hangs strong in the air. No use trying to explain. "Probably."

"Take it."

Night ladles sugar over the leaves. "Uh, uh."

"Why not?"

"Don't need it."

"Take it anyway."

"Why?"

She struggles. "She brought it over herself, isn't it obvious she wants Jade to have it?"

"Ray can keep his money. Jade won't want for anything."

She looks at him as if explaining about red lights and traffic. "Look, never turn down money."

Inwardly he smiles. He has her now. "Quite the mercenary, aren't you?" The kettle burbles, working up a whistle, and he fills the pot. "How much child support you get for Alex?"

She frowns, suspicious. "Why?"

"How much?"

She says nothing.

"That's what I thought." He leads her to the table, sits her down. "And why not?"

"I don't want it, that's why. I don't want anything from him. He and his money both can go straight to hell."

"So, never turn down money, huh? I'll remember that sage advice."

"Except for her treatments. That I'll take." She throws up a hand in seeming frustration. "Something else I have to thank you for."

He doesn't follow. "What?"

"Ray, his letter must have been a good one is all I can say."

"Why, what happened?"

"He's going to pay, that's what happened—he's arranged to have Alex covered under his insurance."

Joy plumes, cold in his belly. "And it'll cover it?"

"Damn right it will—all of it. I'm solent. Christ, I'm on easy street."

"That's great."

She nods. "Yeah, yeah it is. And you did it."

He pours their tea and the smell of it fills the kitchen. "Ray did it."

She watches him sit opposite her and smiles. "Your hair, I like it."

He runs a hand over his scalp, still not used to feeling bristles where for so long he has felt the weight of tangles. "Weird, huh?"

She takes his chin in her hand, turns him. "I'll get used to it."

In fly the girls, ending conversation. They tear out to ride bikes and Night decides it is time to show her the house. He rinses his cup, sets it in the washer. "Let's walk."

Ceridwen faces him, "I've got packing to do."

He fetches her jeans from upstairs on the floor by his bed and puts them in her arms. "Get dressed."

Eyes on his, she slips into them, tucking in the oversize tee. He leads her to the bench by the back door, sits her down.

"We're leaving in three days."

From her shoes he takes balled socks, shakes them out, slips them on her bare feet."

"I don't have time for this."

He puts walking shoes on her feet, ties them.

"I've got movers coming at eleven."

He holds her coat for her, zips it up, grabs his own.

"I've got to get us packed. Do you hear me?"

"I hear. I've got something to show you."

She smiles, canting her head, and it's as if she's tugging a string tied to his aorta. "Or what, you'll arrest me?"

"No, but I may have to cuff you and slap you around a little. It's been a while since I've beaten a handcuffed suspect and I'm getting a little twitchy."

"You know, if I even thought…" In spite of herself she laughs, letting him lead her out. "You are sick."

"So they say."

It's a beautiful drizzly morning. The girls ride ahead, Alex following Jade up the street. Her hand nesting in his, they follow.

"Taking me to see your house?"

He stops. "How did you know?"

"I saw your car and stopped by once." A smile flickers on her mouth. "For just a minute."

What does that mean? "I didn't see you."

"You were busy."

That smile again. As if she knows something he doesn't. "You should have. I could have stopped whatever I was doing."

"Oh, no, I didn't want to interrupt."

At the house, he sees the girls have beat them inside.

"And it has such a big backyard, too." Jade says.

"Oh, yes, it's divine," Alex says in a stage voice, "just perfect for a family."

Ceridwen bites her lip and Night sighs, hangs his head, "Go play in traffic, will you? Go on, out, out!"

Jade leads Alex out, "Would you like to see the back yard?"

"Oh, yes, I must see the garden site. We're all very big gardeners, you know."

Tension between them making him short of breath, he leads her down the hall, smell of fresh paint and carpeting strong on the air. In the master bedroom he opens a window. "Now the carpet has cured, I need to get these windows open."

Outside they can hear the girls chasing frogs in the pool.

Night feels the need to say something, anything. "The pool's a mess."

She comes to stand by him, leaning both elbows on the sill. "I think they prefer it like it is." She shakes her head, smiles. "They're such plotters."

Lightheaded with anxiety, he speaks without giving himself the chance to think. "They probably think I'm going to ask you to live here with us when you come back."

He watches her face and sees something close to fear. She bolts for the door.

He follows her down the hall. "Cer."

She keeps moving, hands up. "No."

He catches her on the walk, cuts her off. "Talk to me."

The girls tag after. Night barks at them and they scurry back inside, giggling. He turns her to him. "Will you tell me what I said that was so wrong?"

In her eyes, hate or something close. "Forget it."

"Tell me."

She sighs, rolling her eyes and he knows he's gotten through. "You think I'm coming back from New York to be your live-in, you're nuts."

"No, no, no…" He takes her arms, "I don't think that." He swallows, looks back at the house, decides to settle for the truth. "Since the first time I saw you I haven't been able to think about anything but you living here with me. Everything I did here you were in the back of my mind. How would you like it? How would you want it? It's like you were here with me the whole time. It's been driving me nuts thinking about it. I can't imagine living here without you."

She looks away and back, eyes stricken. "What does that mean?"

"It means we give it a year. You get Alex well, and when you come back… we see if we feel the same."

"If we do?" He can see she is afraid of the answer.

"Then no hedging our bets, no life rafts, both feet in."

She bites her lip, eyes squeezed shut. "Oh, God." She pulls free, paces, down the sidewalk, back. "We're both failures at that."

He takes her hand, she pulls it away. "We've failed, that doesn't make us failures."

"We don't know we can make it work."

"No we don't. No guarantees in life. We both know that. But we have a year. I'll write you. You write me. It'll give us a chance to make sure... of a lot of things. In a year we'll see how we feel."

"What if we try and we can't? What about Alex, what about Jade?"

"You know how they feel about it. It isn't like we just met, like we've only seen the sunny side of each other."

She grimaces. "Thanks a lot."

"You know what I mean. You can't even breathe without me."

She watches him, eyes making him feel translucent, "You want to do this?"

"I want it, have wanted it." He watches her face, sees worry there.

"I need to think."

He smiles. "You've got a year."

She searches his face, skeptical. "You'd wait. You'd wait a year for me."

"I'll be right here."

Nodding, eyes worried, she takes a breath with an expression like someone preparing himself for a dive far out over rock into ebbing surf. She offers her hand and he takes it. "Well, what are you waiting for? Show me the rest."

• • •

They write, sometimes as many as three letters a week, sometimes two, never less. When her letters come he carries them with him through a shift under his vest. With every movement it chafes against his skin, reminding him of her, of the pleasure awaiting him when, during a lull, he finds time to read it. As he does he feels her close, almost as if she were in the back seat peering through wire mesh over his shoulder.

Ceridwen's letters are long, five pages at least, written on steel gray paper flecked with cotton fiber. The stack of them he keeps on a table by his bed. Sometimes he takes them up and weighs them in his hands, flipping his thumb along the edge as he might a deck of cards.

In them she shares a parent's desolate hell. A year spent in a strange city, child suffering. Through the anguish, the loneliness in her lines, he comes to know her. In her letters she describes long days at Sloan, her search for part-time work, the friends she makes among the parents at Ronald McDonald House. By tacit agreement neither speaks of what they will do when the year is up.

Piggybacked in each envelope is a letter from Alex. At first tentative, later they come to share her fear, the pain of the treatments, the doctors and nurses she likes and those she doesn't, how the brownies he sends help but make her sleep.

Fresh off shift at two a.m., Jade asleep, he sits at the kitchen table and writes them each their own letter in return. In them he tells about the people he arrests. And those he does not. He tells her about a woman in an old Toyota he pulls over to find she has no license. He tells her about the kids in the back seat with smeared faces. He tells her about the baby on the floor in the front, and how she cries when she tells him about tickets she can't pay, and the defiant tone that comes into her voice when she says she has a job and won't take welfare.

He wants her to understand why he bawls her out and has her follow him to St.

Vincent de Paul's, where he buys her a car seat and straps the baby in. He wants her to see the woman's eyes as they flood when he tells her to get on her way. He wants her to understand why he does what he does, why he feels the way he does—about the job, about everything. He wants her to understand what only cops understand— that the job is a chance to do something for the guy on the bottom, for the kids who hurt.

Next day, on his jog by the post office he sends his letter, mail box door clanking shut in the bleak light of dawn behind him as he pads away, mind holding the memory of a woman he hasn't seen in months.

Strange how they grow to know each other through ink and dry paper. Strange how when he holds that stack of rough-edged stationery in his hand he feels closer to her than when they lived in the same house.

• • •

"She's been gone a year?"
Night smiles at Derek in the car parked at his elbow. "That's right."
"And you haven't seen her once?"
"Nope."
"Talked to her on the phone?"
"No."
"Just letters?"
"That's all."
Derek shakes his head, "When she get in?"
Night looks at his watch and his heart lurches. "Couple hours."
"Damn!"
Night fights the churning of his stomach. "Yeah."
"Going to pick her up?"
"Soon as I get a shower."
"Man, a year! You shouldn't have let it go so long."
"We agreed it was best."
Derek nods. "I respect that. I think you're nuts, but I respect it." He drops a hand on Night's arm. "Don't be late."
Night starts the car, "Stay away from those doughnuts. Julie says I'm supposed to keep an eye on you."
Derek raises a hand, shakes his head. "Don't worry about me."
As Night pulls away, Derek raises a raised glazed in salute, calls after him, "Good luck, man."

• • •

At the airport he waits, mouth dry, as their plane taxies to the ramp. What seems an hour later passengers filter out. Jade points them out, but he's already spotted her. She rushes to meet them. Not sure why, he stays where he is, stomach heavy with dread. She is more beautiful than he remembers. His eyes water. He is losing it. He's a basket case and they haven't yet spoken.

He hunkers down to offer Alex his hand. She ignores it, rushes to hug him, hitting him hard, face buried in his chest. She burrows into him, nearly knocking him over. "I missed you."

Horseradish ache rising from nose to eyes, he presses her to him hard as he dares, "Missed you, too, kiddo."

"I got all your letters," she says, voice breathy, muffled by his jacket. "I don't ever want to see another brownie."

They laugh and he wipes his eyes as subtly as he can. "I think we can work that one out."

She pulls away and under her eyes he notices deep hollows, "I'm tired, can we go home now?"

Unsure what Ceridwen intends, he rises, "Sure."

Jade leads her to the car leaving the two of them alone in the crush. She moves closer and he's so nervous he can't see straight. "Is she..."

She nods. "She's fine."

"Where to?" That's what he says. He can't believe it, but he says it.

Ignoring him, she comes to his arms as if it were inevitable, as if there were nowhere else she could possibly go, and in a breath he is nearly too weak to stand. "Oh, God..." The words, involuntary as breathing, leave his lungs as water is pressed from a sponge.

"So long..." She whispers it. "So, so long..." She pushes him away, "Did you keep my letters? I have every one of yours."

He shrugs. "I used yours for grocery lists."

Her hand squeezes his arm hard as she fights a smile. "Oh, you sensitive, sensitive man."

Around them crowds pulse, a current coursing around their islet of two. Amid the crush they are alone.

At last she speaks. "I've thought about what we should do."

His heart stutters. Blood falls stagnant in his veins. More naked he has never been. His voice comes out hoarse, weak, his words inane. "You have."

Her voice is no louder. "Uh, huh. Have you?"

Jaw clamped shut to stay in control, he nods.

"And... change your mind?"

"No." Time whirlpools into a backwater, slowing to nothing. This woman he knows better than any woman. Who knows him. From whom he's hidden nothing. The stuff of his letters was arterial blood. She rejects him, she rejects who he is. Stomach tight with dread, he says the word. "You?"

Her hand falls to his, clamps it in a grasp firm and secure as her eyes. "Why are we standing here? Are you going to take us home or not?"

A TERRIBLE BEAUTY

"St.John takes critical aim at all the teaching theories and experiments that school districts churn out on a regular basis, which totally ignore the abysmal track record of earlier programs and the basic needs of its students. This novel is an inside view of the anger and frustrations felt by teachers in failing school systems."
Booklist

"Descriptions of classroom conflicts, successes, frustrations will touch readers to the core. The teacher and student among you will cheer out loud as this novel progresses…"

National Public Radio
Oregon Public Broadcasting affiliate KLCC

"Agree or disagree, this book is worth reading!"
News Review

After suffering the greatest of personal tragedies, Dai O'Connel is no longer willing to lie. A headstrong Welshman twenty years in an Oregon classroom, he refuses either to lower standards or to implement the feel-good nonsense of Outcome Based Curriculum, and as a result is targeted for dismissal.

Sent to document his failings is Solange Gonsalvás, Oregon's youngest assistant superintendent. Known both for breathtaking attractiveness and her dedication to the job, she is relentless in pursuit of incompetent teachers. Deeply believing she can make the district's schools better, while struggling with her own concept of what school should be, Solange finds O'Connel not at all as she expected. Principled, confident, very good at what he does, Dai is not the kind of teacher Solange forces from the classroom—but more than competence is at stake.

District politicos demand O'Connel's ouster, and if Solange wants the top job, she must take his. Bewildered by the intense attraction she feels for the man, Solange must choose between ruining an outstanding teacher's career and furthering her own, a career for which she's sacrificed everything.

AVAILABLE AT YOUR FAVORITE BOOKSTORE

SISTERS OF GLASS

Karl Latte doesn't like the twenty-first century. Not recombinants, not Ultimate Reality, not Digitally Mastered Immortals. He doesn't like that people are disappearing, or that he stands to lose the only thing in the world that matters to him. Most of all he dislikes the talent he was born with, the talent that's damned him—the ability to see into minds.

A forty-year-old ex-cop with bad knees and an arrhythmic heart, he may be the last man in 2030 L.A. without a satcom implanted deep in his cortex. 21st century Luddite with the skills of a gun-for-hire blackmailed back to take over a case that's left nine agents parted out, he is at once scrambling for his life.

The assignment takes him to Plat 66, a sea platform owned by the genetic conglomerate, Genesistems. His task: find Romy, one of the last surviving first-generation recombinants. Tall, slender, gifted, she's the apogee of genetic perfection—everything he loathes in a woman.

All Karl wants is to go home—but before he can he's got to get Romy off the plat alive. Easier said than done. Genesystems wants them dead, the Army of God is hell-bent to sink the plat, a sadistic cabal is murdering Sisters two a night, and a 21st century demon lurks just out of sight, craving possession of them both.

Most alarming for Karl, as he grows to know this appealing patented life form, he finds his most cherished prejudices teetering as his concept of what is human and what is not skews bewilderingly.

AVAILABLE AT YOUR FAVORITE BOOKSTORE

MADELYNE SIMONE ROVENHAUER'S

THE
Nasty
LITTLE WRITING BOOK

AT LAST,
THE DIRTY LITTLE SECRETS OF MAKING IT
AS A BEST-SELLING AUTHOR REVEALED
BY LONG-TIME NEW YORK PUBLISHING INSIDER!

• • •

THE BOOK THAT WILL TURN YOU
INTO A BEST-SELLING AUTHOR—GUARANTEED!
OR FIVE TIMES YOUR MONEY BACK!

• • •

HAVE YOU EVER WANTED TO PICK THE BRAIN
OF A REAL NEW YORK PUBLISHING INSIDER?

NOW YOU CAN!

THIS BITINGLY SATIRICAL TOME—CHOCKABLOCK WITH LIES AS
IT IS—OFFERS MORE TRUTH THAN ANY DOZEN ORDINARY HOW-
TO-BE-PUBLISHED BOOKS.

MADELYNE SIMONE ROVENHAUER'S
THE *Nasty* LITTLE WRITING BOOK

LONGTIME NEW YORK PUBLISHING INSIDER
MADELYNE SIMONE ROVENHAUER
REVEALS:

•The secrets of 'bonding' with New York editors.
•Mistakes made by 'hack' writers.
•How to know when your muse is calling.
•Which writers to read and which to avoid.
•How watching TV can be your doorway to success.
•Why literary agents want to 'discover' you.
•How to write a best-selling novel without revising.
•What plots are 'winners.'
•What plots are 'losers.'
•Why 'names' are published more often than 'unknowns.'
•How to know what to write about.
•Why clichés deserve a place in the author's toolbox.
•What genre is ripe for 'breaking in.'
•Why NOT to 'write what you know.'
•Why being published is just the beginning.
•Handling fame and wealth.
•How to treat fans.

AVAILABLE AT YOUR FAVORITE BOOKSTORE

ABOUT THE AUTHOR

D.W. St.John lives on Dragon's Back Ridge in Oregon's Coast Range in a home of his own construction with a wife of twenty years and two children. He is currently at work on fiction and nonfiction projects. Communication regarding his work may be sent care of the publisher.

Printed in the United States
1741

9 781930 859173